"Daniel had got to within a yard of the fight ar
rhythmically in imitation punches. His dad's d:
was so beautiful. He knew that when his dad st
go free that it was a virtuous thing. The act of a ,
said softly. 'My dad.' But he also knew that his c
speed, power and elegance was the more import
to do with God he thought."

"With Daniel only a hundred yards away, Tom turned his face into the blast of the
rain and hoped that in the wetness of his face, his tears could not be seen when he got
to his son.

'Ye' oahreet, lad?' was the most beautiful and appropriate thing that he could say.
Calm, dignified, reassuring. Loving."

"What was not planned was the poetry of the movement, the music of the
timing of the passes, the elegance of Pretorious' run as he drifted a yard to
the right to meet the falling ball, the harmony of the players sharing one
beautiful vision. That beautiful vision would be taken on Monday morning
to work by a thousand men who relived those moments in Saturday's
sunlight as they swung their picks in the dark. And some of them knew also,
that in its baroque lines and sweeps it was great art. Or at least as close as
they would get to it."

"Daniel got to his legs and swung a wild fist, but he only caught Gobbo on the ear.
He tried to swing again but Gobbo had grabbed Daniel by the back of his head and
slammed his face into his rising knee with great force. The classes in the playground
went silent. Daniel's head was full of noise."

"Do you two still keep in touch with Jane Russell?"

"St. Bridget's Church sits on a small plateau looking west over the Solway Firth
towards the Isle of Man. It is sandwiched between an old Roman Fort and the
Jacobean Mansion, Moresby Hall. It looks quite romantic when silhouetted against
the setting sun, but it's far enough away from the angry squalor of each of its three
parishes of Lowca, Parton and Moresby not to get grubby. Physically or spiritually."

"And so the procession of pit buses carrying miners from the outlying
villages of Arlecdon, Frizington, Cleator, Pica and Distington had to pass the
Church gate as the mourners were drifting out. And here's the thing. Each
bus in its turn stopped at the gate for five seconds or so to give time for each
of the miners to take off their caps and bow their heads a little. There were
thirteen buses and it took some time for them all to pass."

"'Ivverbody knows old Harry and his Sally, asser.'
You had to know everybody else in the pit or in the villages. You may need to call out
their name in distress, in the dark, a mile down."

"A lonely young boy who had no friends to speak of who didn't seem to
have blurted out to anybody that he had seen his teacher's tits, he was just
the right person to help with something she couldn't handle on her own."

"It looked more like a Constable sketch than a Bewick engraving. However, in his
finished scraperboard, he had not included the stench of the cowshit slurry in the
beck and he had left out the smell of the tar from the tar plant and coking ovens
which were up the hill, not far behind the trees on the right. Although he included the
steaming train and the three men, their dog and the engine driver, Daniel did not
include the fountain of coal or evidence that there were five hundredweight of coal
being stolen by two very nice men from the village, two friends from Lowca School
and their dog 'Beaut'."

"Daniel was sensitive enough to know, by the nature of the silences in the
large congregation, that it was a moving ceremony and that the others on his
pew, his dad especially, were taken along on a journey that he couldn't join
them on. Daniel had bought the ticket, but he couldn't get on the bus."

"'To-day we all witnessed and were nearly victims of, one group of Christians
shooting and trying to kill another group of Christians coming out of a church. This
is an evil beyond my understanding. The spectacular neo-classical façade of that
church had its architectural roots in pagan buildings of ancient Greece and Rome,
two thousand years ago, and is all the more glorious for that. Christianity was
brought to this part of the world thirteen hundred years ago.' Daniel paused for
effect. 'By foreign immigrants'."

"In the fire of the rugby scrum he only had to suspend his cognitive mindset
for the two or three seconds it took to position himself, arse pointing to the
ball in the scrum-half's hands, and strike the ball against the put-in. Sitting at
his painting, the brushes came and went from his hand, the paints in his
palette presented themselves to the hairs of his brush. Daniel witnessed his
father emerging slowly, sometimes hesitantly, in the transcendent paint on
the board."

Lowca

Geoff Stalker

THE CHOIR PRESS

First published in the United Kingdom in 2021 by
The Choir Press

ISBN 978-1-78963-249-1

www.geoffstalkerportraits.com

This book is dedicated to Martha Elizabeth Alexandra and to Rachel Danae

With gratitude to Jessica Seabern, Christopher Thorson, James Shera, Margaret Vechell, Stephanie Leeman, Margaret Davies, Ann Pelletier-Topping and Francis McCrickard

Chapter 1

HARRINGTON – DISTINGTON – PICA – MORESBY – ARLECDON - ROWRAH – FRIZINGTON – WHITEHAVEN – CLEATOR.

Daniel learned to read as a three-year old, nearly four, reciting the names of the Lowca pit buses in their order, over the level crossing at the top of East Croft and West Croft terraces, round past the Co-op, down East Road and round on a tight arc past the ends of the Solway Road terraces, then inside the line of the engine sheds, and back up to form their queue in the order of his recitation.

He hadn't really learned to read the names of the villages on the front of the buses, but his dad, Tom, in his daftness had made up a nursery rhyme.

> "HARRINGTON, DISTINGTON, PICA,
> *All aboard fer Lowca*
> MORESBY, ARLECDON, ROWRAH,
> *Git on't bus fer Lowca*
> FRIZINGTON, WHITEHAVEN, CLEATOR,
> *Harray, we're gaan ter Lowca*"

Tom had convinced Daniel that it was a traditional song, not one of his sillinesses, and that the miners on the buses would indeed sing this song on their way to work.

"Even in the dark on their way to t'fusst shift?"

"Oh aye, but they'd sing 'sotto voce', so's not to wake anybody up on the way."

It was though, Daniel's own personal rhyme, and he sang it to himself on most of the ceremonial occasions of his life, sitting on the toilet, drying off after his bath, going to bed. His dad had made it up, not just as a gesture of love and affection for him, but as part of Tom's own need for order and truth in his life. The pit buses came every day at set times, and in a set order, and that had to be acknowledged; in his life at work, at the Rugby and the Cricket, and most importantly in his family. To support his nursery rhyme, Tom had brought back from work a discarded geological map of the West Cumberland coalfield, and he wrote the names of the villages in big green capital letters on the map, and in red ink he traced the routes the buses would take. It was a beautiful thing.

The changing of the shifts and the ceremony of the buses was integral to the rhythm of the village, the timing of meals, the digging of the gardens, the liberation of the pigeons. Mr Boyle, the farmer, would never have thought to drive his thirty-five cows home from their pastures to their milking sheds behind the houses of East Road during "bus time". The whole process of disgorging three hundred men, mascara eyed, freshly brushed and scrubbed, ready for home, was performed three times a day for the first, back and night shifts.

And on one very cold day, with sea salt in the rain, Daniel, his mam Emily and three other women with kids, were waiting for the pit bus off the first shift.

A beaming smile and a small laugh at whatever she perceived to be a joke disguised Emily's embarrassment at having to take the cheaper, and at times free, pit bus to Whitehaven instead of the normal service bus. It was an indignity shared by a lot of the young mothers, and the pensioners, in the village. If there was space on the bus they could travel for free, or at least the driver could not be bothered taking the money. Sometimes a miner or two would wipe the seats for them, otherwise the wooden slatted benches would leave striped, coal dust marks on young women's coats.

The first dribble of miners made their way out of the pit baths, mostly those from Lowca itself. One of them, 'Billy Vimto', stopped to talk to Emily. Billy was a 'shot firer', the man who set the explosives on the coal face, and in the aristocracy of the mine he was a Viscount, the 'deputies' were 'Sirs' and the ordinary colliers knew their place. Billy Vimto's real name was William Vernon. His nickname, and its ubiquity, was a gesture of respect. It was also a reminder that once back in the village, there were no hierarchies. He had fought in the same regiment as Daniel's grandfather in the first world war. He brought back Madeleine from St Omer as his bride. Speaking rudimentary

French and knowing a thing or two about explosives, he re-enlisted in the army at the start of the second world war and had 'a good war' as a saboteur.

Most Sunday tea times Billy and Maddie would go to Daniel's 'Lowca' grandparents' house with a tin of fresh French pastries which Maddie made instead of going to church. Once when Daniel was there, he got a slice of sweet apple tart. It had vanilla in it, and cinnamon. Its magic to Daniel was that it tasted of several things in the same mouthful.

Billy was a short, dapper man and looked smart even in his pit roughs. It was only six years after the end of the war and, like many of the men, he still wore his army beret. He did not wear it as a badge of honour, like some still did, but to hide a scalp which was a patchwork of blue ragged scars and sparse tufts of grey hair. As he and Emily chatted, he stood upwind to take some of the rain off her. Amid the gentle laughter, the first of the buses circled the end of Solway Road. It was of course, the Harrington bus.

"HARRINGTON" then "DISTINGTON" and then "PICA", Daniel recited as the second and third bus made their turns, in turn.

He wasn't reading of course, he was reciting his own nursery rhyme, but he had the sense to recognise the rough form of his dad's green capital letters and relate them to the white on black of the names on the buses.

"All aboard fer Lowca."

Then as the second wave of buses came round, Daniel returned to, "MORESBY, ARLECDON ..."

"Stop him Emily, lass, he's starting to frighten me."

"Oh, Tom's teachen 'im ter read," she said.

Billy crouched down to Daniel and sat on his right clog. "Daniel, will you read the next one for me please?"

"Rowrah." Daniel disappeared shyly behind his mam's coat. He shoved his right hand deep into his mother's right pocket.

Billy Vimto reached into his trouser pocket and took out a sixpence and a penny. "That's very good," he said, "That's extremely good." He pointed behind him at the next bus, which was across the other side of the road, waiting to make its turn. "I have a tanner and a penny. If you get the name of the village on the bus right, I will give you a penny. If

3

you get it wrong, I will know that you are a normal little boy and I will give you the sixpence." He grabbed hold of Daniel's hand and shook it slowly and formally. "Is that a deal?"

Daniel knew that it would be Frizington, but people were gathering round and he was frightened of the crowding. He retreated further round his mam's back.

"Leave the lad alone yer rotten bugger. Sorry for swearing Emily," said one of the other mothers.

The bus came round into view, and from behind his mother's shopping bag, Daniel very quietly said, "Frizington."

There was a little silence, and without meaning to, he sang out, "Git on't bus fer Lowca."

"I cannot believe what I have just seen and heard." Billy tried to give Daniel the money, but he shied away. Emily was ready with her hand to take it.

"Frizington must be one of the hardest words to learn. You must take the seven pence." Still squatting, he said to Daniel, "That's my beer money for the week!"

"And the rest," said one of the other Lowca miners.

"Aah cannot believe that av seen Billy Vimto giv'n money away."

Emily gave Daniel a tug. "Say thank you."

Stupid boy that he was, he said, "Thank you Mr Vimto."

The small crowd roared with laughter. Daniel thought that they were laughing at him. Emily thought that they were laughing at her.

But William Vernon smiled at Daniel, straightened his beret, and gave a mock salute.

Emily grabbed Daniel's hand and took him round the corner behind the Co-op. The seven pence would get her a return ticket on the main service bus to Whitehaven, with its clean, upholstered seats. From the proper bus-shelter she could see the other young women riding on the front seats of the Whitehaven pit bus as it pulled out. Emily and Daniel stood in the cold wind for twenty minutes before the service bus arrived.

Every Wednesday, Emily took Daniel on the Distington pit bus to visit her maternal grandparents, William and Sarah Carr. William and Sarah were both in their eighties and lived in a small, terraced cottage near the Queen's Head bus stop. All Distington life passed their front window, and nothing ever went unnoticed. The door was always opened before anybody needed to knock. Distington Grandma would have been reading an improving book sitting up straight at the table by the window. Grandad would be sitting in a slightly distressed leather armchair by the fire, smoking his pipe, reading a book from the library. "There's half them books in't library I wouldn't touch, let alone read them," he would say as he put his book down, before his punchline of, "They put them on the top two shelves just so that ah can't reach them." They would all laugh each time he cracked that one, not every week, but most weeks. Grandma would laugh because she worshipped him, Emily would laugh, not because she found it funny each time, but because she knew it was a joke and laughing was the thing to do. Daniel laughed because he was happy as shit to be there.

Distington Grandma and Emily would go into the kitchen and make a batch of scones with Tuesday's sour milk. Grandad and Daniel would split a fire stick between them with the carving knife. First, the one-inch thick stick would be split in two to make half-inch sticks, then each stick would be split in two again until there were sixty-four sticks, each of them eight inches long and an eighth of an inch wide. These "spills" were to be used to light his pipe from the fire.

"That's saved me the cost of a box of matches."

"Harray," Daniel would shout and clap.

Grandad would fill his pipe and let Daniel light the spill, then hold it steadily. They would both stare intently at the small yellow and blue flame and with half a dozen rhythmic puffs the pipe would be lit. There would be several minutes when they would both sit and watch the smoke set off on its way up to the ceiling before turning down in its path to go up the chimney with the fire smoke.

While his pipe was puffing away, William Carr would tell Daniel the news of the day, whether it be of some altercation outside the Queen's Head the previous night, or Churchill's latest mendacity.

"The man is senile and has to wear a nappy, he shouldn't be allowed out into the daylight." Other affairs of state would be related to Daniel as if he were an adult and knew what his great grandfather was talking about. But Grandad talked 'properly' and his voice had a lovely nasal ring to it. Daniel just liked the sound of him talking, and when there was a pause he would think of a question, any question, just to keep him going. He was not trying to be clever but when important national figures were mentioned by name, he would say, "Tell me about Mr Attlee, tell me about Princess Elizabeth, or Stanley Matthews, how far away is London?" Keep talking Grandad.

Only when Daniel knew that he had squeezed all the talk out of his grandad that he could, would he reach under his armchair and pull out the roof slate, the six-inch nail and the piece of chalk. This was the signal for "the drawing of the fish."

Grandad would dust the slate with the cuff of his shirt, and picking up the nail, he would rapidly draw a fish with one movement. His nail would trace a line from the left of the slate in a fluid arc describing the top of the fish to the right of the slate. A little squiggle would outline the tail before the nail would make the return journey round the bottom of the slate to join the line where it had begun, creating an open mouth for the fish, a kissing mouth or a smiling mouth. A couple of loud scratches would make a fin or two, an eye and perhaps some bubbles coming out of its mouth. This was magic as Daniel understood the word. It was all over in three seconds, and a life-like creature was created. And his ancient great grandfather's hand had moved with the speed and grace of a teenage ballerina. With the chalk Daniel would trace with fat white lines the thin, elegant lines engraved by his great grandfather.

"Daniel has drawn a fish," Grandad would shout to the kitchen with feigned astonishment, even though he had 'drawn a fish' every Wednesday for several months. Soon Daniel was adding scales to the fish and seaweed to the picture. Before long he was drawing the fish himself with the nail and Grandad would draw the seaweed.

Each visit to Distington ended with the ceremony of the hot scones, the melting butter and the gooseberry jam, made from the fruit of the two bushes in the back yard. While the grownups drank hot sweet tea, Daniel drank a glass of "Aneurin Bevan's orange juice," as Grandad called it with a wink.

Emily and Daniel had to get the service bus back to Howgate, and this entailed a one mile walk down to the beck and up across the valley to the top end of Lowca. "It'll be two miles for Daniel with his little legs," said Grandma and Grandad from the door. Every time.

'Distington Grandad' used to cut Daniel's hair. He used to cut cousins Harry and Billy's hair until Uncle Harry put a stop to it.

"We don't have enough elastoplasts, Grandad," he said, loudly but gently. "The boys can't sleep if they know y'er cummen."

To lighten things, he pointed to his own balding head. "Look what yer did ter my hair!"

Even Grandma wouldn't let him cut hair at their Distington home. "I don't want our offspring frightened of coming to visit. I don't want the drunks in the Queen's Head complaining about the noise of children screaming."

Nonetheless, he continued to visit Lowca every Friday. He would take a cardboard box tied up neatly with hairy twine. The knot would be secured with a blob of sealing wax. Grandma's best blouses, Grandad's shirt collars and various antimacassars and lace furniture mats would be ironed by Emily. From Grandad's left jacket-pocket he would pull out a pot of Grandma's pressed meat; in these more cosmopolitan times we would call it a 'terrine'. It would make a lovely lunch with some lettuce, tomato and buttered bread. If Daniel hadn't known that his Grandad's hair clippers were secreted in his right jacket pocket, he would have relished his lunch.

While Emily was clearing the dishes and getting the ironing board ready, Grandad set Daniel up on a dining chair, put a rough towel round his throat, and got into the business of cutting his hair. There were always a couple of nicks, and the positioning of Daniel's head was precisely dictated by the pulling of his ears. It didn't hurt really, but Grandad's hands shook with a gentle tremor and he would regularly say, "Yer nearly lost yer right ear there Daniel. Then where would yer be? You wouldn't be able to wear glasses would yer?"

When it was all over, he cleaned up and put the rough towel in the laundry box. There would be a mint humbug or some home-made toffee, covered in 'pocket lint', and there would be an incongruous "Anything for the weekend, Sir?"

By the time they had read a book, or done a page of a colouring book together, Emily would have done the ironing and it was folded neatly back in the cardboard box. The hairy twine would be re-knotted, and then from his trouser pocket Grandad would take out a box of matches and a stick of sealing wax.

"Look at the time." His pocket watch and chain were pulled out.

7

"Half past two," Daniel would say. It was the only time he knew. He took hold of the seal fob on Grandad's chain.

The match would be lit, the red wax would melt in great slow drops onto the knot of the hairy twine, and with a "Ta – Raaah" Daniel would press the seal into the soft gob of wax.

Time would be taken to examine that the letters, "W.C." , William Carr, had been neatly and precisely embossed into the wax.

"A cup of tea before you go Grandad?"

"Yes please, lass."

Now that he was four, pushing five, Daniel was allowed to walk Grandad to the Co-op bus stop. Then after waving to him when the bus pulled out, he would run up the hill back home without stopping.

Sally Cragg was William and Sarah Carr's eldest daughter, Emily's mother, Daniel's 'Grannie'. Strong, beautiful Grannie. Sally had held a small family party for Distington Grandma and Grandad when they both reached eighty. It was on neither of their birthdays. Daniel and his cousins, Harry and Billy, thought that this was as hilarious as things could get. Nobody sang 'Happy Birthday' either. There wasn't even a birthday cake.

Distington Grandma wasn't very well. The three boys were sent out to the garden.

"Yer ken play cricket or else yer ken dig grandad's garden ovver," said Uncle Harry.

Daniel ran, with great excitement, to the shed to get a spade. Harry and Billy just stared at Daniel. They knew how two could play together. At that age none of them knew how three could play.

They didn't have a cricket bat, or a ball for that matter, and they soon drifted morosely back into the party.

Billy and Daniel shared a glass of diluted orange juice in the kitchen. Harry, two years older than Billy and Daniel, went to stand with his dad and his grandad with their backs to the 'black leaded grate'.

"Old Harry, Young Harry, and Young Harry's Son Harry," said Emily pointing. Everyone laughed because it was Emily's joke. Emily didn't do jokes.

Distington Grandma had been taken for a lie down upstairs and the doctor was coming.

Emily took to going to Distington without Daniel for a few weeks.

She would drop him off at Meadow View, 'to help Grandad in the garden' and Grannie went to Distington with her, instead of Daniel.

And then Distington Grandma died. She died in Whitehaven Hospital of a "Stroke", whatever that was. Daniel knew nothing about death, how it happened, or what it meant. He was puzzled. Harry, Billy and Daniel said to each other, "Distington Grandma is dead." And that was it.

Four days later Distington Grandad turned up at Emily's prefab and had to knock on the door. He wasn't expected. Daniel heard the gentle tapping and ran to the door to see if there was indeed someone there. It was Great Grandad, with his cardboard box. All he had in his box, after all the palaver with the hairy string, was a collarless shirt, and a collar. It was his best shirt and his best white collar.

"Aah hev a new bewk, Grandad."

"Wheesht," said Emily.

"Go and get your book Daniel."

"I'll put the kettle on," said Emily. "Do yer want summat te' eat, Grandad?"

"Nae lass. Mebbe a biscuit."

"Sit beside 'es and read 'es yer book."

His finger traced the words for Daniel for three or four pages, then his finger stopped. Daniel read on for a few words then Grandad said, "Poor Grandma."

Daniel stopped reading and slid onto his lap, better to hear him.

"Poor Grandma."

After they had tea and biscuits, Emily said, "Look after Grandad will you Daniel, and aah'll git Uncle Harry."

It was Auntie Elsie who came.

"Would you like a lie down Grandad?"

"Nae lass, ah's read'n some Shakespeare wid Daniel."

Emily had gone down to the phone box and an ambulance arrived soon after she got back.

He died that evening of no apparent cause except sorrow.

Tom was a very gentle man. Not physically gentle. He was as rough and hard as anybody who worked in the pits was expected to be. In his thirties he still had big, heavily muscled shoulders and an athlete's torso. He walked with a slight stoop as if walking into a tough wind; or pushing something.

"Here's mi ede, mi arse is cummen," or "Here is my head, my backside will be along in a moment."

His gentleness was in his soft, teasing humour. His chesty laugh engaged everybody in his small circle of friends at Workington's new Rugby League Club, and at the Cricket Club, where he was the First Team scorer. People felt comfortable in his presence, told him daft jokes, told him secrets and gossip.

He was a check weighman at Micklam pit, and with six fountain pens, loaded with black, red, blue, green, purple and amber inks, he logged the mine's produce in huge leather bound, marbled edged ledgers with his 'copper-plate' hand. In this minor outpost of the West Cumberland coalfield he did the weighing and the counting of one-ton bogeys of coal and shale. Also, there was a deep-bed clay which could be fired at 1,400 degrees to produce linings and flues for the blast furnaces and Bessemer Converters of the steelworks five miles up the line in Workington. This clay was the gold dust of the mine.

The Micklam mine was a drift shaft of about 38 degrees from the horizontal, where narrow gauge bogeys could each carry one ton of stone. Each had to be shunted by hand, shoulder and backbone into three sidings. These were interchanged with 'the empties' for the down journey, before the next train of bogeys was to be brought up. They each had to be labelled and sorted 'coal', 'clay' and 'shale'. Then they were weighed.

The weighing, the accounting, and the recording were Tom's responsibility, as was the despatching of the cargo to the brickworks a mile or so up the line. These bogeys were pulled by a diesel version of 't'laal ratty' of Ravenglass fame.

It was a simple enough job, complicated only by the fierce storms which would billow up from the Solway Firth, a few hundred feet below.

In more egalitarian times Tom would have been a small-town accountant, but he would have missed the physicality of pushing the bogeys into line, getting things into order, being known as a 'good grafter'.

Tom took every opportunity to do overtime at Micklam, two or three times a month whenever there was a safety inspection or if the electricians needed to "wire a new seam" or as Tom sometimes said to them "changen' a leetbulb, asser".

From when Daniel was five or so, whenever his dad had to do any overtime, he got the chance to take him some extra bait, a 'corned beef sandwich and a rock cake' was favourite, for Tom, and indeed for Daniel. Being allowed to eat with his dad while the winching gear was working almost made him wet himself with joy.

Tom loved to watch out for his lad getting on to the path which ran along the side of the small gauge line. It was more than half a mile away, but he could recognise his son's gait, carrying the 'OXO' tin with his sandwiches and cake. Daniel would hold the box with both hands out in front of him and the closer he got to his dad, the quicker he walked until the last hundred yards he would be running at full tilt and Tom would make a pretend rugby tackle.

Sometimes the other men at the mine top would shout, "Ooh's the' ga'an on Daniel lad?" and he would reply, very formally, "Good afternoon, Mister."

"Did yer bring me any bait? 'Er is it oah fer thi' dad?"

"It's all for mi dad. Mister."

And Tom would try very hard not to weep with pride.

Every so often Daniel would get to his dad, just as the steelworks at Workington were opening their blast furnaces. Tom would know when they would 'tip oot' and he would take Daniel fifty yards or so to the full gauge link line to see this explosion of light. Sometimes on cloudy days the whole sky would glow vermilion, scarlet, magenta.

Once, at the end of summer, it had been sunny for ages and the sea was flat and glassy and reflected every flame and spark, doubling the glory on the shallow Harrington Bay. The lines on the main railway were turned to straight and true gold, and those on t'ratty to a gentler, wavy, silvery blue.

There was another time when the whole coast was sheathed in a dense sea mist.

"We won't be able to see it Dad."

"Wheesht, bide yer time."

And as he said that, the mist took on a glow which started in front of them as a slow, dancing, yellow stain and spread out into deep purples above them and pale pinks to their left. Fierce reds were to their right, and what had been the explosions of the furnaces, were taken in by the fog and given back out as a sigh, a singing, the humming of a half-forgotten hymn. Daniel turned about as if dancing to a tune, and behind them everything was blue or green, different each time he blinked. Tom's pit head buildings and their rows of bogeys were a fairy castle and its armies.

Tom held his son's hand. Then he took him back to the winch shed and made a quiet cup of tea.

"Ye'd best wait on and ga back yam wi' me." Maybe he had seen the same fairy castle as Daniel had.

"We divvn't want the 'bogey men' to git yer," he laughed.

If, on his way back home, Daniel could cadge a ride on t' ratty, or even better, to hold the wheel and pretend to steer the train, his small life was fulfilled. Sometimes they would see a large freighter a mile out to sea and Tom would say which country the ship had come from. Sometimes there would be lambs in the field on the brow above the cliff. And they just needed looking at.

For the first couple of years Daniel found school equally exciting and couldn't wait to tell his dad, and his mam, about "hundreds, tens and units", long division, and to sing the "song of the day", or recite a poem the class had learned. Tom kept an old "draft book" of his pit-head calculations, still leather bound and marbled edged, and when Daniel went to see him at work he would let him play with the numbers he had written down, let him add up those long columns to see if he got the same answers. A tick in green ink was the signal that Daniel's sums were as correct as his dad's. That the ink was green was the source of great hilarity. The noise of the winch made it difficult to hear, so Tom made Daniel write the poems and songs in a small hard backed exercise book he kept for the purpose. In a year or two Daniel almost filled each page of it.

Then one spring, the day before Daniel's eighth birthday, he had only been home from school a few minutes when he saw Miss Wildgoose, his teacher, coming up the path. Daniel had no idea why she was going to knock on the prefab door, he could not fathom what he had done wrong. He ran to the bathroom and hid behind the door. Miss Wildgoose was his dad's half cousin, even though she spoke posh. "Maybe my dad's in trouble," he thought.

"Hello Emily, I am sorry to catch you by surprise."

"Is something wrong? We only ever see each other at funerals."

"Isn't that a fact. No, I just wanted a chat about Daniel."

"What's he done now?" Daniel could hear his mam moving the settee and putting coal on the fire. "Have you time for a cup of tea?"

"No, no, I have to catch the 'five' bus. Thank you. No, Daniel's doing really well. It's just that he wrote this story in his Composition Book and it would be useful to know if it's all made up, or if it's written about a real event."

"Is he in trouble? Because he can be a handful, I know. You wouldn't want thirty of him in your class."

Daniel had written a story about his mother putting a tatie pot in the oven for tea. She turned the oven on and then went out, "to do her good works". When she came back an hour later the oven was cold. Switched on. But still cold. It was a new oven. It was a new prefab. She thought about calling the council, but she didn't have fourpence for the phone at the Co-op. A man from across the green, Mr Johnstone, was an electrician at Number 10 pit. He had come over and looked at the oven and saw that it was indeed switched on. But cold. Above the oven was another, bigger, switch. "You need to turn it on at the mains, Emily, lass," said Mr Johnstone. When Tom had come home they all had eaten the tatie pot, but Tom had said that the mutton was tough.

That was the story Daniel wrote.

The only true bit was that Tom had once complained to Emily about the "mutton being tough."

"His handwriting isn't neat. His little hand was going ninety to the dozen trying to catch up with what was going on in his head."

"He writes more neatly at home."

"I typed up a copy, I was thinking of sending it off."

"None of this is true. Jackie Johnstone has never been in this house without Tom being here."

"He shouldn't be writing stuff like this at his age." Things between Emily and Miss Wildgoose were not going well and it sounded like Daniel was in trouble. "... at this stage in his development."

"You can come and have a look at the oven if you like, it's spotless. It has never broken down."

"If it's all made up it's one thing. If ..."

13

"Why would he say that I had no money? Here's me purse, look for yerself."

"I don't think that is what Daniel has written."

"And Tom has never complained about my cooking." Daniel could hear his mother's tears welling up. She cried a lot did Emily.

"It really is a wonderful piece of writing." Miss Wildgoose was struggling with Emily, "Such imagination ..."

"He'll get 'imagination' when I catch him ... "

"I'm sorry Emily ... I'll have to go for my bus."

It was a good while before Emily went looking for Daniel. And she found him, still in the bathroom.

When Tom came home, Daniel was still in the bed to which he had been sent. There had been a very loud argument, with some very loud tears. Daniel could have listened to every word, but he put his head between his pillows. He could not work out what he had done wrong. Laying in his bed he had decided to retire from writing to concentrate on his sums.

Tom poked his head round the bedroom door. "Cummen hev yer tea son."

Tea was taken in silence. Daniel was so glad it wasn't a tatie pot. It was sausages. But the living room and the kitchen had been cleaned, "spotless". Daniel worked so hard to not say that the sausages were tough.

Then out of the silence his mother let rip. "She's not coming into my house sneering. I knew her mother better than you did. She was nowt better than a farm gate hooer, mair at yam on a haystack than in her own bed."

Tom got up from his seat and went and brought Emily's coat and scarf from the hall.

He did not have to say anything.

With a wail she charged out of the kitchen door into the damp night.

Tom and Daniel did the dishes and cleaned the kitchen.

Tom picked up a ball of rolled up paper from the coal scuttle by the fire. He carefully unrolled it and flattened all three pages with the palm of his hand. "You had better read it out loud to me. I can't read your handwriting." Tom talked properly and precisely when he was angry, but this time Daniel knew that his father was sad.

Daniel read his story to his father as properly and precisely as he could.

It was several minutes before Tom turned to look at his son.

"Your mam will be back in five minutes. Why don't you get bathed and into your bed for when she gets home?"

"I am sorry about my story Dad. I'll say sorry to Mam when she gets back."

"You will do no such thing."

Again, he was proper and precise. "Tomorrow you will be eight." He took a deep breath. "And life will not be any different. And you won't be any different."

Miss Wildgoose continued to be lovely, but Daniel thought that she might be embarrassed about her 'engagement' with his mam. Did she think she had "snitched" on him by showing his mother his stupid story?

Daniel still thought that his teacher was great.

She could play the piano without looking at the music, and that was cool enough for him. She was tall and pretty and dressed 'in clothes she didn't buy hereabouts'. But she had strayed unknowingly into the minefield that was Daniel's family.

As for his handwriting, Daniel took the obvious route of writing like his dad, with his copper-plate hand. He relearned how to 'draw' his letters, precisely, with uniform sizing and the right italic lean. He wrote rubbish of course, because he was now scared of what would come out of an uncontrolled pen. The slower he wrote the more was caught in the sieve. He no longer had his hand up all the time in class, not that he would ever get an answer wrong, but sometimes he knew the answer because he had worked it out properly, and sometimes he knew a better answer because it came out of his mouth before the thought. It was thus plain that there was no way that Daniel should have, or could have, worked out that better answer if he had consciously thought about it for some time. And that frightened him. It's where the 'tough sausage' would have come out if he hadn't stopped it.

Miss Wildgoose was always kind, but Daniel knew that she knew that he had turned off the tap. She never mentioned it though.

Daniel did have an escape route through his Auntie Gwen, who was only six years older than him and was still at Lowca School. She was in

Mr Proud's senior class. She would leave at the end of the year at fifteen, like all the others who had 'failed' the eleven plus. Gwen had to do homework once a week and the work took the form of a newspaper cutting, or a magazine article which came with four or five questions. Some of the questions were perhaps political, or maybe about the National Health Service or some would involve writing a letter to a bereaved relative or to a newspaper. But the questions were always open-ended and Gwen was, "buggered with all that."

Would Daniel do her homework for a tanner?

"I'll do it for a shilling."

"You'll do it for a tanner 'cos you know that I wouldn't manage a shilling, en' ah'd hev te' owe it t'yer. Will yer dae it or what?"

Daniel was of course dying to do it.

They wrote about the polio epidemic which was abroad at that time and about not being able to go to the swimming baths.

To a question about Workington steelworks, they wrote about the new Jane Russell brassieres being designed by a structural engineer who designed bridges and railways. This engineer's invention allowed Miss Russell's unusually magnificent bosom to bounce naturally in a film. 'The Outlaws', the film was called. "If I didn't have to pay you so many sixpences, I could afford to buy meself a Jane Russell bra." But it was Gwen who had seen the film, Gwen who had read about the film in magazines, and Gwen who had seen the adverts for the brassiere. It was Gwen who was able to make the connections, not Daniel.

They wrote about the Suez crisis without either Gwen or Daniel knowing, "where the fanny, Suez is." Daniel copied a map of the Middle East from the Daily Herald. He 'coloured in' the Mediterranean in blue and the Red Sea in red. They pissed themselves laughing at that. Daniel tried to draw a camel, but it looked like a dog. He drew a pyramid quite well, but he put it in Saudi Arabia.

They wrote about television without anybody they knew in the village having one yet.

They wrote knowing that Daniel wouldn't be marked for it, it would be Gwen who would carry the can, and they both knew that nobody would take it round to Emily.

Gwen didn't tell Daniel or anybody else how well these 'homeworks' were received by Mr Proud. Or indeed what Mr Proud thought of Gwen's change in handwriting style, but Gwen and Daniel had a lot of laughs on Sunday evenings. Mr Proud must have known that Gwen was getting someone else to write up her homework for her, but he would have regarded that as an important and appropriate life-skill to learn, for someone who aspired to a Jane Russell brassiere.

Daniel struggled at school for some time after the altercation between his mother and Miss Wildgoose. Lessons were still exciting, and maths was always fun, but he felt that he was somehow betraying his mother whenever he engaged enthusiastically with Miss Wildgoose's classes. Writing slowly and neatly and handing in mundane essays and stories was just as much hard work as writing well. Writing neatly and precisely didn't come easy to him and it took twice as long to do. Sometimes he had to work through the morning break so that he could finish what he was doing. Miss Wildgoose would stay in the classroom and have a cup of tea delivered to her. But she didn't, couldn't, engage. Daniel was comfortable 'just doing the work as requested' but he missed the engagement, 'the divil inside 'ev 'im', where all the jokes and funny remarks came from, where the occasional exotic word he didn't know that he knew sparkled in a sentence or made what he wrote sound more like what he would say. He knew that his mother was wrong to behave in the hysterical way that she did with Miss Wildgoose, but he also knew that she was ashamed and embarrassed about it. She had stopped asking Daniel about school, did not ask him about his lessons. "Did yer come top in yer sums, lad?" used to greet him almost every day when he came home from school and it was a great burden to him. But now the question was never asked, and he missed that.

Daniel gradually learned to understand the hurt and embarrassment his mother felt when Miss Wildgoose came to the house with his story. Miss Wildgoose was, being a teacher, an authority figure of sorts, but also a member of his dad's family. His story had highlighted all his mam's vulnerabilities; impoverishment, incompetence with ordinary things, and most of all, moral respectability. After all, she had won a scholarship to Whitehaven School in the twenties when it was all but a private school. Her name was on the honours board in Mr Proud's classroom. She went to church quite regularly. And now her infant son was writing rubbish about her and holding her up to ridicule.

Daniel understood all that.

17

So, in the early summer, when the school was taking a trip to Edinburgh, Daniel understood that he couldn't go. Miss Wildgoose understood that also.

Emily and Tom had had a couple of arguments about it. Tom had insisted that Daniel should go. "When do you think we could ever tek him to Edinburgh? He's ga'an, and that's that."

But Emily knew that by the time the trip came round, Tom would have forgotten about it, and besides, he was doing less overtime and she could play the 'not bringing enough in' card.

Daniel was not too bothered. He didn't understand what Edinburgh was. He knew that it was a big city, was the capital of Scotland and had a castle. But, none of those things meant anything to him.

So, on the last Friday in June, three busloads of Lowca school children set off in warm sunshine at 'nine sharp'. Daniel hid behind the boys' toilets to watch them go, and still pretended to himself that he was not too bothered.

He was either going to go back home and stay indoors just to annoy his mam, or he was going to stay out all day and make her worry.

The school had what was laughingly known as a playing field, but it was let out to Mr Boyle, the farmer, to paddock his milk dray horse. 'Everest' was a runt Clydesdale. Tracey Smith, who lived three doors away from Daniel, came out to stroke him. Daniel didn't know that anybody else from his class was not going on the trip. Her dad had been a prisoner of war and suffered "setbacks" which meant that he wasn't always at work.

"Why don't you stroke him?"

Daniel didn't want to say that he was scared to, so he hesitantly stroked Everest's nose. Its head reared up a little and they both giggled. He stroked its nose again and Tracey stroked its mane.

"When mi dad came out wid me yistieder, he calmed Everest doon and I stroked the hairs on its hooves."

In a rush of false courage, Daniel bent down and flattened the hair on its right hoof. He didn't think that he impressed Tracey as much as he impressed himself. All he got for his bravado was a handful of horse shit crumbs.

"Where were yez gaan?"

"Gaan t't' ghyll."

"What for?"

"To get a swing on t' rope widoot anybody push'n 'ez off."

"Can ah come en hev a swing?"

"If yer want."

"Bye Everest."

The horse nodded as if in assent. They giggled again.

Getting to the ghyll involved scrambling through a hole in a hawthorn hedge and at another fence holding some barbed wire down so that they could straddle over it. On both occasions Tracey showed her white knickers. She did the same again on the rope swing when the old hammer-handle they used for a seat pressed against her arse. The knot of the rope gave her a tail.

"Double up?"

"If yer want."

"You sit on it fusst, an' I'll sit on you."

They didn't swing high or fast, partly because the rope was pressing into Daniel's very painful erection. Did Tracey know that? As the swing came to a slow hover, they both jumped off.

"Race yer t't den."

The den was a small arched clearing with a canopy of interlocking willows and a hazelnut tree. In this warm weather the floor was dry and grassy, nobody had been here for some time. Daniel sat down and "adjusted himself" without Tracey seeing. She sat down beside him, then lay down flat on the grass.

"You can lift mi skirt up and look at mi knickers if you like."

Daniel blushed; his erection became even more painful. Within minutes they had each persuaded the other to undress.

"Shoes and socks as well," one of them said.

Daniel touched, then nervously rubbed her fanny. She held his cock. Only for a few minutes. Well, seconds really. She tried to kiss him, but that was too much for them both. They both jumped up, hysterical with embarrassment. They ran through the stream and back. They each pretended that someone was coming up the ghyll. They dressed in seconds.

"I'm ga'an yam, I need the lav."

Daniel held the barbed wire for her, but once she was over the fence, she was off.

Daniel didn't want to go home, and instead walked to 'Number 3' beach. There was nobody there and he could lie on the rocks and wave to the passing trains. The tide was quite high and had splashed over the flat sandstone slabs creating dark carmine pools, an inch or so deep with warm, soothingly warm, salt water. His socks, sandals and shirt, rolled into a bundle, made for a good pillow and he lay flat on his back and sweated onto the hot, dry stone. He fell asleep for a few minutes, maybe more. The salt from his sweat, or maybe the sea salt dust on the stone woke him with the stinging of his back. He got up very stiffly and looked down to see the pattern of his body marked out in red, damp stains. A round one for his head, a triangle for his torso and six little patches for his thighs, calves and heels.

The tide had receded to below the pebble stones, to a couple of acres of coal dust and sand.

Daniel thought of building a sand-castle but the rough, oily sand on 'Number 3' beach would sting, so he collected a few round cobbles and bowled out 'Len Hutton'.

Daniel was hot and hungry, but Tracey Smith had played with his cock. There was a lot to take in on his climb home.

Tracey's, and Daniel's, undoing happened at the same time, as he walked in the back door, just before tea.

Muddy feet under clean socks.

No rational explanation. Confession was inevitable and quick. Mothers compared notes and the punishment for each of them was probably the same.

When Tom came home, he got the full account of his son's depravity, garlanded with whatever damning details were available.

"Why wasn't he at school?"

There was no answer from his mother that Daniel could discern.

From his bedroom cell the shouting was too loud to hear. He covered his head with his pillow, but "I told you that he was going on the fucking trip, yer nasty little shit," was audible. Then there was, "You don't bring enough money in for treats and trips, I haven't had ..."

From then on it was the same old argument his parents had once a week, but this time it was repeated at full volume.

After half an hour the noise died down. Then there was another half hour of silence, broken by Tom, knocking on Daniel's door. He waited for Daniel's response.

"Aye."

"Git drissed son," he said quietly, "But wash yer feet fusst."

Emily was in the kitchen staring out of the window with damp eyes. Tom picked up her purse. "Ah gev yer the five-bob for the trip, git it oot." He threw the purse at her. "Git it oot," he shouted.

The five shillings paid for Daniel and his dad to go on the bus to Whitehaven, have "sit doon, knife 'en fork, fish and chips" and see a cowboy film at the pictures.

Alas the bus back to Lowca got in just as the three Edinburgh trip buses were disgorging their load.

Tom saw Miss Wildgoose, and Miss Wildgoose saw Tom.

"Sorry Tom," she started to say, but Tom and Daniel scuttled round behind Boyle's farm.

Daniel was ashamed as well.

"Dad," he said, "I have had a much more exciting day than if I had gone to Edinburgh." He realised his lack of tact and tried to fix things, "I mean going to the pictures and that."

"Mnnnn."

On the Monday, Tracey sneaked up behind Daniel in the playground at morning break. "Did you get a good hidin' as well?"

"Aye, ar got belted." He was a bit embarrassed at being reminded of their naked tryst.

"My mam went mad, me arse is red raw, aah won't be ont'swing fer a bit." They both giggled silently. "My dad thought it was funny though. He keeps asken me to take me socks off and show 'im me clean feet."

"Is yer dad orright?"

"Aye! Cheered 'im up nae end. He's back at wuk temorrer."

"Next time 'es a bad fettle, let us kno'."

Laughing makes everybody look beautiful.

On that same afternoon Miss Wildgoose caught up with Daniel at playtime in the school corridor. "I wonder if you would think it was an exciting thing to do if I asked you to write a story about what you did when the rest of the school was in Edinburgh."

Shit! Shit again! How the hell did she know about him and Tracey?

21

Had she grilled Tracey, or was it all round the school?

"I promise you, I won't show it to anybody, however good it is."

"Does it have to be the truth Miss?"

"If it's true to you, then that is true enough."

Daniel didn't really understand what she was talking about, but he was no longer in a state of panic.

"You promise Miss." He touched her cardigan. "You won't show anybody?"

"Cross my heart and ..." she did the thing with her hands. "Well, just write me a nice story, like the ones you write for Gwennie Cragg! "

"How do you know?"

She put her hand gently on his head.

"Yes Miss."

Daniel wrote about stroking the chuff of Everest's hoof and getting his hand covered in horse cack, as if he had been on his own and not with Tracey Smith. He wrote about going to Lowca beck, by Anderson's farm, where he sat there listening to the water, or at least its little silences, without the noise of other people and cousins around. He wrote about knowing that the 'babbling brook' was full of cow shit and piss slurry and it was still lovely, and gentle to hear. He didn't mention that he still carried an erection from what he had really done earlier that morning. He wrote about following the beck to the shore then walking towards Number 3 beach to lie on the vast sandstone slabs, hot with a month of sun, and waving to the mainline trains without feeling like a twat or being laughed at by any older kids. He did not write about turning over to lie on his tummy to hide and ease his still tumescent cock. He wrote about all the effluence from the pits, the farms, the steelworks, the "cankerwatter" from the tar plant and the engineering works on this, the most polluted shore in the whole country, and he wrote with his bad handwriting that all that he could smell from the pounding waves near to were oysters, mussels, herringfish and mackerel shoals, the cleanest, most cleansing of smells. And he wrote that he could only do any of those things if he was on his bloody own.

When he had finished his story the next day, he gave it to Miss Wildgoose in a sealed brown envelope, reinforced with his dad's sellotape. "There's some rude words in my story Miss. I can write my story again if you think it's bad. But please don't show it to anybody."

He reached to touch her again but pulled back his hand, "or send it off somewhere."

"Shall I read it now, while we have a bit of peace, then we can burn it together, and nobody else will ever see it or read it. How's that?"

It took her just a couple of minutes to read it, but then she spent another couple of minutes staring at what Daniel imagined was the last full stop.

"I know that I promised, but I cannot bring myself to burn something like this. It is very good as you well know." She hesitated, "But it is also very beautiful."

She looked at Daniel and her vermilion lips made a sort of smile.

She put the story very carefully back in the envelope. "You must show this to your mam and dad, especially your mam. She will want to read this and understand better who her little boy is, and what he can do sometimes."

"I think she knows exactly who I am and what I get up to Miss."

He really wanted to blurt out that the story was all lies and bollocks and that on the fateful day his story was supposed to be about, he was with Tracey Smith dancing nakedly and gigglingly in a muddy stream down in the ghyll. If he had made eye contact with Miss Wildgoose at any point, he would have told her everything.

But he didn't and that was fine. Daniel felt that his story was gift enough for her.

Of course, he couldn't show his story to his mam and dad because they would know full well how dishonest it was. Besides, it would have opened up fresh wounds. They had wanted a nice ordinary little boy and Daniel promised to himself that he would try and pretend to be one.

He scrunched the story into a ball and put it into his pocket. After school he went home by the ghyll, sat down under the tarzan swing and tore his story up into little stamp sized pieces. Each piece was rolled up to a pea sized ball and it was thrown into the stream. Daniel's little armada would float down the stream for half a mile and then navigate its way down the beck and into the sea. Maybe the tides would, bit by bit, carry his story up the coast to Number 3 beach and be cleansed by the waves crashing onto the sandstone slabs. Or maybe all those little balls of paper would just rot in the mud at the bottom of the ghyll.

CHAPTER 2

————

Daniel did not notice it immediately, but over time he stopped taking his dad his extra bait to Micklam. There were fewer opportunities for Tom to do overtime. Then once, in early summer, when Daniel was nine, he went as if to go to Number 3 shore, through Forster's farm and down to Micklam's main buildings. He had his trunks and a towel in a brown paper bag. Tom must have seen him coming while driving t'ratty and by the time Daniel got to the railway lines, Tom, his engine and eight empty bogies were waiting.

"Y'on yer own?"

"Ah was gaan t't shore. Mebbe Harry and Billy are there."

"Does yer mam know yer 'ere?"

There was a sadness in his voice.

"Ah didn't bring yer any bait."

"Ah'm not stopp'n."

"You haven't stopped fer a long time," Daniel said.

There was a short, enunciated "No."

"Shudda mebbe ga yam?"

"Aye, yer mam'll be worried."

Harry and Billy were not on the shore anyway. On his way home he heard their voices, with the three Gibsons at the rope swing in the ghyll.

He didn't try and join them.

Over the next couple of weeks when Daniel was staying up a bit later, his mam and dad's fights and arguments, and their tender conversations also, all seemed to be about Micklam.

Uncle Harry came to the house, and they talked about Micklam in dark tones.

Grandad came.

Daniel asked questions in an oblique way, but got no response except, "There's nowt wrang, lad. Divvn't worry."

"Then why hez Grandad been round. Eh?"

"Grandad's been roond cos he's yer grandad."

"Then why are we all so unhappy?" he wanted to ask, but instead, "Is it cos ah's bad?"

"Course it isn't."

He could always tell when his mam and dad were lying; they tried to talk proper. There was a lot of 'enunciating' being done throughout that early summer.

It took until August for it to come out, well, enough of it for Daniel to understand the bare bones of his dad's travails at work.

Tom worked with three men at any given time on Micklam's pit top. Sometimes the three changed, one or two at a time, but for almost a year, the three men stayed who they were.

Les Thornton, Len Clayden and John Dee.

Tom didn't just understand the numbers, the additions and the subtractions, of his job in separating the fireclay, the coal and the shale. He understood the mathematics, the rhythms, the music of what was coming out of the pit and up the shaft.

"Things wurrent reet."

The first thing he did was to requisition three extra ledgers from the main office.

"Summat up?" asked Lennie Coombs, the pit manager.

"Just need te mek sure ivverything's reet." He paused. "It's owt about nowt Lennie." But he did convey that there was an 'it' that was concerning him.

"Hev yer got enough colours? Ah ken git yer some purple ink, wud yer like some pink ink, Tom asser?" Everybody in the office laughed, not just at Lennie's little joke, but at Tom's fastidiousness, his copper-plate hand and his multi coloured logs.

From Brents' stationers in Whitehaven, he ordered some sheets of A3 graph paper.

He began making charts and graphs of the output of the pit.

He did pie charts and 'manhattan graphs' of the pit's output from the statistics of the previous six months.

"Some bugger's pinch'n coal," he had said to Emily, to Grandad and to Harry.

"Look on," he said. "There's a twelve per cent drop in the production of coal. A nine per cent increase in the production of shale, and a two per cent increase in fireclay."

"Where'st miss'n one per cent?" asked Harry, laughing a little at Tom's discomfiture.

"No!" he stressed. "Look here, all they need to do is swap six inches off't top of a coal bogey wid six inches off't top of a load of shale. Neaboby in't sheds 'er ganna check, as lang as they git their clay."

"Oh't coal is just shunted off ter Wukkinton wid'oot anybody look'n," realised Grandad.

"Hoo much coal duz thou reckon's gone miss'n?" said Harry.

"Eighteen point six tons since t'fuss't a' February."

"Bugger me," said Old Harry and Young Harry together.

"How'd they git it oot?" asked Young Harry.

"Round't back of John Pit, naebody would see them," suggested Grandad.

"Who would they sell it to?"

"Hutchinsons," said Harry, "Oa't four of t' brothers could just drive up en git it shifted in five minutes."

This of course was all conjecture by three men who had never pinched a thing in their lives.

"Hev ye reported it?" asked Harry.

"Nut yit."

"Yer can't report it," said Grandad. "Len hez 'is mother and three young sisters te look efter."

"John's just got married," said Tom.

"Then shop Thornton," said Harry. "'E's got a car 'n'all."

"A van," said Tom.

"Ye can't shop just yan er'them, 't'others would git it 'n'all."

"I hev copies of oht'three bewks. Ah keep them in't airing cupboard."

"Naebody wud speak t'yer if yer did shop them lad," advised Grandad.

"Y'ev te dae what's reet, whativver," said Harry.

There was a communal "Aye," signalling that nobody had a clue what to do. Trust, reputation, integrity, communal responsibility, were the ropes which kept both the pits, and the Lowca community itself, tied together over the years. Those ropes saw them through the war and through the new dawn of Attlee's government, the NHS, prefabs with fridges.

They were the same ropes which threatened to hang Tom.

Nothing got sorted in a formal way. Tom had a quiet word with Len Clayden, but Len had pretended not to understand what he was talking about. Les Thornton had been his friend right through school. They started work at Micklam on the same day.

"Ye've seen nowt."

"Fer fuck's sake stop it now Les, while yer hev a chance. What'll Len and John dae if yer git caught?"

"If you shop us, yer mean."

"Ah will if it ga'as on."

And that was roughly where it was left for some weeks. Tom kept up with his stratagems of making copies of the official ledgers on single sheets of file paper and filling in his own books and his charts when he got home.

Tom, Grandad and Harry seemed to draw closer. Emily seemed to drift further away. None of the three of them really drank, so going to the Ship Inn for a pint, or to the Legion, was never an option. They couldn't talk openly about it anyway. Sundays and Tuesdays with the colliery band wasn't on because three of the players worked at Micklam and all the others were from the pits and the various dependent works in the area. They were all imbued with the same tight values as Tom, Grandad and Harry anyway. Their certainties were communal ones.

Tom kept a close eye on the numbers, and for a week or two, nothing was untoward. Les, Len and John returned to being friends as well as colleagues. They exchanged kindnesses, brought cakes in to share, swapped fags and shared intimate stories about village girls and Whitehaven women.

Tom didn't let his guard down in the secretive manner of his copying and transferring of the day's data, and though he told his jokes, and his cricket stories, he never gave anything away to anybody else at Micklam, or his family, or anyone in Lowca.

Then the "numbers" started to drift again.

He mentioned this one late Sunday afternoon at Meadow View, when Emily, Grannie and Grandad, Harry and Elsie joined with him for card games in the parlour. Daniel was in the kitchen by the fire pretending to read. Harry and Billy were playing marbles in the yard.

Mrs Vernon had left some French pastries and they took precedence over the whist and the pontoon.

"Whativver ye dae Tom, we'll back yer," said Auntie Elsie.

"Mind on, yer'll be tarred wid't same brush if they git caught," said Harry.

"People will turn agin yer whativver ye dae," said Grandad.

"And ah'll turn agin yer if yer dae owt te harm yer family," warned Grannie. "There's yer lad in't kitchen needs te know that his family is honest. And ah need tae know who wants another coffee."

The orders taken, Grannie went into the kitchen, "What are ye readin'?"

"Nowt much, another book aboot poncy boys in a private school bullyin' each other."

"Can yer help me wash these cups while ah mek fresh coffee?"

"When ah grow up ah'm ganna write a book aboot Billy Hawthorne and the Gibsons ga'an birds nestin', en Harry an' Billy git'n stuck on Number 3 beach at high tide ..."

"You just write about yersel' lad. That'll mek a grate bewk."

On the following Tuesday, Tom was finishing his shift as usual, just before five. He had done his books and had them in their 'suitcase' for delivering to Lennie Coombs to be signed off and put in the safe. He had eight bogeys of fireclay and twenty odd men cadging a lift from the shaft to the changing shed by the number two furnace. Another twenty men walked behind on the track, not much slower.

Les Thornton, Len Clayden and John Dee were left behind to check the miners' tags, secure the winching shed, order the forty odd bogeys in their sidings, and lock the big metal gates which secured the entrance to the mineshaft.

Lennie Coombs knew that something was up with Tom, but he couldn't find the space to address him among the six secretaries dressing and preening and laughing to go home.

Tom thought about saying something, but he wasn't good at this sort of thing.

He said "see yer" to Lennie and smiled at the girls.

"Tell Emily we were asken efter 'er," said one of them.

"Will dae."

He took the slightly longer route home, by the farm, and for no reason at the time he looked across towards the pit top. It was nearly a mile away, but he could see six figures moving quickly around the sidings. He could recognise each of Les, Len and John from the way they moved, but the three others were not people he knew. They moved quicker than any pitman ever did after a shift.

Emily had made a reasonable tea, a kind of shepherd's pie, but nobody seemed to be eating much as Tom told his story of the day, of how the girls in the office sent their best wishes, about not getting the chance to talk to Lennie. He then described seeing three extra men in the siding.

"They musta been theer afore a'ah left wid't' ratty." He looked at Emily, as if for some sort of confirmation, "They musta been waitin'. Watchen 'ez."

"You have to leave, pet."

They were both beyond tears. Daniel thought about crying on their behalf, but he reasoned that the best thing that he could do would be to eat up his dinner, then offer to do the dishes.

"All three of us will do the dishes," said Tom, "Then we'll oah ga'a fer a walk."

The walk was, of course, to Grannie and Grandad's.

It was still light. The sun was setting in a blaze of reds across the Solway just north of the Isle of Man. The tops of the mountains behind and beyond Pica bounced the colours back and it occurred to Daniel that this was a very important day.

Tom explained to Grannie and Grandad that in the morning he was going to go in and see Lennie and hand his notice in.

There was no discussion.

Grannie hugged Tom and kissed the side of his cheek.

Grandad hugged his daughter and shook Tom's hand very formally.

Daniel stepped backwards to allow the grown-ups to do what it was that they were doing.

As they went out through the door Grannie hugged his head from behind. "You are a very lucky little boy."

It didn't feel that way to them when they got home. Daniel was sent to have his bath while Tom cleared the living room table, and with his best Parker pen and black ink, set about writing his letter of resignation. Emily helped him with a few choice clichés normally associated with these things.

"With immediate effect."

"... thank you personally for your professional support down the years ..."

"... look forward to maintaining cordial personal links ... "

When Daniel got out of the bath Tom had gone out to put the letter through Lennie's letterbox. He only lived on Solway Road.

When he got back, he gave his sad son a hug and sent him off to bed.

Daniel hadn't had any supper, but he didn't think that his trivial needs were important in the context of that night.

Tom's resignation meant that the family didn't qualify for immediate financial support. If the three men ever got caught pinching coal and were sacked, they would qualify for the dole immediately. Tom, honest and honourable Tom, had to wait for three months before he could apply for special family support to cover the cost of food for 'dependent child.'

Daniel, the dependent child.

Emily and Tom's optimism and their joint belief that Tom had 'done the right thing' lasted well in the early weeks. So much so that they could both, secretly as far as Daniel was concerned, take part in the ceremonials of the Family Christmas Present Swapping. Tom was the eldest of ten, and he took his duties seriously now that his dad, John, was no longer alive to oversee the proceedings.

There were a lot to buy for, and from Daniel's point of view there were a lot to receive from. 'Gosforth Grandma' was in mourning for a long time after Gosforth Grandad's death. Apart from Richard and Walter who were not much older than Daniel, all Tom's brothers and sisters were grown up and they were all popping out youngsters of their own by the year. The presents were usually small. There were tins of toffees or chocolate, books from the twins, Elizabeth and Eleanor, a ball of some kind from George, that sort of thing. 'Gosforth Grandma' and Richard counted as 'one' for the purposes of the sums. Tom had a mathematical phrase for the logistics; 'ten factorial'. However, the Family Christmas Present Swapping solved the problem whereby each of the ten, plus Grandma, gathered at 'young John's' with pillow-cases full of wrapped and labelled gifts.

John and Mary's living room acted as the 'sorting office' and their kitchen acted as a 'tea and cake factory'.

Margaret, the second oldest, was a little different. She was already on her way to half a dozen kids of her own, and had caught the knitting bug, so all her gifts were knitted. There were multi coloured scarves, 'arran' sweaters, 'cable stitch' pullovers, cardigans with leather buttons, quite a lot of balaclavas, and once, to great hilarity, a woollen bra and panties for Shiela who 'had the figure for such a thing'.

"Wid oah these babbies, ah divvent knoa when she gits time ter knit," said George.

"Or where she puts t' knitt'n needles in't' babby mek'n process," said Tom.

Apart from the jollity of "Family Christmas Present Swapping" parties, Emily was determined, Tom's unemployment notwithstanding, to "Show the Flag". She amassed a 'same as last year' array of gifts. She took a bit more care in the wrapping and labelling. She had tried to bake a fruit loaf and a tin-ful of fairy cakes, but they 'hadn't worked out' and Mrs Vernon came to the rescue with some of her elegant 'Tartes Tatin'. That everyone recognised that Emily was making a special effort only served to embarrass her more.

Nobody mentioned 'the unemployment', nor indeed, Tom's moral dilemmas. However, George's gift to Emily and Tom was a cardboard box containing two plucked pheasants. In a brown paper bag there was a substantial salmon, rolled up in a couple of pages of a dirty magazine, "just ter git Emily ga'an". There were remarks about the legitimacy of his 'purchases', and where, for example, had he bought the salmon?

"Caught it mesel. Tickled it oot'et Calder wid' me tickl'n fingers." He demonstrated a rather rude gesture, which brought a rain of slaps from Elizabeth and Eleanor.

They had all been born and brought up on the farm at Barngill, just a mile east of Lowca, but they had moved to the middle-class rurality of Gosforth just after the war. They had all lost the harshness of the Lowca accent and most of the idiosyncratic vocabulary. But they all shared, if not Tom's and his father John's huge nose, then the genetic trait of cavernous sinuses, and the soft, echoing modulation of their speech.

If they were all talking together, as they did at funeral wakes, they offered the base line to the sound of the general throng.

Emily and Tom got back home just as Grandad dropped Daniel off from taking him to the Workington Reds' game. They had cast aside the pretence that he didn't know where they had been, and what for, and he helped to hide all the parcels from himself in the space above the airing cupboard.

"I hope I don't find all these presents before Christmas!" he said, as they closed the cupboard door together.

CHAPTER 3

Tom knocked on a lot of doors in Whitehaven and Workington looking for a job appropriate to his aptitudes and skills. He wore his suit and took the bus for the first few weeks, but eventually accepted the realities of his situation and started walking to interviews, sometimes ten miles each way, and once, to Maryport, there and back.

All three of them started full of hope. But come the new year Emily was the first to crack. She cried every day. She screamed and shouted every other day. She gave up on trying to make good meals out of nothing.

Worst of all was the regular, "It's all yer dad's fault."

As the hardships and the small humiliations piled up, they lost their togetherness.

Every time Daniel was slightly naughty it was, "What have we done to deserve him?" In his early childhood the same phrase was used as an expression of joy.

Tom still looked strong and fit. He was walking over fifty miles a week, but his shoulders started to sag, and the lean in his posture became more pronounced.

He was ashamed and was belittled with fierce regularity.

Lennie Coombs never went to the house to query Tom's resignation in the first weeks, or subsequently to see how his erstwhile friends and colleagues, Tom and Emily, were. Emily had worked in his office as his personal secretary for five years. 'Micklam' was how Emily and Tom had met. The remainder of Tom's pay and his 'holiday money' were dropped off by a secretary from Parton, not someone from the village who was known and could possibly be invited in for a cup of tea. Those small things became big things.

Tom sometimes wondered if Lennie knew all about Thornton's scam, but was too weak to do anything about it. "Maybe Lennie was gitt'n a cut?" he once asked out loud.

Sea coal and the wood from broken tar barrels kept the house warm and the fire was a source of entertainment. The choice of radio station was always a point of conflict and silence was the constant compromise.

It was one evening 'watching the fire', four months in to their 'confinement', that Emily got up to answer a knock on the back door. Tom heard the lowering of his wife's voice and reacted by jumping up and dashing to the door.

Les Thornton was at the coal bunker struggling to tip a sack of coal in.

Tom charged violently through the kitchen and shoved Emily into the chairs and table. He scrambled over the railing steps to land four feet below, onto Thornton. He pinned him down in the blackness, in the coal. Thornton was the first to scramble out of the bunker, trying to escape. Daniel was standing in his underpants and vest at the top of the steps and for a second or two he started to cry, but he was soon taken over by the thrill of a 'full on' fight. Tom jumped after Thornton and with a large cobble of coal in his right fist started belting him, first into his ribs, then round his elbows and arms. He caught him one glancing blow to the side of his head and one full punch to the forehead which shattered the lump of coal. Thornton threw a few blind punches in the light from the kitchen door, then he struggled free to run to his van.

In the light from the front windows of the prefab, Tom, in his socks, chased after Thornton and in a flying tackle from behind, hit him with his right shoulder into his buttocks to explode him into the paving slabs of the front path. Thornton's body shuddered and ground into the path for four or five yards before it stopped. Tom jumped to his feet and knelt astride him, both knees pressing inwardly into his ribs. Tom was about to rain more punches on him when he just stopped.

Tom did not know what made him stop.

Thornton cringed slowly into a ball waiting for the next blows. Tom stood still, apart from his heaving chest, and allowed Thornton, Les Thornton, his erstwhile school friend, to crawl to the safety of his van.

Daniel had got to within a yard of the fight and his arms swung round rhythmically in imitation punches. His dad's diving tackle only just missed him. It was so beautiful. He knew that when his dad stopped and let Mr Thornton go free that it was a virtuous thing. The act of a good man. "My dad," Daniel said softly. "My dad." But he also knew that his dad's flying tackle in all its speed, power and elegance was the more important event. It had something to do with God he thought.

"Y'oh'reet Tom asser?" It was Mr Elliot from next door.

"Aye. Oh'reet Wilfred." Tom gasped.

Daniel skipped in his bare feet to hug his Dad.

"Grate tackle," said Mr Elliot.

In later life Daniel would see many great tackles. He would see Gus Risman tackle Billy Boston into touch two yards in front of him when he was still a child. Then once, when Daniel himself was playing against Coventry, David Duckham flew past him to tackle Charlie Bend from behind, with the same elemental elegance with which Tom had felled Les Thornton.

Tom, in his gasping, knew that his tackle and his grace in letting his friend go free were two parts of the same, single spiritual act and he had to keep on breathing heavily to hold back some tears.

Four months of pain, loneliness and despondency assuaged by one transcendent moment?

Not really.

Daniel had sidled up to his dad from behind and gently caressed his still, clenched fist.

There was coal dust and some blood and Tom wiped his hands on his shirt.

"Git drissed, en put yer coat on, Daniel."

When Daniel was dressed he went to the bathroom and shared the basin of hot soapy water with his dad. He washed his face and his hands and took on some traces of the blood and coal silt from Tom's dirty water. Tom and Daniel used opposite ends of the same towel to dry off.

Emily was still in a state.

"He was oney tryen' ter help," she wailed "When did you last bring owt in?"

Even Daniel was ashamed of her.

"Stop yer twinen' and git roond 'en git Harry te help yer clear oot ivvery last speck 'e coal dust oot'er that bunker."

"We need the bloody coal."

"We need te git oah that coal oot. It's Micklam coal."

"Coal's coal," she shouted.

"If the' find Micklam coal in oor shed, a'ah'l be ga'an te jail," he cried, "Ye' useless lump."

Tom stormed out and started shovelling Thornton's coal back into his sack. Daniel held the sack mouth open for him.

At this point Mr Elliot came up the path, this time with his coat on. "Owt ah ken dae te help lad?"

"Aye, ye can asser. What's left 'er t'coal in't bunker yer ken tek it yam and put it on yer fire."

"Ah'm up fer that."

"It's stolen coal Wilf, and Thornton's tryen' te frame 'es wid it."

"Micklam coal is it?"

"Aye. Ah'm tekken' it back te the bastard."

"Te Parton? D'ye need me te cum wid yer?"

"Nae, ah've got me lad."

Mr Elliot picked a handful of the coal up into his hand to hold it to the light. "Tis 'n'oah asser."

Tom had filled Thornton's sack and was gasping again. Mr Elliot dashed back to his own house and emerged with a thick leather pitman's yoke. He put it on Tom's shoulders and helped him get the sack of coal aloft and balanced.

"Ye'll hev te carry it a coupla times Daniel lad."

Daniel had no concept of the scale of what it was that his dad was going to do. He understood that he was going with his dad to take the bag of coal to Les Thornton's house, to Parton, in the dark.

Mr Elliot had run back into his house again and came chasing after them with two large flashlights. "Batteries might be flat, so just use yan at a time Danny lad."

The rhythm of his Dad's boots on the tarmac road guided Daniel's stride.

He kept his light steady until they got out onto the main road down to Parton. He turned it off when they had the streetlights, past the Ship Inn, past the Co-op bus stop and over the railway lines of 'Number 10' pit. Down past East Croft and West Croft Terraces. He turned the torch on again at the Brethren Chapel.

Some cars came up the hill with their lights on and put them on 'main beam' right into their eyes. They must have been a curious sight. Tom started to falter as they crossed the bridge over Lowca Beck. He sat on the sandstone parapet but kept the sack perched on his shoulders.

Daniel tried the second torch and it shone brighter than the first and up got Tom again.

Daniel knew that Parton wasn't far away and told his Dad in confident tones. "Nut far noow dad! Keep ga'an. Eh."

"Fower 'undred yards, count me steps out loud fer 'ez lad."

Daniel did, and to please and impress his dad he counted down from four hundred, three hundred 'en ninety-nine, three hundred 'en ninety-eight . . . "

He counted to the rhythm of his strides and it felt like singing.

When Daniel got down to '. . . a hundred 'en eight . . ." Tom stopped.

"We're here," he said, trying not to gasp.

He let the bag of coal drop off his shoulders right by the white door. One of the curtains of the front windows of number 129 opened quickly and an attractive woman put her face to the glass. Then Les Thornton's face appeared. He had a bandage round his forehead which covered his left ear. He had a terribly bruised eye, not swollen, but black.

The curtain was just as quickly closed, then the light was turned off.

Tom emptied the coal out of the sack and with his foot he spread the coals all over the pavement.

Daniel grabbed the sleeve of his dad's jacket and they turned and walked away.

Tom walked quite quickly, as you do when a load comes off your shoulders. Daniel had to walk and run to keep up with him.

Daniel struggled to get up the hill but hid his strain. Tom was profoundly weary. Even Wilf Elliot's yoke felt heavy. "Race yer up ter't' Ship, Dad."

"Riddy! . . . Stiddy! . . . Gaa!"

But neither of them had it in them to quicken their cadence and they laughed.

Both of the flashlights had failed, but they were, by now, close to the lights of Lowca. It was still only just after nine o'clock and Daniel was surprised to see so many people milling around the village.

"Back shift off, t'neet shift on," mumbled Tom.

"Hoo's tha' ga'an on Tom?" Half a dozen men came out of the Ship and greeted Tom as if all the village were out for a stroll in the evening light before going home for a cold supper and a dry sherry before bed.

One of them called back, "It's past your Danny's bed-time."

Daniel was frightened a little about going into the house, but Emily was radiant, with her best frock on, a pot of tea on, with a half packet of biscuits which Auntie Elsie had brought round.

"I've run you a bath."

She said, "I'm sorry," as much to herself as to Tom and they kissed standing up.

"Mam," Daniel exclaimed.

Daniel had milk, again from Auntie Elsie.

"Bed."

"I'm all dirty."

"Thank you, son."

"T's'oahreet Dad." As if it was no big thing.

Tom's heroics on that trip to Parton never materialised into anything.

He thought that Lennie Coombs or someone from 'head-quarters' at Workington might pay a visit to check what coal there was in the bunker so that they could ascertain if it was indeed Micklam coal, or 'Number 10' coal. Even though the shafts of each pit were only a mile and a half apart, the coal was from entirely different seams. Lennie Coombs would have known and understood what had happened to Les Thornton's face. That nothing was done confirmed to everyone at Micklam that "summat wuz up" and so "nowt wuz sed, asser."

Mattocks' delivered all the coal to Lowca, and they only delivered 'Number 10'. Hutchinsons' had the contract for Micklam coal but they picked it and bagged it directly from the Workington depot. If any of their coal trucks came anywhere near Lowca there would be "ructions on."

"The great Lowca coalfield war!"

The bunker had been brushed out clean and then swilled out with the bucket and mop.

Uncle Harry delivered a wheelbarrow of coal, Number 10 coal, to scatter on the concrete bottom in case there was indeed a visitation.

Then Tom put a padlock on the latch of the bunker.

"It's a sign ev things when y'hev te lock up a bunker in this village," said Harry.

"Thanks Harry. Ah'll top it up wid some sea coal," said Tom.

"Ah want te see Lennie Coombs's face when y'oppen't door fer 'im," said Harry. "'E'll hev te knock on yer door te git te see in, ye promise te roond up ivverybody frem Ghyll Grove te cum'en look at 'im."

Everybody wanted that to happen, but it never did.

Thornton having the shit kicked out of him by Tom was perhaps the best solution. Len Clayden's mother and three sisters, and John Dee's new wife would be none the wiser.

But Tom still didn't have a job after all those months.

By now he had given up on finding a job "with a pen" and was looking to take up anything at all. He got one or two temporary labouring jobs for three or four days at a time, and he lived in hope that they might lead to something more permanent.

"They're shit-shovellin' jobs and naebody ken shovel mair shit than me," he would exclaim with a false jollity.

Every week there was the small hope of a job in each of the local papers, and every week there was disappointment and rejection. He was an educated, fastidious man, and what was he doing giving up a good job at Micklam?

That Tom was reduced to applying for basic labouring jobs meant that he had no chance of getting them. If he had to write a letter of application or fill in a form, he did so in proper sentences with his copper-plate handwriting. They would be the first to be thrown in the bin.

Emily never went out of the house, except to see her parents, and even then, she took the path through the ghyll where nobody would see her. She never called in on Harry and Elsie because they seemed such a happy family.

Tom said nothing. He got used to saying nothing. No silly jokes, no teasing. He looked for jobs, he picked coal off Lowca beach at low tide. He picked mussels. If a rowboat came into Parton, and he had a sixpence, he brought three mackerel home.

He was never a proud, articulate, witty and upright man, ever again.

CHAPTER 4

Throughout this time, Daniel was not much help to his mam and dad. He spent too much time indoors and getting on their nerves. He didn't go "out to play" much. He had had enough of "schoolfriends" by the end of the school day. Maybe this was part of the natural cycle of growing up, of being nine, and becoming more independent. Maybe his peculiar family situation made him less confident, less trusting.

Nobody in the village ever mentioned Tom's situation with Micklam, or indeed the beating he had given Les Thornton. Everybody in Lowca knew, but they were always too embarrassed to mention it. Daniel was never overtly teased about it.

But nobody ever knocked on the door, with a ball in their hands, asking Daniel to come out to play.

Then Daniel did an awful thing.

Once a year, when the weather got warm, the junior part of the school went to Allonby for a day trip.

Allonby was about fifteen miles up the coast, had vast flat sands, a playpark, and some shops which sold balls, fishing lines and unflyable kites.

The trip would cost two shillings, and that was out of the question at such a time. Daniel never even mentioned it at home. But when the day for the trip got closer, out of spite, he prayed for rain. He prayed for rain in Church on the Sunday morning before the Friday of the trip.

He checked with Tracey to see if she was going on the trip.

"Ah hev'n't missed a trip since that time wi' thee." She hit Daniel in the chest with her fist and laughed. "Me mam wouldn't dare nut send 'ez." She must have understood. "Yer nut ga'an ah suppose."

"No."

"Hev yer got another lass lined up fer't' ghyll?"

She knew that Daniel didn't and couldn't, and she put the palm of her hand on that part of his chest which she had just punched.

When Mr Hall noticed that Daniel hadn't paid for the trip, he kept him in the classroom at playtime. "Daniel; the Allonby trip?"

Daniel burst with blushing, he struggled to breathe with the embarrassment. Why couldn't Mr Hall just forget it and leave him alone.

"Will you be coming with us?"

A whispered, almost inaudible, "No, Sir." It was all that he could squeeze out.

"Why not? I can make the arrangements so that your mum and dad don't have to pay."

He could see that Daniel was on the verge of crying. That was the worst thing that he could say when Daniel was trying to hide his shame, trying to pretend that everything in his family was fine and dandy.

Daniel wanted to say something along the lines of, "Leave me and my family alone, it's nowt tae dae wid thee." He blew hard to stop the tears. How could he say at such an age that he loved his mam and dad so much that it hurt his head, that it made his shit bleed, and that he knew that he was the only thing that kept his family from going mad in this shitty fucking world and in this shitty fucking village. He understood that he wasn't old enough or big enough to carry all that.

But he couldn't articulate that.

"Don't like Scotland. Sir," was all that he could mumble. He stared at Mr Hall's cardigan with its leather buttons. "Where the buggery did that come from?" he thought.

Mr Hall must have had the same thought as he took his time, and a deal of care, before he said anything. Instead of saying, "Allonby is nowhere near Scotland, you stupid boy," he came up with, "If you think really hard about it I am sure that you, of all people, can come up with a plan."

"I have made alternative arrangements for that day. Sir."

Though Daniel couldn't see Mr Hall's face, he knew that his teacher had stifled a laugh at his silliness and pomposity. Mr Hall was sensitive enough to change the subject by asking Daniel to take the wastepaper basket to the bins. As he picked up the basket, as an afterthought Mr Hall said, "If you do eventually come on the trip, I will bring a rugby ball and I will organise a touch rugby match on the

41

beach. I will play on one team and Miss Wildgoose will play on the other, how's that?"

How did he know that Daniel had dreams of Miss Wildgoose playing rugby with her skirt tucked into her knickers, as if for skipping?

Tom and Emily never mentioned the trip. On the Friday, they got Daniel up out of bed a little later than usual, gave him a good breakfast and, when they knew that no other kids would be around in the village, they sent him off on a spurious errand to his Grandad. Daniel got a second breakfast of toast and milk from his Grannie.

"Can ah hev a lend of Gwen's bike please?"

"Aye, she doesn't use it much. Yer might hev te pump the tyres up. Where yer ga'an?"

"Just a bike ride, might tek some paper and dae a drawin'."

"Why don't yer ga te Pica or Lamplugh 'en draw the mountains?"

"Might dae."

Daniel did indeed have to pump the tyres up. He gave the bike a good wipe down. He had never had a bike of his own, and this was fun to him. He was going to take the saddlebag off to make it look less 'sissy'. The lack of a crossbar was embarrassment enough. But his Grannie brought him some jam sandwiches and a small bottle of water.

"Theere's a pencil and some white writing paper if yer want te dae a drawin' lad."

So, the saddle bag stayed, and he was ready for an expedition.

"Ah'll tell yer mam what yer dae'n lad." As he mounted the bike, she gave him a clean hankie.

Pica or Lamplugh sounded a great idea, Pica AND Lamplugh sounded even better.

But Daniel didn't go there. He needed to go 'somewhere else'. He needed to go to a lot of 'somewhere elses'.

Workington docks sounded fun. The Western Fells are beautiful, they would be hard to draw. Workington docks were ugly, dirty, and would be perfect for him.

He got to Workington too quickly. Gwen's bike was three or four years old and had been used only occasionally by her, so one of the many ideas floating in his mind was to carry on to Maryport, perhaps find the factory which his dad had walked all the way to. Where he still could not get a job. Where he walked all the way back to Lowca from.

It was his intention to find some significant place in the works, and piss on it. Piss on it with a full bladder, maybe fart as well.

By the time he got to Maryport, and tried to find his way around, he was at Maryport docks anyway.

He had no particular affection for docks or harbours. Daniel had never been on a boat. However, in the one art shop in Whitehaven, paintings of boats in harbours seemed to be the fashion. Harbour scenes in framed prints. The front covers of 'How to Paint' books were of Cornwall, the Mediterranean, or of the Thames in London.

Whitehaven harbour shipped coal and phosphates. Workington harbour shipped railway lines.

What Maryport harbour shipped, Daniel had no idea, but the boats were not small, or brightly painted. The six boats in Maryport harbour were each 'sixty footers', and they were the colour of slag heaps, had big diesel engines spewing out black smoke from their constantly chuntering motors. One of the exhaust flues on one of the boats had once been painted a bright crimson, and the cabin on the boat next to it had recently been painted vivid orange. They were dirty now.

The morning cloud disappeared. There was a metal cargo container plonked onto one of the harbour walls, and if Daniel sat with his back to it, nobody could see him. It never occurred to him that a lone, nine-year old boy on a Friday morning would look a little conspicuous in a working industrial harbour.

Daniel had not reached the stage in his life where he could "look, measure and mark" and make an accurate reproduction of what was in front of him. But he could draw a boat. He could draw a harbour wall and some single storey buildings, and he could draw a crane. In the end he managed to incorporate three boats, 'each in front of the one behind', a crane, a wall and some buildings into the rectangle of his paper. He wasn't pleased or displeased with it. He was pleased with the three little men he had drawn, carrying sacks. He was pleased with the reflections of the boats in the water, more for the fact that he had made an attempt to draw the reflections with squiggly horizontal lines, than any illusion of the surface of water that he may, or may not, have been trying to create.

Nonetheless he had spent more than an hour not doing anybody any harm, and no harbour master, policeman or truant officer arrested him for being bad. A triumph of sorts.

Two of his sandwiches made a nice early lunch and he was ready to try and find Matteson's building yard with his full bladder.

Daniel cycled round most of the streets of Maryport before finding a road sign to Dearham. His grandad's sister, Aunt Leah, lived in Dearham and his mam had taken him on a visit there once. They had taken three different buses on the way there, but only one on the way back. How they had both laughed. But Daniel didn't go to Dearham, he found a small copse in which to have a discreet pee. And having no further items on his day's agenda, he decided to turn about and go back home.

The road from Maryport to Workington is straight and flat and is separated from the sea by the west coast railway line. Cars, lorries and buses get up a good speed, and when they pass small boys on girls' bikes, they cause a great draught, and it is difficult to keep pedalling straight. The first few big vehicles caused him problems and he got a little frightened. He got off and tried walking his bike, but that was just as nerve racking. He got back on his bike and ploughed on as fast as he could to try and get to the peace of Workington's back streets, but in an instant the afternoon sun just disappeared and down came a heavy rainstorm. The turbulence of the traffic then came laced, not only with the rain, but with the shitty, muddy spray from the big wheels. He was soaked to the skin in just a few minutes. He was pedalling like buggery, gasping for breath, frightened and a little lonely. Daniel was able to grasp the irony of praying for rain, in Church, on the previous Sunday. He took only a little pleasure in the thought that if it was raining in Flimby, it was probably pissing down in Allonby as well.

Billy Millington had been sitting on the back seat of the Allonby trip bus and was standing up, looking out of the back window at the rainstorm, and the spray from the back of the bus.

He had tried to attract the attention of the driver of the lorry behind by waving at him and pulling faces. All to no avail. He finally gave the man 'two fingers' when, for only a second or two, he saw what he thought was Daniel riding a bike through the storm, bouncing up and down through the puddles and pot-holes on the verge of the road. He sat down and tried to join in a song with the 'lads at the back'. It was an Elvis song which began with "It's one for the money ...", but between them they could only muster the first three lines.

"Ah think ah just saw Danny rid'n a lasses' bike."

Nobody was taking any notice, so he repeated his line. John Baxter responded by standing up to look out of the back window, and Billy rejoined his position.

"Where?" said John.

"Oh, it wuz way back."

They both sat down.

Five minutes later in a lull in the fun, John told Kenny Melvin. Kenny told his twin brother Herbert. Later still Herbert told Billy Keay and Billy told Billy Millington. Thus, the circle was complete.

"Daniel wuz riden his bike te Allonby."

"Ah kno' that, asser."

And from that conversation, "Daniel wuz rid'n his bike te Allonby," became accepted fact. Witnessed first by Billy Millington and corroborated by John Baxter, the Melvins, Billy Keay and most importantly, authenticated by Denise Cowan.

Denise said, "He 'asn't got a bike," but that was ignored.

So, when the bus got back to the school, it was Denise, supported by the 'lads at the back' who informed Mr Hall and Miss Wildgoose that Daniel was seen riding a bike to Allonby, no doubt he was trying to join his classmates on the trip.

There was much to do in the rain for Mr Hall, Miss Wildgoose and the other teachers. The re-uniting of children with their mothers, the cleaning up of the litter, and Jeremy Stone's right shoe, from the bus. The collecting of the skipping ropes, balls and the cricket gear into the P.E. bag.

"What did you make of the story about Daniel?" said Mr Hall.

"The usual rubbish."

Mr Hall was giving Miss Wildgoose a ride home in his new green Morris Minor. When all duties had been done, and they were both in the car, Miss Wildgoose said, "We should go to the house to check that he's all right."

"He can be a strange boy. I wouldn't put it past the little bugger."

"His dad is my half cousin. You couldn't meet a nicer man. He resigned from a 'pit top' job at Micklam because some of his workmates were stealing coal. They've hardly had a penny coming into the house for six months or so. What that poor lad is going through I dread to think."

"He's bright as a button."

"He used to do Gwen Cragg's homework. She's his auntie," said Miss Wildgoose.

"The one about the Jane Russell bra?"

"That's him."

When they got to Ghyll Grove, she said, "You knock on the door, the mother's scary."

"Hello, I'm Mr Hall, Daniel's teacher."

"Oh yes." It was Tom who answered the door.

"Is he at home by any chance?"

"He's gone fer a bike ride . . . he'll be wet through, ah bet."

"Some of the children think that they saw him on a bike in Maryport."

Emily appeared behind Tom. She disappeared back to the kitchen just as quickly.

"He was go'an to Lamplugh,"said Tom.

"It's probably something or nothing," said Mr Hall, "We just thought you should know."

"Thank you, that's very good of yer . . . . Mr Hall."

Tom knew immediately that it was the sort of thing that his son would do, and he kept the door open until Mr Hall got into his car. Miss Wildgoose gave Tom a tentative wave from the car.

Mr Hall got back to his car. He had decided that he had to find Daniel. "Fancy a ride to Maryport?"

Janet Wildgoose put her hand on Chris Hall's sleeve by way of assent.

Emily was having one of her screaming fits.

"Ah've got a useless bloody husband who can't git a job, and a bloody son who sets out te mek me life a misery."

Tom breathed a long sigh and bent his head.

There was more, and worse, of that sort of stuff, and within minutes she had her coat on, her hat, and a polythene rain hood draped over her hat and tied under her chin. She was still screaming and ranting as she got to the back door. But the slamming of it behind her triggered a silence as she negotiated the rain, the long, wet grass of the back garden and the gap in the hedgerow. She was on her way to her own mam and dad, on the other side of the ghyll.

It would be a wet and very muddy journey.

It would be a wet and muddy journey on the way back as both her mam and her dad, particularly her dad, shouted at her, "Ah'm ashamed of yer. Yer a useless mother wid'oot any feeling fer yer son, 'oos somewhere oot theer gitt'n sokken wet."

"He's been out all day, just te embarrass 'es."

"He's bin oot oa'h day 'cos 'is muther doesn't love 'im properly. Git oot."

She looked to her mother for respite. "Yer dad has said ivverything ah wanted tae say. Go home."

By the time she got home, the house was empty.

There are several routes through Workington to get on to the Harrington Road. Daniel took the road past the train station and past the steelworks to Moss Bay. There was a bus shelter near the Workington Rugby Union Club and he took refuge there, not just to get out of the rain but to eat his remaining sandwiches. The saddlebag was, alas, full of water, two quarters of bread were floating on the top. His drawing and its backing card were entirely under water. He saw the funny side. Well, he made himself see the funny side. It wasn't the worst thing going on in his life.

He was only wet.

With that thought, the rain not abating, Daniel allowed himself a "Bugger this" and got back on the bike.

Sadly, he had a flat tyre.

Daniel didn't bother trying to diagnose the cause of the flat tyre. He made no attempt to fix it. The flat tyre was part of the same inevitability of his life. For a moment he put it down to God's revenge for praying for rain at Church.

"All right, you've had your laughs, now stop it raining," he said to himself out loud so that if God did indeed hear him, and the sun came out, he might be dry by the time he got home. "Me knackers won't be dry for a week, though," he thought.

The road home went past Mrs Troon's house in Harrington and he managed to summon up enough gasp to run past it without being seen.

He took the short cut through High Harrington and turned right onto the last drag to Lowca. It was uphill for at least a mile, the rain came horizontally off the sea, up the cliffs and across the moors. He could taste the salt.

Tom had already set off walking to Maryport to somehow look for his son. When Emily had stormed out, he had started to cry. Disgusted with himself for being so weak he tried to put his walking shoes on, but one of the laces snapped. In his panic to get out of the house he sealed his shoe onto his foot by wrapping layers of Sellotape round the lace-holes and the sole of the shoe.

He set off in a dash out of the back garden and into the school field.

"Stupid fucker," he shouted at himself. His boy was on a bike and would be on a road at least, and he didn't want to miss him in his own panic. He ran back past the house to get on to Ghyll Grove. He turned north up the hill past the 'British Legion Club'. The lights were on in the gloom and the rain. A couple of early drinkers had their backs to the window. He quickened his pace in case they turned and saw him in his shame.

When he got to the school, he had a look inside the gate and ran round the back to the playing yard.

Back on the road, clear of the village he was able to start running. He hadn't run for ages, and with his loose shoe he didn't have the pace he once had. The rain from the sea was so heavy that he was already wet through, the left side of his face was stinging. He didn't look but he wouldn't have been able to see the winding sheds of Micklam two fields away. His lungs were burning fiercely and he was glad. Was this an atonement or something?

He tried to work out where his lad would be, and when he thought about him, wet and lost somewhere, he started to wail and cry out loud. He wailed in short quick gasps which couldn't be heard in the screaming of the wind. His legs now joined in with the agony of his lungs. Soon, up the slight hill towards Mill Lonning, all Tom's pains came together in one long howl to chime with the gale. He was scared to stop running and so only gave a quick glance down the lane to see if Daniel might be there. The road to Harrington was downhill now, but it didn't ease the pain. He tried to run even faster. Tom had no idea how it might happen but the thought that Daniel might be dead came to him. An accident of some sort. Or the wrath of God. Why else would God send this awful wind?

There was no traffic on the Harrington Road. Daniel could just push his bike up the hill with his head tucked down behind his right arm.

He took a glance up to see how far he had to go to get to the top, and there, half a mile on, where Mill Lonning meets the road, was his dad. His unmistakeable dad, 'Here's me heed, mi arse is cummen." That dad.

"What was he doing?"

"How did he know I would be here?"

"Am aah in trouble, again?"

The pot-holes on the edge of the road were evaded subconsciously. Tom didn't really see them. He did not see the hawthorns in the hedgerow, how far they were bent, pointing like fingers.

It took some moments for Tom to see his son. Four hundred yards down the road, there was the small black shape that just had to be Daniel. Tom tried to cry out his son's name, but it wouldn't come out between his gasps.

He tried to run faster, but this was as fast as he could run.

He cleared his eyes and saw the shape of his little boy, his unmistakeable little boy, bent double from the rain, hiding his head behind his arm and the handlebars of his bike.

Tom tried again to call out.

Then he stopped.

He straightened his wet jacket and fastened the top button of his shirt. His fingers struggled in the cold of the rain.

He tried to calm himself down, to stop his gasping, and to make himself presentable to his son. To be worthy of his son.

He tried to be dignified, as much as he could, and walk in an upright relaxed gait.

By now, the little figure with the bike was moving more quickly, more upright.

"He must have seen me," Tom thought.

He tried to stop crying; but he couldn't.

With Daniel only a hundred yards away, Tom turned his face into the blast of the rain and hoped that, in the wetness of his face, his tears could not be seen when he got to his son.

"Ye' oahreet lad?" was the most beautiful and appropriate thing that he could say. Calm, dignified, reassuring. Loving.

They didn't hug or anything. For the first hundred yards neither of them said anything.

"Let me tek yer bike lad."

"No, dad, it's me sack 'er coal," is what Daniel thought of saying but he couldn't articulate that and carried on pushing Gwen's bike.

Tom then told Daniel about Mr Hall, knocking on the door, and Miss Wildgoose making a small wave from Mr Hall's car.

"They said that some kids on the trip bus had seen yer on't' road te Allonby."

"Ah didn't ga anywhere near Allonby. Ah just went te Maryport."

Daniel let his father take the bike.

He sheltered behind him, not to get out of the blast of the wind, but to allow his dad his dignity.

"Ah tried te find that place that wouldn't give yer a job, ah wuz ganna pee on the door."

"That wouldn't hev bin very nice."

"Couldn't find it anywez."

"Yer mam's upset."

"Ah's in trouble again, ah suppose."

"Aye, we both are, lad."

The wind was so loud that they didn't hear Mr Hall's car pull up beside them.

Miss Wildgoose wound down the window. "Hello Tom, get in the back, we can put the bike in the boot."

"Hello Janet, we are too wet to get into anyone's car." Tom shuffled closer to the car so that his shoes were out of Miss Wildgoose's line of sight.

Mr Hall leaned forward and down so that he could be seen. "You found the little lost boy. We've been up and down to Maryport. How did we miss you?"

"Ah wuzn't lost. If yer'd tell't me ah wuz lost, ah would hev come ter help yer look fer 'es."

Nobody laughed.

"Were you going to Allonby?" said Miss Wildgoose.

"Naah," Daniel said. "Don't like Scotland."

Mr Hall smiled.

"Thank you so much for all your efforts, it's very kind of both of you," said Tom, poshly. "You two must have had a troubled, and long, day. You should get on home." He gave a knowing look and a smile to 'Janet'.

"See you on Monday Daniel." Then, as an afterthought, Mr Hall dipped his head again and added, "Perhaps we should all stick to the story that you were nowhere near the Maryport road and that the boys on the back seat of the bus got it wrong. Well meaning, but wrong."

"Very wise," said Tom. He held back on an errant 'asser'. He didn't want to embarrass 'Janet'.

He smiled again to 'Janet'.

When Tom and Daniel got home, Emily was hysterical with joy. She hugged them both and was shocked at how wet they both were.

"Git outa them clothes. Ah'll run yer a bath." She was crying a little bit, but not scary crying.

The hot water scorched Daniel's skin.

Carbolic soap used to come in brick sized blocks and was the staple of the pit head baths. It was very cheap, but with the very soft water of this part of Cumberland it made beautiful, creamy, fragrant water. Daniel held his breath and sunk under the water for as long as he could.

By the time he got out of the bath, dried himself and dressed, the house was a'buzz. Tom didn't bathe, he had just dried himself off with the best towel and changed his clothes, and Grannie and Grandad had brought round 'fish'n chips fer five', a large bottle of 'Dandelion and Burdock' and a bowl of cold rice pudding.

Everybody was happy, nobody got told off. Daniel knew that though he was innocent, he had been the cause of a great deal of pain.

But nobody said anything throughout the meal except, "Put the rice puddin' in t' oven," and, "Sorry, we haven't got any vinegar."

What a feast.

After the rice pudding they had tea with no milk. Tom and Emily had grown to prefer it that way. Grannie produced a wagon wheel out of her handbag. She cut it up into five.

"I'm too full," Daniel said.

Everyone feigned a theatrical, shocked face.

"Ah think that aah'll ga ter bed."

"It's only seven o'clock," said Tom.

Daniel gave everybody a kiss and went to his room.

By that time in his life he could recognise that particular silence of his parents weeping in the living room. He knew that Grannie and Grandad were weeping too.

This was confirmed, after about ten minutes, by the way Grandad broke the silence, and said, "This will be ovver soon Tom. Aah promise."

Two or three minutes later he repeated, "Aah promise, this'll be ovver soon."

CHAPTER 5

Six months from the day he resigned, Tom got a note summoning him to go to the 'Labour Exchange'. He thought that he must be in trouble and put on his interview shirt and best tie. He put on his tweed sports jacket that he hadn't worn for ages, and on his walk to Whitehaven prepared himself for yet another humiliation.

"There's a job at Sellafield Mister … erm, Tom, isn't it?" said the lady behind the counter.

"What? Er … yes," he stuttered.

"However, I have to inform you that the job is on the 'risky side'."

"That doesn't matter," he said. "Can you put me forward for it please?"

"I haven't told you what the job involves. I haven't explained the risks to you."

Tom wanted to shout at her that he would take the fucking job, that he had been out of work for six months, that his wife had lost twelve pounds in weight, that his son had become morose and introverted, that he would wring her fucking neck if she didn't tell him what he had to do to get this job. Whatever the fucking job was.

But he bit his tongue and sat up straight with his best grateful expression on his face.

"It is working in a labouring capacity with low level radioactive material. … . Tom. Are you willing to proceed with the application?"

"Yes," he replied, successfully holding back a diffident 'please'.

"You will have to work periods of overtime, whenever it is required." She looked at him questioningly, and after a silence she said, rather abruptly, "Well?"

"Sorry, yes, of course."

"Overtime," he thought to himself, "I'd fuck even you for overtime."

"Good," she said.

Tom smiled to himself that her "Good" could have been the answer to both his spoken, and unspoken, statements.

"You will have to start work at eight in the morning." As she filled in a form, "That's tomorrow morning."

Tom dismissed three or four witty rejoinders from his mind and continued to work on his gratefulness.

"Can you report to the main gate in your work clothes and present these three papers? One of these forms is a security clearance form, and you must answer all the questions honestly. You will have to be interviewed by the security people before presenting this form." She reached over another piece of paper.

'... to a Mr Hannah."

Tom sat still, waiting for her to say something else. But she had nothing more to say. "Tom" had been processed.

After a second or two, she looked at him. "If you have no further questions, that will be all." She could have said his full name and something polite and cheery at the end, but it 'didn't come out'.

Tom walked to the bus station to get the bus timetables from Lowca, or perhaps Howgate, direct to Sellafield.

He wrote all the times down in his usual neat hand.

He decided to splash out and get the bus home.

He had walked so far.

When Daniel got home from school, the house was spotless. There was a fire on. Emily was sitting by it.

"Tom!" she called. But he was in through the hallway door anyway.

"Helloah lad. Aah've gotter job."

Daniel just looked at him. His dad had been out of work for so long and he had been rejected so often, that Daniel didn't quite understand the full implications of what he had heard. He didn't speak. It didn't occur to him to ask what the job was. It didn't really matter what the job was or where his dad would have to go.

"Grate!" was the only thing that would come out. There was another impotent silence.

"Can ah dae owt?" he said. He looked to his mother, but she was just poking the fire. He thought that he should be jumping up and down cheering and whooping.

"Aah knoah lad!" seemed an incongruous response. But they both knew what it meant.

"Run roond to tell Grannie and Grandad and see if they could lend ez some money fer mi bus fare te Sellafield temorrer mornin'."

"Sellafield eh?" He could speak now. "Will ye hev te wear a white coat? Will ye be splitt'n attems?"

"Wid'n 'ammer 'n chisel."

They could both laugh now for the first time.

Daniel wanted to hug his dad and say something tender and meaningful, but their laughing was loving enough.

"Aah'll git ga'an ter granda's"

And off he ran. Out of the back door and through the fence. "Aah've gotter job," he said to himself. He said it again at every second breath as he ran faster and faster through the school field's long grass and Everest's old turds. "Aah've gotter job," he sang as he scrambled down through the ghyll past the swing rope and up through the fence into Ghyll Bank and its two rows of prefabs. He ran even faster past Denise, Margaret and Maisie who were playing with an old pram in Mrs Paradine's garden. "Aah've gotter job." By the time he got to the end terrace house on Meadow View he was gasping. The back door was open, and he burst into the kitchen.

"We've gotter job," he said to the empty kitchen. Grannie and Grandad were in the living room and he had to announce it again, but this time proudly as, "My dad's gotter job."

Daniel gasped his message and Grannie and Grandad went scurrying in their own excitement; Grandad to the parlour bureau to get a proper white five-pound note and Grannie to the kitchen to put together a string bag of three sausages, half a fruit cake and four tomatoes.

Old Harry put the fiver in an envelope and folded it into Daniel's hand and then folded his grandson's fingers into a very tight fist round the envelope. He then theatrically put Daniel's fist into the right pocket of his shorts. Grannie put Daniel's left arm into the handles of the bag, up to the crook of his elbow.

"Off yer ga'ah," they said, almost in unison.

Next morning, Tom had gone by the time Daniel got up.

He had caught the Howgate bus, and six Lowca people were at the bus stop with him.

It was pitch black and nobody spoke, except one, "Oa'h'reet Tom."

He presented his papers at the Sellafield main gate. "You're a bit early."

"Sorry."

"Nae bother."

He was ushered into the 'Security Offices'.

He sat in a bentwood chair at a formica table. Opposite him was a youngish man in a black uniform with black buttons.

Each of the twenty security questions, which Tom had answered in his best handwriting with his best Parker pen, were repeated to him by the man. He looked directly at Tom, all the time he was answering the questions.

An older man had his back to this interview. He had his feet on his own formica desk. He leaned back at an alarming angle, his chair teetered on its back two legs.

At the end of the formal questions there was a small silence.

Then, without turning around to face Tom, the older man said, "Yer an asser marra frae Lowca?"

"Yes. I suppose."

"Do you know a Mr William Vernon?"

"Billy Vimto?"

"Indeed," laughed the man. "Welcome to Sellafield! ... Tom."

He was ushered out with two different security passes and one small, artificial leather wallet.

He had a job.

These were the things that the family didn't have in the house after all that time with Tom out of work. Shoe polish, a yard brush, scouring pads, sandpaper, glue, brillo pads, aspirins, mustard, fat for the chip pan, shampoo, envelopes and writing paper, chamois leather, butter, pepper, furniture polish, bleach, cough medicine, baking powder, elastoplasts, knicker elastic, sellotape. Stuff that gets used but never replaced.

Emily had lost confidence going into shops, she was always afraid of not having enough money in her purse. She didn't want to be seen making calculations on bits of paper. It took several months to "put stuff in drawers."

Daniel's shoes were too small, Emily's needed mending, and Tom needed new boots with rubber soles for work, instead of the steel cleated boots he had used at Micklam.

Tom was making more money at Sellafield than he had done at Micklam, and even with the added bonus of 'twenty-four-hour shifts' every couple of weeks, Emily still took a long time to adjust. Sometimes Tom 'brought home' a lot more money, but he was still only identified as a labourer.

The prefab felt empty and lonely for Emily. Prefabs were a brilliant architectural and social solution to the Post War housing shortage. However, by the mid-fifties they had taken on a bit of a stigma in the press and this hit Emily hard after the shame and the privations of Tom's unemployment.

When there was a chance of a three-year-old semi-detached council house in Vale View, she called the council without telling Tom. She talked to Edward Calthorpe who was Lowca's Councillor, and it was he who told Tom that there was a good chance of getting the house Emily wanted.

There was an argument of course, but they were both still thin and dark eyed and neither of them had the energy to fight.

"It's mair rent," Tom said, "And hoo' dae a'ah knoa that this job's ganna last?"

"It'll save yer a mile each way ga'an te Howgate ivvery day."

The 'walking bit' was never an argument for either of them. The distances he had walked looking for work were a measure of Tom's love, and Emily knew that. She might just as well have said that he needn't kiss her so much if they moved to Vale View.

Tom gave in.

The house in Vale View was a mess. How could one old couple create such a hovel out of a newly built house?

Tom and Emily could never have contemplated divorce or separation. But leaving the prefab and moving into a new house, a new house which had no ghosts, was the saving of their love. They blitzed every room. First there was the cleaning, the stripping of wallpaper, the scrubbing of the floors, the scraping of the paint, the filling of the cracks in the plaster. This they did together. Daniel was used as the unskilled labourer or he was sent out to play to get him out of the way.

At weekends they could wallpaper and complete the painting of a whole room together.

Daniel was at first consulted on the colour scheme for his own room, then completely ignored. He didn't mind.

He scraped the glass in his bedroom window of all the errant paint left by the previous owners. First with Tom's discarded razor blades, then with wire wool, then with a new chamois leather. The south facing view through his window took in the whole of the valley from Common End in the east, with the chimneys of Pica not quite visible on the 'tops' behind. A patchwork of fields and ghylls directly opposite took in twelve farms as well as the hamlets of Barngill and Howgate. Two miles away across the valley, the far horizon above hid the Western Fells, but only just. The road from Common End to Moresby Parks traced a long arc for four miles, only interrupted by the pumping station and three cowering farmhouses. At night, car headlights danced between the trees and hedgerows of the road. Daniel was old enough to know that on that bit of road, when a car's lights stopped and then went out, someone was shagging somebody they shouldn't.

The western part of the valley offered fewer opportunities for social adventure, guarded as it was by St Bridget's Church. Almost next door there was Moresby Hall, a Jacobean Mansion of great splendour and dark history. There was the Whitehaven harbour wall with its little lighthouse perched on the end. In the distance, some six miles away, was the great nose of St Bees Head ploughing into the Solway Firth. It was Daniel's constant reference point, but in that constancy, there was eternal change. The weather, the angle of the sun, the tide, the surface of the sea, the occasional freight boat anchoring out off Whitehaven harbour. Daniel looked for echoes of those times standing with his dad looking north from Micklam to the steelworks and the eruption of the furnaces. Daniel understood that moving to this new house was an act of desperation by his mam and dad and that learning to love this new landscape was a gesture of love and support.

Tom let the back-garden grow "Te see what comes up." But whenever Daniel needed to get out, away from the wallpaper and the smell of paint, he would go out and cut some roses hard back to the ground. For the fun of it, to get himself scratched by the prickles, to get sweaty and exhausted, to be not useless. Then, as the soil warmed up, and nothing of any worth sprouted through the soil except cooch grass, Daniel got into digging. What a cleansing thing. There was a patch of the roughest land to the side of a twenty yard, paved, garden path. It had been used as a dump for old broken bricks, empty tins of baked beans, cast iron hinges and half of an old farm gate.

Grandad joined in the fun by offering to bring barrow loads of pigeon shit, collated from the five pigeon hulls on Meadow View, but only if Daniel could 'manage a bit of double digging'.

"Whit Week next week," said Emily, and that was the contract signed.

"A'al cummen show thee how."

Old Harry understood that Daniel needed to do something challenging and pointless but physically fulfilling. He had been worried about Daniel when Tom was out of work. It went unsaid that 'learning how to work' was a rite of passage for Daniel and that this process was full of ironies in the context of the pain of Tom's long stretch of unemployment.

"Git ivverything oot fusst," he said, "A'ah'l fetch a barrer."

There were the twisted vines and roots of ten climbing roses which had made a mess of the wire fence. "Ga reet t't bottom, t'roots'll grow back be' Frider if the' duzzn't."

Daniel turned the farm gate into firewood with a sledge-hammer and chucked the hinges into Grandad's barrow. They loaded up the rubble, and the bits of metal, and a solidified bag of builders' cement. They made three trips to the slag heap, and with a nod to the driver, they tipped their excavations into the 'dozer's path. On the third trip, Grandad had a bottle of brown ale for the dozer driver, Arthur Bedale, who lived on Vale View as well.

Arthur turned his engine off and jumped off his seat to accept his bottle.

"This is my Emily's lad, Daniel."

They shook hands, very formally.

"How's yer dad?"

"He's very well, thank you."

"Tell him that he's a good man. A'ah knoa what went on at Micklam."

With that, a wind came up off the Solway and clouded everyone in coal dust and shale dust. Pockets of heat from the permanent fire which burned slowly inside the slag heap made small whirlwinds of the ash. Zephyrs. One of the old tin cans from their load blew across the flat top of the tip. Daniel grabbed the barrow to stop it blowing over and that was taken as a signal to leave. They would go back and try to get the double digging done.

In the time that it took Daniel to dig a fifteen-inch deep trench, 'Old Harry' had gone to Meadow View and loaded up with pigeon shit. He filled the trenches himself. The stuff had an awful stench. Daniel covered the manure with scrunched up newspapers.

Grandad had a bucketful of seed potatoes and he placed them a clog's length apart.

"Won't it affect the taste of the taties?"

"There's mair muck in them newspapers than wot's under them." Grandad stood up to straighten his back.

"Nitrogen," he nodded as if either of them knew what he was talking about.

They laughed.

They rushed to finish before Tom got home. Daniel was brushing the path with the new yard brush when he came.

Emily, who had been watching all afternoon, made two mugs of 'Camp' coffee for her dad and Tom. She brought them out on the new tray, with a plate of chocolate digestives.

Tom gave her a sharp stare. She had to boil a fresh kettle of water, before she could bring Daniel a cup.

It took several months for Emily and Tom to get the house on Vale View in order. It took even longer to fill the cupboards and drawers. The old curtains from the prefab were the wrong size of course, but they would do for the four windows at the back, which faced across the valley. Upstairs, there was Daniel's bedroom and the bathroom, and the dining room and the kitchen were downstairs. Nobody could see in through the back windows except for the drivers of the coal trains a hundred yards away and perhaps Mr Botterell on his tractor ploughing his field beyond the garden hedge. Nobody could see the curtains, plain and dull stuff from the days of rationing, too dour to look at and too thick to see through.

Emily made a special effort with the curtains for the windows at the front of the house. These rooms and the front door faced onto the Vale View road as it turned up the hill to meet Meadow View. There was a small triangular 'green' filling the corner, good for small children's games. Though there were rarely any cars on the road, the people traffic was always busy, and they were always nosy.

Emily's first attempt at the curtains for the front room, and 'the master bedroom', as she called it, missed the target when the fabric she bought was a couple of inches too narrow. It was half the price of the full-size fabric, but there was always at least a four-inch gap when the curtains were drawn.

This caused her great pain. It was bad enough that people, "Could see in as we went aboot ooer business," but she thought that everybody would know that she was an idiot for not buying the right sized curtains, and that they would be laughing at her.

This was not true of course. Everyone in their corner of Vale View "knew who Tom and Emily were, and what their story was."

Besides, each of their new neighbours had their own tales to tell, or indeed to not tell.

It took another month of Tom's new wages to create the cash for proper curtain fabric to be bought. And with a couple of Tom's sisters, "gitt'n stuck in", matching cushions were made from the old fabric.

How posh was that!

Tom's sister Margaret corralled Sheila, Elizabeth and Eleanor, and Gosforth Grandma to make a 'prodded mat' as a housewarming gift. A prodded mat is made from thin strips of old fabric woven into the warp and weft of strong marine hessian, tied neatly in a double knot, and trimmed to a uniform length. "Two front knuckles" was the family length of choice.

Formal patterns, as in the style of patchwork quilts, were most favoured. However, with the twins' influence, a more 'pointillist' or 'Jazzy' pattern was the order of the day.

With all the contrasting colours there was a shimmering brilliance to it, particularly if you walked across the carpet at speed as Daniel did. To everyone's annoyance.

The thing was ten foot by six foot and filled the space between the settee and the two armchairs.

Daniel used to lie on it with his cheek on the carpet, staring at the individual pieces of fabric and trying to imagine if they might be from one of Auntie Sheila's dresses, or Eleanor's blouse, or Grandma's scarf.

Alas, the open coal fire spat sparks out all the time. The mesh fireguard was no defence against the vicissitudes of 'Number 10 coal'. "Micklam coal didn't spit," Dad once joked.

"That's not funny," said Emily, "nut funny 'et oa'h."

Chapter 6

"Tha' kno'as that some folks ga' off 'n git religion, well aa'h think oo'er Tom 'ez been 'en got radiation." That was Old Harry about Tom.

Tom was a man of precise habits. So, when one Sunday afternoon he went off to the Miners' Welfare Hall to mend a trombone, Emily and Daniel expected him to be home by six. He often cooked a light supper at that time, perhaps his 'signature dish' of 'egg 'n crumb' [bread-crumbs, chopped herbs from their new garden, mixed with eggs to bind into a patty, fried in butter, served with bits of leftovers from the day's lunch].

"Ga'a t't' Welfare lad en see what's up." Emily was not so much worried, as hungry for her husband's little culinary treat. It had become a weekly ritual since they moved to Vale View.

["We ken afford two dinners noow!"]

'The Welfare' was closed and there were no lights on. Daniel ran back home. He assumed that his dad would be there when he got back.

But he wasn't, and now his Mam was worried. Worried enough to put her coat on.

She sat down again, still in her coat. She poked the fire.

With an 'harrumph' she got up and went out of the front door.

Now Daniel was worried.

He was young enough to fear that both of them could get lost, disappear, never to be seen again, but old enough to be embarrassed by such infantile thoughts.

Within minutes they both came in through the front door, with Emily still chuntering away.

"Yer kno'a where 'ese bin? 'Ese bin ter chutch."

She threw her coat over the end of the bannister.

"On 'is o'an."

"How awful!" Daniel laughed. That was so much better than disappearing under the waves off Parton shore whilst picking sea coal, which was one of his apocalyptic scenarios.

"Nae supper then?" Daniel asked.

"A'all mek yer some supper," Tom said.

"Barley loaves 'en fishes?" Daniel laughed. Emily didn't. Tom did.

'Egg 'n crumb' and fried tomatoes, some of Mrs Vernon's green tomato chutney.

Nobody mentioned Tom going to church again.

Well, until the following Sunday, when he, "Pulled t'sem trick again." As Emily put it.

Emily didn't go regularly to church, though she thought that she did. She was miffed that Tom went on his own, without even asking her. And it was 'Evensong', never 'Matins'.

Within a couple of months Tom's late Sunday excursion was embedded into the pattern of the family's weekend. Nobody ever asked him what had happened, that from a point where he rarely went to church, to being, on the face of it, a devout and committed Christian.

"A'am happy ter cum wid yer ter chutch if yer want ez ter."

"No lad, it's best as it is."

"Nivver been t'll evensong."

"It's same ez Sunday mornin', kneelen' 'en singen."

"The new vicar's oa'reet."

"Aye."

And that was the sum-total of any engagement Daniel had with his dad on the matter.

Soon Tom was enlisted into the 'Bible Study' group on Tuesday evenings. He would dash in from work through the back door, go upstairs for a quick bath, a hot bath if Emily remembered, a change of clothes, then out through the front door with a pork pie or a sandwich in a paper bag to eat on his walk to church.

Daniel was always careful to make sure that he was in bed and out of the way when his dad got back around ten.

It would start with Emily telling Tom that there had been, "nowt on telly".

"Wot's wrang wid t'wireless?" Tom would reply.

Then Emily would bring in a tray of tea and biscuits before proceeding to list all the things in the house that Tom had, "left undone which ought to have been done!"

"A'al dae it temorrer when a'ah git yam."

Then there would be an angry exchange before they went to bed.

Emily didn't really want to go with Tom to church on Sunday evenings, and certainly she didn't want to go to Bible Class, but she was angry that she had not been taken into his confidence. She was angry that 'Church' and 'Piety' were her patch, her domain, and Tom had invaded her territory.

Actually, it was Daniel who had been the regular churchgoer in the family. Not every Sunday, but he only missed "Chutch" if there was something pressing to stop him. It was his world which had been thrown into confusion. He had worried that whatever was the nature of his father's Damascene experience, it had never happened to him. His dad had always been a good, strong and virtuous man, and Daniel was aware that he himself had certainly never been that. "How could this 'church' thing make him a better person?" he worried, "How could he be an 'even better' person?" Daniel had been going to church most Sunday mornings for three or four years and it "hasn't made me any better".

He wanted to know if there had been some spiritual change in his dad which made him such a 'sudden Christian', and if so, what did it look and sound like? "Wuz it summat like watchen t'steelwuks frae Micklam that time, Dad?"

"Wheesht," he interrupted, not letting Daniel finish his question.

It also occurred to Daniel that in those very darkest days, perhaps when his dad had that hundredweight of coal on his back, or walking, still jobless, from Maryport, or looking for his 'lost' son in the rain, he had cried out, "Get me and mi family oota this shit, 'en a'al become a proper Christian 'en cum te chutch ivvery Sunder."

Daniel wanted to find a way of telling him that he understood, that somewhere on his stupid bike ride, or in the night, when he was hungry, that he had also made a pact. Daniel's deal was, that when his dad was ever back in a job and that their family could afford a coin for the collection, Daniel would go to church every Sunday. It was a decision to "commit". The word "commit" had a special resonance in Lowca. Miners had to commit to going to work. To commit to turning up on time, whatever the shift they were on, to commit to work even on those days when they were frightened or couldn't face the agony of uniquely aching shoulders when they were "on't pick". No miner ever wanted to be thought of as "not committed". Those were dangerous people to know, in the dark.

Daniel's deal was not that he would stop being bad, or that he would try and be a better person, just that he would "commit" to go to church. Without fail. Every Sunday.

Daniel could never articulate profoundly intimate questions about his dad's 'new-found church-going' any more than he could ask him about sex and stuff. He understood that his dad would not be able to articulate any meaningful answers to such questions.

Daniel left it at that.

Up to the point where Tom started going to 'Bible Study'. Daniel's bedtime reading would usually be bits of the New Testament. The Old Testament had no meaning for him and he had no interest in St Paul, or indeed any of his letters. He just read the Gospel stuff, whispered it to himself silently in bed, enjoyed the poetry of it. Memorised the best bits.

Thus, it was a bit much when Tom, not knowing that his son did indeed read the Bible, came in and took it.

"Dad, yer pinched me bloody Bible."

That threw both Tom and Emily.

"Don't use that word with the Holy Bible," screamed Emily.

"A'ah need it fer Bible Class lad."

"Aa'h need it ter save mi soul!" Daniel laughed. Emily didn't, Tom did.

"It's the family's Bible, not yours," chuntered Emily.

Tom must have told the Reverend Nidd about his little family spat because the following Sunday morning after the service, as Daniel was trying to sidle out of the door past all the handshaking, there was a "Young Mister Daniel." Nobody had ever called him that, so he didn't respond, "Daniel!"

He looked round.

The vicar's finger beckoned Daniel to squeeze between the robust figure of Mrs Collins and the skeletal Mrs Haley.

"Some homework for you." It was a brown envelope and Daniel knew that it was a book inside. In his blushing, he knew that it was a Bible. The Reverend Nidd knew more about him than Daniel wanted him to know. He stuttered out a "Thank you." But he wanted to shout out, "Mind yer own business, yer nosy bugger."

The Reverend Nidd was a portly, affable man. In just a few weeks of Tom starting to go to church, he had recognised something in him. Then one Sunday evening he took him aside on his way out after the service and suggested that he would enjoy the Bible Study on Tuesdays. Tom was a bit nonplussed. He had never said anything to anybody at church, even the people he knew. He just turned up, sat down and stood up a few times, sang as best he could, then went home.

But those in the congregation who knew Tom would have told the vicar who exactly he was. He was the checkweighman at Micklam. It wouldn't have taken the vicar long to piece together "the story".

"You don't come to Evensong with your father?"

"No, I come in the morning," Daniel said in his 'Sunday Best' tones. He held the vicar's gaze.

"Yes, I think that is what I have just said."

"Dad comes to Evensong … In the evening."

"Indeed."

"A'ah think that's just the way Dad and me want it."

"Mmm!" he smiled. He knew when he was beaten.

He tried to persuade Daniel to join the choir, but he wasn't having any of that. "All that dressing up and having to sing properly," Daniel said out loud.

Reverend Nidd was taken aback by this small boy's rudeness. "I dress up and I think that I sing properly." There was no reaction from Daniel, "You would enjoy it, and you know that you have a beautiful voice."

"A'ah can't read music."

"I think that you can."

"A'ah can't afford a frock."

"They are not frocks, as you put it, they are called surplices. And the church provides them for free."

"A'ah just don't want ter."

"That's okay then. But let me know if you change your mind."

Daniel tried to turn and go, but the vicar said, "Your father is a very impressive man."

"Aye, ivverybody sez that," Daniel said. He didn't mean to sound sarcastic and he was uncomfortable in this conversation and its intrusion into his family's 'private stuff'.

With that he turned away from "Mister Nidd" and ran out through the main doors. He didn't stop running, even up the hard hill to home.

Daniel had been taken to Sunday School when he was five or six, to Holy Joe Stackpole's Brethren Chapel at the bottom of East Croft Terrace. It was 'clap and sing and listen to a story' and was great fun. Something happened, perhaps untoward, perhaps just some perceived sleight, but Emily transferred Daniel to 'the proper church' at St Bridget's. This involved a tough mile walk down to the beck and up the sharp hill to the church, but there were half a dozen boys and a couple of girls and soon there was a rota of mums to take "t'laal gang" every Sunday morning. And bring them back.

Some of them stayed on after the Sunday School for the main church service. This was the bit that Daniel liked. The singing was louder and better, the grown-ups seemed to know the words and the organ gave Daniel, at least, a tune to sing to. The scenes in the stained-glass windows were great to stare at while the mumbo jumbo was going on. Also, the vicar and his sermon from the pulpit was just somebody else telling a nice story. More than that, the church itself was the nicest room for miles. Warm, full of light, stuff on the walls to look at, and permanently clean and tidy. In the environs of Parton, Moresby and Lowca, that was a rare and beautiful thing.

When the Reverend Nidd first came, with his soft Yorkshire accent, and told everybody who exactly St Bridget was, when she had lived, and why she was considered a saint, his 'flock' warmed to him immediately. He was unpretentious when taking the services, not just in the sermons, but when reading the banns or calling the congregation to pray for the sick and dying. He was quick to explain to the people of Parton who Joe Bloggs from Moresby was, or to those from Lowca what was happening in the Church Hall in Parton. To Daniel, this was great, because the church started to fill up and sing the hymns louder, which meant that he could sing at the top of his voice, on the back pews, without anybody seeing that he was a prat.

One Sunday morning while Daniel was dressing for Church, Tom shouted from downstairs, "His 'vicarness' wants yer te tek a test efter Chutch terday."

"Oh shit," Daniel thought, "He's going to try and show that I'm a fraud. He must know that I am bad, vicars are supposed to know our souls. I bet he's going to ask about my wanking."

Daniel sweated all through the service. Didn't sing a note.

On the way out, he was so busy trying to sneak past the Reverend that he didn't see Mrs Nidd. She had both her hands on his shoulders. "Daniel," she smiled, "I have some currant slices and some orange juice for you."

She took him to the vestry. It was full of rubbish, old hymn books, the choir's surplices just scattered after the day's use. The one plain, leaded window was filthy.

"Even our house is nicer than this," Daniel nearly said out loud.

At the plain table in the middle of the room sat the dreaded Fleetwood twins, Elaine and Audrey. They were from Low Moresby, went to Moresby school. Their dad was the Church Warden. He always took the collection plate round on the side of the church where Daniel sat. He would stare intently at the plate of coins before Daniel put his threepenny bit in, then he would stare at it even more intently afterwards. When the plate came back to him where he stood in the aisle, he would stare at Daniel.

For a period of weeks Daniel took to staring straight back at him. Square on.

Then he just ignored him.

Elaine and Audrey were fiercely identical, but Elaine looked attractive, Audrey not so. They were like two sketches of the same person. The first attempt was fresh and lively, the second, more accurate but a bit dull. Daniel could have erotic thoughts about Elaine, even here in the vestry, but Audrey's constant presence just dampened things a bit.

"Daniel is taking the test with you," Mrs Nidd announced.

Daniel knocked a prayer book off the top of its pile.

"Do you two masturbate as well?" he thought. Before his mind could frame the thought of how exactly the twins would do such a thing without any of the equipment, the Reverend himself swept through the door and in the same movement removed all his 'frocks' and threw them on to the top of the prayer books.

Daniel had picked the prayer book he had knocked over, up off the floor, then he placed it carefully on the vicar's surplice. He put it in its place on the top of the pile, where he would have put it if there had not been a thin layer of the vicar's robes. He patted the top of the lone book.

The vicar stopped what he was going to say and watched Daniel performing his own personal liturgy with the prayer book.

Then "Elaine, Audrey, Daniel, do you know each other?"

"Yes," they said.

"No," Daniel said.

"Surely you know each other?"

"Ah knoah Elaine, 'en ah knoah Audrey, but ah divvent knoah which is which."

Everybody laughed except Elaine. "We know Daniel," she said.

"Right then." The Reverend Nidd reached into a briefcase and after a bit of ratching about, he brought out a large brown envelope; from it he pulled three sheets of paper. He placed two papers on the table where Elaine and Audrey were sitting. Then he placed another paper on the opposite side. "Daniel, can you sit here?"

"Ah wud, but ther' isn't a chair."

"There must be a chair," said Mrs Nidd. A sharp look from the Reverend sent her out. "I'll go and try to find one. There must be more than two chairs in a church." She mumbled her way through the door, then rather inaudibly from the end of the aisle, "It's a church, it's full of pews. People come to a church to stand, to kneel and to sit."

Ignoring his wife's bleatings, he looked at each of the children in turn, "Thank you for staying on." He brushed some cake crumbs, some drips of orange juice and a currant from the table, "I know how bright each of you are." The twins gave a small nod to each other. "So, I thought that you might like to take this exam. Well no, it's more of a quiz really."

He straightened the papers to align them with the table edge. "It's a bit of fun really, and I hope you will enjoy it."

Mrs Nidd came in with a tall stool. "This is the best I could come up with." Then she added rather sadly and slowly, "I'm afraid."

"It should only take an hour or so. There's a quick quiz on bible stories, then there's a small essay entitled, 'The greatest act of Christian kindness'. That sounds very exciting. What do you think it could be?"

Daniel tried to sit on the stool, but it left his arse just an inch below the table top and he struggled to write, bent over double.

70

"I'll stand," Daniel said," Why don't you have the stool, Mrs Nidd?"

"What a great act of Christian kindness itself, perhaps you could write about that."

Mrs Nidd gave her husband a withering look. "You sound like a Methodist."

The first half of the test had simple questions about the Gospels, their miracles, their stories. There was none of what Daniel thought of as "the St Paul rubbish".

When Daniel read the Bible in his own bedroom, huddled under the blankets with his torch, it was a private, almost sinful thing. He mostly read the Gospels because the words sounded great. When he whispered them aloud in his bed, he knew they were true, because they 'sounded' right.

So, when the first question was about Christ healing a blind man, Daniel was able to decorate his answer with "As long as I am in the world, I am the light of the world." Daniel thought that this was great. He knew that the sentence was somewhere near the story of the blind man and when could he have used the quote in the general gossip and conversation round the milk crates at school?

Warming to his theme, on a question about the raising of Lazarus he was able to answer that he was buried in a cave, but was also able to drop in, "Lord, by this time he stinketh." Daniel remembered pissing himself when he had first read that.

And on the last question, about the Resurrection, Daniel was not sure that he got the question right because there was a bit in Luke about Jesus, after he had been resurrected, asking for some food and getting a piece of broiled fish and a honeycomb. That never rang true to him. He never knew what 'broiling' was. He thought first that it must be a spelling mistake, then he thought that it must be what his mam did to Parton herrings instead of cooking them. The other thing which didn't ring true was that if you were the Son of God and had just been miraculously raised from the dead, the first thing that came to mind would not be, "I'm famished, owt to eat?"

By the time he got to the second half of the paper the twins were being irritating. They had thrown out all thoughts of answering the questions independently and honestly. When Mrs Nidd got down to the business of making herself a cup of tea they knew that they were not being supervised properly. They whispered to each other constantly and wrote corrections in each other's papers. They had decided openly that the 'greatest act of Christian charity' was the 'feeding of the five thousand' and were going to each write the same essay.

Daniel knew in his bones that the founding of the National Health Service was the greatest act of charity in the history of the world, Christian or otherwise. The NHS was still in its infancy, but it had seeped into the lives of all Daniel's family already. From the gentle caring of his great grandparents at the end of their lives to his own caesarean birth after his mother had been in labour for forty-eight hours. Emily had been in and out of hospital ever since Daniel's birth with a series of ailments. Her health was a constant backdrop to their lives. That her appendix, her stomach ulcers, her diabetes could be cured without anybody having to worry about the cost, probably saved the family. Some months after Tom had been out of work, Emily had suffered a burst appendix and had been in Whitehaven Hospital for more than a week. In family rows and fights it was constantly referred to by Emily, "Aah cuddev died ev peritonitis".

The content and form of Daniel's essay was not all his own idea. All the colliers at 'Number 10' pit walked more surely to their work and young girls got pregnant more joyfully without the fear of death at the time of their confinement. It was constantly alluded to in all the grown-up conversations that Daniel was party to in his Grannie's parlour, or on the bus home from the rugby on Saturdays.

Daniel wrote a sentence about "millions and millions of souls saved from pain, saved from death, saved from the prison of ill health." He was pleased with that line and and it got him started.

He wrote, "There was nothing Jesus ever did to match the scale of that kindness." But he crossed the sentence out rather roughly. Not the sort of thing to write when inside a church.

He wrote instead, "There has not been anything in world history since 1948 to match it." As if he was any good in the History class at school.

All this poured out of Daniel and through his pencil. Faster and more rhythmically than if he had tried to say it.

"Would you like a cup of tea now Daniel?" whispered Mrs Nidd.

"Yes please," he whispered back.

She made it with milk and half a spoon of sugar without asking Daniel how he 'took his tea'.

"It's lovely."

She saw Daniel looking round to see if there was any currant cake left, read his mind, and produced a ginger snap.

"Me handwritin's nut ser good."

"You write very quickly."

"If ah ivver thowt aboot wot ah write, ah wouldn't write owt."

She took his empty teacup. "I think I know what you mean."

"Bye Elaine, Bye Audrey," he said as he held the vestry door open, "Sorry. Ah got that wrang way roond. Diddent ah?"

As he came out of the west doors Daniel let a great shaft of oblique sunlight in. Over by the old Roman fort he saw the vicar sitting on the stone stile. Daniel waved to him, but he saw that he was praying.

When Daniel got home, Tom asked, "Hoo'd yer git on?"

"Oah'reet," he said and joined in the helping of his mother with the dinner.

When Tom returned home after evensong that night, he asked Daniel again, "Did yer dae oah'reet at that exam?"

"It wuz oaney a bit a' fun," he replied.

Three or four weeks later Tom came back from his bible class. Emily and he were whispering a lot in the kitchen, but Daniel couldn't be bothered trying to listen in to them.

He put some coal on the fire, exchanged the usual pleasantries with his dad, he assured him that he "hadn't done his bloody crossword." And went to bed.

When Daniel came home from school the next day the living room was spotless. It smelled of furniture polish and dust.

The fire was set, but not lit.

The kitchen was clean. A ham hock was soaking in the big pan.

Emily was cutting up carrots and potatoes, "Can yer tidy the dining room please lad?"

"What's gaa'n on?"

"Nowt's gaa'n on." Daniel didn't want to start a fire by saying something crass like "the house is not normally this clean and tidy." For all that his mother was quick to tears, she had been through a lot in recent years.

"Table-cloth as well," she said.

"Bloody hell, iss't Queen cummen 'er summat?"

"Watch yer language in the presence of ladies." There was a lightness in her tone. If she wasn't going to tell Daniel what was going on, it would be best not to push it.

"Gaa up ter Mrs Vernon and see if she hez a jar 'er chutney?"

Tom didn't seem surprised when he came home and saw that Emily had 'made an effort'.

Tea was surprisingly excellent. The ham just needed to be pulled apart from its bone and slid on to the plates in soft unctuous lumps. The potatoes and the carrots had been boiled in the same pan as the ham and just needed a little pepper. Mrs Vernon's crab apple chutney was a master stroke.

There was no conversation during the tea and Daniel was comfortable in the silence.

"Light the fire lad," said Tom. "We'll dae t'dishes."

Daniel lit the fire and sat in his dad's armchair to toast his feet. There was more whispering in the kitchen. Daniel was full.

Emily and Tom came in and sat together on the settee.

"Yer oah'reet, stay theer," Tom said.

Emily took a deep and deliberate breath. "You know that exam you took for the Reverend Nidd?" She was enunciating, talking proper, was Daniel in trouble again?

"Well," she took another breath, "you passed."

She waited for Daniel to react. "You passed with flying colours, you came top or summat, and you have a scholarship to go to a big public school near London."

Daniel didn't understand what she was saying and waited for her to get to the point of her story.

But there was no 'story'. There was only that one bald statement and Daniel had to go back to it.

Was he being sent away to a public school? He started to sweat.

Why was he being sent away?

How bad had he been that his mother and father wanted to get rid of him?

He tried to look out through the window but could see nothing for the uncontrollable flood of tears.

He wasn't crying, it was just tears coming out of his eyes in a fierce torrent. He couldn't breathe in or breathe out, he made no noise but for the wailing inside his head.

How could the vicar, a great vicar, come into their village, come to send young children from their families? Daniel had never been bad with him, why was he, of all people, trying to get rid of him?

If Daniel heard his mam say that he would be able to find and make friends with other boys in the dormitory, or if he heard his dad say that there would be good rugby teams to play in, then they did not register at the time. If he had heard his dad say that he would be buggered in the arse by a housemaster, then that would not have registered either. All he knew was that he was being sent away. How could they after they had all been so strong, the three of them, when his dad was out of work?

When his dad walked for a hundred miles a week?

When Daniel pretended that he had had enough to eat by leaving a crust of bread on his plate?

When his mam lost all her dignity and sense of self and was too frightened to go into shops?

When Daniel walked with his dad and his sack of coal to Parton?

When Daniel biked to Maryport to piss on the door of a factory which wouldn't have his dad?

When he pretended that his shoes still fitted his feet?

Daniel felt sick only for a moment before he vomited violently through his tears and on to the fire. The ham, the potatoes and the bile exploded on impact with the hot blazing coals and kindling wood and spat sparks and sick out onto the carpet. As Emily jumped on to the hearth rug and Tom jumped to hold his son, a second, more violent spasm hit Daniel, but this time there was only a large gob of bile. It hit the grate. Tom put Daniel on his hands and knees as he retched again.

"Stay there, son."

Tom went for towels. Some to clean up the mess. Some to put round Daniel's shoulders as a gesture of love and comfort.

Emily ran Daniel a bath with the hot water that was being saved for Tom's evening bath.

Tom stayed with Daniel. His left arm around his son's shoulders, his right hand mindlessly cleaning the hearth with a messy towel.

Daniel had his bath and went to bed.

Emily was angry. She was angry that the evening which she had worked so hard for had not turned out according to her plans and dreams. She was angry that the meal she had cooked had turned out so splendidly only for it to be vomited up by an ungrateful son all over the fire, the hearth and the carpet. She was convinced that Daniel was perfectly capable, if he put his mind to it, of vomiting at will just to spite her.

Emily had been a Grammar School girl and though she found it to be a difficult experience, both educationally and socially, she enjoyed the distance she was allowed from the roughness of some of her contemporaries. She liked her name being on the Lowca School Honours Board. She had imagined all sorts of doors being opened for her after the Grammar School, but she only ended up being a secretary at Micklam. A pit.

She had married a checkweighman from the same pit, but for all his skills and diligence, Tom hadn't earned any more than an ordinary collier. That agonising time of Tom's unemployment had nearly killed her with all the resultant humiliations. Her rough contemporaries from Lowca School must have enjoyed laughing at her. The opportunity for Daniel to get away from Lowca was too good to turn down she thought. "My son Daniel is a scholarship boy at Harrow," she had imagined saying.

"What have we done to deserve him?" she shouted at Tom as she stormed off to an early bed.

Tom put his head round Daniel's bedroom door, "Y'er oahreet lad?" but Daniel was seemingly asleep.

Tom had seen Daniel's tears for those few seconds before he was sick. Tom knew that his lad was in great pain and he was angry with himself that he couldn't understand why. The Reverend Nidd had told him at Bible Class that Daniel's essay on the NHS was outstanding and that "My next sermon will be themed on 'Lord he stinketh.' "

Tom had watched his son go hungry when he was out of work and he had watched him lose his sharpness, his brightness and his readiness to talk. He had seen Daniel pushing his bike up the long hill from Harrington in the howling rain and had screamed to God, or whatever, with the pain of his love and his shame.

Tom went back downstairs and cleaned the hearth and the carpet again. He put a couple of lumps of coal on the fire. He had at first thought that Daniel's scholarship was a blessing from God. He had thought that the job at Sellafield was perhaps God's answer to his Harrington prayers. That his son would vomit with fear at the prospect of being taken away from this most miserable of places and this most fragile of families was hard for Tom to grasp. He tried to pray but could not articulate what he wanted to say. He settled for just trying to remember and account for all the things that he had put his boy through over the last year or so and to try to imagine what Daniel was afraid of.

He eventually fell asleep and woke up to the cold of a dead fire and open curtains.

He quietly opened the door to Daniel's bedroom. There was still enough light in the day to see that Daniel was curled up facing the window.

Tom did not want to disturb him whether he was awake or asleep.

Daniel had heard his dad.

He stared out of the window watching the light go.

He didn't get to sleep for such a long time. He tried to think of other things, Tracey, or even Elaine for goodness sake. But the images of being sent away, of perhaps saying goodbye at Whitehaven train station swam through his mind unbidden. Worse still was the image of returning to Lowca after a year or a term away. How would Harry and Billy react? How would he feel if Ralph Coulson, John Baxter or Billy Nevis didn't ask him to play touch rugby with them in the school holidays?

What idiot would think that a rough young boy from a place like Lowca would fit in to a posh public school? How would a boy who already had difficulties getting along with the other kids at school, kids who spoke with the same accent, who played the same games, how would he cope with the primal politics of a dormitory? How many boys would he have to fight to be able to sleep through the night?

When he did eventually get off to sleep, he was soon woken by his dad putting his head round the door again. It was now pitch black and Daniel closed his eyes in case his dad could perhaps see that he was awake. Minutes later Daniel heard his dad close the back door on his way to work. Daniel sat up in his bed and looked through the window to watch him go. He couldn't see him of course, but he watched long enough to see a bus, with all its lights, stop at Howgate. He knew that he would get on the bus and go to the upper deck to 'have a breakfast fag'.

Daniel got dressed as silently as he could, and without cleaning his teeth he went downstairs. He took a swig of milk from the bottle and two scones from the bread-bin. He wasn't running away from home. He just couldn't face any more talking. He just wanted to be, 'somewhere else'.

He followed Tom's path towards Howgate down to the beck and waited under the rail bridge until the sun got up. When there was enough light, he edged his way up into the small wood and followed the rail line westwards until it touched the edge of the beck. He sat on the rail and listened to the beck. The beck didn't smell at this time of day.

Daniel got to school an hour early and he was determined to act as if nothing had happened. "Actually," he thought to himself, "nothing has happened." His parents had thought that he should be sent away to a posh school, and here he was, sitting on bricks in a narrow gap between the temporary wooden classroom and the outside wall of the school toilets eating a disintegrated scone for his breakfast with nothing to drink. He got up and went to the school gate and stole a bottle of milk. He came back to his little lair and drank the milk. He hid the bottle between the bricks he was sitting on.

"How could anybody want to take me away from all this?" he laughed to himself.

He walked across the field towards his old prefab but before he got there Tracey came out of her house and waved to him. Daniel was going to tell her about being sent away, but he was for a while, too happy to.

"He's bin in that sulk fer a week noow," said Emily.

But it wasn't a sulk. Daniel just couldn't face discussing 'it'. 'It' being the concept of his mam and dad wanting to get rid of him. More than that, he just couldn't talk, about anything. He was like Emily had been when Tom was out of work. She couldn't go into any of the shops in the village. She was so ashamed that she could only buy the cheapest stuff. When she tried to work out what she could and couldn't afford, she just panicked and ran out of the shops in a state.

Daniel had frozen up also. Was he so unlikeable that even his parents didn't seem to want him around? There wasn't anything he could say to that. He had been to see Grannie and Grandad a few times. He would go each time with a prepared statement in his mind, but he never was able to get it out of his mouth.

"Maybe Grannie and Grandad are part of the plot," he thought.

He wrote a note to them, a very formal note with his address written out on the top right-hand side of the paper. He began the letter with "Dear grannie and grandad". He immediately rewrote the initials so that it read "Dear Grannie and Grandad,"

The letter went something like ... "My mam and dad are trying to send me away to a public school. I don't want to be away from my family and friends. I don't understand why this is happening to me, can I stay with you until it all blows over? I am happy to sleep in the shed if that is the only room available."

He finished the letter

"Thank you for your consideration,

Yours sincerely,

Your loving grandson,

Daniel"

He never sent it.

Once when he got home Emily showed Daniel a small pile of new underpants and vests which she had bought for him.

Daniel wanted to say something eloquent like, "You haven't bought them for me, you have bought them for the school I have no intentions of going to." The phrase was almost in his mind, but he couldn't quite get the words out and he ran out of the back door.

"You can't run away from it ..." Emily shouted after him.

Daniel stopped.

He wanted to turn and shout back at her, "If I actually did run away, would that let you off the moral hook? Would it let you get rid of me without having to feel guilty?" Of course, he couldn't get those words out either and he turned and carried on running down to the beck.

He watched the water in the beck until he saw his dad coming down the path from Howgate. Daniel's plan had been to catch him on his way back from work and to walk back up the hill to home with him, perhaps say something meaningful to him. But he was with two other men in work clothes. He was talking. He looked happy. So, Daniel hid behind the hawthorns and got home a few minutes after him.

Dinner was crap.

"If you don't like it just say so."

Tom didn't rise to the bait of cracking a friendly joke and the table was cleared and the dishes washed with uncharacteristic haste.

Daniel disappeared upstairs to read something.

He may have nodded off. There was a loud knock at the front door, then the sound of friendly chat moving from the hallway to the living room.

A few minutes later Tom knocked on Daniel's door. Daniel sat up straight on his bed.

"The vicar's here, he would like to talk to you."

Before Daniel could react, Tom said, "No, that's nut reet. The vicar's here, wud yer like ter talk wid 'im?"

Daniel smiled for his dad. He wanted to say that he would, but even that wouldn't come out.

He started to get up, but Tom put his hand on Daniel's shoulder, "Yer divvent hev ter."

They went downstairs together. The vicar stood up and shook Daniel's hand very formally.

Emily was already out of the room. Tom exchanged a nod with the Reverend Nidd and went into the dining room. He closed the door behind him.

Daniel told himself to look the vicar straight in the eye. He knew that his mam and dad must have got in touch with the vicar and asked him to come to the house and, "sort him out."

They both simultaneously made the same hand gesture to the other to sit down on the settee.

Daniel wanted to say, "Before we get going, I have a question. Tell me, where did you get the nerve to come into this village and try and take children away from their parents?" But of course, that, of all things, didn't come out.

Daniel was so focussed on maintaining eye contact that he didn't see the vicar take a cricket ball out of his jacket pocket. It was a bit worn. If Tom had been in the room he would have said that it was, "forty overs old".

He fiddled with it a bit with both hands.

"I was a decent cricketer when I was a kid, my oldest brother played for Yorkshire, and I rather hoped that I might give it a try. I had two games for the second team, didn't get any runs, then one day I was asked to travel with the county team as twelfth man against Northants. My brother was playing and I had just got home from university." He stopped talking.

Was he expecting Daniel to make some comment?

"I couldn't even get into the university team," he said, almost to himself, "And here I was, nearly playing for Yorkshire."

He gave Daniel the ball. Well, he just put it into his hand.

"The twelfth man always got on the field, the old pros always needed a 'spell off', for a fag or a pee or a lie down. Anyway, all the big names were playing. Johnny Wardle came on to bowl and took four wickets just after tea. They, Northants, were nine wickets down and I was fielding at square leg just behind the umpire and I took a diving, one handed catch. You wouldn't think it looking at me now, would you?" He laughed, patting his tummy and for the first time looking directly at Daniel.

"It gave Johnny a five-wicket spell and won us the game and stopped them batting out a draw." He paused again. "I took a good catch in a County Championship match."

He paused again.

"It was the end of the game. I thought that I would keep the ball as a memento of my catch. I put it in my kit bag. It was a small suitcase, I didn't have a proper cricket bag. When the rest of the team came back into the changing room Johnny was looking for the ball with which he had taken five wickets. He was a little angry when he couldn't find it. He was searching around other players' bags. I told him that I thought that I gave the ball to one of the umpires. He charged out of the door and came back five minutes later with his 'triumphal ball'. The umpires must have just given him any old ball and he was happy."

"So, there you have it, Daniel, you're handling stolen property. I am ashamed that I stole the ball, of course, but more than that I am ashamed that I didn't understand that Johnny Wardle would want to keep all the balls that he took five wickets with. He must have taken five wickets loads of times. He was a top-class international bowler. Why would he bother about such trivial matters? But you know, most of the top players have these small rituals and I just didn't understand that."

"I was twelfth man a couple more times, but never did anything. Just wasn't good enough."

He paused again. Daniel put his fingers round the ball with an off-spinner's grip, but his fingers were too small to get round the seam.

"It seems like I am just not good enough in this job either," he started again. "It seems as though I have caused you a great deal of pain. I'm sorry about that. My church is a mile from each of the three and a half villages in my parish and I don't understand what I have come to. I am from rich Richmondshire, nowhere near the industrial heartlands of Yorkshire. I got sent here because it was thought that a Yorkie would have a natural empathy with a cluster of mining villages. But I don't. I am from a long line of farmers and bank managers, never been near a pit. What I can see though is that there are moral values in the way miners look after each other which are way stronger than anything you could find in my divinity class at Oxford. Honesty, sometimes in the form of painful truth, is in Lowca's blood. There are real Christian values to be found here. And I come along with my dog collar and think that the right thing to do is to take you away from your family and all the good people around you."

He looked at Daniel as if looking for a response.

"Just because you are clever."

Daniel looked away from his gaze.

"For what? You'll go to university. *Nae bother asser!*"

He laughed at his own attempt at the Lowca accent. "But you should be proud that you have made your stand. You must follow your own path, even if it seems stupid at the time."

Daniel nodded to him.

"Your parents think that I am here to persuade you to take up the scholarship, well I'm not. I am here to apologise to you. I know it has caused you much anguish. I'm sorry. We will tell your mum and dad that we had a meaningful conversation and covered all the pros and cons and that we have both came to the conclusion that there are as many fulfilling opportunities in life here in Lowca as there are in Harrow."

"Sounds oareet."

"I have got you to talk at least," he laughed.

"You tell them," Daniel said pointing with his thumb to the dining room door.

"You must keep the ball."

"Oah ta. Rev."

The Reverend Nidd went to open the door. Daniel was half expecting to see his mam and dad on their hands and knees with their ears to the door. They weren't. They were in the kitchen. The kitchen door was closed also.

"Tom, Emily," he called.

They came in. Daniel got up and put his ball on the window-sill.

"Tom, Emily, I became a priest because I wanted to do God's will and do good in the world. There doesn't seem much evidence of that yet. This evening I think that I have, at last, done a little good. Daniel is not going to Harrow. He is going to stay here in Cumberland to find love and enlightenment. I now see that my job is to support him in that arduous quest."

The four of them were still standing politely in the middle of the living room. Neither Emily nor Tom understood what the vicar was getting at. The vicar gave way to the strained silence.

"As for doing God's work, I believe that God would, at this moment, want us to pray."

Daniel knelt on the rug by the fire and Emily and Tom moved awkwardly to join him on the floor.

"No! Noooh! Let's sit on the chairs. Please."

Emily, Tom and the vicar took up the spaces in the settee and Tom's chair. Daniel turned from kneeling to sitting where he was.

The Lord's Prayer was mumbled in unison.

The Reverend Nidd intoned blessings on the "Community of Lowca", which had everyone sitting up straight, then there were blessings for the family and Daniel, "this most courageous of boys . . ."

Emily and Tom were none the wiser, but they both felt touched. Emily nearly cried.

The vicar stood up, breaking the silence again.

"Tom, I have been at St Bridget's for nearly two years now, and do you know a funny thing? I have never been into any of the pubs. I remain an outsider and Daniel has persuaded me that it is up to me to make the first steps into the community. I am in desperate need of a pint Tom, would you join me for one, or maybe even two in 'The Ship'?"

"Yer keepen yer collar on?"

"Good idea." He took off his dog collar and loosened his shirt.

Daniel was shocked that it was a little strip of white plastic and not something which went all around the neck, like a polo mint.

As 'Mr'Nidd and Tom went out of the front door Emily said to Daniel, "The Ship is in fer a shock."

But Daniel was out of the back door with his cricket ball.

CHAPTER 7

In Mr Hall's class, the curriculum was Maths and English. Very little Art or Music. No Science or French. Geography and History, what little there was, was just another excuse to write an essay. There was an 'eleven plus' to pass. For boys like Daniel it was a duty more than an opportunity. Failing the exam would be failing his family. Mr Hall was the kind of teacher who dutifully made an effort to talk to each child in his class at least three or four times in the course of the day, but it was always about school-work. That's not quite true. He would read the class a story at the end of every Wednesday afternoon, a story from Dickens, or Robert Louis Stephenson, sometimes easy bits from Shakespeare. He could do all the accents and characterisations. He made the children laugh. In the winter months, the classroom lights would sometimes be turned off, a candle would be lit, and he would tell ghost stories. However, the class had to write an essay about it on Thursday!

There were twenty-eight in Mr Hall's class and the regional average for getting into the Grammar School was 15%, so four or five getting in from Lowca School was a good number, notwithstanding the usual social and class stereotyping. Nonetheless, twelve were selected to attend Mrs Troon's "drill class" in Mr Proud's room after school every Tuesday and Thursday. For added personal pressure on Daniel, there, behind Mrs Troon, were three large oak Honours Boards, in the middle of which was Daniel's mam's name " Emily Polgrean Cragg 1931" under the heading 'Scholarships.'

Though selected, Tracey Smith opted out of the class. Going to the Grammar school was not an option for her and her family. There was no way that Mr and Mrs Smith could afford the uniform, the P.E. kit, the dinner money, the dreaded school trips. Mr Smith was ill again and missed a lot of work.

"Ah'd like to come to t'classes, ah would enjoy them, and Mrs Troon isn't as scary as ivverybody sez, but if ah passed it would knock my dad out, wid oh't guilt 'n that. Ah divvn't want ter dae that t'll him."

"Ah sometimes think that ah want ter fail, just ter git ivverybody off me back," Daniel said.

"Ah think that ah'd look nice in a shop assistant's uniform. Me mam thinks ah look a tart anyhow."

Thus, all the good boys and girls stayed on after school for Mrs Troon, and sixteen children were told at the age of nine that they were not worth bothering with.

Tuesday was maths, well not real maths, but different forms of arithmetic. The sums were quite easy, it was working out the question, with all the complications of 'apples and oranges', 'train times from Edinburgh to London' and 'the average temperature of the Sahara Desert in winter.'

Thursday was English, and the writing of an essay, a story, a composition.

Mrs Troon had a formula for an 'eleven plus essay', and she laid out the structure.

- A very interesting and intriguing first sentence about something the pupils knew about in their own personal lives within which there was an approximation of the truth.
- A paragraph giving the background to the story, with lots of descriptions and adjectives.
- The introduction of more than one person to the story, with suitable dialogue to show that they could punctuate speech.
- Two sides of a given scene, argument, event, fight.
- A funny or sad outcome of the story.
- An interesting and intriguing last sentence, or paragraph.

On the first Thursday the students had to come up with four very inviting first sentences which were roughly true.

Daniel excitedly scribbled a few of the hundred ideas that came to him in those first few moments.

- "Stanley Matthews broke my nose," was the first one.
- "My grandad had thirteen horses shot from under him in the First World War."
- "Mr Churchill wasn't as good as people made him out to be. Both my grandads said."

- "There's a Roman column which can be seen at low tide on Parton beach. It is covered in cuvvins now."

Over the next few Thursdays the stories got written and rewritten. Mrs Troon didn't tell her class what to write, but she asked questions and gave them options to consider. There were no options when it came to grammar, punctuation and structure. Daniel listened to the other kids as they talked to each other about their stories. They seemed to have better essays and they were about more serious and important themes.

"Stick to what you know," said Mrs Troon. "Examiners can spot flannel from a mile away."

So, Daniel's initial efforts changed to:

"Stanley Matthews didn't break my nose like I sometimes say. I had a nosebleed when I tried to head the football which he had kicked past the post in trying to score a goal playing for Stoke City at Workington in the F.A. Cup. For three seconds people laughed at me until Mr Matthews shouted to me, "Are you okay son?" then somebody gave me their hankie."

"My grandfather had thirteen horses shot from under him in The First World War. He was a Hussar. There are five of his "war pals" from the same Regiment still living in Workington and Maryport, including William Vernon. Grandad and Mr Vernon sit on an old park bench in Mr Vernon's garden, drinking hot tea with 'carnation milk'. They talk politics. They don't like Mr Churchill because of his mistakes in the First World War. He wanted to machine gun the miners during the General Strike."

"You might get a vindictive Tory examiner," warned Mrs Troon.

"The Roman column on Parton beach got there because it fell down the cliff from the Roman Fort next to St Bridget's Church. Two Roman soldiers might have leaned against it talking about the beautiful local women and the ugly local men, the funny looking sheep."

"The names of Lowca and Pica both have their roots in vernacular Roman," said Mrs Troon. "You should try and get that in."

"You can adapt any one of those stories to fit any of the questions. The questions are only there to get you started, not to catch you out."

Daniel spent so much of his time, walking home from school, daydreaming on the toilet, in wakeful early summer mornings imagining himself into any of these scenarios. It was better than reading comics.

In the end, nine pupils passed that year, Maurice Dicks, Denise Cowan, cousin Billy Cragg, John Baxter, Billy Nevis, Ralph Coulson, Elaine Menton, Daniel of course and … Tracey Smith! The 'wild card' girl who was not in Mrs Troon's 'study group' because she was afraid of passing.

The Headmaster, Mr Smith, went into the classroom with Mrs Troon in tow. Mr Hall was given a sheet of paper and he read out the names of those who had passed.

The room was silent.

Mr Smith, great big fat Mr Smith, moved closer to the heart of the class, "We have never had as many as nine pass before, I think that it is a record. Whitehaven Grammar School will not know what has hit them."

The class tittered a little nervously. Mr Hall laughed and nodded.

Angela Williams was the first to start crying, well, quietly sniffling. Soon there were three or four in the class dabbing their eyes with their sleeves, the cousins Billy Brampton and Alan Brampton.

It wasn't the sense of failure, most of them knew that they would not pass, but they perhaps hoped. It wasn't that they were stuck at Lowca School for the next four years, some would have quite liked that. Certainly, most of them, even those who had passed, were scared about going to the Grammar School with all those snobs, having to wear the silly green caps and berets. Angela's weeping evoked a silent empathy round the class because the world had decided to separate these children from each other for the rest of their lives. A line was drawn between the Grammar School pupils and the Lowca School pupils and they would inhabit different worlds. Some friends would try to stick together, but it wouldn't last beyond the first couple of terms.

There was a unique sorrow for those families who were divided by the eleven plus.

"'Well done' to those who passed, well done to those who didn't pass. You are still wonderful and unique Lowca lads and lasses, don't ever forget that, but most of all a huge 'Well done' to Mrs Troon and Mr Hall, the best teachers it is possible to have."

Well that got everybody sniffing. Even Mr Hall had a hankie in his hand, just in case he had to "blow his nose".

Mr Smith nodded to those who had passed, "Go on home now and tell your mams and dads."

Daniel got up out of his seat and turned to head to the door at the back of the class, and, true to form, Billy Millington stuck out his foot to try and trip him up, but he didn't get his timing right and Daniel was able to stand on his ankle with some force before he turned to him to say a false "sorry asser".

Mr Hall glowered at him. Then he and Mrs Troon both smiled at him. Daniel looked at them both but didn't know if it was appropriate to smile back.

"Be back before two, you are still at Lowca School and you still have lessons," shouted Mr Smith.

The results had been posted at Micklam, Number 10 pit and the Coking Ovens before the class was told, and Daniel's mam already knew, but a trip to Meadow View was in order. He had to tell his grandparents, but they already knew also. Billy had already been round to tell them. Daniel got a congratulatory 'wagon wheel' and a bottle of lemonade.

He couldn't be bothered going back to school. Life would be complicated enough before the end of term, so he went down to the beck to look at the water and the stones and had a proper weep.

It was well understood that for the remaining few weeks before the end of the school year, "the Grammar School Swots" would have a hard time, would be "fair game". The words 'tradition' and 'rough and tumble' disguised some serious bullying of both the boys and the girls.

So, the following day Daniel got to school with just a few minutes to spare and snuck into his class line ready to be marched in single file to the classrooms.

"In yer lines," bellowed Gobbo Gibson to all the strays.

It may have been a new and innovative education policy throughout the country, or it may have been a unilateral educational experiment devised by Lowca School, but it was maybe a mistake to appoint fifteen-year-old 'prefects' to organise and police the ordered entrance to the school classrooms in separate class single files.

"Empowerment" was one of the words. "A bit of responsibility before they leave school and enter the adult world," was how Gwen had heard it when she was a prefect.

These innovative social arrangements had not factored in Gobbo.

At nine o'clock on a windy summer morning, Gobbo was just a bully with militaristic overtones. When he shouted "In yer lines," at the very top of his voice, he meant a very rigidly straight line. The children, however, understood that a line could take many forms. Class 3's organic, slightly wavy line was a suitable expression of their corporate mind-set, but it was a line, nonetheless. The previous day's eleven plus announcements may have created a little disunity.

Daniel did not hear Gobbo come up behind him. Gobbo smacked Daniel on the right side of his head with such brutal force that his legs buckled under him.

"In yer fuckin' lines, fuckin' Grammar School Swot."

Daniel got to his legs and swung a wild fist, but he only caught Gobbo on the ear. He tried to swing again but Gobbo had grabbed Daniel by the back of his head and slammed his face into his rising knee with huge force.

The classes in the playground went silent.

Daniel's head was full of noise.

Daniel was lying on his left side on the tarmac floor and all the other kids had gone. Gobbo had gone. Daniel could only see out of his left eye. There was a small pool of blood the size of a saucer on the playground floor. Daniel retched as if to vomit.

"He's going to be sick," he heard a girl's voice say.

"Let's git Mr Smith er Mr Proud."

"No let's git 'im yam." Daniel knew that it was the voice of Joyce Southland from four doors up.

"He was in a fight before school missis."

And that remained the official version of events for Daniel's mother, and he was not too sure of his facts at the time to disabuse her. Vomiting on his bedroom rug just served to give her more pain.

That night Tom came home from work and asked Daniel what had happened.

"Git drissed, we're tekken yer t' t' doctor's."

"No Dad, it's only a black eye. I'll be all right for school in the morning. Please don't make a fuss of it."

Daniel was very keen to go into school the next day. His mother was even more keen. The joy of Daniel getting into the Grammar School was a rare beacon of hope for her. She couldn't handle the state her boy's face was in, particularly now. She made Daniel a fried egg on toast for his breakfast. She had never done that before. It was supposed to be something triumphant. It was supposed to be the one thing that they could share. They had both passed the eleven plus and now her son was going to the Grammar School like she had done. She had imagined that they would enter a warmer, more trusting relationship. She could help him with his homework. She could tell him stories. She would make him great breakfasts and Daniel would tell her about the teachers who were still there from her time.

And now she couldn't even look at him. Her son looked like something from the newspapers in the war. Whatever pasting he had got to make the whole side of his face into a huge blue bruise, she knew that he probably deserved it.

Daniel came out of the front door of the house and Ian Leeming and Joyce Southland were there waiting for him.

"Bloody hell!" was not the reaction to his black eye that he really wanted from Joyce.

"Does it hurt?"

"Of course it will hurt," said Joyce. Then, rather incongruously, "Can I touch it?"

Joyce was a close friend of Gwen. They both went to the "tanner hop" in Harrington every Friday night. Ian fancied Joyce. He edged his way between Joyce and Daniel. When they got to the end of Vale View, he suggested that they took the short cut through the Ghyll. "Might save young Daniel here a bit 'ev embarrassment!" Joyce shot him a withering look but didn't say anything.

"Ah'm up fer that," Daniel said.

It was more difficult than he thought, picking his way down through the Ghyll, but Joyce went ahead of him and held his hand. She held Daniel's hand again when he tried to get through the gap in the barbed wire fence on the other side. She kept hold of his hand when negotiating Everest's piles of shit. She only let go when Ian ran on ahead.

"Gwen got felt up et wuk yisterder."

"Ah didn't kno'ah."

"Factery floor manager. Tell't her ter git summat oot'et' store-room." She looked closely at Daniel's eye. "Are yer sure yer oah'reet?" She held his hand again, "follered 'er in, touched 'er arse."

"What did Gwen dae?"

"Kneed him in't knackers, then locked 'im in't cubberd. Gev't key ter yan 'et machinists."

She let go of Daniel's hand as they laughed. "Yer'll be oa'hreet frem 'ere," and she skipped off.

"Thank you," Daniel said, too late to be heard.

Daniel got to the school yard and they were all there. Mr Smith, Mr Hall and Miss Wildgoose. His heart sank at the thought of all the attention which was probably heading his way. He found a space by the back wall and Tracey joined him. Daniel could look out over the field without ostentatiously hiding his eye.

Tracey leaned over the wall to get a look at him. She gave his elbow a gentle squeeze.

"Daniel," said Miss Wildgoose. He turned to face her. She tried to maintain her smile, but her shoulders dropped.

Tracey let go of Daniel's elbow and edged away, just a couple of feet. She tried not to cry.

"Who gave you the black eye?" said Mr Smith. He knew very well who had given Daniel his black eye, his swollen face, why else were there three teachers on duty?

"A cricket ball sir."

"Did this 'cricket ball' have a name?"

Daniel tried to say, 'Gunn and Moore' but he got mixed up and what slipped out was, "Bryant and May."

Even Daniel, himself, had to stifle a laugh.

"'Bryant and May' make excellent cricket balls. I shall call the M.C.C. forthwith to see if England will be using 'Bryant and May' balls in the Test 'Match' on Thursday," said Mr Smith, pleased with his little pun.

Everybody else in the playground was trying to act normally, as if nothing had happened at the same time yesterday, as if Mr Smith and two other teachers were 'on playground duty' every morning. But some were trying to listen into the conversation and wondering why on earth Mr Smith, Miss Wildgoose and the boy with the horrible black eye were wetting themselves with laughter.

Mr Smith gave Miss Wildgoose a key. "Take the lad to my office will you, there's a First Aid box in the bottom right-hand drawer of my desk. There's some Vaseline and some haemorrhoid ointment in there, mix them up and massage his eye with it. I'll sort this lot out."

Mr Smith's office was in a small annexe to the main school buildings, but it was surprisingly roomy. "Enough room to swing an admonishing cane."

Miss Wildgoose sat Daniel down in the chair. "That's a big chair!" she said. They both sniggered at the reference to Mr Smith's size. "Tell me if this hurts." She was so gentle. Her free hand cradled Daniel's left ear. "Well done on passing. I sent your mam and dad a card yesterday, from what I heard I didn't think that you would be in school today."

Mr Smith came in. "Nurse Wildgoose, next time I get a black eye I will come to you first."

A nod sent her to her classroom holding her greasy fingers aloft.

"Still not going to tell me the truth?"

"No sir."

"That can sometimes be noble, but more often, telling the truth is nobler still."

"Yes sir."

"Going to Grammar School is the best revenge."

"Yes sir."

He put the rest of the ointment which Miss Wildgoose had made into an empty aspirin bottle and gave it to Daniel.

"Thank you! Sir."

"When you go to the Grammar, give my best wishes to Mr Colley. He was a very good footballer."

"Yes sir."

The following Monday Mr Hall's classroom was all abuzz because on the Saturday, all the kids who had 'passed', except Tracey and Daniel, had walked the four miles to Harrington to knock on Mrs Troon's door. They had bought between them a bunch of roses and a big, hand-made 'thank you' card.

"Oh, how wonderful and thoughtful. Nobody has ever done this before." She opened the door and invited them in. "You won't tell anybody that 'scary Mrs Troon' had to get her hankie out".

"Did you come on the bus?"

"We couldn't afford the bus AND the flowers," they chorused.

"Sit where you can, I'm sorry about the mess, I have just made some chocolate cake. Denise and Billy come into the kitchen and help me, please."

Warm chocolate cake was a great treat, but she also had real Coca Cola. Wow!

Mrs Troon told stories of previous 'scholars' as she called them, and what they were now doing with their lives. She gave each of her 'little visitors' a 'Platignum' pen. Not only that, she ordered a taxi to deliver them home. "Mind on, don't just dump them at the Ship Inn, take them each to their own houses." She gave the taxi driver some money, "There's more than enough."

Only Denise had ever been in a taxi before, as she told everyone twice, and the journey back to Lowca was taken in silence.

In the playground on the following day those same seven gathered together like sheep at the crouching of a dog. They were not afraid that what had happened to Daniel would happen to them, or that the rest of the school would chant something about "grammar school swots and snobs", or that they would break off all their Lowca friendships, even before the end of the term. But there were no more impromptu games of cricket, or touch rugby, not even a co-ed game of 'barthedoor'. Worst of all there were no more games of skipping, that most glorious of spectator sports, where even the senior girls tucked their skirts into their knickers. It was just that this little group were different now. They no longer belonged here.

Daniel's black eye, and the ugliness of Gobbo's assault, gave him a bit of protection, a kind of inoculation. Nonetheless Daniel played safe, and at break times took to wandering round the school looking for, and finding, corners to hide in. With a book or with some paper to draw on, he was content. A week or two later, when his eye had turned yellow, he wandered past the school's front gate and down the alley towards Mr Smith's office. He found Tracey in a girly-fight with Helen Cobbett. Helen was fifteen, and big for fifteen. Her sister Sue, who was in

Tracey and Daniel's class, was acting as both Helen's second, and her look-out. Helen had grabbed Tracey's hair from behind and was yanking her head from side to side. It was so much more vicious than any boys' fight. All this was performed silently.

"Why don't you just scream?" Daniel thought.

He moved towards them and grabbed Helen's two fists with half of Tracey's hair in them. He bent her finger ends, nails and all, back into a tight spiral and into the palms of her hands. He squeezed tighter and tighter. Tracey's body was pressed into Daniel's. Her left cheek, wet with her tears, pressed into Daniel's left cheek. For a moment he forgot about Helen's fingers and felt Tracey's warmth and dampness. He may have pressed his cheek back into hers a little. Helen's head tipped backwards. Her knees buckled. Three heads tight into each other. Daniel was hurting Helen, delighting in doing so. In the midst of all the hair and the clenched fists Daniel thought that he was going to kiss Tracey. Her cheek, her closed wet eye, her open mouth.

"Hey up our Helen, I think yer wetting yersel'."

Daniel let go of Helen's fingers and she pulled backwards before turning to run off out of the front gate of the school. Sue ran in dutiful pursuit.

Sure enough, there was a tiny patch of dampness on the floor. It may, or may not, have been Helen's wee.

Tracey let go a full torrent of sobbing and Daniel was now embarrassed. She wiped her face with the sleeve of her blouse. Tears, snot and all.

A few minutes passed without Daniel saying anything, he was still standing there like a lump.

"Hev yer got a hankie?"

"No."

"Watch that naebody comes." And she took out the bottom of her blouse from inside her skirt and blew everything out from her eyes and her nose. With a sniff, she stood up straight and tried to smile at Daniel.

She tucked herself in, shoving the crumpled, snotty bit of her blouse into the top of her knickers.

Daniel stared at Tracey as she buttoned up the top of her skirt.

"Thanks fer that. I suppose I hev te strip off again and let yer feel 'ez up?"

Daniel couldn't say anything.

"Not at all, my love, the touch of your warm damp cheek was thanks enough," might have been a good response. Or, "Yes please." Perhaps she would have laughed at, "What? Here by the school gates?" or "Are yer mam and dad at home?" These thoughts were all passing through Daniel's mind at the same time, but he couldn't get his mouth to say any of them.

"A'ahm ga'an t't lav, te sort misel oot."

She walked away.

"I'm sorry I didn't have a hankie," he shouted after her, but she was round the corner of the 'Senior Class 2' and out of sight.

At the end of school Daniel caught up with Tracey at the bottom of the school paddock.

"Why didn't yer just bugger off home today?" he said, "Your head must be very sore."

"Ah can't tell me mam, she'd tell me dad. Me dad will git in a state."

As she squeezed through the gap in the fence to her own back yard, she ignored Everest as he came plodding and nodding over to her.

Tracey stuck her head back through the hole, "Divvn't tell anybody asser."

"I won't."

"Promise."

Daniel's walk to school from the new house in Vale View was longer, the short cut through the Ghyll didn't save much time. Daniel missed squeezing through the gap in the old prefab's fence and finding Tracey near at hand.

In the classroom, after assembly and prayers, Mr Hall gave out a newish set of comprehension books. When he came to Tracey he bent over and whispered something to her. She went quickly out of the door, skipping a little as she pulled her socks up. She didn't return to class and Daniel just knew that she was in some kind of trouble. What that trouble was, he couldn't fathom. Mr Hall had never whispered anything to him, certainly never anything which would send him out of the classroom.

Daniel made a complete mess of the 'comprehension'. He read the text several times without having his brain plugged in. When Mr Hall did 'the questions' he would normally have had his hand up with all the answers.

Daniel avoided his gaze. "I have answered enough questions in my years at Lowca School. No more answers," he thought to himself.

Mr Hall honed-in on Daniel from his 'black eye' side and he had to turn round in his chair to see his teacher properly.

"Daniel." Mr Hall winced a little when he got a full-frontal view of Daniel's face. He pressed on, "Why do you think the Doctor in the story turned the injured man on his side?"

"I don't know Sir."

"Come on. Of course you know."

"No Sir. I just don't know anything anymore."

Daniel stared at him. He twisted even further round in his desk and stared at him with his clear eye. A little water, not tears, seeped out of the cleavage of his black eye. He wanted to wipe it away with his sleeve, but he allowed one small drop to run down his cheek.

Mr Hall stared at it. He may have thought that Daniel was being rude, or insolent. He may have thought that Daniel resented him personally for having the shit kicked out of him by Gobbo, when staff should have been on duty.

Daniel didn't want any more crap and he gave in. He made a guess. "To make sure that he could breathe properly."

Mr Hall was going to ask Daniel a follow up question, but he paused. Then he looked away.

At that point Tracey came back into the class and sat at her desk.

At morning break, she went over to Daniel. She knew Daniel would have been in agony all morning wondering why she had gone out of the classroom and why she took so long to come back.

"Mr Smith's ga'an round to see me mam and dad at twelve o' clock. I hev te be theer as well."

"Why?"

"Ah dunno."

"Aaarrrgh ..."

"Ah mebbe still might be gaan t't grammar."

"Wot? Great."

"Ah don't know, Ah don't really understand."

"It would be great if you could."

"Hope 'e doesn't want 'is dinner. We've on'y got bread 'n 'iffit."

"Good morning Mr Smith."

"Good mornin' Mr Smith tae thee yersel."

Mrs Smith had a tray of tea, ready and waiting in the "funeral best" white Wedgwood service.

There was a small plate of ginger snaps.

The three adults sat round the coffee table; Tracey had to sit by the door to the kitchen.

There was a freshly made fire.

"Tracey is a very clever girl with a strong mind of her own," said obese Mr Smith.

"Don't we know it!" said Mrs Smith.

"I have some options to put before you as a family." Three sets of documents in brown folders were put on the table and the cups and saucers were shuffled around to accommodate them.

"With your war record, your regiment and your medical condition you are in a position to get a series of grants and bursaries for one or other of two public schools. These schools are very prestigious, but they are both in the south of England and transport to and from the schools is not included."

"Ah'm nut gaan t'll a public school. Ah'm nut sleep'n in a dormitory wid a bunch ev other lasses," shouted Tracey.

"Wheesht lass."

"An' ah'm nut leav'n me dad either."

"A stong mind of her own indeed." Mr Smith, the headmaster smiled. "Option number two is perhaps more favourable then. Tracey can stay at Lowca School for four or five years and if she works really hard, we can try and get her through a couple of exams and get her into the Sixth Form at the Grammar School to do 'A' Levels." He picked up a third folder and opened it out on top of the others.

"Then there is this."

He gave the document to Tracey's dad. "We can access a series of small scholarships, again military related, to pay for all of Tracey's uniforms, shoes, P.E. kits, school trips and even her dinner money, and she will be able to take up her place at the Grammar School."

"They won't be cast off uniforms, will they?" said Mrs Smith.

"No, as you can see on page three." He pressed his finger down firmly on the relevant paragraph, "There would be a new blazer and skirt, and all the other stuff for 'the start of each academic year up to the value of thirty-eight pounds'. So, she would be a lot better dressed than most of the kids."

"Will ah hev newer clothes than Denise?"

Mr and Mrs Smith both tried to interject that they liked that last option. They both started to talk at the same time; and both retreated, perhaps in case each would have said something different.

"You would need a letter from your doctor, your G.P., or perhaps better, your specialist. There would be a lot of form filling."

There was a pause. "I am sorry that I have come at such short notice, and I know, that even though this is all for Tracey's benefit, it is all an intrusion into your family life, an invasion of your privacy."

There was another silence.

"This is a proud family, we divvn't want any handoots," said Tracey's dad.

"This isn't charity Mr Smith. You earned every penny of this in Tripoli and in Italy. Think of it as a war pension paid through your daughter. And you must also remember the part Tracey played in winning the scholarships."

Tracey went behind her dad and cradled his head. "We'll think about it Mr Smith," she said. "Sir."

"I got four medals 'for courageous use of a pen', "laughed Mr Smith, "But we both fought." He paused, "Well, I don't know about you Mr Smith, but I did my bit so that the Traceys of this world, the Beckys and the Billys, could all get an equal chance. Where would you be now, if you don't mind me saying, if it wasn't for the National Health Service?"

"Can we read these papers?" said Mrs Smith, "Perhaps get back to you on Monday. That won't be ower late will it?"

"No, Monday would be perfect." He stood up. "Can you come at four o'clock? I can get Mrs Troon to join us. We can return your lovely hospitality."

From inside Tracey's arms Mr Smith said, "This must hev tak'n a lot a wuk on your part."

"Thank you for the tea, Mrs Smith. If anybody asks, please tell people that I only had two ginger snaps."

There was some awkward handshaking, which finished with Tracey laughingly shaking her dad's hand.

"You should be back in your classroom in ten minutes young lady."

On the Monday, Tracey asked Daniel to stay with her after school while her mam and dad went in to see Mr Smith and Mrs Troon.

They walked round the empty school. It was ten minutes after the bell had gone and there was nobody about except the four of them in Mr Smith's office.

"Ah doan't want ter just hang around ootside on me o'an while ivverybody is inside talkin aboot ez."

"Is ivverything oahreet?"

"Aye, dad went te see his specialist on Frider. Dad wus worried that if he got better ah might lose 'the scholarship'. "She did a funny sign with her two hands.

"Will yer dad git better?"

"Nah, nut fer a few years. Ther' ganna put him on some new pills."

"He's allus seemed oahreet ter me."

At that point Tracey's parents came out of the front gate looking for her.

"Hello Daniel! Hev you two been doon't ghyll 'bird's nestin'?"

Mrs Smith gave him a dig with her elbows, "Leave the lad alone." She turned to Daniel, "Do you like your new house, Daniel?"

Daniel didn't understand the reference to bird's nesting. "Aa'h'll hev ter gaa. Seeya Tracey. Bye Mr and Mrs Smith." He walked as fast as he could without running.

"Tell yer mam and dad we were asking after them."

"Wot d'yer mean 'bird's nestin' Dad?"

Mrs Smith gave her husband another dig with her elbow, "See! You and yer filthy tongue."

CHAPTER 8

Mrs Eccles and Mrs Bruce from across the green persuaded Emily to re-join the Mothers Union.

"We'll walk theer t'et Chutch, git sum exercise, 'en Vicar's wife'll run 'es yam."

Emily had been a stalwart before Daniel went to school and during his time in the infants' class. She had been secretary for most of those years. So, after only a few weeks she was asked to take up the job again. She was delighted to say "Oh! I don't know," which was taken by all the "Mothers" to mean "Yes". She had been a "Grammar School Girl" from the village and that still meant something to her contemporaries. Emily rather enjoyed writing the minutes of the meetings. She took pride in her sentences. She liked to read her minutes out loud in proper, enunciated, English. Her duties as Secretary got her out of cake baking.

So, every Thursday, Emily had a new connection to the ordinary realities she had once enjoyed, "Before Micklam".

Tom had a 24 hour shift every two or three weeks. These were usually on Thursday through to Friday, to give the men a long weekend to recover.

When there was a clash, Gwen was happy to babysit Daniel for half a crown. "Nae less."

"But yer wukken. Y'ev plenty 'er money cummen in."

"So 'ev you."

Gwen stuck to her guns.

Daniel was of an age to be embarrassed about needing a "babysitter", but he understood that he was too young to be trusted with an open coal fire. As long as Daniel was in bed by eight, and didn't object to her playing her records, Gwen was happy too.

Sometimes she would bring a friend.

One night, Angela Farthingale and Joyce Southland came round. They shared cigarettes and got a second packet of custard creams out

101

of the pantry. Angela wasn't allowed to smoke at home and Joyce didn't smoke but took a puff or two just to be sociable.

Daniel took two biscuits, "Ah'm ga'an ter bed."

"Ah'll cummen tuck yer in, in a bit," said Angela.

Everybody laughed.

The records Gwen played were mainly 'English Pop', rather than 'American Rock', Alma Cogan rather than Billie Holliday, Tommy Steele rather than Chuck Berry.

Daniel was asleep soon enough.

He woke to the sound of the toilet flushing in the bathroom.

The door to his bedroom opened, light came in from the landing.

"Daniel." It was Joyce. "Are yer awake?"

He didn't answer. He pulled the blanket up to his neck, he didn't want her to know that he didn't have pyjamas ["We'll buy yer some next time we shop"].

Joyce knelt on the floor by his bed.

"Gwen said that yer wanted me ter teach yer hoo te kiss."

"That would be very interesting," he said. 'Very Interesting' what sort of answer was that?

"I mean yes."

"Good," she whispered.

He felt Joyce's hands gently press his ears.

Her 'pony tail' hair fell around his face.

She brushed her lips against his right cheek.

"She's missed," Daniel thought.

Then she took the lobe of Daniel's right ear into her lips. He could smell her talcum powder.

"Yer ken put yer arms roond'ez if yer like."

She was wearing a little cardigan made of the softest imitation angora wool.

"Joyce." It was Gwen shouting, "Joyce, Emily's back ... git doon quick, asser."

Joyce was away and down the stairs in a flash. She was able to open the front door for Emily, Mrs Eccles and Mrs Bruce.

"Did yer have a nice time at the pub?"

"Yiss lass, t'vicar's wife got drunk on barley wines. Then we all danced on't tables," laughed Mrs Eccles.

Gwen and Angela were already standing in the living room.

"That's a nice fire lass," Emily said, "Did the little bugger upstairs behave hissel?"

"Hez the'r bin somebody upstairs oa'h this time?" laughed Joyce.

Everybody said 'hiya' and 'goodneet' to each other at the same time.

"Did yer leave 'ez any biscuits?"

The following day was the last day of the school year. The morning classes had been a little unruly, and Daniel thought it was wise to try and find Tracey. He waited in their usual trysting spot near Mr Smith's office.

"Danny-boy."

It was Gobbo, who had snuck up behind him.

"Wot's this aboot you coppen a feel 'ev Joyce Southland's tits?"

Daniel stared at him. His back was against Mr Smith's office wall.

"She tell't 'ez."

Daniel still stared back at him in fear, in silence.

"She said that yer unhewked her brassiere wid a flick 'er yer thumb."

Where had he got all this?

Gobbo put his left hand on Daniel's shoulder, he flinched as he thought it was the start of a punch.

"She said yer felt her up." He grabbed Daniel's right wrist. "Let's smell yer fingers ..." He let go, "Yer musta washed yer 'ands," he laughed, "Aa'h wuddner washed me hands fer a week."

Daniel laughed because he didn't know what the hell Gobbo was talking about. Also, he hadn't been hit by him yet.

"We're ganna hev a game 'er 'Slap Touch'," he said, "Yer ken be in my team."

"No," Daniel said, "Aa'l be on't other team." He caught Gobbo's gaze. Gobbo turned away. He seemed disappointed. Maybe he had been trying to make a gesture to Daniel.

Mr Proud played No 8 for Workington Zebras, and had once played for the full R.A.F. team. "Daniel, you are on my team."

Daniel turned and smirked at Gobbo. It was all he could do not to put his tongue out.

It was seven-a-side. 'Slap touch' is touch rugby, but with heavy duty, open palmed slaps. It was a 'Lowca thing'.

The rest of the school had to clear the whole of the main playground. Daniel was the only boy playing who wasn't in Mr Proud's senior class. Billy Nevis, Ralph Coulson and John Baxter, all better players than Daniel at that time, watched the game from the field.

"Don't knock on, don't miss a tackle and pass the ball before Gobbo hits you."

"Yes Sir."

Daniel didn't play all that well, but Gobbo never got near him, or near enough to slap him when he had the ball. And just once, in one glorious second, Daniel intercepted one of Gobbo's passes.

They carried on playing for twenty minutes after the rest of the school went into their classrooms.

Mr Proud was very keen on the niceties of the game. "Well played the other team," he shouted at the end of the game. Everybody shook hands with everybody else. Gobbo tried to break Daniel's fingers when he shook his hand. "Gabriel!" said Mr Proud.

Gobbo ruffled Daniel's hair, "Did yer like me given yer that interception pass?" He looked at Mr Proud for some approval. "Aa'h did it on purpose."

"Yes, Gabriel," said Mr Proud.

As they made their way up to the classrooms Mr Proud said, "How is your Gwen?"

"Grate," Daniel said.

"How is she doing at 'Smiths'?"

"Oa'hreet."

"Do you two still keep in touch with Jane Russell?"

CHAPTER 9

On that first day of Grammar School, as Daniel and all the other new 'grammar school swots' waited for the half past eight bus, all looked splendid, cleaned and polished, scared shitless. All their green school blazers were a size too big. Those blazers would define them for the foreseeable future but for the time being they had to survive two, maybe three, years of growth, wear and the stains of adolescence. But Tracey's blazer looked as if it was made to measure. She knew that she would get another new one the following year. Her blouse was a proper white shirt and not a school issue one. When it was buttoned up to the top button it sat neatly and precisely round her neck.

"Are yer nervous?" she asked.

Daniel nodded.

"What are yer most nervous aboot?"

"The huge numbers. So many people nut ter knoa."

"A'ahm scared of nut bein' able ter dae the wuk. Wot the bollocks is Shakespeare all aboot enniwez?"

"Yer'll be fine," Daniel said. "Yer just scared of oht'other pretty girls. Ah wunder how many will be better look'n then yer?" he teased.

"Will yer meet up wid ez ivvery break time en look efter ez again?"

"Aye," he said. "Yer divvn't hev te sit beside ez. Ah ken look efter yer frae a bit away."

"Mebbe yer'll find another girl te feel up."

Daniel looked at her and smiled about that day in the ghyll, but even then, he knew that they would just nicely drift apart. They were in different classes, she would have friends from her class who Daniel would never get to know. She would have different teachers, she would read different books.

Over the years she got lovelier. First her legs wouldn't stop growing, longer and longer, and then it was her arse. She wore the most expensive of the school skirts and the fabric rested more caringly round each buttock. The line of her knickers, her still regulation school knickers, always cruised gently and precisely over her bum. She never seemed to get her pants stuck in the crack of her arse, or twisted asymmetrically, high over one cheek, low under another.

Her lips were always naturally red, but they just seemed brighter, year by year. She was once told off by a new teacher for wearing lipstick. Tracey said that she wasn't wearing lipstick. In front of the class the teacher took out a hankie and wiped it roughly over Tracey's mouth to try and prove that she was lying. But the hankie was left clean. Her lips were left redder and wetter.

Daniel wished that he had kissed her that time in the Lowca School yard.

Chapter 10

When Harry Cragg met Sally Carr, it was in the early months of the First World War. Sally was a nurse, she wasn't trained or qualified. She was just a willing girl who could cope with great spurts of blood and handle crying men. That's all they could ask for at the time. Harry was a Hussar. He rode the front right of four pairs of horses pulling the gun carriages. The family fable went that in his four years at war he had thirteen horses shot from under him but had survived without "a scratch or a hole".

So, when in later life Sally would say that they only ever saw each other in uniform before they were married, it defined their proud romance, but perhaps hinted strongly that they both went to their wedding night as virgins.

There is a photo of them at that time, both in uniform indeed. Did either of them have, or would they ever need, other clothes? It is a "studio portrait" and they both have that fixed look demanded by a five second exposure time. Harry is handsome, in a boyish way, no hint in his eyes of the horrors he had seen in the trenches of the Somme. Sally is stunningly, hauntingly, beautiful. Her hair is combed neatly and tightly against her head, perhaps to an equally precise bun at the back. Even in the photo's sepia tones, it is plain that she wore no make-up. Daniel, as a child, could never reconcile the nice, wrinkly old lady, dying soon, with the lovely girl in this photo.

Lowca was a grim place for them to settle after their wedding. Three coal mines, a tar plant and 'coking ovens'. Coal dust and soot covered everything, and after big storms, salt from the Solway Firth rotted bricks and trees. But Harry had grown up a mile or two outside the village in one of half a dozen scattered cottages, laughingly known as "High Lowca". He had a job with a pick down 'Number 10' pit and this came with an end terrace house and its huge garden.

The pride of Sally's house was "The Parlour." It had a red marble fireplace in which there was rarely a fire, but there was always paper, sticks and coal ready if someone important stopped by. There was "The Bureau", a glorified writing desk which held all the family papers, various death certificates, important photos, Harry's medals, and strangely, the best tea service. The best face of the curtain fabric faced outwards, for any nosy buggers passing the window. There was a bookcase with Trollope and Shaw for Harry and 'owt and nowt', mostly poetry, for Sally. Their five children were born, grew up and left home without really going into the parlour.

It was to the parlour that the marital bed was brought when Sally came to her last few weeks. She was in her sixties. Daniel was frightened to ask what was wrong with her. He was eleven and old enough to know that one didn't enquire too closely into women's health issues. But this was different. He was a little frightened. He had just started grammar school and popping in to Grannie's after school was a good excuse to not go home.

"Can I make you a cup of tea Grannie?"

Daniel's presence allowed his grandad to go for a walk, shop at the Co-op, visit his sister in Barngill.

"Coffee lad, please."

As he boiled the kettle Grandad turned to him as he went out of the door, "Light a fire will you Daniel, lad, she won't let me dae yan as it's ower early fer t'expense."

Soon it got to be a regular thing, and Daniel began to feel that he was needed.

He would light the fire, make her coffee, he brought two biscuits.

"Did you get all your sums right today lad?"

"I don't think calculus and quadratic equations count as 'sums' Grannie."

He would hang up his still undamaged school blazer and tell her about his day. As his visits moved to the routine, he would be asked to bring in the rough chair and sit and read to her. Sally's glasses no longer worked for her to read. At first it was the newspaper, The Daily Herald usually, but on Thursdays, the Whitehaven News. Daniel's English Class were doing 'Ten Twentieth Century Poets', so he offered to read from that.

"Only one mind, you have to let the poem sink in," she said. "I couldn't do with these poetry readings they do now, allus one poem on top of another."

Sometimes she would ask Daniel to read a poem a second or third time "and think on now, ENUNCIATE."

If she at any time dozed off Daniel would bring the bureau lid down and do his homework with her prized 'Parker Ladies Fountain Pen'.

One late afternoon, Daniel arrived and the bureau lid was already down. "There's an old magazine on there, reach it ovver please."

It wasn't really a magazine. It was eight pages of very faded newsprint and on the top right-hand side of the front page was the date, May 1892, and the glorious price of 3/4d. There were five of them, each more tattered than the others.

"Money was no object to you, was it Grannie!"

"There's a poem in here aah'd like you to read." She found page five and handed it over to him, reverently, with both palms supporting the fragile sheets.

"It's not in proper English."

"No, it's in Cumberland dialect."

"I thought I wasn't supposed to 'talk Lowca'."

"Just read the damn thing," she cried with some irritation.

Daniel's first attempt wasn't very good. "Let me give it another go."

The poem was about a long walk from a cottage to Church for a Christening one Sunday. It was a hurried Christening, "T'laal thing wuzn't rete, nut rete at oah." ... And the sunshine on the way back from Church made, "ivverybody squint their tears oot." The second stanza described a return visit the following Thursday for the funeral of "T'laal lass." There was some rain, and on the journey home the small family laughed and let the "damp weeds in't lonning, and the bare hawthorne, dae their wailin' fer us."

Daniel read it well at the third attempt. He was going to read it a fourth time, but his eyes had filled with tears. He moved to wipe his eyes before he remembered that he carried a hankie in his pocket now that he was a grammar school boy.

"Do you see who wrote that?"

"Er ..." he checked the magazine with great care, the paper was almost falling apart. "Sarah Bristow."

"That's your grannie."

"You are my grannie."

"No. Your Great Grandma, Distington Grandma. My mother."

"Not Sarah Carr then?" He looked back at the magazine and its date. His great grandmother had written movingly and precisely about the death of a baby under her maiden name, "Nivver." He was surprised and a little resentful, "She would tell me off for not speaking proper. She would tell me off for owt aa'h did. She nivver used to tell Harry and Billy off. It was allus me."

"She was always telling people about you. "

"She wrote dialect poetry? She wore a black coat and a funny black hat," he said. "Great tatie pots though, and rum butter. I don't suppose you could do that without thinking Cumberland."

"There's a poem in each of the other magazines."

"Gooseberry jam and melting butter on hot scones."

"Handle them things very gently Daniel, son. The paper's very old," she said. "Like me."

"These'll see us through the week, eh?" He made a neat pile of them.

"Tidy things up a bit lad, then put a lump on the fire before you go."

So, he was going then.

"Does that mean that the baby in the poem was your sister?"

"Noooo lad!" she said. "I am the oldest, I was born a year after my mam and dad were married."

Daniel knew that he had taken a wrong turn with that question, that he had troubled her. She turned her head and gazed out of the window.

"Straighten up the pleats of the curtains lad. Ah hate bein' in here, it's supposed to be just for posh. For visitors."

"I'm a visitor, Grannie."

He fixed the curtains as well as he could. He tidied up a bit and stacked the fire. Her eyes were closed when he left the room. He put his blazer on and sat in the kitchen until his grandad came back.

Grandad came back with Gwen. She was seventeen now and beautiful. She was a 'different beautiful' now that she could afford to buy her own clothes. There was always make-up, a lovely perfume, high heels which made her elegant, self-confident. She picked a "wagon wheel" out of the biscuit tin. "Split it wid yer," she said, "Ah'll walk yer yam."

She did; and talked dirty to Daniel all the way. About boys she fancied.

When he called into his grandparents' house after school the next day Daniel found it full. There was his 'grandad' Harry and his uncle 'Young Harry', Gwen and, strangely, his mam.

"What's up?"

"The Doctor is with Grannie."

Suddenly everybody was 'enunciating'.

"It's bad eh?"

"Not good lad," said Uncle Harry.

"Not a good time to discuss aspects of Rococo Architecture with her then?"

"Why couldn't I keep my fucking mouth shut?" he thought. Just this once? He couldn't tell them that he only said it to stop himself crying. Old Harry broke the silence with a forced laugh, "Go home and make your dad's tea. Your mam's been here all day and I bet it's a tip."

Emily gave her dad one of her stares.

Daniel successfully negotiated the silencing of a "No change there then!" He had said enough. Gwen went with him, the youngest and the wisest.

On the way to Vale View she tried to explain 'cancer of the ovaries' to Daniel without really understanding it herself.

"I know where ovaries are on a diagram. We do Human Biology at school. Don't know where they are on a body though."

"Ah think yer'll find oot soon enough." She pushed Daniel away with a giggle.

"Couldn't put me finger on one."

They laughed.

Then Daniel said, "Will it be long?"

Sally died on the Friday and Daniel never got to read the other magazines. He did not read his great grandmother's other poems. On Sunday Tom took Daniel to see the body, still in the parlour, but already prepped by the undertaker.

The fire was lit even though it was still morning. The visit was a rite of passage for Tom as much as it was for Daniel. A formal thing involving father and son. Tom did not know the rules and protocols for such a visit. He did not know the rules and protocols of being a dad either. He wondered if Daniel had perhaps covered it in one of his lessons at Grammar School or had read about such occasions in one of his 'bewks'. Daniel was a little frightened to go into the parlour, but when he saw the body of his grannie lying there, as if she had just nodded off, he held back an urge to say "Hello Grannie. Ye'oah'reet? D'yer want ez te read summat te'yer?"

After much shuffling of feet, Tom motioned that they should both kneel down and pray. The Lord's Prayer was the only thing they could come up with.

They were still kneeling when Daniel suggested that he should "read a poem or mebbe a bit frem't paper."

He stood up and dared to look at his grandmother properly, to look at her to remember. She was still wearing her glasses, something Grandad had insisted on, and her skin had tightened a little around her eyes and her mouth. She was the Sally of the wartime photo. Serene, full lipped again.

He brought the desk lid of the bureau down to get his great grandmother's magazines. Tom was disturbed that his son was ratching where he shouldn't.

"The poems aren't here!"

Daniel looked to the fire and knew instantly that they had been used as kindling with The Whitehaven News.

"Some idiot's burned them." And for the first time in his 'good boy's life he used the "fuck" word.

"Fuck." Not loudly.

"Hey. Think on now where you are."

Tom wasn't angry, just sad again. This strange son of his, with his ostentatious cleverness, his fighting and his silences. He had only aspired to father a normal son. He yearned for the dignity of the ordinary, the invisible. Someone who could get a job in an office, avoid the pit. Perhaps play cricket for Whitehaven, or maybe even rugby for Workington.

Not someone he didn't understand. Tom thought that it was all his fault for being out of work for so long and that his son, his beautiful son, his "clever as fuck" son, had never really recovered from all that trauma, the hungry times, his 'angry mam', those long weeks without him really talking. In spite of the 'fuck word', Tom was just as glad that his son could speak now.

So here his lad was, opening his big mouth, swearing in front of his grandmother's body.

"I'm sorry Dad."

"It's alright lad, it's just the grief."

"No, it isn't."

They both knew that it wasn't, and they each took their different sorrows out of the parlour.

Shame is a funny thing when you are eleven. Like most of the boys Daniel knew in that last year at Lowca school and that first year at grammar school, he carried a permanent aura of shame, rooted in the onset of erections and the uncontrollable nature of wet dreams. It was shame that led to all those fights with his junior school friends who had not passed the eleven plus. Ashamed that he would move on to learn exotic things and that they would stay at the village school to wait, bored with fear, until it was time to go down the pit. Shame that as a 'Lowca scruff' he would have to fight all the posh boys at the grammar school. It is an all-enveloping shame not always related to specific sins and failings. So, he was not mortally ashamed about saying 'fuck' for the first time beside his grandmother's body, or even after reading her mother's poem to her, but he was deeply ashamed that he had put the seed of the idea that her mother may have had an illegitimate child, and that this was what the poem was about. "A very shitty thing to do," he said to himself, quite often. But his atonement was very much at hand, he would go and get a sack of sea coal off the shore.

He was pleased with his 'grate idea, asser'.

He snuck out of the back door away from everybody, especially his Dad, and went out to the toilet for a pee, then checked into the coal shed to confirm that there was indeed only a couple of days' worth of usable coal available.

He went home. He changed into his rough clothes and checked the view to St Bees Head. He saw that it was a low tide. He didn't really need to do that, anybody who lives near the sea has a feel for the tides. But there was rain on the way from the Isle of Man, he was going to get salt wet anyhow.

He had a hessian coal sack which could hold a hundredweight if he could fill it, and he had an old leather shopping bag. He had his rough old bike with only the one pedal. He had ambitions to upgrade the thing with another pedal, but for carrying a hundredweight of coal it was very fit for purpose. He could free wheel all the way to Parton beach. He couldn't ride back up that steep road anyway, even if he had both pedals and no hundred-weight load of coal.

He had to duck his head to go under a bridge of the west coast rail line. There was a blast of damp wind as he hit the shore. He had to hide his bike and sack in some blackhite bushes. The sea was two hundred yards away, and still on the ebb. Nobody was going to steal such a crap bike, but a big black bag of ready picked coal was booty indeed. With his leather bag he scrambled through deep pools and large rocks, all covered in bladderwrack, mussels and cuvvins. The seashells would cut your hands to ribbons, so you couldn't use the rocks for support. He pretended that his bag was a rugby ball and that he was Gus Risman, sidestepping, selling dummies. He did scissor moves with Tony Paskins. He made it to the sea in no time, and only fell into a pool once.

The West Cumberland coalfield has several seams of the purest anthracite. Most of the seams come out into the Solway a couple of miles out, but small potato sized coals wash up on to the shore on a regular basis. Black shale seams also wash up and it is wise to know the difference between the two. Coal is a little bit blacker with a crystalline glint on the surface, shale is duller, slightly heavier and though, like coal, it is rounded by the turbulence of the sea, it is usually flatter in shape. Other pebbles were made of the local sandstones and the ancient wash from the Lake District fells.

Daniel could fill his leather bag in about ten minutes of careful picking, and back at his bike, transfer his treasure to his coal sack.

Ten trips in two hours would almost fill the sack and Daniel was a wet, happy, scratched, atoned boy. The hard bit was getting the sack and its cargo wedged under the crossbar and straddling the bike chain and pedal. A redundant spoke from the front wheel was unscrewed and threaded through the sack's top and wound round the crossbar for added stability, and off Daniel went. Under the rail bridge, over the two beck bridges, round the bottom of the slag heap and then on up the absolute bugger of the hill. It was raining heavily now, but he was soaked to the skin anyway, and the rain washed the salt out of his cuts and grazes. He had to stop a couple of times to catch his breath, well,

114

several times, and by the time he made the last stretch up to Meadow View, what muscles he had at that age were trembling.

It was getting dark. Grandad's now, not Grannie's, house had all the lights on, so there must still be visitors. He couldn't get the spoke out of the sack and off the crossbar and he had to lean his bike against the toilet door and pick out his coal, handful by handful, from the sack to the coal shed. At some stage, early in this process, Grandad came out of the back door and managed to pick out the spoke from the sack. He picked up the hundredweight sack and put it closer to the shed. He could quite easily have picked up the whole "fucking" sack of coal and tipped it into the bunker. Instead, the two of them, coal by coal, emptied the sack, with the odd mussel and whelk, and hung it up on a nail on the door. Uncle Harry had been watching from the kitchen window, and in her turn, Gwen.

By now, Daniel was weeping again. With shame? With exhaustion? With, what his Dad had called grief?

"I've got some cold rice puddin' inside."

"No, ah'd better git yam."

"Reet ooh lad."

St Bridget's Church sits on a small plateau looking west over the Solway Firth towards the Isle of Man. It is sandwiched between an old Roman fort and the Jacobean mansion, Moresby Hall. It looks quite romantic when silhouetted against the setting sun, but it is far enough away from the angry squalor of each of its three parish villages of Lowca, Parton and Moresby not to get grubby. Physically or spiritually.

Daniel had to get the afternoon off school to be at his grand-mother's funeral, as did his cousins, 'young Harry's son Harry' and Bill. They were each in their school uniforms. They could have changed, they had the time to, but they didn't have good funeral clothes to change in to. Daniel did not dare to sing out the hymns. He was just glad that he got through the service without weeping or having to use his hankie.

But one thing stood out and stayed to haunt Daniel. The service ended at about one o'clock. In the pits it was time for the 'first shift' to knock off and the 'back shift' to clock on. And so, the procession of pit buses carrying miners from the outlying villages of Arlecdon, Frizington, Cleator, Pica and Distington had to pass the Church gate as the mourners were drifting out. And here's the thing. Each bus in its turn stopped at the gate for five seconds or so to give time for each of the miners to take off their caps and bow their heads a little. There were thirteen buses and it took some time for them all to pass.

It was then that he cried, but as a hundred other people from the congregation were crying also, it didn't matter.

Daniel realised that he had seen this before with the pit buses. Not perhaps the ordinary service buses. But anyone being buried at St Bridget's was more than likely known to more than a few of the miners on their way to work.

In this case it was Harry Cragg's girl Sally, Young Harry's mother, old William Carr's daughter.

Harry, the First World War man, the Hussar, the Labour Party man, the Secretary of The Lowca Colliery Prize Silver Band.

"Ivverybody knows Old Harry and his Sally, asser."

You had to know everybody else in the pit or in the villages. You may need to call out their name in distress, in the dark, a mile down.

CHAPTER 11

Miss Klein gave a short talk on Van Gogh and Gauguin; on how the Post Impressionists differed from the Impressionists.

She illustrated her lecture with half a dozen colour postcards of the two artists' work which Class 1A passed around the class. More amazing than the paintings was the fact that you could get postcards with paintings on them.

"Yes, Daniel."

"Where did you get the postcards, Miss?"

"These two I got at the Prado in Madrid, this one I got in Amsterdam and these at the Tate."

Oh, how exotic.

Everybody in the class thought so, and started asking her about Madrid, travelling about Europe with friends, what the food was like, what her friends were like, was she rich?

"Back to Van Gogh." She had a way of looking round the whole class and in just a few seconds make eye contact with each student. "This may look just like an ordinary painting of a chair, but it is in fact a painting of the chair used by Gauguin when they lived and worked together."

Christopher had his hand up, but before he could ask his question Miss Klein had answered it, "Good question Christopher, Gauguin was a fellow artist, another 'Post-Impressionist'."

She had a book and showed the class the self-portrait Van Gogh painted with his ear in bandages. She told the drama of the 'cutting off of the ear' and presenting it to his "girl-friend".

"A prostitute miss," said one of the boys, "'I saw it on the television!"

Class 1A sneered a collective, "Yeeau! ... Posh Boy."

"Back to Van Gogh and the chair ..."

"How do we know it's Gauguin's chair? Did he write the title on the back of the picture?"

"Another very good question Christopher."

She dashed to the store room and brought out another book.

"And have I got a great answer for you?" Brandishing the book she said, "Van Gogh was a troubled man." She looked to a group of six girls who were sitting together at the front, "Yes girls, all men are troubled, aren't they?" All the class laughed, "But most evenings Vincent wrote to his brother Theo, telling him of all the paintings he had made."

"Just a minute . . ." she licked her finger, to thumb through the book.

Daniel had always been repulsed by seeing people lick their fingers like that, such lack of class, so many germs. His mam had scolded such bad manners out of him. But Miss Klein had big red lipsticked lips, there was always a little wet drool in the corners of her mouth, and she licked her finger so slowly. Daniel looked closely at the pages of her book to see if any of her lipstick had stained the paper.

She found, then read, the relevant part of Vincent's letter which did indeed authenticate the title of "Gauguin's chair."

"A few days before we parted," Miss Klein paused to bring every-one into her 'story'. "This is when Gauguin and Van Gogh stopped sharing a studio." She licked the corners of her lips. "When illness forced me to enter an asylum, I tried to paint "his empty place". It is a study of his armchair, of dark red-brown wood, the seat of greenish straw and in the absent person's place, a lighted candlestick and some modern novels."

"That's a very sad story Miss," said Christine.

"So, there is proof, Christopher, that the painting is indeed of Gauguin's chair."

"Thank-you Miss. I believe you now."

"That's very noble of you Christopher."

She gave him a sharp look and folded the book slowly and reverently.

"This book is the collected letters of Van Gogh. You may dip into it if you ask me nicely, but only after washing your hands."

Some of the class put their hands up but were ignored.

"I want you all to paint a chair that may or may not have a particular resonance with a family member or friend." She looked at all the class again. "Your homework is obviously to do a drawing for next Tuesday's lesson."

"Can it be a sofa, Miss?"
"Can it be a brick wall, Miss?"

It was, perhaps, a measure of that strangeness which so disturbed his dad, that doing a drawing of an old cheap chair at that particular point in his life was the most exciting thing that Daniel could think of doing.

He would do a drawing of the rough chair, the one he had used to bring in to his Grannie's parlour so that he could read to her.

His Grandad wasn't too sure about Daniel using the parlour to do a drawing, particularly of the rough chair.

"We hev proper furniture fer yer to draw." He put the rough chair by the fireplace. "That old thing should hev been scopped out ages ago."

The bed had been taken back up to the bedroom and the parlour looked very empty. There was a shaft of sunlight flooding the room and Daniel moved the chair right to the middle of it. If he squinted and looked through his eyelashes he could do a drawing of just where the light was settling on the seat, the padded panel of the back, the legs and the struts which kept them together. Then there was the shadow cast by the chair on the carpet.

He had 'the good armchair' to sit in. He had the reverse side of a square of some old wallpaper, some pencils, and he was off.

He could handle the complex perspective, it was just maths after all. He had a large rubber to get rid of any mistakes, and it was just a drawing, an examination, an enquiry. He wasn't making a pretty picture. He wasn't making art.

When it came to the transferring of the drawing to good painting paper in the art class, Daniel didn't make a conscious decision to include the bed that Grannie had lain in. It just happened. Nor indeed to include Grannie herself, neatly tucked into the folds of the eiderdown. He made the eiderdown in his picture, of a plain ivory coloured material, totally unlike the chintzy flower-patterned blanket that his Grannie had actually worn on her bed.

He could do the perspective of the bed, but his life was hard enough at that time without having to paint flat, printed flowers in the special complexities of tucks and folds, receding to a point, through the window, and into the back garden.

His grandmother's head, shoulders and arms were quite difficult to draw from memory, but her face, silhouetted against the window, with her glasses halfway down her nose, was quite easy. Easy in the sense that it just happened at the end of his pencil, with no cognitive planning or calculation. He knew what she looked like, so there was something guiding his hand. When he drew the chair for homework he was trying to examine it and find out what the thing looked like. These were two very different processes at play, and he wasn't yet ready to fully understand either.

Turning the drawing into a painting wasn't just filling in the colour between the pencil lines, especially on his grannie's face. He couldn't seem to get the flesh colour to make her seem alive, awake, ready to listen to Daniel read to her. He kept working on the rest of the stuff and coming back to her face, maybe the glasses she was wearing stopped him seeing her eyes. But she always wore glasses and he could now understand why it was so important to his grandad that she should wear them to her grave.

Christine McGann, who Daniel quite liked, leaned over his shoulder and said that the light on the chair "represented God ...". Daniel went right off Christine.

Denise Cowan, whom he worshipped, just asked him, "Is the figure in the bed alive, dead, or in some transient process?"

"I don't know." Well Daniel didn't know, he didn't know what she was talking about.

At that point with a violence and speed which surprised him, Paddy Fielding leaned heavily on Daniel's shoulder and with a large, loaded hogs-hair brush he painted a wavy multi-coloured line right across Daniel's painting from the top left to the middle right.

"She's dead now, bitten by SUPERSNAKE ... HisssssSSS ..."

Daniel froze, he didn't know what was happening. He didn't know things like this happened. It was a new school to him and nobody knew the rules. Not the school's rules, but those rules that came from all the other kids, from all the other schools, from all the other gangs and groupings. Those rules. The cruel unwritten rules.

Daniel stood up, he flailed his arms in the hope that he would hit Paddy in some way, but Miss Klein had already beaten him to the task.

With even greater violence than Daniel had felt from him, she had

Patrick Fielding by the collar of his new blazer and the arse of his short pants and lifted him, pushed him, ran him to the art room door with only the toes of his shoes touching the floor. A girl opened the door just in time, or surely Miss Klein would have used Paddy to break through the frosted glass window of the door. The same girl closed the door behind them as quickly as she had opened it.

Oh! Miss Klein!

The class cheered, clapped, laughed, it was all the same noise.

The door opened, and as slowly and as calmly as you like, Miss Klein walked back in.

It was her slowness, the slowness of her licking her finger to turn her page, her grace, which silenced the class enough to hear the squeak of the door as she closed it gently behind her.

Only her breasts betrayed her breathlessness.

"Back to work," she almost whispered.

After getting everybody settled she brought to Daniel's table a beaker of water, a natural sponge, and a man's hankie.

"Let's see if we can mend this."

Delicately dabbing with the wet sponge, alternating with the dry handkerchief, she took away most of the traces of the "snake".

"Don't touch it until it is dry, you can rescue it. But whatever you do, don't start another painting until you have finished this one."

She put her hand on Daniel's head. "Otherwise the Philistines win, don't they?"

"Yes ... Miss."

"Perhaps you could spend the last twenty minutes bringing some sense of order to the chaos which we laughingly call the store room."

"Wot?"

"Tidy the store room up a bit will you lad."

"Yes Miss."

The store room smelled of cricket bats. More specifically of linseed oil and oil paints. There were two wooden wine boxes full of tubes of oil paint in various states of squeezedness. They had wonderful names like Phthalocyanine, Quinacridone, Alizarin Crimson, Rose Madder Deep. Daniel wondered if there was a 'Rose Madder Shallow' and laughed a little to himself. A tear nearly came out through his nose. On the shelf above the wine boxes were packets of new, unopened tubes, and cardboard tubes full of brushes. This narrow wall had four shelves, all stacked with different paints, brushes and solvents. There were thirty or so boxes of watercolours, ten colours each in little half inch mosaics. There were palette knives, delicate little things, and scrapers for scraper-boards and engraving. There were coloured pencils, oil pastels, ordinary pastels, conte-crayons and fat chubby wax crayons, not to mention the hundreds of different graphite pencils.

This wall of shelves didn't need tidying up at all, it just needed its boxes and packets straightened out neatly. The long wall at the back had two half-moon windows, high up, just below the ceiling. There were only three shelves. The shelves were two-foot deep to accommodate three or four different types of paper and several different sizes of each. Elephant, A2, A3 and, wonderfully, A4 sheets of "Handmade Watercolour Paper, Heavy Duty". Again, it was just a two-minute job straightening them up.

Miss Klein hadn't really wanted or needed Daniel to tidy the place up. She was just giving him a little space to get himself sorted out.

The other narrow wall was full of art books, art history books, books on architecture, books on how to do stuff. It had some brand new, gloss black, Thames & Hudson books, state of the art colour printing on themes such as 'Giotto to Cezanne', 'History of English Painting', 'Modern British Sculpture'. And quite literally on the top shelf there were eight or nine books with the word "Nude" in the title!

At that point Miss Klein burst through the storecupboard door.

"Are you okay? You have done a good job in such a short time."

"Nice books Miss."

"I sent Patrick Fielding to Mr Jones's office, but he may or may not have gone there. There's ten minutes to go before the end of school, I wonder if you want to slip out early in case he is waiting at the gates for you?"

"I'm okay miss."

"Come on now, he is twice your size."

"I am not running away from him."

"That's very brave, but not very sensible now, is it?"

"Aah will just have to deal with whativver happens, Miss. He may be scared 'er me after what he did ter mi picture."

She laughed; and Daniel laughed with her.

"I'll be okay, miss."

Daniel left the art room with the rest of the class.

Daniel got home without incident. He took an alternative service bus to Howgate and walked the short mile difference. He pretended that he had homework to do and went upstairs to read a book. He was nervous about the next day at school. His class had P.E. first thing in the morning and it would be Rugby. It wasn't summer, so it would be Rugby. The Grammar School still had the trappings of its origin as a fee-paying school. It had its snobbery, its school uniform, boys wore short trousers until they were sixteen and it was still stipulated that girls had to wear navy cotton knickers and plain white brassieres. "Knicker Inspections" were made on a termly basis by Miss Poulton, the Deputy Headmistress. It also retained its "house" system for competitive intramural sports. 'Marshall', 'McGowan', 'Walker' and 'School' houses wore red, green, yellow and blue rugby shirts respectively. So, the thirty or so boys in the 'A' and 'Alpha' class streams would play 'reds and yellows' versus 'greens and blues', or variants thereof, every Wednesday morning. Mr Colley would put a notice on the door to the changing rooms announcing the teams he had picked and the positions each of the boys would play on that morning. It seemed to be his rule that no boy should play in the same position two weeks running. This notwithstanding, small boys were usually selected as backs and the tall and the fat were to be the forwards.

So that evening Daniel prayed that he would be playing in the opposite team to Paddy Fielding. He wanted to be able to see him coming. Daniel prayed for that, properly, on his knees. He took time out to clean and polish his boots. He cleaned his laces too.

By the morning he was scared.

He ran to the changing rooms after school assembly and sure enough he was playing full back for the 'reds and greens' and Paddy was playing No.8 for the 'blues and yellows'. He got changed very quickly and hid his new blazer in his kit bag, just in case. For all the impending trauma, whichever way it went, Daniel's mam and dad could not afford another blazer for the foreseeable future.

From then on, he would be under the watchful gaze of Mr Colley.

In refereeing the game, Mr Colley's rule of thumb was not to blow his whistle too much, to keep the game going, and have the little bastards run themselves silly until they were thoroughly knackered, then make sure that every boy showered properly without any "unsavouriness".

However, in the ensuing maelstrom of play, any doubts Daniel may have had about Paddy's intentions were dispelled by three tackles on him when he was only marginally connected to the ball. One of the tackles was a 'clothesline' round the neck while he was trying to catch a pass. Daniel struggled to get up from that. Another was when he caught a high ball. Daniel was not tackled by Paddy, but it was Paddy who was the next player "in" and he stamped on Daniel's ribs, tearing two small holes in the back of his shirt with his boot studs, leaving three long, bleeding wheals in his flesh.

Daniel tried to get up quickly to show that he was tough, but he stumbled over the first boy who had tackled him. Daniel's immediate thoughts were that he was in serious trouble, not just in this game, but for some time in the future. And that he might not actually get through this grammar school life without being seriously hurt.

Later in the game Daniel stood forty yards behind a line out. Was he just soft and over-reacting? "How do I get my own back if I am out in the wilderness of the pitch, on my own, vulnerable and visible?"

"Fuck the game," he thought. "I have to go after him."

The opportunity came just at the next scrum. Paddy's team had the ball and it was at his feet. Paddy picked the ball up and ran forward. Daniel sprinted up to the scrum. He was hidden by two of his own team's players. He had some momentum and got into a position to hit Paddy, really hard. However, the ball popped out of Paddy's hands and, by luck, into Daniel's arms. Within that second, Daniel butted Paddy's left cheek as hard as he could with his forehead.

Paddy's head jolted violently. He fell backwards into the mud.

Mr Colley blew his whistle.

Behind Daniel, Paddy Fielding was flat on his back on the ground and he had blood pouring out of his eyebrow and his cheekbone. He pressed his hands to his face, but the blood continued to seep through his fingers. Daniel saw this. He needed to put this image of Paddy, in pain, rolling on his back into his memory as vividly as he could. Daniel thought of how his dad had once stood up after his tackle on Les Thornton and allowed the man to escape to his van. One beautifully articulated blow was more powerful than two. It was implied that there could be much more to come.

If necessary.

Daniel half remembered all that, as he stood, sweating, and slightly out of breath.

"Look closely, and remember," he thought to himself. The only expression of triumph he allowed himself were his two clenched fists hidden in the pockets of his rugby shorts.

Mr Colley took out a hankie and pressed it to Paddy's wounds. He rolled him on to his side and told Billy Wheeler to run and fetch Mrs Lowther.

The other kids gathered round to gawp at Paddy.

There was the odd glance towards Daniel. Daniel maintained his 'concerned and sympathetic' expression throughout.

Mrs Lowden arrived just as Paddy was coming round, and sitting up.

"Let's have a look at you." She peeled away Mr Colley's hankie. "You will need a trip to the hospital for a few stitches. Still, you haven't any looks to lose, have you? None of the girls across the road will be weeping tonight, will they?"

With that, and with the help of two "Sick Notes" she took him wobblingly off the field, and on Mr Colley's orders, they got on with the rest of the game. He stared at Daniel for a second or two. But Daniel avoided his gaze and went back to his position at full back.

"Fuck'n Yesssssss."

"You wanted to see me Sir?"

Mr Colley was pouring himself a cup of tea in his cramped office. The Royal Worcester tea service didn't sit well with all the rugby balls, corner flags and team kit bags.

He saw Daniel staring at the floral teapot, two matching cups and saucers and a plate with four rich tea biscuits.

"Standards dear boy. Standards."

"How do they not get broken in here Sir?"

"Who would dare?" He ate the first of his biscuits without 'dunking' it. How posh!

"What happened out there with Patrick Fielding this morning?"

"I'm not sure Sir."

"Look me in the eye and tell me that it wasn't deliberate."

"You mean the clash of heads Sir?"

"Was it a clash of heads or was it a head butt?"

"I don't really know. I came up with the intent of hitting him in the ribs, and I admit that I wanted to hurt him, to wind him, but then the ball popped into my hands and my head came up."

"But you hit him in the head very hard. How come?"

"I braced myself because I thought he was going to hit me hard. I think that I had my eyes shut when our heads clashed together." Daniel paused. "That's not quite true Sir. My eyes were open, and for a fraction of a second my brain told me that the harder my head hit his, the less it would hurt me."

"Your brain told you this?"

"My brain tells me a lot of rubbish Sir."

"Indeed." He took a swig of his tea, looked at Daniel intently over the rim of his half-moon glasses. "Off you go son."

Daniel just got through the door when Mr Colley called him back, "You only get one chance with me young man. Tell your brain to shut up for a while."

"Thank you, Sir."

"You haven't asked how Patrick is."

"No Sir."

Paddy was off school for a few days. Daniel saw him going into Assembly on the following Tuesday morning.

"How are you feeling?" Paddy was a mess. His eyeball still had some blood in the bottom left corner. He still had five stitches just above his eyebrow and seven in a gash an inch below his eye. The left side of his face was blue, red and yellow, with streaks of purple on the side of his nose.

"Or is that 'Rose Madder Deep'?" Daniel thought.

Daniel was trying to be nice to Paddy, but by approaching him first in a friendly way, Daniel thought that perhaps he would get the message that he was not afraid of him.

He offered his hand, "No hard feelings Danny-boy. I know it was an accident."

Daniel offered his hand in turn. "Of course."

They shook hands, perhaps a little pompously.

As they waited in the corridor outside the Art Room door, Daniel made a point of queueing up beside Paddy so that when Miss Klein opened the door with "Come," she could see them both, almost arm in arm.

Miss Klein's jaw dropped, her shoulders dropped, her breasts dropped. "What on earth happened to you Patrick?"

"It was an accident Miss." Paddy beat Daniel to it. "Playing rugby."

Daniel moved on to his chair and table, but he knew that her eyes were on him. Most of the class were looking at Daniel or at Paddy. They all knew what had happened in the Art Class on the previous Tuesday with Paddy's 'snake'. They all knew what had happened in the rugby game on the Wednesday morning. It was a shock to them to see Paddy's face, and a bigger shock for them to see Paddy and Daniel coming into the Art Class together as if nothing had happened.

"Oh! he was so brave coming into school looking like that!"

It was the quietest of art lessons, none of the usual creative hum of a good class working. Miss Klein didn't even tell her class a lovely artsy story at the beginning.

Daniel got on with rescuing his painting. He was making 'the eiderdown' look very realistic, as he did with the 'wrong side of the curtains' in his Grannie's parlour. He wouldn't finish it in that lesson, he thought that it would never really be finished. It wasn't that he had lost his original 'vision', or that Paddy had painted that bloody snake on it. It was that Miss Klein had 'mended' it, had got rid of most of the traces of the 'snake'. For all her best intentions she had violated the painting as much as Paddy had done. Apart from some finishing touches the following week, the painting was good. For someone of his age, it was really good. But it was no longer Daniel's. No longer totally his own.

Daniel desperately wanted Miss Klein to come over to him, to see his progress, just perhaps to be with him for a minute or two during the lesson, but she paid him no more attention than she did any of the boys and girls in the rest of the class.

Daniel would walk alone to the bus station at the end of school, perhaps he would get the bus to Howgate on a regular basis and walk that extra mile. It was no bother. He could do his homework during playtimes, and in between all this time killing, he would have lessons. He would 'listen to the teacher' but he wouldn't ask the teacher his usual "hands up" questions.

Everything could and would be quite normal.

But there would be no more snakes on his pictures or on his quadratic equations, and nobody would kick their studs into his ribs, or 'clothesline' him every time he played rugby.

There was a new freedom for him in that.

When the class had cleared up the art room at the end of the lesson Daniel tried to make eye contact with Miss Klein as they lined up by the door, but she was busy with something. Daniel was at the back of the line and as he went out of the door, he ushered out two girls ahead of him so that he could turn to look at her again, and for a fraction of a second, he caught her looking at him, so sadly.

"You're playing at fly half so that I can keep my eye on you." Mr Colley pointed a theatrical finger almost touching Daniel's nose.

Paddy was excused rugby, but he was allowed to run the touchline, and was even given a proper flag to do it with.

Paddy's 'House' was paired with Daniel's 'House', so there was an excuse for Paddy to offer ostentatious support every time Daniel touched the ball. Daniel had decided to play 'a passing game', and to eschew kicking the ball. This decision was arrived at because his team's best players were the two centres outside him. Also, Daniel knew that he wasn't any good at kicking.

This stratagem made Daniel look unselfish and, in the context of the previous week, virtuous. His team didn't score any early tries, but Daniel took the pass and gave the pass with great elegance. Instead of wiping his nose on the sleeve of his shirt, he had a hankie in his shorts pocket, and blew his nose every time there was a lineout or a scrum. Just like Gus Risman or Harry Archer at Workington Town. Daniel called the moves, even though it was always the same move. He passed the ball to one of the centres. But he ostentatiously called the moves hiding his mouth with his hand, so the opposition could neither see, nor hear the call. "I look so cool, and I am doing nothing!" he thought.

Hadn't run more than five yards at a time.

In the last ten minutes of the game, after Mr Colley had succeeded in his weekly plan of refereeing the game so that every boy had run himself off his feet, Daniel received the ball from the scrum half and, instead of passing, he just ran straight and there was nobody there to tackle him. He scored a try.

Right at the end of the game, the same situation occurred. This time he flamboyantly made a dummy pass, ran through the defence, then passed the ball for somebody else to score. He had done the same thing a thousand times playing touch rugby in the playground at Lowca School with an old soccer ball or a shoe, but scoring two tries in a proper game, with a proper blown up rugby ball, would most likely get him more crap. One try was enough.

Daniel was waiting in the queue for the showers, his towel tightly round his waist, his ribs still ablaze with the long scars of Paddy's studs. He couldn't really see them without a mirror, but each evening they had left a stain on his new school shirts.

Emily never mentioned it.

"You didn't make any tackles today," said Mr Colley.

"Didn't dare to Sir."

When Daniel had showered, Paddy was waiting with a tube of 'germoline'. "Mr Colley said you have to put some of this stuff on those cuts to your ribs. They're septic, he said."

"Oh thanks."

"Mr Colley says you have to get the ointment back to him next Monday and not to use it all up."

Paddy looked at Daniel's scabs.

Daniel looked at Paddy's bruised face.

On the following Monday morning break-time, Daniel went to see Mr Colley to return the ointment.

"Thank you for this, Sir. My mother said that it was very kind of you."

"I am tempted to say, 'keep it' because I get the sense that you will get several shoeings in your time at this school." He paused, "but I think you already know that don't you."

"I won't deserve all of them, Sir."

"You are a Lowca Lad, are you not?"

Daniel nodded.

"I saw your old headmaster, Mr Smith, on Saturday."

"Oh heck."

"Not at all, he had a very high opinion of you." He waited for a response from Daniel. "He said that you were a young man of great character and that I should keep my eye on you."

"Mr Smith said that you were a very good footballer, Sir."

"That's very nice of you to say that," he smiled gently and genuinely. "But I shall still keep my eye on you."

"I must go Sir, I have Miss Morgan for French. Thank you for the ointment."

Daniel turned and ran.

Daniel would go into the next Art lesson and complete his picture. He would paint the window frames and make them straight. He would paint the reverse side of the curtains and make them look like the front of the fabric was facing inwards. He would 'pay attention to the edges of things' and darken the back walls to emphasise his grandmother's face in profile. He had tried to paint his grandmother as she was when he read her mother's poems to her. But he had ended up painting her as she looked when he had visited her on her deathbed with his dad. As she looked when they had mumbled 'The Lord's Prayer'. Just before Daniel had said 'Fuck'.

It would be a good picture though, painted with great care and attention to detail. It would be the best thing that he could do. It would not though, be the great work of art that Daniel, in his naïve arrogance, imagined that he could paint. The chair in his picture was just a chair, and the light falling on the chair was just light.

And that was good enough.

Haunting the painting though was not his grannie, not Sally Cragg. The "lighted candle in Gauguin's chair" was Sarah Bristow, his great grandmother when she was young, before her pain.

How did Sarah Bristow, the poet, fit into the semi-rural industrial landscape of West Cumberland? What had she gleaned from her limited schooling and even more limited family background that encouraged her to think that the writing of poetry, the writing of poetry in her local dialect, was a viable option for someone of her class. After her schooling had finished at thirteen she had gone into service in a large town house in Cockermouth. What had given this girl the courage to write real poetry in, of all places, Wordsworth's Cockermouth?

Did she get crap for it?

Did she get crap for her audacity and presumption?

Did she get even more crap when people saw that her poems were, nonetheless, good? Good enough to be published.

"What is this servant girl doing writing? Does she do this poetry thing in this house?"

Sarah Bristow can only have been in her late teens, or twenty at the most, when she wrote the poem that Daniel read to his grannie. So, what had happened to her, that sixty years later she was a black clad matriarch, with no hint of the exotic, no signs that, for a time, she had explored places where most people don't go, don't dare to go? Sarah Bristow wrote poetry in a West Cumberland dialect, the language of all the people she knew, the language of her landscape and of her time. Yet, as the old woman, Sarah Carr, she ruled her family with her strong tongue and insisted that her great grandchildren, "have their roughnesses educated out of them".

Daniel didn't understand all that.

CHAPTER 12

Tom had really missed his rugby when he was out of work. When he was still at Micklam he used to take his son, as a special treat, to big games. They could be Workington Town against St Helens or Hunslet, places Daniel couldn't find on a map, or against big city teams like Hull, Leeds or Wigan. Each such romantic sounding places. Sometimes he would take him if the team had a spectacularly good or famous player. Sometimes he would take him if Emily just wanted Daniel out of the house.

Tom could not afford to go to games when he was out of work, nor could he afford treats for his son. So, when he got the job at Sellafield, making the pilgrimage to Workington Town on Saturdays was perhaps as significant for him as starting to go to church on Sunday evenings.

He re-joined the congregation of about a dozen supporters who stood above one of the corner flags just where the Derwent Park stadium steps started to bend round to the curved terracing behind the posts on the south side. It was the perfect place to see the games from. The perfect place to see half the tries from. And it was only ten yards from what was laughingly called the 'refreshment facility'. A redundant caravan was painted in white with a blue hoop, Town's livery. It sold "Oxo's, pie's, tea'se, coffee's and cold drink's"[sic]

"Git 'ez summat in a proper bottle," was the cry from the gang if anyone offered to go to "t'caffy de parry" for a pie or a drink.

"A cupper gravy, asser."

Some of Tom's gang had played at a high level in pre-war local rugby, one of them had played Rugby Union for a Wartime Army team. Mostly they were just guys from all over West Cumberland who enjoyed each other's high level of debate and wit. Tom would have his little stories to tell before the kick-off and at half time his chesty laugh was contagious. He held the group together though with his fastidious mind. His match programme would be covered with notes in blue biro on the points scored, tackles made, tackles missed. With his red biro he would make notes on individual players, how the half backs, Roper and Archer, orchestrated the attacking plays, how the defence controlled the gain-line.

Five minutes before the end of each game, Tom would call out, "What 'er we givv'nt Ref?'

"A smack in't gob, asser!"

"A cauliflower ear!"

"A gonner ear!"

Eventually they would settle for a six or an eight or a 'five point five' with all the solemnity and professional rigour of Olympic skating judges.

"Mr T.C.Eaves of Lancashire, seven point five," Tom would announce. "Any notes or pertinent remarks?"

"Duzzen't knoa t'offside rules."

"Can't keep up wid play."

"Let Sol Roper 'en Harry Archer git away wid murder ... gaa' back 'en give 'im a ten."

All this so that at the beginning of the next home game Tom would be asked, "Dae we knoa this ref Tom?"

"We gev 'im a five against Widnes."

"That's 'im. Good in't fusst half, rubbish in't second."

Then, whenever the referee was near enough to hear, there would be orchestrated calls of, "'er yer 'ere fer't duration, ref?"

"Does yer nurse knoa thet yer hevent tekken yer pills terday, ref?"

"Is yer other eye med 'er glass 'en oah, asser?"

"Yer bein' paid fer both halves ref, nut just yan."

Informed abuse would be more effective in keeping the referee honest.

At the end of the games they would shake hands and disappear from each other for two weeks. None of them knew each other well enough to know what part of West Cumberland they came from. None of them talked about work. Some of them had been in the War, some were in the pits or the steelworks.

The rugby at Workington Town was their reward for surviving the privations of the 'forties'. It was as much a part of the new social and spiritual fabric as proper new schools, the NHS, and yes indeed, prefabs.

That Workington had such a good and successful team was not accidental, or a matter of good fortune. Rugby, both League and Union, was part of the soul of the whole area. Football rarely got a look in. Soccer was a pastime, "a kickaboot". Men whose hands could wield a pick for eight hours a day found a sensual pleasure in the soft curves of a proper leather rugby ball. Even when they were nowhere near a rugby pitch, if you threw them a ball they could be watched clasping it to their breast, absent-mindedly tracing the lines of the stitching with their loving fingers. A soccer ball would only be bounced. You couldn't play 'keepie-uppie' if you were wearing clogs.

Most of the villages in that coastal line from Maryport to Egremont had amateur teams of one code or another. So, in the forties, fifties and sixties, when Cumberland won the occasional Rugby League Championship, or when they would beat Australian or New Zealand touring sides in front of crowds of twelve thousand or so, it was a surprise, but never a shock. And when "Northwestern Counties" Union team beat the New Zealand All Blacks at Workington, the same twelve thousand people, Tom included, came to watch, and to shout the same informed abuse.

Going to the rugby with his dad was, initially, Daniel's gesture of support for him after his troubles. He didn't have to stand with his dad at the matches, or with Tom's friends, "The Brains Trust", but he did. He kept a discreet and respectful five yards distance though.

They used to get the one thirty bus from Lowca, which got to Workington before two. Tom usually had a little shopping to do before they walked to the ground. A pound of sausages, liver, or a bantam chicken would fit into one of the voluminous pockets of his greatcoat. A couple of magazines for Emily. 'The People's Friend' or 'Woman's Own' would be secreted into one of the inside pockets. Some hairclips, or perhaps some scented soap "well wrapped up please." He was of course going to the rugby game. These were bought if Emily asked for something, or even if she hadn't asked.

On one of these pre-match trips he bought Daniel a sixpenny 'Autograph Book'. It looked very posh for sixpence.

"Yer divvent need ter cum shoppen wid 'ez. Ga'a on ahead 'en git some autographs. Aa'h'll see yer 'et usual spot." Tom gave Daniel his entrance money.

This worked great for Daniel for a few games. His plan was to get one autograph per match from each of the two teams as they came through the players' entrance beneath the main stand.

Bill Martin was a great 'second row', didn't play for Great Britain, or England, but was good enough, in Daniel's opinion.

Mr Martin was standing outside the players' gate with half a dozen team mates and Bill Iveson, the Manager.

"Can I have your autograph please Mister Martin?" Daniel said in his best enunciated voice.

"Nut now lad. 'Evvent got time. Cum back efter't match."

He was the first player who had refused Daniel's polite request. Daniel understood that he was not entitled to intrude into someone's life and expect them to take time out to write their signature in a book.

He understood that. His errant mouth did not.

"How long does it take you to draw a cross?"

As soon as he said it, he was appalled with himself.

He turned to walk away as smartly as he could. How could he say such a thing? Bill Martin was one of his favourite players. He understood the 'liturgy' of the pre-match. On his own Fridays, before Saturday games, he polished his own boots, also he laundered his laces, went to bed early. On 'match day' he had a light, meat free, carbohydrate breakfast, then three hours before kick-off, the raw egg. He understood all that. He wanted to turn and say, "Sorry, Mister Martin, good luck in the game today."

But all the players with Bill Martin were laughing at him, and Mr Iveson had been angry with him and had said, "Git after him and sign his bloody book."

Daniel did not know that. So, when he saw Bill Martin chasing after him, he turned and legged it. He really shifted, slaloming and sidestepping through the oncoming match crowd. The other players were now wetting themselves, because, in his best 'match day' shoes, club blazer and flannels, Bill Martin couldn't catch the little boy.

"If yer catch the little bugger, offer 'im a contract," shouted one.

Daniel didn't know that he was being chased so that Bill Martin could sign his name in Daniel's bloody 'Autograph Book'. Daniel was still under the impression that he was going to get a clip round the ear for being so dreadfully rude. However, he was mortally afraid of the shame of being caught. He was afraid of being caught and having to face up to himself and his embarrassing behaviour. Most of all he was afraid of embarrassing his dad.

His dad wouldn't be able to stand, with dignity, with his friends from the 'Brains Trust'. And he had been without dignity for so long.

Daniel had got as far as the train station before he had the nerve to turn around to check that he was no longer being chased.

He gasped for such a long time. He was sweaty and dishevelled.

He stood in the phone box by the station. He pretended to be making a call. Eventually he calmed himself down and straightened his clothes. He used his hankie to dry his hair.

The Maryport train had just got in and disgorged a crowd of fans going to the game.

At ten to three he made his way back to the ground and saw his dad queuing at their usual turnstile.

Daniel joined him with as much nonchalance as he could muster. Bill Martin would be rubbing liniment into his hamstrings and would not be thinking about Daniel or autographs.

"Did yer git anybody good?"

"A'ah went t'et library. Hev some homework te dae."

"Dae yer hev membership?"

Shit! That was a good question. "Just dae'en research."

As they got through the turnstile Tom asked Daniel to return the shilling entry fee he had given him. Daniel scrabbled around in his pocket for the money, but Tom, playfully, shoved his son's head away. "Just kidd'n lad. Divvent tell Mam. Eh?"

"Oah, ta!"

Daniel was in a bit of a bind now. Spending half an hour in Workington Library sounded like a great plan. He might be stuck with it.

"There's some grate Art bewks," he told his dad. "Ter just look at."

Wouldn't bump into Bill Martin there at two o'clock on a Saturday either.

Workington Library was usually quite full on Saturdays. It was, quite delightfully, noisy from the general rustle of kids with their mothers and old men arguing about what was in the papers of the day.

Spread around the tables and chairs were sixth formers working for their A'Levels. On that first Saturday the only space available to Daniel was on a large 'dining' table set in an alcove of three walls of books. He had an armful of art books which he had taken down at random from their shelves.

He vaguely looked for paintings of religious scenes. "Not 'Religious Paintings'" he told himself. He wasn't interested in objects of veneration like 'Icons', but "paintings which were illustrations of passages in the Bible."

The other students were all writing in their notebooks from the texts in their own pile of books. Daniel was soon embarrassed that he was 'only staring at the pictures' in his books. The others were preparing for their exams, but he was initially only passing time in the warmth of the library. So, when he happened to find a full colour illustration of Rembrandt's 'Return of the Prodigal Son' he took out his autograph book and started drawing that small section of the painting where the hands are placed on the prodigal's back. He used his best school fountain pen, the one he had filled up freshly that morning to be used for autographs. It wasn't a good drawing, but by doing the drawing, however ineptly, he was taken closer into the painting. He saw things in the construction of the hands that he would not have seen by 'just looking'.

At twenty to three he put his pen and his little drawing in his jacket pocket. He put the books back on their shelves and set off for the rugby.

Two weeks later he was back in Workington Library raring to have another go at the hands in 'The Prodigal Son'.

He couldn't find the book on Rembrandt which he had used. He went to the counter.

"I can't find the big book on Rembrandt," he moaned.

"I'm not surprised you cannot find it," the nice lady said, "Coz it's oot."

"Pardon?"

"Somebody has borrowed it," she said. "That's what we do. We buy bewks. We put the bewks on't' shelves. Then people cum in 'en borrer t'bewks."

She smiled, "Job done!" She reached behind her and from the middle of three piles of 'bewks' she handed Daniel another great big book, "There's yan 'ere on Rubens," she said, "Another artist beginnen wid 'R'!"

"Grate," he smiled back, "Ta!"

The same space at the same table was free and Daniel plonked himself down. Some of the students from two weeks previously were there in their same seats. Two girls looked up and smiled. Two boys glowered at him for being a disturbance. He smiled at them.

Daniel took out his fountain pen and opened his book.

The pages fell open right in the middle of the book. There it was, the kind of picture he had been looking for, a big, full colour reproduction of Rubens' "Raising of the Cross".

It was a triptych. Daniel checked the details to the side of the illustration and translated the centimetres into imperial measure. He let out a small "Phew" to himself. The middle panel was about fifteen feet by ten. There were about eight figures in the scene, and a dog. Christ was nailed to the cross, naked except for a conveniently placed loincloth, looking for all the world like a second row jumping in a line out. There were three or four other semi-naked figures, built like forwards, muscles all over the place. Daniel drew the guy right in the middle of the painting who was lifting Christ. He looked like a prop.

It was all wonderful stuff, and his little drawing of this huge biblical scene was so much better than the drawing he had done of the prodigal son and the father's hands.

Daniel thanked the nice lady for picking out the book on Rubens. "Hev yer got any mair 'nice 'R's' fer 'ez next time?"

She looked puzzled, but she smiled because Daniel was smiling.

He caught up with his dad as he was approaching the ground. They queued together.

"Git any autographs?"

"Bin t't' library." He took out his autograph book and showed him his drawing of Christ and the man lifting him.

It was another of those shocks that made Tom worry about his son.

"Put it away lad, we'll look at it when we git yam."

Something very beautiful happened in that game. Towards the end of the first half Brian Edgar had charged up the middle of the field dragging a posse of Wakefield Trinity's would be tacklers with him towards the half-way line. He passed the ball out of the tackle and Sol Roper and Harry Archer moved the ball very quickly through soft, delicate hands to Ray Glastonbury on the right touchline. As the Wakefield defence drifted across the field to tackle him, Glastonbury put in a high crossfield kick towards the middle of the twenty-five-yard line. At which point Piet Pretorious, 'Town's South African full back, caught the ball at full pace, without breaking his stride, to score under the posts.

The big crowd broke into a sustained roar.

A man, standing behind Tom said, "Anybody got a hankie, lads? A'ah think a'ah've just cum." In the laughter another said, more quietly than his friend, "That must be what it's like ter play the violin."

"What yer ganna put in yer bewk Tom, efter that?"

Standing where they did, 'The Brains Trust' could see that Piet Pretorious had set off on his 'middle of the field sprint' before Ray Glastonbury had received the ball from Harry Archer. They could see when Glastonbury got the ball that the Wakefield full back had to move towards the touchline to cover any break. They could see that Glastonbury's kick was targeting that space on the twenty-five-yard line vacated by the Wakefield full back. They could see all this and knew that it had all been planned and practised. Rehearsed. That Piet Pretorius, the Springbok Rugby Union full back, was the perfect person to catch a high ball. That Ray Glastonbury, the Welsh winger, would concern the Wakefield defence so much that their full back would have to cover him. That Brian Edgar, captain of the Great Britain Rugby League team, would always gather round him enough worried defenders to clear space in other parts of the field. That Roper and Archer and their fast hands could orchestrate such a bold and visionary move.

What was not planned was the poetry of the movement, the music of the timing of the passes, the elegance of Pretorius' run as he drifted a yard to the right to meet the falling ball, the harmony of the players sharing one beautiful vision.

That beautiful vision would be taken on Monday morning to work by a thousand men who relived those moments in Saturday's sunlight as they swung their picks in the dark. And some of them knew also that in its baroque lines and sweeps it was great art. Or at least as close as they would ever get to it.

Daniel stepped back a yard or two to let his dad make his farewells to his fortnightly friends. The road to the bus station was uphill most of the way. Tom and Daniel each walked as quick as the other, too fast for conversation, but they had just enough puff for the odd laugh.

There were ten minutes to the half-five bus. "Tell you what Daniel, why don't we split an ice cream?"

"Oah grate Dad."

They crossed the road to Tognarelli's, still slightly out of breath.

Tom handed the cone to Daniel for the first lick, "Fusst ice cream fer yer in eighteen months, eh lad."

"Wuth't wait eh dad?" Daniel knew that the ice cream came with baggage. "Oah reet noow, eh?"

The bus was almost full. There were women who had shopped and men who had also been to the rugby match. Tom knew most of them and he smiled and nodded to each. They all knew Tom. A voice from the back of the bus broke what ice there was with, "Grate try Tom, asser, Eh?"

Tom turned, smiled and nodded again.

Tom and Daniel talked about the game. Daniel had always seemed to talk like an adult, but he knew his rugby and he bounced his observations back and forth with his dad. He wasn't afraid of disagreeing with his dad's views and Tom was happy to be challenged. He was happy that his lad could talk freely. During 'the redundancy' Daniel hardly talked at all.

Tom was very proud that his son was clever. That he was at the Grammar School and seemingly doing well. He loved what engagement Daniel allowed him with his homework.

Daniel's drawing was more of a difficulty. He was obviously gifted in some way. The drawing of the Rubens painting which Daniel showed him in his 'Autograph Book' was shockingly good, but Tom understood that his lad was off on his own into a landscape where Tom could not follow. And that frightened him a little.

When the bus came past the end of the 'John Pit' slag heap, there was a blast of light from the low sun. Tom took out his match programme and pretended to read his notes. He didn't want to see the silhouette of the Micklam pit top.

Daniel saw this and knew.

"Grate try, Eh?"

When Daniel next went to the library 'his' Rembrandt book was there and the painting of the 'Prodigal Son' was still on page 203. Why should he have expected that it wouldn't be?

This time he was armed with not just an HB pencil, but, luxury of luxuries, a 2B and a 6B pencil.

The painting seemed more vivid to him in the weeks since he had made such a bad drawing of it. The kneeling of the son, the all-enveloping embrace of the father, standing, old. Daniel was too afraid of drawing the face of the father and of the head, in profile, of the son. Instead he drew the hands again.

This second time he very consciously paid more attention to the marks of Rembrandt's brush strokes and the lumps of light paint which defined the knuckles and the sinews in the backs of the hands, and of the thin watery strokes which outlined the fingers and defined the shadows cast on the back of the 'Prodigal Son'. It was such mundane detail which put the hands so close to the surface of the back, the palms so gently pressing.

This was love.

This was love so precisely articulated. Daniel's drawing had not repeated or recreated Rembrandt's eloquence, but his drawing had allowed him to see it more clearly.

He didn't see Rembrandt's painting as a metaphor for himself and his dad, it never occurred to him that it should. He didn't know what a 'Prodigal' was, or what the lad had got up to when he was away to warrant such a beautiful forgiveness. Daniel was quite keen to do some 'prodigalling' of his own, as soon as he could find out what was involved.

There were loads of nudes in the books that he explored on those Saturdays at the library. There were paintings which were a thousand times more erotic than anything in Malcolm McConnell's dirty magazines, but he didn't look at them too much. He was carrying enough guilt. He was genuinely looking for something more substantial. Transformative.

He flirted a little with Georges Rouault's paintings on biblical themes. They had great slashes of black outlines and vivid luminous reds and blues. There was a strong hint of the stained-glass window and were as close to abstract painting as anything else being done at the turn of the century. He did the pencil outlines of the brushstrokes in his little book and when he got home he redrew them on white writing paper. For the colours, he used his dad's inks. Tom didn't mind, just as long as he didn't touch his pens. With the white of the paper shining through the reds, the yellows and particularly the greens, the picture was as luminous as a real stained-glass window. One drawing of Christ blessing someone gave him quite a thrill, but it was an 'artsy' buzz, not a religious one. Daniel was a little concerned about that. The word 'piety' is much misused, but Daniel was genuinely trying to be a better person. He wanted desperately not to make his mam cry so much or embarrass his dad so regularly. He never missed going to Church every Sunday morning.

But it wasn't working.

Chapter 13

Daniel liked his Great Aunt Eva, his grannies' younger sister. She was very beautiful in her old age. She had married well and dressed well. Some weeks after his grannie's funeral he bumped into her on Lowther Street on his way home from school.

"Do you like cake Daniel?" she said.

"Yes."

"Pull your socks up and come with me."

Daniel pulled his socks up, straightened his school cap and walked at a pace to keep up with her.

She was wearing a fawn tailored suit and had the line of her stockings running perfectly over her legs and ankles. She was sixty, looked fifty. She wore perfume. Daniel had no idea if it was expensive perfume or cheap stuff, but it was subtle and exuded a little class.

She took Daniel to the Wheatsheaf Hotel for 'afternoon tea'.

"I am taking my nephew out for tea Jeremy, so two 'afternoon teas' with a glass of 'pop', we'll both have the lapsang, and mek sure there's an éclair for each of us in the cakes."

"Yes Mrs MacKenzie." The restaurant was quite full, and she got a smile or a wave from someone on most of the other tables.

"I think I'm your great nephew," he said, stressing the 'great'.

"Shut up lad, if some of these buggers think you are my nephew it'll knock years off me." She laughed like a schoolgirl and Daniel could see that her eyes were those of her older sister, and he could talk to her without feeling on trial.

When 'afternoon tea' was served she made Daniel smell the lapsang souchong in the pot. It smelled of road tar or a dying bonfire.

"It smells very exotic for Whitehaven," he said.

"I'm so glad you said that. Most of our family would just turn their noses up."

They laughed again as they both ate their chocolate eclairs at the same time and Daniel had said, "Race you."

"When are you going to read me some poetry? Sally loved you reading to her."

Daniel told her about the one poem of her mother that he had had the chance to read and about the loss of those old magazines, probably used for kindling in the parlour fire.

Aunt Eva told Daniel that just before the Second World War the BBC had written to her mother and asked her if she would be willing to come to Manchester so they could record her reading her own poems and be interviewed about them. They wanted to make a series of programmes about "Vernacular Poetry in the North." They were going to put the recordings in a 'sound archive'.

"Arthur, Sally and me were very excited for her, but she wrote back and thanked them for their interest but that she was an old woman with a growing family around her and that the poetry was written at a time she would not be happy to revisit."

Daniel started to ask her about the poem about the dead little girl, but she said, "Let's not think about that lad."

She talked about her son Ian who had gone off to London to work in the same bank as her husband Ernest. "Ian plays for the Bank rugby team."

Just then two of her friends came over from another table and they started chatting. Aunt Eva patted Daniel on the knee, "You must get the six o'clock bus Daniel." She turned to her friends, "This is my nephew Daniel." She gave a theatrical wink and her friends laughed. "He's Emily's lad."

Daniel thanked her for the lovely tea and turned to go. Eva smiled, her eyes laughed, "Thank you for being such a handsome and charming 'date'."

Everybody laughed.

Chapter 14

So, in the end, Daniel's painting of his grannie was an insignificant thing, it was not an atonement at all. Even if he had shown it to, or given it to, his grandfather, it would have been a hurtful reminder of Sally's painful end. His mother would have cried.

When his painting was done, he took it over to the drying shelf, a slatted, wooden, home-made construction placed above some double radiators. He placed it next to Denise Cowan's picture, then got a cloth to clean his part of the table. Denise very theatrically crossed the room to move her work to the other side of the shelf.

"Transienting it away from my picture are you Denise?"

"You are no better than Gabriel Gibson," she huffed.

"Gobbo."

"Whhatt?"

"Gobbo." Daniel said. "It's GOBBO Gibson that I am no better than."

She blushed and turned her chair and her back to him.

By the time he had washed his brushes and returned to his seat, there was a big, heavy book on Vermeer on the table. It was open near the middle and had a bookmark from Amsterdam laid across the pages. There was a full colour reproduction of a painting of a girl reading a letter, standing by a window. In the picture a soft light bathed the plain room and highlighted the figure.

Daniel looked across to see Miss Klein and this time caught her gaze.

It was a very new book and he sniffed the pages and touched the image of the painting.

The text outlined the background to the painting, when it was painted, who it was painted for, that it was a 'Protestant painting' in its simple composition as opposed to a more complex, flamboyant painting by the very Catholic Rubens. The writer argued that the ostensible subject of the painting was not necessarily "a girl reading a letter by a window" but that the real subject was the light coming into the room, with a secondary light bouncing up from the letter to the girl's face. That the painting was about several moments in time, at least the length of time that it would take the girl to read the letter, but in the meantime, there was ample time to gaze at the picture. It was a painting to be tasted, savoured, bathed in, "smell the girl's perfume perhaps," because the girl will move soon enough, and her transient world would not be the same again. "Bloody hell!" cried Daniel to himself. "Sodding Denise Cowan might be right. She's a snobby, pretentious, stuck up little bitch. She's from the same rough part of Lowca as me." He hated the idea that Denise could see something that he couldn't see.

The writer then argued that this most simple painting was a profoundly religious painting, more spiritual in fact than Vermeer's biblical scenes. Christ! Daniel didn't have to admit to Christine McGann that she was right as well, and that the light shining on the rough chair in his picture was indeed 'God', as she had said. Daniel couldn't do that. It would end up with him crying twice a day like Christine did.

He went back to looking at the gorgeous painting again, it was so much better than reading such bollocks. He turned the pages and looked at other paintings.

What he did get though, was that what a painting is about is not necessarily what the title is, or indeed the stuff that has been painted. Daniel now understood that perhaps his great grandmother's poem was not just about the death of a baby, but about being a girl on the verge of womanhood in a particularly raw place and time in the world.

"Mebbe aah shudda just painted a chair for homework, like aah wuz tellt ter," Daniel thought.

The "Post Paddy Fielding" ostracism was not a big thing, but it did last a long time. Twice Daniel sat behind Denise Cowan on the bus home and she got up out of her seat and moved to the front, taking her usual friends with her. He started taking the bus to Howgate and walking home.

Maybe, he thought, he wasn't being ostracised for hitting Paddy at all. Perhaps nobody talked to Daniel because nobody liked him.

Daniel was never keen on the school dinner thing anyway. The food was quite good, but it was five shillings a week. At 'dinner' the children sat at tables of eight and day by day he found that he was usually the one sitting beside an empty chair or two. Nobody hit him or tried to bully him overtly. There was no individual animosity towards him that he could put his finger on. It seemed as though Denise, some other girls and yes, Paddy too, had decided that Daniel just wasn't worth bothering with, and everyone else was happy to go along with that arrangement. The other kids were all new to the Grammar School as well and were each trying to make their way as best they could.

Not going to school lunch and keeping the five shillings a week for himself seemed the obvious solution.

After a few days of wandering the school at lunchtime he found the perfect sanctuary by hiding in plain sight in a third form classroom next to the Head's office, two classrooms down from the staffroom. It wasn't where kids would want to hang around with each other and it was not where teachers would expect to find errant pupils. Some desks at the back right of the room could only be seen by those teachers who were on lunchtime duty if they opened the classroom door and poked their head round it. Daniel could do his homework, read a book or just stare into space until the afternoon classes began. Sometimes he was close to nodding off.

He wouldn't be really hungry until the middle of the afternoon anyway.

A few weeks of this went fine until Daniel was 'sussed', by of all people, Miss Klein.

"All the staff know that you hide in here instead of going to lunch."

"I'm not hiding, I'm doing my homework in peace and quiet, Miss."

She sat down in the desk next to him. She had brought a cup of coffee, a banana and a Mars bar.

"Mr Colley told me about the rugby match where you hit Patrick Fielding."

She put the coffee and the Mars bar on Daniel's desk.

"I didn't put any sugar in your coffee. I didn't know how you liked it."

It was beyond Daniel's comprehension that a teacher would bring a cup of coffee for a student, and a Mars bar.

"I don't understand Miss."

"You are not telling me you are not hungry."

He took a sip, "It's lovely Miss."

"And the Mars bar." She shoved it further towards him.

"Mr Colley said that you head butted Patrick on purpose, but that "he had it coming." He thought that it was a very good head butt, if there are such things."

Daniel was eating his first bite of the chocolate bar and couldn't reply. Not that he knew what to say.

"Anyway, I have some good news for you." She started peeling the banana for herself. Shit, he quite fancied the banana. "Mr Lincoln wants to put your painting in the 'Gallery'. Framed an'all."

The school had twenty framed paintings or drawings, by current students, on strategic walls in the central part of the building, round the assembly hall and the school offices.

"Isn't that wonderful?"

"I'm not too sure Miss." Daniel had got enough crap as a result of that picture. He didn't want any more. "Hitting Paddy Fielding was both an accident and deliberate. It was only the last half of a second that was deliberate. I wanted to hurt him, and I'm glad I did it." He shoved the coffee and his half-eaten chocolate back towards her.

"Don't take on so. I understand," she said, "Anyway it's all forgotten now."

"No, it isn't, nut by me it isn't. Aah want ivverybody ter remember." He was upset. "Even if it means me missin' mi dinner."

She shoved the coffee and the chocolate back to him, "Finish your coffee! If you don't finish the Mars bar, I will have to eat it ... and I'll never forgive you for that." Daniel laughed a little, but he was nearly in tears. "The banana is for you as well."

When he was certain that he wasn't going to blub, Daniel said a quiet, "Ta, Miss."

"What about your wonderful painting then? That will show them all, won't it?"

"I am not too sure I want it in the 'Gallery' Miss. I would rather do a better one." He sipped his coffee. "Thank you for the food Miss. The coffee is very nice."

Daniel told Miss Klein about his grandmother and about Sarah Bristow, his great grandmother, and about her poetry, and that her poetry was all perhaps lost when his grandmother died.

"I don't think my picture would be missed by anybody if it was used to light a fire. Do you Miss?"

"Well, actually I think that it would be missed. I would miss it." She pinched back the remaining half of the banana and ate it, one bite.

"There was some other good news," she said, "but you will probably be stubborn about that too. Mr Lincoln thinks that it would be a good idea to let you be part of the Art Club. It's mainly for the fifth and sixth formers, but you are as good as any of them." She looked straight into Daniel's eyes to gauge a reaction. "You will get to use oil paints and to make prints and to use all those crayons and pastels you tidied up for me."

"I would like that very much Miss."

"And nobody else from your year will be there."

Neither of them knew how to end the conversation but after a minute or so the bell went anyway.

"I have a question and you don't need to answer it if you don't want to." She paused when the bell sounded a second time, "When you hit Patrick, did you enjoy it?" Her right hand made a fist and there was a tiny one-inch punch, "I mean the physical bit at the point where you hit him? Did it feel good?"

"Yes."

"Art Club" was after school on Tuesdays and Wednesdays and any day in the second half of lunchtime.

The night before his first attendance Daniel was as nervous and scared as he was before the "Paddy thing".

He was the last to arrive and there were five older students buzzing about. They each turned to look at Daniel as he came through the door. Daniel blushed. He froze by the door for a few seconds. Mr Lincoln and Miss Klein were leaning on a windowsill laughing about something.

"Are you Daniel?" said Mr Lincoln.

Everybody smiled.

Daniel was very conscious of being the only person wearing shorts. The draught from the doorway behind him chilled his bare legs.

Miss Klein made a small gesture with her eyes to indicate that Daniel should join the other students.

There was a table in the middle of the studio. There was a blue stoneware bowl with four or five peaches in it. There were three more peaches on the table, placed with care, as if they had just spilled out. Half a dozen sketching desks were arranged around the "Still life with peaches". Daniel knew enough to recognise the references to Cezanne, but not enough to understand them.

Miss Klein introduced Daniel to the others. Daniel gave a nervous nod to them.

There was classical music playing on a tape recorder. Daniel half recognised it as something he had heard his grandad's band play, but this was the full orchestral version. That was comforting.

The students were laughing about something when Mr Lincoln addressed them.

"Tonight, peaches in a bowl, they are not all yellows and reds, look to the shadows. Same rules as last week, no outlines, just the colours of your pastels. We will take a break in half an hour. Work quickly, don't worry about mistakes. ENJOY."

Daniel had never used pastels before; he was worried about getting a mess on his good shirt. As if she could hear Daniel thinking, Miss Klein appeared behind him with a small apron for him.

He did not understand the rudiments of colour. He had never seen a colour wheel. He did not know about colour opposites and he struggled to reach a graspable image by the time the class had to take their break.

"I think I've drawn a banana," Daniel said quietly.

"You do talk then." Carmen Twentyman looked like Grace Kelly, but Grace Kelly never wore a red and white striped butcher's apron. "Would you like a cup of tea?"

"Where from?"

"You sit down."

She turned to go to the sink and Daniel saw her bottom in the gap at the back where her apron did not meet. She was wearing the same type of bottle green skirt that all girls had to wear, and he could see the line of her pants across her arse.

Arne Arneson had put a kettle on. Christine Bayley was hand washing a very varied collection of mugs. Mr Lincoln put some custard cream biscuits on a plate. The two teachers and the half dozen students sat together on some desks and chairs. The music was changed to some form of jazz, and Daniel felt so sophisticated. The other students were taking a trip to London to visit "The Tate and The National" and seeing a play on the Saturday evening. They were taking the overnight sleeper train after school on Friday, and there were jokes about the sleeping arrangements.

"Oh! Didn't I tell you? Miss Palmer is coming on the trip to make sure that none of you get up to any 'arrangements'."

For three or four seconds there was shocked silence before Miss Klein started giggling. Then they all laughed. Daniel was too young to go. He could not have afforded to go anyway. Daniel thought that he would have wet himself before they got to Crewe if Carmen Twentyman was going to be sleeping in the next compartment to him.

By the time Mr Lincoln had called, "Back to the fun," Daniel realised that he had not eaten his biscuit.

"Is it Dan or Daniel?" asked Arne.

"Most people just call me a cunt," Daniel whispered, but Arne roared with laughter and broadcast Daniel's remark to everybody. "You're the lad from Lowca and I know who you are. And, as long as you don't break my cheekbone, I'm your marra." He paused, "Asser."

The second half of the exercise was to bring "drawing, form and space" to what Mr Lincoln called "the underpainting." Daniel was given some coloured wax pencil crayons, a fistful of any old colours.

He was more at home now. Drawing was his thing. He saw things in lines. Strangely, to Daniel, Mr Lincoln and Miss Klein sat amongst their students to draw with them.

The swishes of all those pencils working on the papers did not move in rhythm with the jazz on the tape machine, but it felt like it did.

David Dixon reached over to Daniel. "A bit of putty rubber," he said. "for your negatives." Daniel nodded as if he knew what he was talking about.

What a magic bit of stuff, like chewing gum. Daniel was now able to erase his smudges, clean up his lines and make white highlights on the rim of the blue bowl.

After about forty minutes there was a natural closure as one by one everybody seemed to finish. Daniel was still working when Mr Lincoln called to him, "Woah! Stop right there, you'll lose all that freshness, your drawing is finished. Soon you will learn to listen for when your work says to you 'I am done now,' "

"Thank you, Sir." Daniel thought that he knew what "Sir" was talking about.

They all pinned their drawings on the wall. "Christ they're good," thought Daniel. Both the teachers' drawings were obviously more elegant and vivid, but it was so exciting seeing everybody's work. Only an hour's work or so. "This is the real thing."

Daniel thought that his drawing wasn't bad.

But Arne punched Daniel's shoulder and said, "Grate Asser!"

Carmen smiled at Daniel and took her apron off. He blushed again, uncontrollably.

Carmen unpinned the sketches and laid them in a line across the desks. From the storeroom she brought out a small bottle of clear liquid. She unscrewed it to let Daniel have a sniff. He pulled back, it was violently pungent.

"Fixative!" she said.

She also had with her an instrument consisting of two small metal tubes held at right angles by a hinge. She put one of the tubes into the liquid. She took a deep breath and blew through the end of the other tube, producing a mist like a hair spray. Her mouth formed a kiss. She did Arne's drawing first, then her own. She was bending over the drawings so that the spray came down vertically and evenly. Her skirt was stretched tightly over her bottom. Did Daniel see lace on the line of her pants? He looked away in case anyone saw him staring.

"Would you like fixative on your picture?"

"Yes please."

Daniel made a policy decision right there and then. Whatever Carmen asked him, he would reply 'yes please'. Would you like a cup of tea? Yes please! Would you like a custard cream? Yes please! Would you like to untie the straps on my apron and touch my bottom? Yes please!

Daniel would very much like to touch her bottom, what was next in the process he wasn't so sure. From the limited range of books on the subject which he had read, the next steps seemed to be very enjoyable.

Miss Klein saw Daniel in his blushing. "See, you are just a gentle softie at heart, aren't you?"

"This was 'grate' Miss. Thank you."

Each of the students was given a peach from the 'still life'. Daniel had never eaten a proper peach before, except out of a tin, sliced, and smothered in syrup.

He missed the six o'clock bus, and rather than wait twenty minutes for the next one he decided to walk the coastal path between the railway and Bransty cliffs and through Parton before the steep hill home. He had done his homework at lunchtime as usual, so he left his satchel in the art room for safe keeping and could walk freely and lightly. He had much to think about. Sitting beside Mr Lincoln, drawing as if he was an equal. He had learned about 'underpainting', shape, line and colour. About getting a free cup of tea and a custard cream, and about Carmen Twentyman's bottom.

It was dark when he got home. His mam and dad had been worried, but he had a fresh peach to share.

Daniel was up early the next morning to make sure that he got the school bus with plenty of time to spare. He was very full of himself. After all he had sat in a circle, drawing with Arne, Miss Klein, Carmen, Christine, Mr Lincoln and the others. He had been picked for a team. It was with this in mind that he let everybody else get on the bus before choosing a seat at the front with empty seats all around.

Before class registration he went up to the art room to see if he could retrieve his satchel. He tried the door and it was open. He walked to the drying rack where he had left it, but it wasn't there. Somebody might have put it in the store-room, he thought.

The key was in its hole and he opened the door outwards.

Daniel was hit by a blast of sunlight through the half-moon windows. There, standing facing him was Miss Klein. She was standing quite still. Her hair was silhouetted against the light and sparkled with tiny rainbows. Daniel saw her hair before he saw her breasts. Miss Klein was naked from the waist up. She remained still, holding something black, an underskirt or something. He saw her looking at him, a little startled, and he tried to hold her gaze. But against his will, he dropped his eyes to her breasts. Wonderful and full breasts. Such full breasts on such a thin frame, her nipples pointed upwards and outwards. He could smell the oil paints to the right of him and he could smell her perfume and her warmth coming from the space between her breasts. She turned slightly to put her slip on the paper shelf behind her and picked up her brassiere. Her left breast caught a slice of light on the profile of her nipple and stayed for a second or two. Turning back to face Daniel, Miss Klein put her arms into the straps and reached behind to fasten the clip, stretching her breasts higher and tighter to her chest. Her left hand cupped her right breast with finger and thumb cradling the nipple and laid it gently into the cup of her bra. She took her left breast with her right hand and as Daniel looked up to Miss Klein's face, he saw the blues, the greens and the pale purples of her neck and sternum. He caught her gaze again. He held it as she put on a blouse and buttoned it from the neck to her waist and tucked it into her skirt.

There was the slightest of smiles, the tiniest glint of dampness in the right corner of her mouth.

She closed her eyes for a second or two, no more, then she picked up her slip and eased past Daniel. She put her hand gently on his hair and moved it slowly down to caress his ear.

She closed the door silently behind her.

It cannot have been more than a minute from Daniel opening the store room door to Miss Klein closing it. But he remained in that minute for such a long time. He breathed in the smell of her perfume and of the linseed oil. He bathed in the inviting warmth of her breasts as they moved in and out of the sunlight. The wetness of her lips and the caress of Miss Klein's hand on his hair. He knew that this was a special catalogue of gifts which had been presented to an eleven-year-old and he thought that it had something to do with God.

It took him some time to start thinking again. Something very large had happened to him, but he had to get back to reality. He had to start breathing properly again, walk again, find his bloody school satchel.

His satchel was at his feet under the bookshelves.

He tried to walk calmly but he was desperate to run and to make the registration in time. As he got to Room 11b the class was coming out of the door on their way to school assembly. Mr Mogg, unpleasant Mr Mogg, was at the door.

"I'm sorry I'm late Sir."

"I am sorry I am late Sir. I am late because . . ."

"I had to see Miss Klein." Daniel couldn't believe that he said that.

"I had to see Miss Klein. SIR!"

"I had to see Miss Klein. SIR."

"Why did you have to see Miss Klein? Pray tell."

"I had Art Club last night and I had to make sure that my picture was put away safe, SIR."

"You are in the Art Club? Why would Mr Lincoln want someone like you in the Art Club?"

Why was Daniel getting all this crap? He had never been late for a lesson in his life. The other kids in Mr Mogg's registration group were late all the time. All they ever said was, "been to the toilet Sir." And he just nodded.

"I think I have been invited to join the Art Club to help make the other students look good. SIR."

Mr Mogg knew that Daniel was not being self-deprecating. He knew that Daniel was being a smartarse and taking the piss out of him. He stood, as if to attention. His brown brogue shoes, his three-piece suit, his starched white collar and double cuffs stood to attention also. His face turned quite red. He stared at a point several inches above Daniel's head.

"See me immediately after school Mr Rembrandt."

Daniel was so glad that Mr Mogg had been a prick. Everything was back to normal and he could take more time coming to terms with what had just happened, not just first thing in the morning with Miss Klein, but at the Art Club the previous evening. Even the peach was a new beginning.

Daniel reasoned that he should no more take any unwarranted crap from his 'Form Teacher' than he should from Paddy Fielding, but he did not know how to defend himself against his teacher's sarcastic barbs. He was afraid that he would say a stupid thing. He was afraid that he would clam up and not be able to say anything.

As it turned out, when Daniel arrived for his "detention" the man was a little lamb.

"Mr Lincoln says that you are quite promising."

That rather knocked Daniel out of kilter. "Oh! That's very kind of him."

"He said that you were an honest little drawer." Mr Mogg looked at Daniel for a reaction. "Of course, I told him that you were a little snot who wasn't to be trusted."

Daniel still didn't react.

"That was my little joke." Daniel still didn't react. "Go on, off you go."

"Thank you, Sir."

No mention of Miss Klein then.

Miss Klein behaved perfectly normally in both the standard art lessons and the Art Club. She continued to tell great stories in the art lessons. Once she described Caravaggio's wild 'after hours' exploits as if she had seen him and his mates in the pub on Saturday. Then she would show his paintings of heads being sliced off. She showed a print of "Supper at Emmaus" and had the class set up a tableau vivant of the scene, closing the main curtains and shining a dramatic spotlight on the scene. She was careful to leave Daniel out of these small dramas.

Then, as if with an infant class, she would have the class chant, to the tune of "God Save the Queen", the word C-H-I-A-R-O-S-C-U-R-O.

Then with Christine McGann, posing as Mary Magdalene, [God she liked that] holding a candle in the darkened art room. The class had to draw her using ordinary teachers' chalk on black paper.

The Art Club was fun, and sometimes there was a full complement of the twelve students. It was Miss Klein who kept everyone jolly and enthused. Mrs Lincoln's home-made Gingerbread Men, Fairy Cakes, Cream Crackers with Cumberland Rum Butter, all were used as variants on the custard creams for the "coffee break".

"It's like the dormitory of a blooming boarding school here," said Mr Lincoln chewing the head off his gingerbread man.

Miss Klein's warming cups of tea and coffee kept the group together. Mr Lincoln's cakes reminded the class that the Art Club was a privilege. It certainly was for Daniel.

Daniel drew and painted his socks off in the next few weeks.

Mr Knipe, the woodwork teacher, was on a sabbatical for a year as the town's Mayor but he came in one evening and posed in his black suit, his Chains of Office and his pipe. "I miss the smell of the school and the adolescent jokes. Tell me the really bad ones going around." The class had to draw him with their school fountain pens.

The skulls of a sheep, a badger and a trail hound dog were brought in by Peter Dennis, from his dad's farm. The exercise was to draw them on grey paper with white pencil crayons and charcoal. Everyone talked about the group going out to the farm at 'lambing time' to sketch, perhaps a birth if the timing was right. The girls were very keen until Peter described the squeamish realities.

When the staff room and the headmaster's office got fresh flowers, the old flowers were sent up to the Art Club to do some serious botanical drawing. David Pflaumer picked all the petals off some dahlias and made a collage of a passable nude. He laughed more than anybody when two days later all the colours had faded to a sludgy brown. "Lasted longer than most birds in my sad life."

The school seemed to be as proud of the Art Club as it was of the Rugby XV or the Cricket and Hockey XI's.

And all the time Miss Klein continued to be her own, particular, self.

Except that she sometimes changed her perfume. Daniel thought that he detected three different ones, and sometimes the scent seemed to come from her ears or her neck. This disconcerted him a little because at night when he turned the light off he could make himself remember the smell of the linseed in the oil paints, then successively Miss Klein's perfume.

So, when, during the ordinary art lessons, she leaned over Daniel's shoulder to point something out in his drawing, he knew when she was wearing her 'store-room' perfume and all was well in his wonderful new world.

He had promised himself that he would never, ever, mention 'the denouement in the store-room', or in any way taint his memories of those wonderful moments. He sensed that Miss Klein had made the same promises, for she taught Daniel in the same way as she taught the other pupils. And that seemed comforting.

At the end of one lesson, she said, "If I bribed you with some cheese sandwiches, a packet of crisps and a 'wagon wheel', would you help me with some jobs when the bell goes?" Daniel was able to respond with "Salt and vinegar crisps?" without there being any baggage in his answer.

"Only got cheese and onion, I'm afraid!"

"Oh! Okay then."

The rest of the class left the art room and Miss Klein smiled at Daniel and told him what she wanted him to do.

Daniel had to get all of the work from both of the day's classes sorted out and stored in the students' individual folders before the cleaning lady came to do the floor and the tables. Miss Klein was busy sorting out the content of several folders in the corner by the door.

The cleaner smiled at Daniel, "Have you been naughty, pet?" She assumed that he was in detention. She could have no idea how much of a shock he felt. In his young mind he had been very naughty, wonderfully naughty.

"I'm allus bad."

She smiled and left with her bucket and mop.

"Can I help you with what you are doing Miss?"

"That would be lovely."

On the tables there was a ream of large sheets of greaseproof paper, a glass of water and a natural sponge, a large roll of water based sticky tape, some scissors and a pile of drawings.

"I need to put each of these drawings between two sheets of greaseproof paper, then seal them up with the sticky tape."

Some of the drawings were of male nudes, 'life studies' as they would be called in the Art Club. But there seemed to be a consistent theme. There would be a chalk, pencil or ink outline sketch with one, or sometimes two, small patches of the sitter's body painted or drawn in great, almost photographic detail. There would be a hand-written line of comment, sometimes a couple of lines of poetry, and sometimes there was something cut out or torn from a book or magazine and stuck to the picture. One, Daniel remembered, "Your magnetic movements still capture the minutes I'm in" was something that he planned on using one dreamed of evening to impress Carmen Twentyman, but it turned out to be a Bob Dylan line.

"Are they all the same model?"

"Yes."

"From an art class, "life class" sorta thing?"

"No."

They got on with putting the drawings in a row and Daniel took her resounding 'No' as a rebuke.

He cut the tape and watered the glue with a wet sponge and sealed three sides of the envelope of greaseproof paper, then he laid each of the folders on the tables to let the tape dry.

There was one drawing which showed the outline of the figure's penis and balls, but the detailed drawing was of the hip bone sticking out sharply, stretching the skin, catching some soft light. The painting was just too beautiful to not comment on, even though he was embarrassed by the penis. The paint had glints of gold and shiny lines of dark red and drips of the palest of pinks.

"What's the paint made of?"

"Wallpaper paste, nail varnish and eyeliner mostly, with a bit of biro thrown in."

The next drawing was quite large. "This is . . ." she hesitated, "This WAS my boyfriend." There was another pause, "John."

The figure was face down and the detail of the painting formed a cross down the line of the spine and across the small of the back.

"That's egg yolk and honey mixed with powder paint. I had eaten a breakfast of poached eggs and toast off John's back, it seemed like a good idea to do a drawing of it."

"Didn't you cut him with your knife and fork?"

"I didn't use a knife or a fork, I used my imagination. Now use yours 'cos that's all I am telling you."

They consigned the drawing into its envelope and Daniel placed it with the others.

"Besides, egg yolk was used all the time before oil paints. It was called 'Tempera' paint. Honey was used to slow the drying process. I was going to bring some egg yolks into one of the Art Clubs, but it stinks the place out when it's drying, and Mr Lincoln wouldn't have it."

The next batch of drawings were of a female nude, all front on. Daniel knew that they were of Miss Klein even though she didn't include details of the head or the face in any of them. He wasn't embarrassed, he felt rather privileged, but he thought that Miss Klein might be ill at ease.

To laugh it off he said, "Go on, I bet you painted this with a pork pie and a pickled egg."

"With a name like Klein, that is unlikely."

They both laughed. She knew why she laughed, but Daniel didn't.

"Look, he was my boyfriend." She hesitated to talk further, she had either told too much or not enough.

They 'enveloped' another two drawings, one of the man's bottom and thighs and another of the back of his neck.

"He wasn't my boyfriend, that demeans him. He was my lover, he was my ..." she couldn't get her words out.

"I'm sorry Miss, I shouldn't have asked."

"We wanted to get married, properly married, English married with a white frock 'n all. But my parents wouldn't let me marry a Catholic, and his parents wouldn't let him marry a jew, a yid, a kike."

She sat down. Daniel felt that he had to sit down too.

"So, we lived together. We lived together for two years, seven months and four days."

She turned to Daniel.

"We lived together as husband and wife ..." she nodded to him to stress how difficult this subject might be for him to grasp. "If you know what I mean."

"It happens all the time in Lowca," he said. "but it's usually somebody else's wife." She roared with laughter and a little relief. "That's one of my dad's lines. He uses it all the time in one way or another."

"I would like to meet your dad."

"No, you wouldn't." Daniel didn't want to talk about his dad in this context. "I'll do yer a drawin' ev 'im fer homework," he said.

They stared at the next drawing.

"What happened with you?" Daniel said, not really knowing what his question was about.

"To John? To us? To John Ennis McGee? John Ennis McGee died three years, four months and two days ago."

Daniel didn't know how to react. He tried to say, "Oh! I am sorry." But it just didn't come out.

All he could manage was, "How did you meet?"

"At Art College. But it wasn't until we left and had bumped into each other at the Tate. I was in my first year of teaching and I was taking a party of snotty third form kids round and he was showing his boss and some foreign clients round. He was a graphic designer for a publisher and we met outside the toilets downstairs. We were both escorting our charges to more important things than Henry Moore and Barbara Hepworth."

"He said, "It must be crowded in there." "

"I said, "Why didn't we fancy each other at the Slade?" "

"He said, "Seven o'clock at the White Lion in Pimlico?" "

"And that was it."

Daniel wanted her to keep on talking, but he couldn't find the questions.

"We should have that cuppa tea and the cheese sandwiches now."

"Should we put this 'foot' away first? It might be harder than the others." He wanted the nudes of herself left out and picked another drawing from the pile. A cardboard shoebox had been cut and opened out flat to make a cross. The drawing of the lower leg covered the three vertical panels.

"Hairy legs! I suppose the hairs are 'your John's' real hairs?"

"Plucked one by one with eyebrow tweezers one happy Saturday night after a takeaway curry. I used some of the curry in the picture. Some rich colours in curries."

"Never eaten curry. What is the rest made of?"

"Shoe polishes, some scuff paint and the lines are made from the different wools from some of his socks. Stuck down in the right places." She went a bit distant, "Sometimes I imagine that I can smell his feet in that drawing."

"And the curry!"

"Tea or coffee?"

She made a proper pot of tea, plain pale green cups and saucers and a brown teapot. "Fourth form still life!" she said. "Chutney?"

"You still seem very alone in the art class. Any more problems with Patrick?"

"He leaves me alone."

"Denise Cowan?"

"She still hates me." Daniel told her about the musical chairs whenever he got on the school bus. "I know that she encourages the others to ignore me. But I don't mind."

"She doesn't hate you silly. She has a crush on you."

"Funny way of showing it. She always turns her back to me in class."

161

"Only because when you look at her, she is afraid of wetting herself. Give her one of your big laughing smiles next Tuesday and I bet she'll either faint or run to the toilet."

Daniel blushed again. He was okay with Denise hating him, he wasn't comfortable with being her friend or wiping up after her every time he smiled.

"Carmen likes you. She told me last week that I had to promise to let her know, 'Wherever in the world I am, when that boy has his sixteenth birthday ...'. I wouldn't wait up though, women are very fickle."

"Miiissss." Daniel felt very awkward. "Can we do the other drawings please."

She cleared up the dishes. "Mr Knipe is making me a thin wooden crate to store them in." They only had a dozen or so to do. "He is such a nice man."

It was dawning on Daniel that these drawings were some of the most wonderful things that he had ever seen. They were emphatically not quirky life drawings using a hotchpotch of strange materials. They were personal and meaningful statements. He would have liked to have spent time looking at them and relating them to those little lines which were written on them. And here he was, helping to pack them away, to hide them, and he didn't understand.

They did three more which were done on cardboard from big household packing boxes. Some of the cardboard still had traces of printing on the boxes and half torn labels. The images were bolder, the paints were "Household paints, kitchen doors, window frame gloss white, pinks from the skirting board, undercoats and floor paints." She turned to Daniel, "We were making our nest and saying "sod you!" to our families."

Then came a large sheet of the purest, thickest watercolour paper. Thick and stiff as card. "It must have been very expensive," Daniel said. A head filled the paper. It was a thin face against the background of a white pillow. The eyes were closed.

"That is John dying."

Daniel let out some involuntary noise and his eyes flooded, "I am sorry." Sorry for her loss. Sorry for his tears. Sorry for being there.

"Apart from knowing John, that is the proudest thing in my life."

She took a deep breath. "The thing of which I am most proud in my life. Sorry! He didn't ever see it. He was morphined up to his eyes. Don't cry. I have come to terms with it now, but if you blub, then so will I. So, take a deep breath and help me through this."

They both blew as if blowing out candles, and it worked. It halted the tears and made them giggle a little.

"How did you make it? What 'stuff' did you use on this one?"

"The nurses' red, green and blue fountain pens, the Doctor's 'graph markers'. As I sat at his bed drawing, all the staff tried to bring me some different kind of pen, pencil or marker. The daughter of the man in the next bed brought her crayons and one of the matrons brought in a watercolour set just like the ones we use here at school. A nurse let me have some of his blood sample for the shadows in his eyes, his nose and the outline of his ears. This bit here, see! There is some of his snot and a lot of mine, mixed with a lot of tear juice. There's even a few drops of his wee in the cheeks, here, and his forehead. Some of the colours are obviously not permanent and will fade, but that's life."

She took a deep breath, "Or not, as the case may be."

"His parents came to visit. In spite of all that they had said, the 'Jewish thing' and all that stuff, they seemed like ordinary, normal people. I didn't want any more fuss and anguish, so I picked up the drawing and went to the hospital canteen. I wouldn't have wanted them to see it. It would have hurt them. Besides, I didn't want them to know that it existed."

Daniel knew that Miss Klein didn't ask him to 'help after school' to sort out some classes' work and tidy it away. He somehow knew that she couldn't open up her folders of drawings of her former lover alone. A colleague from the staffroom, Mr Lincoln, or any other teacher would not have understood, or rather would have understood too well. "Come up to the art room and I will show you some drawings of an old lover's cock." It wouldn't have gone down well in an elite, snooty Grammar School.

A lonely young boy who had no friends to speak of who didn't seem to have blurted out to anybody that he had seen his teacher's tits, he was just the right person to help with something she couldn't handle on her own.

"When I came back from the canteen his parents were sobbing into the sheets of John's bed. John had gone. John had gone when I wasn't there. I went round to the other side of the bed, cradled his head into my face and arms and just let go. I just let go."

She just 'let go' while Daniel was sitting beside her.

He sat and witnessed her sobbing for her.

"I'll do these last four," he said. He took out a hankie to offer it to her, but he saw it in time and quickly put it back in his pocket.

Daniel was sure that what was left of her drawings was as wonderful as all the others, but he didn't look at them really. He did a neat job with the folders and laid them out to dry on the spare tables, but he left her last drawing of John, "That's John Dying," on top of its folder. Daniel sat down opposite her. She had stopped sobbing, but she was still bent over in her chair, head on hands, hands and elbows on knees. From that position she said, "When John got the diagnosis, that he only had a year, or months, we tried for a baby..."

"Tried for a baby 'like rabbits' as my dad would say."

'You stupid big-mouthed twat', he told himself. He had started to say "I am so sorry ..."

"Your dad did not say that, you just thought of it here and right now." Miss Klein took a deep breath. Daniel sighed.

"Like rabbits indeed, like dogs, like baboons in the zoo, like ..." The conversation was getting a little bit inappropriate, "Well, you know what I mean."

"I don't know wot yer mean, actually, and ah' don't suppose aah'll know what you mean exactly until you send Carmen to me for my 16th birthday."

That really did make her laugh. It made Daniel laugh. It made her give Daniel the hug that had been hanging in the air for some time. To her it was a 'thank you' hug, and Daniel received it in such spirit, but his left cheek was pressed into her right breast, her ripe full breast.

She pulled away.

"In those last few days with John at the hospital, in the moments he was awake and could think and talk, he asked me to make sure that I was with him at the end. We made a little plan that when the time came, that I should talk to the Doctor or one of the nurses and close the curtains surrounding the bed. He wanted to slip away in my arms. Me in his arms if he was able, cheek to cheek, breast to breast. For three

164

days I wore blouses which buttoned up at the front, or loose-fitting tops which I could just slip out of. I didn't wear a bra for all that time and that was not comfortable at all for someone like me."

She looked at Daniel to see if there was a reaction, a blush or something. But Daniel just wanted to keep on listening for her. He just wanted to hear her talk.

But in the silence, he came out with "Ah ken imagine!" and he laughed at his own joke. "Quite often!"

"Then his bloody mother got in the way and John and I missed our pledge to each other ... Bloody Woman!"

"Did his mother get her tits out instead?" Oh Shit.

Daniel thought that he had made her sob again with his gobshite stupidity. But she was laughing hysterically. "Oh, thank you, thank you, thank you." She squeezed Daniel's head with her hands. "You know when they say that if someone is bullying you, or a boss is giving you a hard time, that you should just imagine them naked, or in their underwear? Well now I can imagine that woman 'with her tits out' as you say. She won't be able to give me a hard time. Any more."

"I'm sorry, I thought my stupid remark would give ... "

"You know that after John's funeral, the very day, she had organised a van to come to our flat to sort out John's stuff to take away. I couldn't believe it. Fortunately, my dad was with me, and John's boss from work." Miss Klein's voice tailed off and Daniel didn't hear what she was saying.

She took a deep breath and turned to Daniel. "Thank you for finishing the packing off for me, you must think that I am just a silly woman."

"I didn't put your last drawing of 'John' away properly, I would like to look at it again." Daniel paused as she blew her nose and fidgeted with her blouse. "Why are you packing all this wonderful stuff into a box? Why isn't it all framed and on the walls of a gallery somewhere?"

She stood up, straightened her blouse and tucked it into her skirt. Daniel had seen her do this before. He felt warm and comfortable and just a few months older.

She seemed to ignore his question and he started tidying up the table and picking up bits of paper from the floor. So, when she did speak, he was a little startled.

165

"I'm getting married," she said.

"Bloody hell, where did that come from?" he thought. He couldn't think of anything to say. He was just a boy and things like that never came up in conversations in the P.E. changing rooms.

"I have met this man, also called John." She was looking at the painting which Daniel had fixed in his mind as 'That's John Dying.' Miss Klein wasn't talking to Daniel, she was addressing the painting, she was talking to her first 'John'.

"He's an aerodynamics technician in the RAF. Not at all 'arty' or anything. I have taken him to the Tate and the National a couple of times, but after an hour he is ready for a coffee somewhere. When we went to the Tate first, he could handle the Turners and the John Martins, but the Henry Moores and the Picassos seemed to make him angry." Miss Klein never raised her head or her eyes to Daniel. She moved closer to her painting.

"He is tall, and I suppose that he is even better looking, and I love him. But he is not John." Daniel was about to say something stupid again, but she angrily corrected herself. "I have to get a grip of the name thing. It will hurt and fluster both of us."

"He is being posted to Colorado in America on an Air Force exchange thing. We would have married anyway, whatever people think. His posting just brought things forward a bit. I do love him."

Daniel let her stare at her painting.

He sat down in case she wanted to carry on talking.

Again, without looking at him, "I can't take the baggage of these pictures into my marriage." She said it as if Daniel had suggested that she should.

"I must put them in Mr Knipe's wooden box and forget about them." For the first time she looked at Daniel, but only briefly.

"I will have to take the box with me. But it will be just that. A box. Won't it?"

"Yes," Daniel said, as if he understood all the emotional and spiritual complications of what she was saying.

"My new John will know that the box will have drawings of my first John, and of me from another life. But if he has not seen them, and I will make sure that he never does, then they will be no more 'paintings' than the Rembrandts he didn't see when we went to the

National?" She said it as a question, and Daniel took it as that.

"Isn't there a funny philosophy question about a cat in a fridge?"

"Do you mean 'Schrodinger's Cat'? I don't think that there was a fridge involved."

"Ah think ah wus thinken aboot Puss in Boots," he said, deliberately letting his accent out of its box.

Miss Klein smiled.

She sat down again and they both looked at "That's John Dying".

They stood and just stared at it.

"Why does he look so alive even on his deathbed, and I couldn't get my drawing of my gran to look alive, however hard I tried? Is it because I can't get the colours right?"

They both got to work tidying the art room up.

"You wouldn't think that Mrs Evans has been in here and made the room spotless." She put some books away in the store-room, but she carried on talking.

"The glib answer to that is that you are very young and I am old, and after years of practice you will learn and understand. The true answer is harder to give and it's about something deeper, it's about your gifts and my gifts as artists, it's about how we stay connected to the truth."

She stopped what she was doing and turned to Daniel. "The more profound truth is that it is just the way it comes out at the end of your brush and sometimes there's nothing you can do about it. That is just the way it is. I drew John in the last hours of his life and was clinging on to him being alive, alive in spite of his pose on the pillow, alive in spite of all the morphine, alive when I thought that I was pregnant. I wasn't." She stopped and took a breath. "And I thought that he would remain alive inside me. That's just the way it is. From what you told me, your gran had been dead for some weeks when you did that painting, and it's a mark of your gifts that you could not, however hard you tried, make her look other than dead. That's just the way it is. We will pose it as a question to everybody tomorrow at Art Club. In the meantime it's dark already and I will have to get you home."

"Can I be around when you put the paintings in Mr Knipe's box?"

"Let me think about that. Heavens! Look at the time. Let me think about getting you home."

"I'm okay to get the bus Miss, honest."

"Nonsense, I live in Cockermouth, Lowca is only a detour."

"Lowca is a shithole, no I'll get the bus."

"You will not, I am taking you home."

"Perhaps you could drop me off at Howgate."

In the ten minutes of the journey in her car, Daniel was exhausted, spent, but he knew that the time helping Miss Klein was just as life changing, just as life enhancing, as that morning with her breasts and her perfume and the sunlight.

"Thank you, Miss."

"No, I wish you would let me take you home."

"No Miss, I meant thank you for letting me help you."

She pulled into the entrance of Mr Mossop's farm and he got out. A hundred yards down the lane he looked back and her car lights were still there. Ten minutes later, through the comforting blackness, across the beck and up under the railway bridge, the lights were there again still.

He got home. His mam and dad were watching 'Tonight'. He mumbled some kind of greeting to them before he ran upstairs. From his bedroom he could see her car pulling away.

Can car lights pull away sadly?

CHAPTER 15

It might have been on the following Friday night or the Saturday night that Tom was watching the television from his chair by the side of the fireplace. Daniel got out a sheet of writing paper and a black biro to draw him.

Daniel sat in the chair beside the TV. "Homework," he said, "Just carry on watchen' t'telly."

Tom was used to acting as his son's unpaid model. Daniel had done dozens of drawings of him. The drawings usually went straight to the bin. This drawing, just of his head, was for Miss Klein and it was quite good. Daniel's biro ran out of ink halfway through and he had to use another one with a thicker point. He was still very pleased with himself.

"Who's that supposed to be?" said Emily, when she came back from her bingo. She immediately regretted saying it. It was a very good drawing.

The next morning, Daniel jumped out of bed to look at it. The second biro he had used was blue. It must have looked black in the yellow light of the living room lightbulbs. He couldn't take it to show Miss Klein. She was gone to America before he could do another.

CHAPTER 16

Miss Morgan and Miss Palmer had both taught Emily before the war.

Miss Morgan's French lessons had her pupils set out alphabetically from front right to back left. Daniel's desk was in the middle of the back row. The class hubbub calmed down to a quiet rumble as she appeared outside the door, peering in fiercely through its glass panels. She had a round, almost spherical head with a tiny face in the middle of it. She had tiny eyes and a small permanently pursed mouth. It was part of the folklore of the school that she had been a French Canadian who had come to England to pursue an ambition to be a ballet dancer. Daniel could see that she had once been tall and poised. She was obese in the way that old athletes are overweight, the fat dispersed around the major muscle groups, in Miss Morgan's case, around the legs and particularly the ankles, also round the neck and shoulders. There was no sign of a Canadian accent though.

Daniel was determined to do well in her class. Emily had been in Miss Morgan's class in her later years at the school. She spoke of her teacher often, with the occasional 'mot juste' thrown in, but there was never any warmth.

Miss Morgan stood outside the door for some time, but none of the pupils on the front row, the 'A's to 'D's, made a move to open the door for her. So, Daniel took it on himself to walk down the middle aisle, to loud whispers of "teacher's pet" and "creep", and he opened the door for her. She had been carrying two armfuls of exercise books and textbooks. She stood for a few more seconds staring into the class. Instead of offering to carry her books the last few feet of her journey, Daniel beckoned her in with a courtly gesture of his right arm.

She plonked her books loudly on her desk and turned on Daniel, "You insolent little gutter snipe." The class erupted with laughter, "Stand outside in the corridor, and if the Head comes along, you will tell him that people like you do not deserve to be in this school."

Daniel dutifully stood outside the door.

Of course, the Head, Mr Evans, did indeed come along. He told Daniel to go and stand outside his office.

When he had done his rounds, Mr Evans summoned Daniel in to stand to attention in front of his desk.

He asked Daniel in a kindly manner why Miss Morgan had ejected him from her lesson and why she had placed him outside the classroom.

"I was sitting at the back of the class, Sir." Daniel took a deep breath to stop the trembling in his lips. "Nobody in the class opened the door for her, so I came from the back row and opened the door for her."

"So why did she put you outside the class?"

"I should have taken the books from her and carried them to the desk. Sir."

"So, what else did you do?"

"I think that I opened the door for her a bit theatrically, Sir."

"Show me!"

Daniel went to the office door and demonstrated his gesture.

Mr Evans took out a thin A4 file from his desk and thumbed through it.

"Are you the boy who is in the Art Club?"

"I'm in the Art Club, Sir. Yes Sir."

Then he did an extraordinary thing. He gave Daniel three whacks of the cane with his right hand, and with his left hand he gave him a catalogue from an exhibition of the drawings of Barbara Hepworth.

"Perhaps you could let me have it back sometime next week with a page of your thoughts. No more than a page. I would be interested in your views."

"Yer've nearly brocken mi fucken fingers 'en noo yer want mi ter read yer fucken bewk yer sadistic basterd," Daniel almost said.

But the 'bewk' looked quite interesting.

And the Headmaster was smiling benignly at him.

So, he bit his tongue and was able to continue his Grammar School education.

His right hand stung like hell, so he had to open the door with his left.

Daniel was no longer afraid of Miss Morgan.

He did try to be good at French, but over the next two or three years there were countless variations of, "I don't know why I am expected to teach French to 'gutter snipes' who cannot be bothered to speak English properly." These barbs were aimed, not just at Daniel, but to half a dozen of the class, some girls too.

Once, when researching an essay on Claude and Poussin for Art History, Daniel discovered that in the eighteenth and nineteenth centuries France was a polyglot country with twenty or so identifiably separate language groups ranging from Basque in the south west to Flemish in the north. Actual 'French' as it is known today was only spoken in Paris and various university towns. It took Daniel weeks of waiting to incorporate this nugget into a French essay. Miss Morgan first scribbled all over it, then tore it in two before she gave it back to Daniel.

At the end of the lesson Daniel approached her desk. "Did I get all my verbs mixed up again Miss?" She glowered at him. "Silly me! Miss."

In three years, she never once acknowledged that Daniel's hand was up, or asked him for an answer.

He gave up trying. It was the only dignified thing to do.

He didn't tell his mam of his difficulties.

Miss Morgan's friend, Miss Palmer, also taught Emily. She taught maths. She took a shine to Daniel when the school used one of his 'scraperboard' drawings for a 'School Christmas Card'. She had been a high flying 'proper mathematician' at university and was 'seconded to the military' during the War.

"I have had lots of compliments about your card, Daniel."

She read the relevant bits from two of her letters.

"Thank you, Miss, that's very nice."

"That last one is from a friend from my university days. He is an art historian at Durham University. Perhaps you could do another 'scraperboard' drawing, and I will send it to him."

"Yes, Miss."

"Durham would be a good university for you to go to."

"Yes, Miss."

Daniel told Miss Palmer that it would take him a month to do the scraperboard. He was going to do it in the manner of a Thomas Bewick engraving.

One sunny evening on his way home from school, in his "getting the bus to Howgate" days, he crossed the iron bridge over the beck. The sun was setting rather dramatically. Daniel decided to waste a few minutes and walked a bit downstream.

There is a point on the beck where St Bridget's Church and Moresby Hall can be seen silhouetted against the sky as if they are the one building. The beck curves round a flat cow meadow and on the other bank runs the 'Lowca Collieries Railway' line. On this evening, a coal train of eight wagons had stopped. The short, dumpy engine, called 'Warspite', still had its steam up, and its little clouds drifted across the sun. This was the perfect scene for his scraperboard drawing. Daniel had his sketchbook in his satchel. There was a tree stump to sit on and there was a fence post to lean his drawing on.

This was so much better than going home.

Daniel only had a couple of pencils and the colours of the setting sun were beyond him, but he could outline the shadows cast by the trees and the train on the field. He could draw the train and its wagons pausing in the wood on the bank of the beck. He could draw the light from the sun as it was reflected in the beck.

It wasn't long before Daniel noticed that the sun had gone down behind Moresby Hall and that two men, Peter Rundle's dad 'Trotter' and Billy Springfield's dad Cornelius, were talking to the driver of the train. 'Beaut', the Rundle's border collie stared up at the driver and wagged its tail fiercely. Daniel had cuddled Beaut when it was a pup. He had fed it with biscuits when it was learning to 'sit up and beg', or 'come ter heel'.

Daniel included the group in his drawing. While he was concentrating on drawing each figure as precisely as he could, he became aware that something very strange was happening in the sixth wagon from the front. He couldn't take his eyes off the figures he was drawing to look and see what was going on. Daniel hurriedly finished the drawing of Beaut with a few squiggles of his pencil.

The sixth wagon had a small fountain of coal coming out of it. About four individual coals per second in a steady rhythm. In graceful, silent curves each lump would go up into the air for about five feet or so before plummeting a dozen feet below, then splashing into the beck. Daniel looked back to see the men still chatting by the engine. They seemed unaware of the suspension of the laws of physics which was happening only forty yards away. How long this fountain had been happening he had no idea. Daniel was not too sure how long he stopped his drawing to just stare at it.

There must have been several hundredweight of coal laying flatly on the bottom of the beck.

It must have been Mr Rundle who gave out a short, loud, whistle. Beaut came to heel. At the same time the fountain of coal from 'wagon six' stopped. Almost immediately Daniel thought that he saw Peter Rundle and Billy Springfield jump out of the wagon and into the wood on the far side.

That what Daniel had witnessed was a beautifully constructed subterfuge to steal coal from under the nose of the engine driver took some time to sink in.

Daniel rapidly stuffed his drawing book into his satchel. He was embarrassed about hiding behind trees to do a 'poncy' landscape drawing. He was not aware that his drawing could be construed as evidence of an act of theft.

He straightened himself out, buttoned his blazer and put his satchel on his shoulders. He walked up the lonning to home as if nothing had happened.

Daniel tried to whistle a nonchalant tune, but he was too nervous to get his lips in the right place.

"Hey up Danny," said either Peter or Billy as they jumped down out of the wood and into the lonning. Beaut suddenly appeared and shoved its face into Daniel's hands. He bent down to rub its ears and blow into its face.

"Hey up Daniel, lad," said Mr Rundle and Mr Springfield at the same time.

"Yer a bit late frae school arrent yer?" said Mr Rundle. "Been in detention 'ev yer?"

"Ah dae me homework at school Mister Rundle, so'as ah divvent hev ter dae it when ah git yam."

"Are yer gitten oah' yer sums reet?" Everybody laughed, "Hev yer got any nice teachers at the Grammar?"

It occurred to Daniel that, "I have seen Miss Klein's breasts, and they are very nice!" would have been a good response. But he just said that most of the teachers are 'really good'.

174

"Ah like ter see them sixth form girls in their green uniforms," said Mr Springfield.

"The lasses hev knicker inspections 'en brassiere inspections," said Billy.

"Giv' ovver," continued Mr Springfield. "Is that reet, Daniel?"

Daniel nodded.

"Aah cud dae that job asser," he said. "Ah wunder wot exams yer hev ter pass ter git a job dae'en that?"

"Yer would probably need a 'Bachelor of Arse'," said Mr Rundle, and everybody laughed.

"Yer mam 'en dad oareet?"

"Aye."

Mr Rundle asked Daniel about rugby. Did he like Union as much as League? But they had reached the top of the lonning and Daniel gave Beaut a good ruffle. As each of them said warm goodbyes Daniel stepped across the 'upper' rail line. Another engine, "Amazon", was pulling another eight wagons of coal out of Number 10 pit and shunting them slowly eastwards.

When he got home, Daniel went straight to his room to change, and to take out his drawing to look at it. There was a palm-print of coal dust on the left shoulder of his blazer. He bathed in the brief warmth of the walk up the lonning. If his dad had been home from work, he would have told him the story of 'the fountain of coal'.

He looked at his drawing. If it had been a crap drawing, he would have torn it up and he would have been able to forget all about the incident with the Rundles and the Springfields. But it was a good drawing and he put it safely back in his school satchel.

When Tom got home, Daniel didn't say anything. Maybe he could tell himself that he didn't want to open his dad's old wounds. Maybe it was his own moral problem to solve, and he shouldn't burden his dad with it. A trouble shared is a trouble doubled. Maybe God was testing Daniel like he had tested Tom at Micklam.

The truth was that Daniel tried to tell Tom his story when Emily was getting the dinner ready, but his story just wouldn't come out.

On the Saturday morning he went down to the beck to see if there was still a pile of coal in it. But there were only half a dozen small cobbles of coal mixed in the shingle.

Tom lent Daniel some black indian ink and a good pen to work on his drawing and to work out how to make his marks on the scraperboard. Daniel thought about including a few lumps of coal, 'flying through the air', but his skills weren't up to that.

Daniel took longer than he thought making the scraperboard, but Miss Palmer was delighted.

It looked more like a Constable sketch than a Bewick engraving. However, in his finished scraperboard, he had not included the stench of the cowshit slurry in the beck and he had left out the smell of the tar from the tar plant and coking ovens which were up on the hill, not far behind the trees on the right. Although he included the steaming train and the two men, their dog and the engine driver, Daniel did not include the fountain of coal or evidence that there were five hundredweight of coal being stolen by two very nice men from the village, two friends from Lowca School and their dog Beaut.

Miss Palmer sent the scraperboard drawing off to her friend at Durham University. When her friend replied she typed out his response and gave it to Daniel. She wanted Daniel to write to her friend and thank him for his kind praise, but Daniel thought that doing the scraperboard was enough of a kindness.

This triggered a continuing dialogue with Miss Palmer after lessons about the direct and indirect confluence of Mathematics and Art.

Daniel borrowed a book on Mondriaan from the Art Room and showed her his flat colour grid paintings, but he also showed her Mondriaan's earlier sketches of trees. In these paintings, Mondriaan didn't so much draw the trees, but the spaces between the twigs and branches. The 'negative space'.

Miss Palmer excitedly answered by telling Daniel about the invention of the mathematical concept of 'zero', which she described as, "more significant than the invention of the wheel."

"Where would you cricketers be without 'ducks'?"she laughed.

She brought Daniel into a conversation about mathematicians and artists.

About seeing patterns in apparent chaos.

About the poetry of numbers.

About the purity of thought.

That sort of stuff.

CHAPTER 17

It was part of the natural process of things that Daniel would get 'confirmed' at Church.

The confirmation class were all Grammar School boys; cousin Billy, John Baxter, Maurice Dicks, two lads from Moresby Parks and four from Parton. Most went regularly to church on Sunday evenings, but Daniel was the only one who 'did Matins'.

They met once a week on Fridays at six in the upstairs of the church. The Reverend Nidd took the classes without his dog collar on and worked very hard at making them fun. He had a fund of jokes he would tell them, "Did you hear about John Baxter? He got a pair of water skis for Christmas and had his dad drive him all over Cumberland looking for a lake with a slope!"

"Ah didn't!" exclaimed John and they all laughed nervously, knowing that they would all be named in a joke at some time.

"These confirmation classes are not about making you better people or stopping you masturbating, or stopping you cheating when you have a French test, or making you better and more sporting rugby players," he said.

The sound of ten boys blushing is a particular kind of silence. The Reverend waited at least five seconds, maybe more. Daniel thought that he was going to fart with shame.

"I can see that I have embarrassed you all, haven't I?" He waited a few more seconds. "Hands up," he said, and waited even longer as they each groaned silently, fearful of what he was going to ask. "Hands up if you have never cheated at French?"

They laughed a little hysterically and were able to look at each other for the first time since the class had begun.

"Masturbation is normal, it is not a sin in the eyes of God," he said, "So let us get that out of the way first. It's a sin to be indiscreet and embarrass your family, and cheating at French is a sin, and not 'walking' when you are caught behind at cricket and the umpire

177

doesn't give you out is a sin." He asked them each to confess a mild sin in turn.

"Aah pinched a dirty magazine frae Dalziels' shop," said Edward from Moresby. The other lad from Moresby put his hand up. "Aah wuz wid Edward, on't' lookoot!" he said, and they laughed.

Each of them offered up a mild transgression. Daniel confessed to "Just gitt'n in ter ower many fights et school."

"Yan 'er week," nodded Maurice sagely.

Then Billy Morton from Parton said, "Aa'm at Grammar School, ah'm in't' choir, ah'm in't' rugby team, ah'm' in't' history society 'en aah come ter chutch." He took a deep breath, "Ah'm strugglen wid chemistry 'en maths 'en ah divvent hev time ter dae any sinnen. Aah'm missen oot on mi life."

They all nodded their assent and started talking in a more relaxed manner. The Vicar just prodded and poked with a few questions here and there and they all opened up. Even at school none of them had ever been in a proper discussion group.

"If it is okay to discuss it," John was a little nervous, as they could all tell from his uncharacteristically proper enunciation, "The feller 'Kellogg', 'im off the cornflakes, invented them as an antidote to masturbation. Aah read it in a bewk."

"Well somebody should write and tell 'im that they doan't work," said Maurice.

"I hev 'Sugar Puffs', just ter be on't safe side," laughed 'the other lad from Moresby'.

Daniel said nothing. His breakfasting arrangements were best kept as a private matter.

Someone was downstairs rattling cups and glasses. They had been nattering away for more than an hour.

The vicar brought the boys into a couple of prayers, then they all decamped downstairs to the vestry where Mrs Nidd had an urn of tea and home-made gingerbread. "You must all get your own, I am not a waitress," she announced, "And you will all help with the washing and the cleaning up."

"Thank you, Mrs Nidd," said Billy, "This is very kind of you. I am sure we don't deserve it." Daniel had never heard his cousin speak so well.

"They definitely don't deserve it," said the Reverend, "You should have heard what they get up to when they think nobody is looking. I blushed my dear, I blushed."

Even Mrs Nidd laughed.

At another confirmation class it was a hot spring day and the church was very stuffy, so the vicar took his little group out to the field behind the church which had been the site of the old Roman fort. They sat on the grass on the rim of the slope down to Parton. Across the Solway, the fields and the woods were clear to see on the slopes of the hills of southern Scotland. Further south, the Isle of Man was less crisply defined. Billy pointed out four figures walking the coastal path on the top of St Bees Head. Maurice was sure that it was a single cow.

The sea around Whitehaven's harbour wall was flat calm, the small lighthouse at the wall's end was reflected still and clear.

The vicar started them off. "The important questions of life are the same today as they were two thousand years ago when young Roman soldiers sat on this very spot and looked over to the Isle of Man and wondered what life was going to bring them, what it all meant?"

"Amo, amas, amat!" said one of them, "Quo Vadis?" said another, "Et tu, Brute!"

"Gabrocentum," said Maurice.

"Pardon?" said the vicar.

"Gabrocentum. It's wot this spot wuz knoan as."

"Really?"

"Ivverybody knoas that hereaboots."

"We wear our history and our culture very lightly in these parts, Vicar," said Billy.

"Apparently so! Can you write it down for me please?"

"It was mostly a rough collection of conscripted North Africans and men from the Rhine valley round here, Vicar. They were after the lead and the iron ore in the fells. There was coal on the shore for smelting," said Peter from Parton. Daniel had never heard anyone from Parton talk properly before. Even Lowca folk looked down on Parton.

"What has changed since the Romans were here?" asked the vicar.

"We can all read," said one.

"I mean in the landscape, what can we see which is the same, what is different?"

"Naebody ken see 'ez. Except mebbe them hikers on top of St Bees Head."

"It's a coo."

"T'railway line 'en t' slag heap, en t' pits."

"Nut fer lang."

"Thez three hundred year 'er coal still under 'ere."

"There'll be nae coal, nae steelwuks, nae Marchon in fifty years. We'll git ivverything frae Africa, we'll hev nae government."

"I come here sometimes to compose my sermons. It is different every day," the vicar said. "Different every hour. And it's right next to the office." He used his thumb to point backwards to the church. "This magnificent landscape is not the product of a series of fortuitous natural accidents. In such an idyllic setting how can we deny the existence of an Almighty God?"

"Yer sitt'n on an ant's nest Vicar!"

The vicar moved with elegant speed, his hands flailing away at the real and the imagined ants on the front and the seat of his trousers. He found a patch of grass which looked clear of everything. Thistles, ants, fresh cow shit. He felt around on his hands and knees to be sure. He knelt up cautiously.

Daniel got up and knelt in sympathy, partly in case he might be moving into a prayer, but mostly because he thought that it might be funny in some way.

Within a few seconds all of them, one by one, were kneeling.

Daniel was the first to giggle. The vicar saw him, and tried so hard not to laugh, but in the trying, he made things worse and he collapsed to the ground in hysterics. Soon they were all laughing uncontrollably. Only a few of them knew why, but that wasn't the point. They were all caught in the same comic moment.

It took them some time and several attempts to settle down. It only took one of them to break back into a titter for them all to corpse again.

"All right!" the vicar said, "I will take this as some kind of sign and we will say a couple of prayers, then go to the church for some orange juice. Mrs Nidd may have some home-made ice lollies."

Daniel was sucking on a 'Ribena' flavoured ice lolly by the edge of the graveyard outside the church's main entrance. "Is it okay?" asked the vicar.

"Wot?"

"The ice lolly. Sometimes Mrs Vicar has the ability to change the colour of ice without the intrusion of any kind of flavour."

"It's nice," he lied. "It's cold."

"You don't speak much in the class."

"It would be nice ter dae a panoramic drawing ga'an oah't' way frem St Bees ter t' slagheap."

"Is everything okay? You not talking and stuff?"

"Frae Howgate the slag heap is the same shape as St Bees Head. Except back ter front like."

"Are you enjoying the classes?"

"Yiss! Oh aye."

"It's good news about your dad."

"Wot?"

"Your dad getting confirmed."

Daniel looked at him and tried not to appear upset or confused.

"It will be nice for you to have your dad beside you at the confirmation."

Daniel froze again, like he used to. He wanted to tell the vicar that he knew nothing about any confirmation thing with his dad. But it wouldn't come out.

"We go to the pub in Parton for his 'confirmation class'!" he said, "Right after Bible Study. I never knew that this 'vicaring' thing could be so much fun."

"Yer cudda fucken tell't 'ez." Daniel slammed the living room door and went to his room.

On the way home Daniel had planned to confront his mam and dad in a cool, forensic manner about why such an important thing was kept from him and why he had to find out about his dad's confirmation from the vicar, of all people. He was determined to put them on the spot as to how they thought he would not be mortally embarrassed at having his dad next to him at the ceremony, kneeling in front of the Bishop of Carlisle. "Go ahead and be confirmed," he would say, "I am dropping out." He would look at his mam accusingly and say, "Yer've read aboot summat like this in yer 'Woman's Own' and yer expect me ter act oot yer silly fantasies." He would look both of them in the eye. "The 'confirmation' will be the first, and only time that the three of us would be in the same church at the same time." He would wait a few seconds for dramatic effect before adding a concluding, "It's all a bit pretentious and tacky, isn't it?"

But none of that would come out. For several seconds Daniel tried to start his 'speech', but he couldn't say anything. In his impotent rage all that would come out was, "Yer cudda fucken tell't 'ez."

Daniel had one of his sulks for a few days.

Daniel genuinely respected his dad's decision to get confirmed. Tom was the real thing. He was a committed Christian. He was kind, strong and loving. When Tom prayed, he had a precise vision of what kind of God he was praying to. But Daniel didn't need him to be there kneeling beside him when he was at his 'confirmation'. If Daniel was going to confirm anything, it would be to confirm his confusion and his uncertainties.

At the end of the following week Daniel was sitting on one of the low walls in the largest of the school playgrounds. He thought that he saw Tracey wave at him, but he ignored it. He looked up a little later and she was still there by the main gate but this time she was trying to push herself away from a large boy. The large boy was holding on to her arms.

Daniel had gone most of that term without fighting and he was a little scared of getting into a scrap with a lad who looked so big. He was carrying a rather large book on 'El Greco' and Daniel thought of just smashing it down on the lad's head. But when he got closer, he saw that it was David Dixon from the Art Club. Nice, gentle David Dixon. Drew like Degas. Soft gradual tones of pencil grey David Dixon.

Nonetheless Daniel had raised his book to bring it smack on the back of David Dixon's head when his mouth took over and independently asked, "Dae yer need any music ter dance like that?"

Tracey and David turned to see Daniel standing with his heavy book raised above his head.

"Hello Daniel," David said.

Tracey was free to move round and stand close to Daniel. So close that their legs and hips were touching, all the way up.

Daniel lowered his book and offered it to David. "Hev yer seen this? Mr Lincoln lent it 'ez. It's his own bewk."

David was blushing and sweating and embarrassed. He opened the book and pretended to look at the pictures.

Tracey reached down and took hold of Daniel's hand. Daniel was now embarrassed, even more so when Tracey interlocked their fingers.

When David looked up from the book, he knew that Tracey was telling him that she was 'spoken for' and that he should back off.

Daniel didn't know any of this. Tracey was holding his hand and that was all that he could know in that moment.

David handed the book back to Daniel, "He wasn't 'Greek' at all."

"Wot?"

"He was from Crete, which was more 'Venice' at the time." He turned to walk away, "Wudda been all the same ter't' Spanish."

"Thanks," Daniel said, for some reason.

"Thanks," Tracey whispered.

"Aah wuz ganna hit 'im wid mi bewk," Daniel said, "But mi mooth got in't' way. Eh?"

"Walk 'ez ter the bus station efter school, will ya?"

"Meet yer 'ere?"

It was only then that she stopped holding Daniel's hand.

The sun had come out when the two of them met by the school gate. Daniel took his school blazer off and slung it over his shoulder trying to look cool. 'Cool' is difficult when you are still in shorts and you must wear your school cap on your head at all times 'until you are home'.

Daniel was carrying a satchel full of books. So was Tracey.

"No hand holding then?" he thought.

"Thanks! Fer this efternoon."

"Aah've allus thought he was a nice gentle lad."

"Aah knoah. He was just trying ter be cool."

"Just tryen ter find a girl ter like him," Daniel said, "Bin there. Eh?"

Tracey switched her satchel strap on to her other shoulder.

"Give 'ez yer satchel and you carry mi jacket."

They got towards the bus station when she said, "Would yer like an ice cream?"

"Doah'n't hev any money."

"Ah'll buy."

"No. You git yan fer yersel."

"No. Aah won't if you won't."

"We have both been here," Daniel said rather pompously. "The money thing. Eh!"

"Mmmm!" she said.

They missed the Lowca bus and took instead the Workington bus to Brewery Brow. This brought them walking past the Church.

"Yer still gitten confirmed on Thursder?"

"Aye! Thee?"

"Yiss."

"Are yer still qualified ter wear white?"

Daniel expected Tracey to punch him or shove him, but she said, "You are the oaney lad thet's ivver touched 'ez 'er seen 'ez."

Neither of them spoke until they crossed the bridge over the beck. "Yer dad's gitten confirmed wid yer," she said, "That's nice."

"No, it isn't."

"Embarrassin' yer mean?"

"There's that," he said, "But what's hard is that mi dad's a real Christian 'en aah'm just a fraud."

"But yer gaa' te chutch ivvery Sunder?"

They hit the bottom of the hill up to Lowca.

"Aah've tried ter be good. Aah doahn't fight ser much. Aah still read t'bible."

"Well then," she said, "That's mair th'n me." She laughed, "Aah've oaney stopped the fighten." She made silly punching movements with her clenched fists and in doing so she dropped Daniel's jacket onto the road.

"Aah've been gaan te't' library en looken up oah't' religious paintin's ah ken find."

"Are they all big bewks te hit people wid?"

"There's some grate stuff in the world, en it's all very moving, Sistine Chapel en oah that, oah them paintin's ev saints en crucifixions. But hard as ah try ah doan't seem able tae speak ter God, er listen t'll 'im."

They sat on the makeshift park bench opposite the Co-op. It was rare to catch the seat without at least one retired miner's arse on it.

"Dae we hev ter spit?" said Tracey, a little out of breath. "Oah them poor old gits come 'ere just ter gob their lungs oot."

"Dae yer still believe in God?" asked Daniel.

"Aah try hard tae. Mi dad's still alive but aah'm scared that if ah stop believen en prayen that God'll tek 'im away frem ez." She took a breath. "Look," she said, "Wouldn't it ev been better if ye'd just belted David Dixon wid yer bewk?"

"Sorry."

"Aah believe in God. Aah believe in love. Aah love mi mam and dad as hard as ah can, en aah pray ter God ter keep them safe so as ah can love them even better. En that should be enough ter be gaan on wid."

Daniel stood up with the satchels still on his shoulders. "Come on. Eh!"

"Yer ken drop ez 'ere."

"No aah'll walk yer yam," he said, "Aah want tae."

It was still a fair drag up past The Ship and into Ghyll Grove.

"They're not pullin' the prefabs down 'til the beginning of July," Tracey said.

"Hev yer got yer new house lined up?"

"Seen it on a map. It's near't' main road."

They got to Tracey's house. Her mam and her dad looked out of each of the two living room windows.

They smiled. Her mam gave a little wave.

"Aah see what yer mean," Daniel said.

She took her satchel and gave him the wrong blazer. They laughed.

"Thanks fer listenen t'll ez," he said.

"Thursday will be fine." She smiled.

Daniel looked over to the old prefab at number fifteen. In the courtyard of houses around a little 'village green' all the gardens were immaculate even though everyone would move out to new houses near Brewery Brow within the next month or so.

In five weeks, the prefabs would all be demolished. Nonetheless, all the lawns were mown. All the summer bedding was in flower. The geraniums, the sweet Williams, the petunias and the carnations, all swapped from garden to garden, seed tray to seed tray. But they were all the same geraniums, vermilion pink, in everybody's garden because "Uncle Harry" had bought a packet of geranium seeds. They all germinated, and everyone in the close of Ghyll Grove could have thirty geraniums each. Mr Mossop, Mr Smith, Mr Johnson, Mr Iley, Mr Moore, 'the other Mr Smith, not related', Mr Eliot, they all worked at Number 10 pit and would tend each other's garden if one of them was on the back shift.

When they all moved, would they remember to dig up each other's daffodil bulbs, the tulips and the hyacinths? Daniel thought.

But there was nobody out gardening now. It was six o'clock and it was everyone's tea-time.

Daniel turned to go home. Tracey waved to him from her front door.

On the Thursday of the dreaded confirmation Mr Mogg kept Daniel in detention for being a twat.

He was much later home than he had intended and couldn't have a bath because his dad would need the hot water when he got home from work.

"It's oareet mam, aah'll hev a cold bath. We doan't want me ter hev any naughty thoughts in chutch. Do we?"

"Doan't start," she said.

She boiled a kettle. "It'll tek the sting away."

Daniel bathed and put on his best white school shirt. Emily had bought him a tie from the market, but it was a man's tie and looked huge on him. When Daniel tucked it into his school shorts it would have created the wrong impression to the congregation.

Tom got home and while he was in the bath Daniel lied to his mam that the vicar wanted the boys to be an hour early so that they could rehearse the singing and clarify the seating arrangements.

He was out of the house before Emily could argue and before his Dad could contradict him. Daniel wasn't going to give his mam a chance to corral him into making a parade out of the walk to church.

Only Tracey and cousin Bill were not at the church when Daniel got there.

Mrs Nidd gave everyone, the girls and the boys, a bourbon biscuit and an orange juice.

"These are the bishop's biscuits," she said, "The man should be on a diet anyway."

Everyone laughed. Bill came in. Then Tracey arrived in the whitest and newest of blouses. The top three buttons of her blouse were undone, and this created a one-inch wide gap from her neck to just above where her bra would be. A tiny silver crucifix on a chain glistened discreetly in its little chasm for anyone who wanted to take the trouble to look for it.

"Are you all nervous?" Mrs Nidd asked. "Cos Mr Vicar is. Both his bosses are here to check him out."

"His bosses?" said John.

"The Bishop, silly ... and of course, God!"

Just at that moment the vicar came in through the west door. Everyone laughed again and this made him a little flustered.

"Oh!" he said, "We are all here."

"Except his bishopness," said Mrs Nidd.

"Lovely. Are you all nervous?"

"No!" they all exclaimed. And laughed again.

"When you have finished your biscuits." He turned to his wife. "Where did the biscuits come from?"

"The Bishop's on a diet," she said.

"Now that you are all early and on time, can we do a run through the processional bit and fix the seating arrangements?"

All went smoothly and amusingly until he placed Daniel by his shoulders at the very back, "So that you can walk in with your dad."

All the jollity evaporated. Each of the boys and some of the girls fully understood what Daniel was going to go through with his dad and all that stuff.

Daniel did his jacket buttons up. He unbuttoned them.

Mrs Nidd said "John."

Tom arrived just before the Bishop and his entourage of a Canon, a Curate and a driver.

The Reverend Nidd, now tarted up in all his robes and 'frocks', grabbed Tom's arm and placed him next to Daniel.

Tom was wearing his new suit and he was flustered because all the pockets of his jacket were still sewn up. His trouser pockets were stuffed with his hankie, his loose change, his own prayer book, his wallet, the house keys and a packet of crushed cigarettes. He hadn't thought of checking his inside pockets and Daniel didn't feel like helping him with his confusion.

"Mam's la'al legs," was his explanation for being late.

After the little procession they were sat down together on the front left pews with Tom on the aisle seat.

Daniel gave it his best shot.

He sang well but no louder than the others. Tom mumbled to the rhythm of his own inner music.

He made the same noises in the prayers and the responses.

"Thank God only I can hear him," Daniel thought.

The irony that God was probably listening to his dad and not to Daniel was not lost on him. Surely this was the whole point of the exercise. With all his bible reading and his studies of Christian paintings he was nowhere near being able to visualise who or what it was that he was trying to pray to. He had hoped that at some time in that evening's confirmation liturgy he would get some kind of spiritual buzz when the Bishop summoned God to come to the congregation or when the confirmands were being blessed.

Daniel was sensitive enough to know, by the nature of the silences in the large congregation, that it was a moving ceremony and that the others on his pew, his dad especially, were taken along on a journey that he couldn't join them on.

Daniel had bought the ticket, but he couldn't get on the bus.

The ceremony concluded with a procession back down the aisle behind the Bishop and the Vicar, with the girls down one side and the boys, led by Tom, down the other. Nobody else saw the humour in Tom doing the slow march side by side with little Elaine Fleetwood. Daniel was side by side with Audrey.

When Daniel got out through the main door and out into the blazing evening sunset and the sweet air, he left his dad to wait for his mam and disappeared round to the Lowca side of the church. To breathe. However, leaning with his hand on the church wall was Tracey's dad. Mrs Smith had an arm round his shoulder.

"Sorry!"

"It's oareet Daniel lad. Ah just git in a bit of a panic in crooded places." He stood up just as Tracey arrived.

"Yoareet dad!"

Tracey turned to Daniel, "Wasn't that lovely?"

"Lovely," he said.

"Yer didn't enjoy it did yer? Aah thoat it was very movin', the Bishop in all 'is robes 'en that."

"Thank yer fer looken efter me lass last week. Tracey tell't ez all aboot it, yer tekken on that big sixth former." He put his hand on Daniel's shoulder, "Ye'are yer dad's son oareet."

"Here he is." It was the vicar and behind him was the Bishop, and behind him was the curate carrying the Bishop's mitre and robes, and behind him, the Bishop's driver with two flat black leather suitcases.

"Where's your dad?" the vicar asked and, without waiting for Daniel to reply, he turned to the Bishop. "This is the boy I was telling you about."

The Bishop ignored Tracey and addressed Daniel, "Your father must be a source of great inspiration to you."

Daniel tried to work out a smart-arse response about his dad belting the shit out of Les Thornton, but he had the mouth cramps again.

"I believe that you turned down a scholarship to my 'alma mater'?"

He had his 'divvent like Scotland' response ready but his brain engaged his mouth after only a second or so of a stammer.

"I take inspiration from both my parents, my mam and my dad. I have a grate vicar ter talk to 'en ter listen ter. I hev a grate maths teacher, en I hev two grate art teachers, except yan ev them's left, ah think all of us 'confirmands' will have the same story to tell." Daniel was so pleased to get that word 'confirmands' into his rant. He waved his arm theatrically from St Bees Head to the Isle of Man, sitting under what was now a glorious sunset, then with a gesture to the slag heap he said, "And we live here in this glorious world."

Daniel took a breath, "We are all, each of us, upper class already."

The Bishop said "Well," and turned to his helpers to see that they were there at his bidding. "Quite!" he said.

In a smart line, the three of them set off, joined by a small skipping Canon, round the Moresby side of the church and out of the main gate to the Bishop's limo.

"Where on earth did that come from?" said the vicar.

Daniel looked at him but couldn't answer.

"I mean the 'confirmands' thing? Is it a real word?"

"What a rude bugger," said Mr Smith as loud as he thought he could get away with.

Tracey held Daniel's hand, but it was Daniel who linked their fingers.

"Where's the bloody Bishop going?" Mrs Nidd came through the small crowd, "Just went right past me."

Mr Vicar took Mrs Vicar by the arm and whispered something.

Mrs Vicar strode over to Daniel and planted a big red kiss on his forehead. "You beautiful boy."

Still holding Daniel's hand Tracey said, "Heyup, he's spokken for."

The vicar turned to Mr and Mrs Smith, "Would you like to join us to have some of the Bishop's sandwiches, sherry and wine?"

"Sorry asser, got ter git me 'upper class' family yam."

Daniel let go of Tracey's hand and whispered to the vicar, "Would it be rude of me to ask you to invite mi mam and dad? Ah'm in desperate need fer a bit of peace."

At that point Tom and Emily joined the group, "We've just been talken to the Bishop," announced Emily. At which point everyone burst out laughing.

"Poor Mam!" thought Daniel.

"Emily, please come to the vicarage for some of the Bishop's sherry and sandwiches."

Emily looked at him. She was still not sure that the joke was not on her.

"We doan't really drink," she said.

"If you don't drink at least one glass of wine then we won't organise a lift home for you."

"Ah'll hev te' ask Tom."

"Tom has already said yes. Haven't you Tom?"

"Wot?"

"There it is all sorted," said Mrs Nidd. Turning to her husband, "I'll round up the usual suspects." She kissed him on the forehead as well.

"If it's that kinda party we're definitely nut cummen," said Mr Smith.

The Smith family set off round the church, but Tracey came back to Daniel. "I don't pretend to understand the whole of what you said to the Bishop, ah knoah that ye're angry and sad." She took out her hankie and wiped Mrs Nidd's red lipstick off his forehead. She then re-kissed his forehead.

"Ah was ganna say two things. But mebbe ah shuddent," said Daniel.

"Gah on."

"You must stick to the 'love' thing with your family. It's you that's keepen yer family tight together."

"Thank you," she said, "Aah'd kiss yer again but yer've hed enough fer teneet."

"Ah think thet aah split mi oahn family. Drive them up't' wall."

She smiled with her big white teeth and her red, red lips. "Wot's the second thing?"

Daniel was going to say that they could go over the graveyard wall to the old Roman fort and do a little 'bird's nesting', whatever that was. But it wouldn't come out.

"Nowt. Owt 'en nowt."

She ran off to catch her mam and dad.

Daniel took a short cut home via Moresby Hall and the side of the beck. He ran most of the way.

He made some sandwiches for his mam and dad, set out a tray of cups and saucers, the teapot and the milk jug. He covered it with a fresh tea-towel and went to bed. He closed the curtains as far as they could go. He had had enough of St Bees Head and St Bridget's Church.

CHAPTER 18

There were no more 'Sir Galahad' incidents with Tracey in the school playgrounds. She assembled a circle of girlfriends around her who were all 'up fer a laugh'. Tracey always kept Daniel up with the funniest stories and gossip. Her dad seemed to be more healthy, with better medication and membership of a society of prisoner of war veterans. Tracey helped him write hard letters sharing his 'wartime prisoner of war stories' with other former prisoners. Sometimes when Mr Smith had been able to articulate some of the more gruesome and cruel incidents from his prison days, Tracey would just ask Daniel, "Ter sit wid 'ez."

She never shared any of her dad's stories with Daniel and he understood why her little gang of witty and gregarious girls was so important to her.

That her friends were mostly the prettier ones in the year was also important to her. She didn't want her looks to be a source of conflict and stress. She had conflict enough at home. So, the stories she told Daniel were of plans to hold a 'Miss World' contest in school, swimsuits and all, and to have Miss Palmer and Miss Morgan be the judges. She told Daniel who amongst her friends were developing the biggest 'fun-bags', and of girls getting their brassieres mixed up after P.E. lessons. "Gold dust!" thought Daniel.

Tracey's own breasts didn't arrive until her fifteenth birthday, and they arrived overnight, ready for use and fit for purpose, forcing the buttons on her blouse to the limits of the stitching.

For three or four months, in her last summer at school, she lost a little of her elegance as a series of new brassieres were each found not to be up to the task.

Tracey and Daniel still talked regularly, all through those years, but she just got too beautiful for him to look at.

She did fine academically, but she didn't want to go on to the sixth form because that would have involved the prospect, the very thought, of perhaps going to university.

"I've got a job to go to at Sellafield and if I do well enough, I'll get on to management training courses." She hadn't lost her Lowca accent or intonation, but she had lost her 'vernacular vocabulary'.

"I can get a bus from Howgate right through, or the train from Parton."

She was gone then.

They never got to undress together again, in the ghyll or anywhere else. Daniel knew her body well. He had watched it lengthen, swell and shrink, defined by the contours of her clothes and underwear. Seeing her naked again would not have frightened him all that much.

What scared Daniel was her mouth.

If he had kissed her that time in the school yard, he judged that he could have coped with her kissing him now, now that all their equipment was in place and functioning.

Some years later, when Daniel was at Art College, she left an envelope for him at his mam and dad's house. Inside was a postcard she had picked up at the Tate Gallery. It was a picture of Rodin's 'The Kiss'; a white marble sculpture of two naked lovers kissing. It was just larger than life size, very erotic, very hard not to touch. It used to be positioned just inside the main entrance to greet all visitors as they come up the grand steps and into the gallery.

She had written on the back of the card "Tracey X".

CHAPTER 19

These are the purple colours in Daniel's paint-box

Quinacridone Magenta
Ultramarine Rose
Mars Violet Deep
Kings Blue
Spectrum Violet
Radiant Magenta
Viola di Robbia
Manganese Violet
Purple Madder Alizarin
Caput Mortum
Dioxazine Purple
Cobalt Violet
Persian Red
Permanent Mauve

... In the summer holidays before his final year of school Daniel announced to his mam and dad that he would spend the summer break in London.

"Yer nut leaven home be any chance then?"teased Tom.

"No, aah'll hitch-hike ter London 'en git a job fert' holiders."

"Oh, that's oareet then. We divvent hev ter worry about owt."

"Aah want ter spend some time studyin' in't London galleries."

"Yer've done a lotter hitch-hiken then?"

"You have a job lined up aah suppose?"Emily was enjoying Daniel's discomfort and embarrassment.

"Do yer knoa the way ter London?"quizzed Tom.

"Aah'll ask directions on't way."Daniel laughed, "Aah bet there's signposts when yer git somewhere near."

"And where will yer stay?"

"Aah could stay with Auntie Jessie 'til aah found a place."

"Yer doan't like yer Auntie Jessie."

"Aah do."

"She's nut ower keen on thee,"laughed Tom.

Nonetheless, first thing on the Saturday morning after the end of term, Daniel hitch-hiked to London. That's not exactly true.

Daniel set off from the house at seven with a small suitcase containing his best clothes and a tie. He got to Howgate in just a few minutes. However, he had to wait until nine to get his first lift.

A truck to Wigan. The driver dropped him off at a "service station" near Preston. He had another long wait. Daniel was worried that he would have to give up and hitch-hike back home in shame, disgrace and humiliation. His mother would be unbearable. His dad would be disappointed in him.

But Daniel persevered and he eventually got to his Auntie Jessie and Uncle Douglas' house in Mottingham by the early evening. He had not been raped, mugged or murdered on the way and people seemed quite pleased to see him.

They were even more pleased when, by Monday, Daniel had secured a place in an international hostel in Finsbury Park and by Tuesday he had a temporary job at Her Majesty's Factories Inspectorate just a mile away.

The many ironies of his journey compared with his dad's travails just half a dozen years earlier were not lost on him.

Daniel found the "Inspectorate" quite easily. He was nearly an hour early. He walked twice round Finsbury Square but that only used up a few minutes. He was a little frightened at the speed of the rush-hour crowd. He went through an imposing doorway. There was an "Enquiries" sign on a glass door, but the office was not yet open. He stood with his back to the door and watched the steady stream of workers rush past him and build to a torrent just before nine o' clock.

An elegant young woman appeared from nowhere, "You must be the new boy?"she had to shout.

"Yes,"said Daniel, "I think."

"I am Sheila Morrison, what shall I call you?"

"Er' just Daniel."

"Well, 'Just Daniel', I have got two weeks to teach you everything you need to know."

She had dark, brown eyes. Daniel tried to look at her directly but not stare at her. Her high heels made her an inch taller than him. She was in her twenties, slim but shapely. No, she wasn't. She was slim, but with large breasts. She had long black hair which she was always throwing back over her shoulders. She wore a black skirt and a black silk shirt.

Oh! She was Miss Klein!

"Oh Shit!"Daniel thought.

"We must first find you a chair."

Across the corridor there was the door to another office. She burst in without knocking.

"Morning Sheila."There was a chorus of half a dozen male voices.

"Can I steal a chair?"

"You can have mine. I came in an hour early just to warm it up for you,"said a young man's voice. Other voices laughed.

"You haven't got the arse to warm anybody up Matthew." There was a lot of laughing with some comments which Daniel couldn't hear.

She came out of that office with a chair which she held aloft. She may have been holding the chair aloft to clear any of the desks. She may have just been showing off her bottom.

No, she was not Miss Klein. She was nothing like her at all.

Sheila's office doubled up as the Inspectorate's phone exchange. She pointed to a wall of wires in front of which was a shallow oak desk. "You will be here." She placed the chair under the desk and made a slow, elegant gesture with her hand.

"Where are you from, Danny?"

"West Cumberland."

"Sorry. I mean Daniel."

"Whitehaven."

"No! Lost me there."

"Lake District."

"Good heavens. You don't talk Scottish."

"No. It's in the north of England."

"I know silly. I was teasing." She put her hand on Daniel's shoulder.

"We do have a problem. North of England or Scotland, it doesn't

196

matter where you are from, when you answer the phone you have to speak the bloody queen's English."She said the last bit in an exaggerated cockney accent.

"Aah divvent knoa aboot that asser. Mi marrers doon't ginns in Whitevven understand ivvery wud aah cum oot wid. Eh?"

She stared at Daniel. Mouth wide open.

"Just teasing old chap!" he said with a nervous smile. He thought that he might have overstepped some mark.

Sheila giggled. "Tell me what it was that you just said."

She sat close to Daniel to show him how to operate all the cables and plugs of the telephone switching gear.

Sheila gave Daniel the telephone headset, "Here you are, put this on." Daniel turned it round in his hands to work out which was the front and which the back, "It's a one-eared headset," Sheila paused for effect, "It's for people with one ear. That right ear is going to have to come off. But we can wait until Friday maybe."

Daniel tried to reply with a 'Jolly Santa Claus laugh' of "Ho, Ho, Ho."

But it came out as, "Hoah, Hoah, Hoah." And sounded a little sarcastic.

"Quite!" said Sheila.

The phone rang as Daniel got the headset firmly on his head.

"Hello. Her Majesty's Inspectorate of Factories." Sheila had to put her cheek right beside Daniel's so that she could talk into the mouthpiece.

"Hold on one moment."

She put a plug into a socket, Daniel tried not to breathe, "There is a Mister Cook from Killowen on the line for you Mr Jenkin, Sir."

There was a pause. They were still almost cheek to cheek. He had tried so hard to seem intelligent, cool, grown up, but here was his new boss right up beside him. He could feel the wind of her breath on his face. He could feel the warmth of her left hip on his right shoulder. He was worried that he might have bad breath, but since that time when "Gobbo" had kneed him in the face he had difficulty breathing through his nose. Daniel held his breath. He kept his elbows tight to his ribs in case his armpits weren't fresh. He was afraid that in such circumstances a rogue fart would force its way through his tightly clenched buttocks. A very painful erection was trapped in the folds of his underpants.

"Mr Jenkin is in a meeting at the moment, Mr Cook. Can he call you back?" Daniel's face so close to Sheila's.

"Can I take your number please?" She picked up a pencil and wrote a number on one of several small pads on the desk.

"Thank you."

Sheila pulled away.

Daniel breathed out.

Sheila was embarrassed and a little flustered. "I should go and get you some more notepads." She disappeared out of the office door.

Daniel had time to 'adjust' himself properly before the phone rang again. He answered it in his best posh voice and by checking the list of fifty-one names and extensions was able to put his first connection through. He was pleased with himself. He was pleased with his accent. By the time Sheila returned he was in the middle of his fourth call.

She didn't have any new notepads. There wouldn't have been room for them, even if she had indeed gone to get some. She was, however, freshly lipsticked and freshly combed.

"Where were we?"

"You went for some extra note-pads," Daniel said.

"Don't be ridiculous," she said, picking up some of the original pads. "These pads will last you for a week."

She moved her chair to the edge of the switchboard table and made a neat pile of the pads.

The phone rang again.

"You or me?"

"You."

"Good morning, Her Majesty's Inspectorate of Factories." Daniel looked to Sheila for some approval, but she just looked back at him.

"Mr Ellaway? Can I take your name please, Sir?" Daniel ran his finger down the alphabetical list and found the number 7. He put the appropriate plug into the socket. "Mr Ellaway? There is a Mr Doran on the line for you."

When the two telephonees began to talk, Daniel put his phone down and turned again to Miss Morris for approbation.

"Pad."

"Wot?"

"Make your note of who called who." Daniel wrote the names down. "And the time." Daniel wrote the time, 10:43. "On the spike."

"What spike?"

"The spike which will be up your arse if you don't switch the 'hold' button when you get through to an inspector." She wasn't angry with him. "What if Mr Ellaway didn't want to speak to Mr Doran and told you that he didn't want to speak to 'that pillock Doran'? And because you hadn't pressed the 'hold' switch that Mr Doran found out that he was a pillock, something he wasn't aware of until our nice Mr Ellaway pointed the matter out?"

Daniel looked a little crestfallen. "That was quite good actually," she said, "You have a nice clear voice."

"Is that it for the day, then? Are we done?" Daniel smiled to let Sheila know that he was joking.

"What was it you said earlier? You know, that 'Cumberland stuff'?"

"I can't remember."

"Yes, you do. Who is 'asser'?"

"Where I live can be very beautiful." He paused. "Not the mountains and the lakes and stuff. I mean the pits and the slag-heaps and all the pollution. Posh people don't live near us."

"No! Still lost."

"I am not ashamed of my accent, but I don't want to be 'not understood'."

"Okay!" said Sheila.

"The 'Asser Marrer' bit means 'listen to this, my friend'."

The phone rang. "I'll take this, do they drink coffee yet that far 'oop t't' north'?" She added, "Asser Marrow. Oouh."

"Only 'Camp' coffee." Daniel took the hint and went out of the door to find a kitchen, some coffee and two cups.

"There were a dozen jars of coffee, and as many cartons of milk, so I pinched at random," Daniel said using his backside to get back into Sheila's office.

"Oh, my goodness, you will get us both hung, drawn and quartered," she said, "But thank you anyway." She got half a packet of mixed biscuits from a desk drawer.

"Didn't put sugar in."

"Don't take it, I must lose a bit of weight."

"No, you don't."

Daniel had stepped over a line of sorts and they both were embarrassed. Eating a couple of biscuits helped ease things though.

"Your accent is almost a foreign language, it sounds very musical when it has no meaning for me. Just sounds and stuff."

"No, it's not. I mean thank you for saying it sounds musical, but my accent is just as much 'English as she is spoke' as your cockney accent."

"Do I sound 'cockney' to you?"

"No, you sound erudite and well educated." She was more relaxed about that line than Daniel's gauche reference to her slim figure [with large breasts], and she let out an involuntary "Oouh." She smiled.

After the coffee they had to get down to the business of her teaching Daniel how to go about transferring the Inspectorate's files and records into a form which could be used to computerise them. This process was very much in its infancy and nobody really seemed to know what to do.

'Colour coding', was somebody's idea and Daniel had to learn how to analyse a text and put one of six different colours on a grid according to six different areas of concern in offices, shops or factories.

"It's a cricket scorecard," Daniel said.

"Pardon?"

"My dad's a checkweighman. He used to break down all the product of a mine into six different colours and columns of figures. He did the same on Saturdays when he scored at the cricket."

"Oouh," she said again. "I'm sure that there's a witty response to that, but I'll say it tomorrow when I have thought of it."

Meanwhile the phone would be ringing at irregular intervals and Daniel was keen to impress by trying to take all the calls.

The act of putting down all the colours on to the charts had a meaning for him which he did not yet fully understand.

The next morning, Daniel bought a small jar of the cheapest instant coffee and a carton of milk on the way to work.

He was happy to do the lunchtime shift to allow Sheila a proper break. But Sheila noticed that whenever she came back to the office there was never any sign that Daniel had had a lunch.

"Made some extra sandwiches with the end of the loaf," she

announced the next day. "Hope you like the crusts. Hope you like cheese. Hope you like pickle. Cos it's a 'cheese 'n pickle' sandwich."

Sheila shared the sandwich lunches with Daniel but then would "Slip out for half an hour while you hold the fort."

In the gaps between the phone-calls, she told Daniel about her mother, who she still lived with, and her father being a prisoner of war. "He buggered off to Canada within a month of being demobbed."

"That must have been hard for you."

"No," she said, "Never knew him. As a little girl during the war, I ached for him when he was away, but the 'him' that I ached for was nothing like the man who came back. He hurt my mum though, and of course, I got in the way of her finding somebody else."

Then she said later, "After what my dad went through when he was a prisoner, when he came home he must have found my mum and me just too fucking happy for him to join in with us."

Daniel asked, "Do you ever hear from him?"

But she didn't answer.

Daniel told Sheila about Tracey's dad, but that triggered an inquisition about Tracey. "Is she your girlfriend?" Even, to Daniel's great discomfort, "Have you two done it yet?"

They shared stories of their different hardships in the two to three-minute gaps between the phone ringing and the colour coding of the charts. Sheila told Daniel hilarious stuff about her mother's search for another man and her own role as the killer of any of those potential passions. She didn't hold back on the details. There was the time that her mum brought back the father of Sheila's first boyfriend.

"Hello Mr Freeland. Is Mark with you?" I said, "How's Mrs Freeland?" He was up Vauxhall Bridge Road faster than the taxis." She laughed.

Daniel told her about Micklam and Sellafield, but most of the time he told her the family's funny stories, the daft people at school, the rugby. He stayed clear of the deeply personal stuff, his grannie dying, his mam's pain, his lack of friends. He nearly told her about Miss Klein.

He told Sheila that he only came to London so that he could go to the Tate Gallery and maybe the National.

"Get on with ya," she said, "I live just behind the Tate. Well, the rough bit of Pimlico."

"I am going to try and get there tonight after work. Even if it's just for half an hour."

"Can I come with you?" she said, then retracted. "Na! You wouldn't want me with you cramping your style. Besides, it's laundry night tonight for Mum and me."

"I'd love you to come, please come." He sounded a bit desperate. "I don't have any style. Certainly no style worth cramping."

"Let me phone my mum and make sure."

When they were walking from Pimlico tube station, along the road by the river, Daniel noticed that Sheila was shorter than him. At work she was the taller, but she was now wearing flat 'walking shoes'. It was only an inch or so difference, but she seemed more physical. "Closer to me," thought Daniel.

They climbed the grand stairs of the Tate and went through the revolving doors together, giggling.

"I've never been through a revolvin' door," he confessed.

"You don't have to talk posh away from work. You can talk in your normal accent with me."

"Thank you."

"I won't understand a bloody word you say though." She gave Daniel's arm a playful tug.

Then Sheila left her left arm linked inside his right arm. Elbow to Elbow. Daniel tried to seem casual about it. As if it wasn't the first time that he had walked arm in arm with a woman.

"Oouh." She was looking at Rodin's sculpture of naked lovers. "Oouh," she said again. They walked round it slowly. She put her hand out as if to touch the man's hip but withdrew it immediately.

"I don't remember posing for that," she giggled.

He held back from saying that the 'girl' in the sculpture did not have Sheila's breasts.

They walked slowly from gallery to gallery. The Turners and the Constables were a shock to Daniel. He had only ever seen the paintings as reproductions. Mostly black and white reproductions at that. He was astonished at how vivid and rich the colours were, how raw and unrefined the brushstrokes were, how big and exciting the paintings were. He could have given Sheila a very good lecture. He had written the essays at school, but he was sensitive enough to recognise that Sheila was as much caught up in the power of the paintings as he was himself.

"We don't have to see everything," Daniel said, "We can just stop and look at what we fancy."

"I fancy the man in white marble back there," she smiled.

There was a large room. It was dominated by one of Mark Rothko's huge maroon 'Seagram' paintings.

"They were supposed ter be for a posh restaurant on t' top floor of a New York skyscraper. But it wuz thought that they were ower miserable and depressing for t' rich diners. So, these two ended up here at the Tate instead."

"They're not miserable," she said.

"I'm nut keen on them, but that's because aah've only seen them in bewks. Eh? This big they're a different thing, summat else."

"You couldn't look at them while eating your fish and chips."

"But you could look at them after a bottle of posh red wine, or a black pudding, or if you were eating a big steak, or raspberries, blackcurrants," Daniel paused to throw the word in, "or blackhites!"

"What's a blackhite?" Sheila jerked his arm, "Is it something that only you Cumberland people eat in your caves by the lakes?"

"I will tell you when we are alone," Daniel said. "Sorry, I didn't mean it like that. I mean . . ."

"It's okay," she said. "Anyway, I don't think that this painting has anything to do with food, or a restaurant. Freud would say that it's a menstruation thing."

Daniel was shocked. He had never heard the word spoken out loud before. He had read it. But he was also shocked at how shocked he was at Sheila using the word so casually.

"That sea of dark reds and purples and that huge dark streak. Freud would say that, what's his name?" She looked at the information card at the side of the painting, "Rothko! Freud would say that he is afraid of women and afraid of his own sexuality."

Daniel was still reeling from the word 'menstruation' to take in the apparent erudition about a painting Sheila had never seen before.

"That's Billy Freud from Fulham. Works in the same office as my mother. Not that 'Sigmund' fella you are probably thinking of."

It wasn't until she roared her great dirty laugh that Daniel realised that she was taking the piss out of him, as it were.

Daniel tried to recover his ground. "I was going to say that when a painting is in an art gallery, it is the'er to be looked at, examined for several minutes, compared and judged wid other paintings. In a restaurant you can look at them behind whoivver it is ye're hevvin' yer dinner wid." He paused and turned to look at her. Sheila turned from the painting to look back at Daniel, "What aa'h've just sed wud git 'ez a good mark in 'en essay, but you 'er talken mair sense. Miss Klein wud say that a paintin' is just a paintin' ter be lewked at, that's just the way it is."

"I think I am getting a little bit better at understanding you. But slow down for me please."

"Sorry."

"Who is Miss Klein?"

"She used to teach me." Daniel didn't want to go down this route.

"Were you her pet?"

They wandered the galleries and got a little lost. "I really don't know anything about art," he said, "Most of the stuff here, I know nowt about. Nivver seen its like." He recognised some small bronze sculptures by Henry Moore and Barbara Hepworth. Sheila wasn't moved until she saw half a dozen of Moore's drawings of the wartime underground shelters.

She froze.

"Henry Moore was a 'War Artist' and he spent a lot of time in the underground, sketching the sleeping figures. While the bombs were exploding above ground ... " She squeezed Daniel's arm to make him stop talking.

After a while, after a long while, she said, "I know. I know."

She pointed to a small figure. She waited. Then she said, "I could be that little girl."

Daniel wanted to take her on to see other stuff, but she wasn't going to move for a while.

"At various times we would go down into the tube at Pimlico. Sometimes at Victoria," she said wistfully. "We live half way between the two. I can't believe that I've never been in here. Mum used to run to the station carrying me, a blanket and a pillow. I must bring Mum here. She'll cry as well."

They found a seat.

"Thank you for bringing me here."

She re-engaged with his arm.

Then later, "Do you fancy a drink?"

"What, in a pub?"

Her shoulders dropped slightly. Daniel could see that he had reminded her that he was 'under-age'.

"I know what," she said, "'HELP' is on in Victoria."

"I don't quite understand your banter old chap," Daniel joked.

"The Beatles film." She squeezed his arm. "We could probably get you in at half price."

"You mean you and me go to the pictures?"

"The cinema," she said, "You took me to the art gallery, I'm taking you to the 'pictures' as you call them."

She had a new energy. "C'mon. It's not a 'date', we won't be smooching on the back seat."

Daniel shivered with excitement. Emboldened he said, "In that case ah'm nut cummen."

"We'd better run."

There was a long queue at the cinema and they stood in line like so many other 'couples'. Arm in arm, talking about nothing. There was a large majority of excited young girls, noisy, laughing. Some practised their 'Beatles squeals'. The breeze wafted the smells of their perfumes and their hairspray and their cigarette smoke over to them.

"Them." This odd-looking couple.

Daniel had his own excitements and anticipations. He was arm in arm with a girl, a girl who was ten years older than him, who was more beautiful than all the other girls in the queue. She had probably had sex.

Daniel worried that he didn't have enough money to pay London cinema rates. Did he have to buy popcorn?

Sheila saw Daniel take his little plastic wallet out and she jumped ahead to the cashier's window. "Two adults. Please."

She smiled in triumph.

"That isn't fair. You should have let me pay. I'm the man."

"You can pay next time."

The words 'next time' echoed as they tried to find two seats in the huge, noisy throng.

Sheila persuaded another couple to move one seat along and they had seats two rows from the back. Daniel took his jacket off and helped Sheila remove hers. He folded hers inside his and laid them over the back of his seat.

"Thank you. That was very gentlemanly of you."

Sheila sat to Daniel's left. It was too noisy to talk. Daniel waited nervously for the lights to go down. The couple who had moved to allow them their seats were already 'locked in a snog'.

When the pre-film adverts came up it didn't dim the noise or settle people down in their seats. Sheila and Daniel sat upright and silent, like strangers on a bus.

There was a short film before the main feature of 'HELP'. That calmed everybody down.

Daniel's left hand was resting on his left thigh. Sheila's right hand was on her right thigh. The backs of their fingers touched in the dark.

Daniel didn't know what happened. He moved to her as she moved to him and they kissed. They kissed like the lovers in the Rodin sculpture.

Daniel had never kissed anyone before, properly. He had certainly never had someone caress his tongue with theirs. He had certainly never felt in any way wanted before. That someone so beautiful was holding him was hard to comprehend.

How long they kissed, it was such an all-enveloping embrace. Daniel wasn't even aware of his erection. Something more elemental than a 'hard on' was driving them.

The short film ended, the lights slowly came on and Daniel was aware that the ice cream lady was standing in the aisle to their left, two seats on. The ice-cream lady screamed a nasal scream. This triggered 'practice Beatle squeals' in the girls at the front, near the screen. Daniel was aware that the ice cream lady was screaming, not squealing and she was looking at Sheila.

Sheila and Daniel pulled apart. Sheila smiled divinely at Daniel. It took some moments for Daniel to see and to comprehend that her face was covered in blood. There was a line of blood which went down from her lips, down over her neck and into her cleavage. Two buttons on her blouse had been undone and looking down Daniel could see a small pool of blood in the triangle of her breasts and her bra. It was the size of a small glass of wine and he could see the dark reflection of his head on the surface of the blood.

The ice-cream lady ran screaming up the aisle, her ice-creams bobbing up and down in her tray.

The girl from the couple who had moved seats for them, she started screaming.

The couple in the seats in front of them screamed, the boy more than the girl.

All this screaming strangely quieted the rest of the cinema.

Sheila looked down at all the blood on her blouse and in her bra. She started to weep.

Daniel had had a nosebleed all the time they were kissing. He had covered the most beautiful woman he had ever met with his blood. Huge amounts of blood.

The cinema manager appeared where the ice cream lady had been. "I am afraid that I have to ask you to leave." He sounded ridiculous and so formal.

Daniel took out his hankie and wiped some of the blood from Sheila's face. She took the hankie and continued herself. Her tears helped.

Daniel and Sheila were surrounded by a crowd of the curious. They packed the aisle they were trying to escape up.

"You dirty bugger."

"Filthy, disgusting bastard."

"You poor thing. What did he do to you?"

"They should cut his bollocks off."

Daniel brought their jackets. The manager wouldn't allow Sheila to use the toilets. They were packed anyway.

"Can I ask you to leave by the side entrance," said the manager.

Sheila and Daniel continued to walk out of the main entrance.

"This way please." Then oddly, a plaintive, "Sir! Madam!"

Daniel put his jacket round Sheila and buttoned it up. He carried her jacket by its loop so that it, at least, remained unbloodied.

"Take me home," Sheila said.

Her flat was less than a mile away, but they took the darker side streets. It seemed such a long way. Sheila had been to the cinema with a boy who was ten years younger than her and he had bled all over her,

207

ruined her best blouse and bra, been thrown out of the cinema to the squeals and whoops of morons, and now she was having to walk all the way home in shame and misery. And the little twat was still here.

When they got to the main entrance of her apartment block Daniel had his speech already prepared.

He began, "Sheila, I am so terribly sorry. That must have been an appalling thing for you to endure. I won't come back to the office. If I can get my stuff out of the hostel, I will try to get back to Cumberland over the weekend ... "

She put her hand over his mouth, her eyes filled up with tears again. "You really know how to give a girl a good time don't you?" She blurted out a laugh and snot exploded into the hankie. "Come on in."

In the small lift Sheila just put her head on Daniel's shoulder.

"Mum, I'm going straight to my room," she said as she opened her door. She put her bedroom light on and whispered, "That's our code for 'I have a man with me' so don't disturb us." She waved Daniel into her bedroom. "It's the same for Mum when her fella comes calling."

Sheila gestured to Daniel to sit on the bed, "I'll have to take a shower and wash my hair." She kissed his forehead. "First I must soak my blouse and bra."

"Take your shoes off, and your shirt, and lie on the bed." She took her blouse off carefully, undoing the buttons from the bottom up. The pool of blood that Daniel had seen between her breasts had run down in one single congealed line to the waistband of her skirt and then stopped in the form of a thin horizontal line. She looked down at it. She pulled her skirt forward from her tummy and looked down into the space. Sheila looked up at Daniel and smiled.

"Me knickers are okay."

She took her bra off, it hooked at the front. "I had imagined that, when you first saw my funbags, it would be in much more romantic circumstances."

Daniel couldn't think of anything to say, so he just got up off the bed and put his arms around her. He put his cheek into her cheek and she let out a huge sob. He could feel the intaglio of her bra straps in the skin on her back. "Don't even think about it," she said, and smiled.

She was, naturally, a long time in the shower. Daniel heard her open the door to what was presumably the living room and have a whispered conversation with her mother. She came into the bedroom wearing a red towel for a turban and a short dressing gown in shot silk. Blues and reds alternated virulently as her breasts and thighs moved under the fabric.

"It's my mum's," she said. "I could stand like this in front of that big purple painting and nobody would notice."

Daniel was transfixed. He managed to mumble, "Oh! I think they would."

"Your turn," she said.

"Wot?"

"There's enough water for you as well."

Daniel was shocked. He must have looked shocked. "You are not sleeping with me unless you clean yourself up."

That was an important moment in his life.

Daniel had never seen so many soaps and shampoos. "No carbolic here," he thought. He washed, scrubbed and cleaned every part of himself twice, three or four times in some places. He was scared that she had said "sleep with me" and did not know what she had meant or indeed had implied. A small sliver of optimism slipped into his thoughts, and he washed himself again. He washed his nose gently and sluiced inside, as far up each nostril as he could go. At that moment the water turned cold and he had to rinse off chastely.

He dried off using the two new fluffy towels which had been laid out for him. He put his underpants on first, then wrapped one of the two towels round his waist.

In spite of all the promise of his situation, it took a little courage to walk across the small hallway and tap lightly on the door.

Sheila was still in her silk dressing gown. Some ham sandwiches and a pot of tea had been made.

"We haven't eaten since lunchtime."

The 'we' was nice, comforting.

"We are only going to sleep, tonight. I couldn't let you go back to your hostel alone after what you have been through."

They both ate ravenously, noisily. Sheila slurped her tea.

She asked Daniel about his nose, and he told her about Gobbo and the two other times it had been broken since.

"I had it cauterised in March, but I broke it again on the following Saturday."

"What's 'cauterised'?"

"They shove a hot wire up your nose and try to seal the bleeding. Horrible!"

"Can I pay for you to have it done again?"

There was a lull in the conversation. "You get into bed," she said, "On this side." She pointed to the left of the bed.

"You sound like a nurse."

"Good. I'll clear the dishes, and when I come back you have to be asleep, or at least to pretend to be asleep."

As she went out through the door with her tray Daniel made a pretend snoring sound.

He left his underpants on.

Sheila got into bed still wearing her dressing gown. She moved close to Daniel without touching him, but close enough for the warmth of her body to be felt.

After a while, Daniel said, "I'm sorry Sheila."

He thought by the noise that Sheila was weeping again, but she was giggling, laughing. "That is the funniest night out I have ever had. In years to come I shall tell my grandchildren about tonight."

She put her head on Daniel's left shoulder and he put his arm around her.

Daniel woke some-time in the middle of the night. He was folded round behind her and she was naked. He went back to sleep breathing in her perfumes and listening to her breathe.

It was very early dawn when he woke again. Sheila was taking his pants off.

Whatever they did together over the next week or so, nothing actually constituted Daniel losing his virginity.

The 'fluid dynamics', as she laughingly called it, took on many forms.

Sheila had a collection of Beethoven records, the big, heavy stuff of his symphonies and the more intimate quartets.

They moved to their rhythms and cadences, and once, hilariously,

Daniel exploded too early in time with one of those false climaxes of 'Fidelio'.

Such happiness, such bliss, was of course doomed.

Daniel met Sheila's mother once in that first week in the little hallway as she came in from work. They were both polite to each other. Then Daniel was corralled into giving 'the lecture' on Moore's 'Shelter Drawings'. She did indeed weep. Then she treated Sheila and Daniel to tea and cakes in the Tate's cafeteria. She liked Daniel and talked to him with warmth and charm, but Daniel understood that 'Mrs Morris' would do what she could to put a stop to whatever it was that Sheila and Daniel had been doing.

At work, Sheila's own supervisor, and 'dearest friend', Marjorie from Dagenham took her out for a light lunch and 'a chat'.

"How is the young 'geordie' getting on?"

"Brilliant. He's very bright."

"He sounds good on the phones."

"He's lovely to work with, very funny, very attentive."

"Fucks like a rabbit?"

"Wot?"

"Are you fucking him?"

"No! Er, Marjie, don't talk like this. We don't fuck."

"So, you won't mind if I get rid of him."

"You wouldn't. Please."

"Then you must tell him that it's time for him to go. Give him one last blow job and put him on a train to Hadrian's Wall."

Sheila wept.

"You're the hottest girl in the office, you can have the pick of all of them. Gordano wants you as his 'personal assistant' whatever that means."

Sheila nodded.

"Tell him that he can come back when he is eighteen and I will give him a permanent job."

"Can I take a long lunch and go and buy him a train ticket?"

Marjorie slipped two ten-pound notes into Sheila's hand.

Sheila did not come back from her lunch break until well after two o'clock. The phones had been ringing constantly and Daniel had not been able to do any 'colouring in' with the charts. He was worried that when she did eventually get back, she would be displeased in some way. He had used two notepads up and he had a thick pile of notes 'spiked' to prove that he had not been idle. He was also desperate to go to the loo.

Nothing prepared Daniel for Sheila coming through the door of her office, carrying his little canvas suitcase.

Daniel understood everything in an instant. "I presume that this is our 'pack your bags and fuck off' moment?"

"I went home and packed for you."

"You didn't want me in the house again?"

"I hope that I didn't miss anything. I think I put all your books in."

"Aren't we supposed to have a row before we break up. Should I be throwing summat at yer?"

"It's the age thing." She was trying not to cry, and only storing up snot and tears for later.

The phone rang. Daniel thought about letting her deal with it. He turned and used the poshest voice he could manage. When he turned back Sheila was sitting in her chair sobbing silently.

He gave her his hankie.

"Not again!" She tried to laugh. She gave Daniel a scrunched-up envelope. "It's for you," she said, then bent over to wail a little. It was like her joyous 'Oouh' but at a much higher pitch.

"It's a train ticket to Whitehaven. You can go at any time. Is that alright?"

"I don't understand any of this."

"I don't want to think of you hitch-hiking all that way, all those wild places."

"Is it because I'm no good in bed?"

"Oh, my goodness no!" She jumped up and stumbled in her high heels and fell on Daniel awkwardly. "Oh! Noooooooo ... My love."

The phone rang again. Daniel dealt with it.

Sheila had brought her chair over to Daniel and she sat beside him. She put her hand on his thigh, "I am supposed to give you a blow job." She laughed and blew out an involuntary snot. Daniel offered her his shirt sleeve, but Sheila found his hankie and cleaned herself up.

"Mum gave me a hard time. Marjorie gave me a hard time, she was going to sack you anyway. It was her who paid for your train ticket."

She took in a few deep breaths, "Not bloody cheap those tickets." She wiped her face again. "But I suppose you live such a long, long way away, don't you, my love?"

"Thank you for the ticket," Daniel mumbled, "Should I go now?"

"It's probably best." She reached over and grabbed the pen from the switchboard and wrote her address on it. "What's your address in Cumberland?"

"I need to go to the loo before I go."

"Marjorie said that she will send you your wages and that if you did go early she would count it as 'Dentist Time' and pay you for the full day."

"Marjorie is just too fucking kind, isn't she? All heart Marjorie." Daniel went to the loo.

When he came back Sheila had brushed her hair and fixed her make-up. There was a brown paper bag on his case. "I got you some sandwiches and stuff for your journey."

They stood and hugged. She put her cheek on Daniel's lips.

"If I leaned back against the switchboard, you could give 'ez that blowjob. Eh!"

"What if the phone rang?"

"You posh Londoners talk wid a plum in your mouth anyway, asser."

She didn't laugh.

Daniel picked up his suitcase and his picnic. He kissed her gently on her forehead.

"Thank you," he said.

Daniel had been home for two weeks when Sheila's first letter arrived. It was a package.

Emily had opened it.

She gave it to Daniel, in its opened state, with no embarrassment.

There were four separate documents in the envelope. One was a letter telling him that he was still a signatory to The Official Secrets Act and that he would be bound to that Act for all time, or something like that.

"What secrets dae youw knoah. Eh?"

"Why did you open my letter?"

213

"While yer livin' in this house ah'll oppen yer letters," she said angrily.

"It's me who should be angry, nut thee."

Daniel picked up all his bits of paper, "Are yer sure this is all ther' wuz?"

He slammed the front door behind him and walked down the line towards Barngill. He sat on a stack of old railway sleepers.

There was paper money in a closed brown envelope which had the inspectorate's logo on the front. Inside was two week's wages, plus some.

There was a typed letter from Marjorie saying what an excellent worker Daniel had been and that if he wanted a permanent place at the Inspectorate, 'in a year or two', that his application would be looked on favourably. She would be happy to write him a reference or a testimonial.

"I was only there a fortnight," he thought. But he knew all about guilt and he didn't really mind.

There was another sealed envelope. The flap was secure, but it didn't look right. On the front of the envelope was just 'DANIEL' in capitals.

"Dear Daniel,

I hope that your train journey went okay. Was it full of Scottish drunks 'ga'en hame tae Glasgae'?

You live so far away, it must have taken hours and hours.

I topped up your wages to the nearest pound so that there weren't any coins rattling around in the envelope. You owe me half a crown! You can buy us tea at the Tate when you come back to London.

Very soon, I hope.

How is your nose? Be careful not to break it again when you play rugby or do anything else that's equally rough!

Lots of love
Sheila"

Apart from the occasional birthday card, Daniel had never had a proper letter before.

He was disturbed that his mam might have read it but was

glad that there was nothing overtly personal in what Sheila had written. He carried on walking down the line to Barngill and stood on the sandstone bridge straddling the beck. The water was clean and clear.

"Dear Sheila,

Thank you so much for sending my wages to me and for the extra half crown.

The train journey was indeed long and crowded with, mostly nice, Scots. I had a seat. But didn't dare move in case a large middle aged drunk, who thought that I was called Jimmy, took my place.

Thank you for your letter. I didn't think that you would write, but I am flattered and thrilled that you did. I have to warn you though that my mother opens my letters.

I have been heavily into pre-season rugby training and it has been tough catching up with the others who have been at it for a month or more. There's half a dozen of us 'bairns' but the first team are full of farmers, iron ore miners and Sellafield men who glow in the dark. I have had a smack in the nose at each training session and I bled profusely each time. We have 'Sevens' these next two Saturdays and I might be a travelling reserve.

Lots of love
Daniel"

Sheila's reply came within the week.
It was typed.

"Dear Mrs Jonas,

You do not know me, but my name is Sheila Morrison and I was Daniel's supervisor when he worked at Her Majesty's Inspectorate of Factories here in London.

Why are you reading this letter? It is so clearly addressed to Daniel.

Faithfully yours
Sheila Morrison"

The first Daniel knew of the letter was when he got home after rugby training and his mam and dad were in the middle of a row.

Tom had just got back from Bible Class. "There's some sellotape in me box." He put the torn remains of the letter into Daniel's hand.

Tom and Emily's bedroom door slammed.

"Egg 'n crumb? Or d'ye fancy a bacon sandwich?"

Instead of using the tape from Tom's box Daniel used some paper glue and stuck Sheila's letter down on to a sheet of brown wrapping paper. He didn't make a very good job of it and he had left gaps between the little torn sheets such that there were five vertical brown lines and five, almost horizontal ones also.

Emily must have been very ordered in her rage and her embarrassment. Daniel wanted to apologise to her. She must have been mortified when she read Sheila's letter. She was being laughed at, and Daniel understood that he was the indirect cause of her humiliation. Why didn't she just burn the bloody letter instead of showing it to his dad? Was showing it to Tom a kind of confessional? Did she expect Tom to hit Daniel for the pain that he had caused her?

"Doan't give yer mam a hard time, lad. Yer mam just isn't hersel' any mair." Tom sat down beside Daniel on the settee, thought that Daniel might feel too 'pressured' and retreated to his own chair by the fire. "When aah wuz outa wuk she took it very hard. Aah thoat she wuz ganna shrivel away tae nowt. She's lost oall her bounce 'en sense 'er fun. She hesn't forgiven 'es. Aah 'event forgiven misel'."

Tom and Daniel sat in silence for a while.

"Wot's she like? This Sheila?" said Tom. "Sorry, aah shuddent 'ev asked."

"Aah love 'er."

"Ye oaney saw her fer a cuppla weeks."

"Noah. Aah love me mam."

"Aah knoah lad." Tom got up to go upstairs to see Emily.

"Grate tits," said Daniel.

Tom and Daniel laughed together, silently so as not to alert Emily. Tom closed the living room door.

"She's really nice, Dad. So glad aah met her. But she lives in London and aah live here."

"Good lad."

216

Daniel had found a little hiding place in the downstairs toilet in the form of a one-inch gap between the ceiling and the top of the wooden box that Tom had made to soften the noise and civilise the look of the cistern. Daniel could reach the gap by standing on the lid of the toilet, and even if Emily had ever found out about the 'hidey hole' she would never have been able to reach it. If ever Daniel developed the courage to buy a dirty magazine it would be where he would hide that also.

Daniel wrote to Sheila and told her of his mam's discomfiture at reading the letter. He told her about his rugby and his nose bleeds and he let slip that, "I used to have an Art teacher who would have dipped a brush into my blood to make a drawing of her boyfriend."

"Dear Daniel,

I hope that you are the first to read this! I am sorry that my letter caused your mum [mam?] so much pain.

I have good news and I have bad news.

My good news is that I have bought a new blouse. It is a dark, dark red, and yesterday I went to the Tate and stood in front of that big painting and nobody could see me! I giggled to myself and thought of you fondly. I was so pleased, so I got the tube to Oxford Street and ordered myself a new bra in almost the same colour red. As you may have noticed I have to have such undergarments made to measure and constructed by an engineer! [it is a profession you should consider training for, you have all the talents and qualifications required!] I cannot wait to try it on and have you bleed on me again! In the mean-time here is a photo of me in my new blouse.

The bad news is that Marjorie is 'having it off' with Gordano!!!!!!!

They go to a grubby little hotel near Kings Cross every Friday afternoon, shag themselves silly for a couple of hours then Marjorie catches the 7:12 to Dagenham and Gordano catches the 7:25 to St Albans.

The BASTARDS!

He is twenty years older than her. He's bald and fat!

The crap I got from Marjorie when you were here!!!

Please send a photo and tell me all about the Lake District. I looked up Lowca on the Inspectorate's map. Can you see the sea?

Lots of love.
Sheila"

The photo was only 3" x 3" and would fit into what Daniel called his 'wallet'.

But it was lovely. He imagined that he could see the shape of her nipples in the contours of her blouse. Was Sheila telling him that she didn't have a brassiere on? Is this what people did in love letters? Everything in what Sheila wrote was matter of fact and could be understood as just a nice letter between fond friends. But the letter was of a very different kind, in a different context, if indeed those were her commando nipples that Daniel could discern in the photo.

Daniel put the letter in his 'hidey hole' and put the photo in his wallet.

There are no photographs of Daniel from when he was nine to his late teens. The family camera and the rosewood tripod went to the pawnbrokers when Tom was out of work. Tom's 'wedding watch' went soon after.

There were class photos every year at Grammar School and there were rugby, cricket and athletics team photos, but none of them were ever bought. The "samples" were always returned to the school. Daniel thought that he never looked good in them anyway.

He didn't want to go into all this with Sheila. He wanted to write her a love-letter but he was scared that such a thing would frighten her off.

"Dear Sheila,

I can see the sea from my bedroom window!

I can see the parish church about a mile away and it is silhouetted in front of the Solway Firth. There is a long, curved harbour wall coming out of Whitehaven. It has the tiniest of lighthouses on the end of it. Five or six miles beyond Whitehaven harbour is St Bees Head, a great sandstone promontory shaped a little like my nose!

I can look at St Bees Head and tell what the weather is going to be like in an hour's time and I can tell also if the sea is at high tide or low tide. These are important things in this part of the world. High tide means that I can buy four herrings or two mackerel for a shilling from the rowboats at the Parton shoreline. Low tide means that I can take my bike to Lowca beach and pick a bag of mussels from the rocks, or maybe a crab or two. It sounds romantic and picturesque but, in reality, it is quite grim. The sea is polluted by coal sludge and the effluent from the tar plant high above the cliffs. Then there is the cow slurry from a dozen farms either side of the beck.

The Lake District is several hundred square miles of the loveliest landscape on earth. It can be heart-achingly beautiful and fearsome at the same moment. Wordsworth believed that such sublime beauty improved the soul and made us better human beings. However, every person I ever met who lives in the mountains or by the lakes seems to be a twat. You will have to come and judge for yourself.

I am reasonably fit. I train three nights a week for the school or the club and on Saturdays I play for the school in the morning and for the club seconds in the afternoon. On Sundays I walk. I don't stroll the landscape in search of picturesque views or to bathe in the geography of my surroundings. I mostly walk with my head down. I can't say that I think great thoughts or resolve any problems, or even have exotic daydreams followed by filthy fantasies.

I just walk.

I have not had any romantic or erotic encounters. I asked Stella Carey if I could walk her to the bus-station but she sneered at me and said, "Get lost creep."

Daren't ask a girl if she wants to go to the 'cinema', or even to the 'pictures'!

Thank you for the photo. I would like to do a drawing of you in your new blouse. Do you think that it would fit me?

Daniel"

They would write to each other every two or three weeks and neither of them was able to write anything more than fond and friendly gossip. Daniel tried several times to write a proper love letter and articulate his joy in their 'frank and vigorous exchange of fluids', but he always chickened out.

CHAPTER 20

Tom had not intended to go to the match.

Daniel had not asked him. Tom had never gone to Daniel's games unless specifically asked. Daniel had seemed nervous about the Cup Final. He was fidgety during the week and on the Friday night and the Saturday morning he had hardly eaten anything and spent most of the time alone in his room. Workington Town were playing Widnes and Tom was resolved to go to that game. When Daniel had set off to Howgate to be picked up by the team bus, Tom, unusually, had shaken his hand."Good luck, son." However, when he got on to the Workington bus he was overtaken with his own wave of high nervousness. "Butterflies" he whispered to himself.

Without making a conscious decision, instead of going through to Workington for the 'League' game, Tom just got off the bus at The Ellis Ground right by the steelworks. Was going to watch his son play instead. He paid his money at the gate and found a back seat on his own in the middle of the stand. He was early. He wondered if Daniel was already changed into his kit. He wondered also if Daniel was as nervous as he, himself, was. Tom was a Rugby League man and Daniel was Rugby Union. It was a class thing. Part of Daniel going to Grammar School. But Tom understood that the same elemental certainties of fierce physical conflicts pertained and that at 2:45pm on Saturday Smiler Allen at Workington Town and Daniel, here at 'The Ellis' ground, were both preparing for their third defecation of the day.

The stand filled up soon enough and the teams took the field. Tom looked for Daniel. He seemed so small.

Tom hardly heard the referee's whistle blow. He didn't see Daniel catch the ball from the kick-off. Everyone in front of him in the stand, stood up. Some of them were shouting obscenities. A woman screamed "Git 'im. Git the bastard."

Tom stood up, he saw a brawl, like a pub fight. Almost all the players from both sides were piled in, swinging fists, butting heads.

Tom looked for Daniel but couldn't see him. "Just like the little bugger to be in the middle of a fight," he smiled to himself. But still, he couldn't see his son. The ref's whistle continued its 'impromptu', but the fight rolled on. Tom could still not see Daniel and he started to panic. The mass brawl broke into small groups of three or four, swinging arms, wrestling, some kicking.

Finally, Tom saw Daniel, curled up, foetus like, on the floor. The intersecting whitewash of the ten-yard line and the five-yard line formed a crude matrix for the writhing body of his son.

Tom held back the urge to rush on to the field to care for his boy. He held back the urge to weep.

The two teams were eventually separated. A fat man in a tweed suit was tending to Daniel. Daniel was helped to his feet. The fat man put his hand inside Daniel's shirt and felt his ribs. Daniel winced, then pulled away and rejoined his team.

It took some time for Tom to summon the gumption to leave his seat in the stand and seek out the 'fat man in the tweed suit'.

"Is the number two oah'reet?" Tom asked.

"You his dad?"

"Aye."

"Ribs," he said. "The lad can't breathe. He needs to come off."

"Are you the Doctor?"

"I'm supposed to be, but your boy thinks he outranks me. I told him that he has broken some ribs. He told me that he hadn't." The Doctor shrugged his shoulders and turned to walk away.

"Thank you," shouted Tom.

Tom went round to the other side of the pitch where he could walk along behind the railings and a line of spectators. He could remain invisible to Daniel, but somehow be closer to him. As he watched Daniel play on, Tom's own body echoed every movement, twitch and twist of Daniel's.

Tom wondered if it was God who made him get off the bus and come to the "wrong game" specifically to watch his boy having the shit kicked out of him. Tom carried the burden of all the pain that Daniel had suffered when Tom was out of work, out of society, out of touch with the world. He remembered Daniel's disturbing silences, his moroseness, that time when riding Gwen's bike to Maryport, 'to share his dad's pain'. Tom took a very deliberate deep breath and for a moment or two he did what he thought was praying. In his impotent pain all that he could do was to be a 'witness' for Daniel.

Until, in the second half, there was a scrum, and as it broke up, Daniel was left on his hands and knees with blood pouring out of his nose, pouring out of his face on to the mud between his hands. Tom could not bear this. He scuttled to the far corner of the little stadium to be on his own so that he could weep. He sobbed.

Tom knew that this horrible game, this game with no moral compass, this game where Daniel was punched in a scrum not "in spite of his broken ribs", but "because he had broken ribs" was some kind of epiphany for Tom, not Daniel. This was a transcendent moment in Tom's life. He tried to articulate it to himself with some biblical references, "maybe summat in the prodigal son thing," he thought. "Maybe Daniel is gitt'n the crap kicked oot of him en aah just hev ter watch it .... 'En that's just the way things are." Tom had to 'let go'. His boy was ready to 'leave'.

"He left the family when he walked out of Church after his Confirmation," he said. Not loud enough for anybody to hear.

Tom had gone to the game to see if Daniel was a beautiful rugby player, still quick on his feet, sharp witted, elegant in his skills. What he found was that Daniel was still the son who he had seen shoving his bike up the High Harrington hill in the driving rain as if this was to be his purpose in life. Tom understood that this was who Daniel was and who he was going to be.

Tom dried his eyes and his face and prepared to walk back to the stand for the end of the match.

He wanted to shake his son's hand again.

After the doctors and nurses had seen Daniel's X-rays and pronounced that he had, "three broken ribs, but no damage to your lungs," Tom and he were sent to a hospital waiting room while a nurse came to fit Daniel up with a 'corset' to support his ribs.

Tom asked Daniel teasingly, sarcastically, "Did you enjoy the game?"

"We won!"

"That's nut what I asked."

"Ah knoah."

He was on the point of saying something meaningful to his dad, something which perhaps related to his 'Micklam story', but all he got out was, "It's nut just aboot enjoyment . . ." when the nurse arrived.

"Yer ken hev sexy moss green, er yer ken hev green?" She was holding up two alternate styles of 'ribcage support garment'.

Tom's interest in the deep philosophical and moral aspects of high contact sport waned as he helped the little ginger haired nurse tighten and adjust the straps and strings of Daniel's corset.

The nurse sat Daniel down and cleaned up his face and nose with hot water and Dettol. She took the plug of cotton wool out of his left nostril and this started another flow of blood. She pinched his nose between her thumb and forefinger and eased his head and upper body backwards against herself. It hurt. She inserted a new plug of more solid cotton wool.

"There," she said, "You look almost normal." She smiled at Tom.

Daniel was sent into a cubicle to change out of his rugby shorts and socks. He couldn't do it and, humiliatingly, had to ask for help.

"Dae yer want me 'er yer dad?" she laughed.

They both went in and Daniel had to surrender his dignity. With his back to them, Tom managed to get Daniel's underpants on for him, but only after putting them on back to front in his first attempt. The nurse got another larger dish of hot water and washed the mud and blood from Daniel's legs. In all his pain and embarrassment, it was a delicious experience. He put his hand on her shoulder as she put his trousers on. She put his socks and shoes on from the same squatted position before bouncing up to put his shirt on for him, doing up his buttons from the top to the bottom.

"Put 'is stuff in 'is bag will yer?"

Tom left the cubicle.

The nurse then did up Daniel's flies from the bottom button to the top.

"You must hurt all over," she said, tucking his shirt into his trousers.

"Thank you, nurse, you've been grate."

"Helen," she said, "Did yer win?"

"Aye, nae thanks ter me though."

Tom and Daniel left the hospital with some heavy-duty pills and appointment slips for a check-up in ten days. Tom put them away in his wallet. They waited for the bus to go home, but the bus to Egremont came along first.

"Let's go to the clubhouse," Daniel said, "There's a tatie pot supper and you can buy me a pint."

"Aah'll buy yer a shandy."

So here Daniel was, after getting such a brutal beating in the first big game that his dad had watched him play in, and he did not understand that Tom might have suffered more pain during the game than Daniel himself had done. Standing in the hospital bus shelter, Daniel didn't let his dad look after him, take care of him. Daniel had to take control and would not wait for a more ordinary time before he and his dad had 'that first drink together'. And it was not with Tom's friends and his workmates, but with Daniel's friends and team-mates.

Tom was uncomfortable and nervous in the clubhouse. Space was cleared at the end of the row of tables and Tom and Daniel joined with the props George and Neal. Between them they knew some of the same people in Gosforth and Sellafield. George and Daniel talked about music. The game, this most brutal of games, was hardly mentioned. Egremont at that time was a seriously good team with four or five North of England players and a couple who would go on to Rugby League. They had skills and gifts and they were dedicated, but in this particular game they had found inside themselves an apocalyptic rage and a ferocious unity. There was no jumping up and down, no drinking games; it had never been a good "singing club", but there was a profound sense of fulfilment among the players. The girlfriends and wives in their best frocks and borrowed perfumes also sensed that something was good, more important than the cup they had won. At dinner in the clubhouse, with the extended club family and what counted as 'Dignitaries' in these parts, there was a warm and comforting buzz about the room. The only potential conflict was between those who ate their tatie-pots with black pudding on top against those who ate their tatie-pots with just potatoes on top.

After the tatie-pot, the apple pie with custard, but before the cheese, Tom got up as if to go to the toilet but went instead to the bar. He came back with two pints of beer, one for Neal and one for George.

"Thank you fer looken efter me lad."

"Yer divvent efter dae that, man," said George.

"Aah saw what went on," said Tom, "Anywez, aah's gitten this lad yam."

"Aye," said Neal a little theatrically, "Git yam 'Dan-Dan'. It's past thi' bedtime."

As they got up to go, Bob, the lock, the most gloriously vicious of his team's 'enforcers', came over and just put his hand on Daniel's shoulder. Then he walked away again.

Tom and Daniel had to walk quickly to catch the bus and Daniel struggled to breathe.

"Wot'll we tell yer mam?"

"Nowt," said Daniel.

They sat silently all the way to Lowca.

When they got home Daniel announced, "We won 'en aah took Dad ter git him drunk instead 'er me!"

"Ther' wuz a free pint 'en somebody hed ter drink it!" said Tom, as he smuggled the pills into Daniel's trouser pocket.

"Aah'm off ter bed." Daniel planted a rare kiss on his mother's forehead.

Daniel wrote to Sheila to tell her about the game, his ribs and his embarrassment.

"... I am not too sure that the other players were impressed or grateful that I had stayed on. I think that they thought that I was a stupid little twat.

I had so much wanted to write you a triumphant letter, telling you how well I played.

But I am lying in a crumpled heap on my bed unable to breathe, unable to sleep, a little bit woozy with the pills the doctors gave me. I am looking out of the window and I can see the sea. I can see St Bees Head [the tide is in and it is going to rain soon!]

What a pathetic sounding letter this is.

I would like to write a proper letter to you, a filthy letter, a letter describing all my feelings.

I don't think that I know how to write one. I don't know if I qualify to write one to you.

Daniel."

Daniel's letter was written as much to himself as it was to Sheila. In his weeks with her a door into the light of adulthood had been opened and then quickly closed again. He never really got into trying to date girls at school. He still thought of Sheila all the time.

Sheila's reply to his letter came in the form of a postcard, bought at the Tate, of a William Etty nude, sealed up in an envelope. She had written, "Bring your tender ribs to me and I will poultice them on my thighs, my belly and my breasts until they are healed. I will give succour to your tender heart with my lips."

Their weekly letters to each other became thereafter, more relaxed.

It was well into the summer when Daniel got the strangest of letters. Strangest or perhaps most beautiful of letters.

There was no "Dear Daniel" ...

"I have met a man.
He is not beautiful or athletic.
He does not make me laugh.
I love him.
I think that he loves me.
We will marry in September.
Please don't forget me.
Sheila
I wish we had fucked."

Daniel was not surprised by the letter. He was surprised that he wasn't heartbroken.

Nonetheless after a week or two he decided to make her a wedding present. He would paint her one.

He cut up twenty-five squares of paper, each two inches by two inches. He discarded them for being too sharp edged and instead tore up some other squares. This he did very carefully so that they were as square and as straight as he could get them, but they had soft, gentle edges.

On each square he wrote, with an italic calligraphy pen and black indian ink, the erotic lines which had been swimming in his mind for almost a year. He had not had the courage or the liberty to articulate them precisely.

He wrote the words with as much care and precision as he had torn the paper.

The words described a series of sensual images related partly to Daniel's memories of their couple of weeks together, partly to his fantasies of perhaps fucking Sheila for the first time but also related to context, to music, to smells and touches, to words which they would both think of at the same time but never say.

When Daniel had written all the words, he put the little squares of writing in order from top left to bottom right. Five squares by five squares.

He stuck the squares down on a sheet of black paper leaving a small gap between each of them. The gaps were not precise and uniform but were one eighth of an inch, or so.

He then painted over each square with a series of red or purple fluids. There was blood from his nose, blackberry juice, shoe polish, lipsticks [Gwen's], wood dye and wood varnishes, nail varnishes, cobalt violet watercolour paint and quinacridone magenta oil paint.

Some of the words were still partially legible, some were obliterated completely.

The black of the indian ink is permanent, and the words would always be there as they were written. However, the pigments of all the other dyes and stains would fade over time. Some would fade in a matter of weeks and the words would then be legible. Other pigments would take years to fade before the words are re-revealed and could be read.

Daniel sandwiched his gift with two sheets of greaseproof paper and two sheets of rigid card.

He posted it to Sheila with no accompanying letter. She did not reply.

Chapter 21

Tom was lost.

Tom and Emily were lost.

But it was Tom who was doing the driving and it was Tom who had the map.

It was Tom's fault that they were lost.

They were going to Londonderry for Daniel's and Sandra's wedding.

The old Triumph Herald was new to them. It was their first car. Micklam Brickworks had put Tom through his driving test just after the end of the war without giving him any lessons. He had driven various "shunting trucks" round the Micklam buildings but had rarely ventured out onto a main road. They had never driven anywhere further than Carlisle and here they were driving to Stranraer, taking the ferry to Larne and driving to Derry. Or even Londonderry. Whichever! When they crossed into Scotland at Gretna Green, Emily wondered out loud, "Why couldn't they 'ev eloped te 'ere and saved ivverybody a lot 'er bother?" Then again, "Nivver bin abroad."

"Scotland isn't abroad." Tom was nervous about whether he had the driving skills to get on a ferry, whether the old car would survive the pitching of the waves, whether he would make a fool of himself. But it was the middle of July and the weather was hot with no wind and a dark blue sky. The drive through the gentle hills of south west Scotland had been beautiful. They kept looking to see the sea of the Solway Firth. Would they see the mountains of the Like District? They did. Would they see Lowca? They didn't. And they were optimistic and happy. Tom managed to park properly on the boat, "Nae bother. Eh?" The Irish Sea was like glass.

On the boat they had pie and chips by a window. Emily said, "If some lass 'ez the courage ter marry 'im, we should 'ev the courage ter be theer fer them." Tom squeezed her hand under the table.

It was July 1972 and a lot of people were being murdered in Northern Ireland. Daniel had phoned Tom and Emily from Sandra's house on the Monday and suggested that it might not be wise to make the journey to Londonderry after all.

"Yer dad hez a new suit!"

Daniel had not invited anybody else to the wedding and the fact that he didn't have a 'best man' hung in the air as both an irrelevance and an embarrassment.

On the Tuesday, Daniel and Sandra had been shopping in 'The Diamond' in Londonderry town centre and two shops had "exploded" within a minute of each other. Though they were at least a hundred yards away they felt the blast. Daniel had felt that half second of "vacuum silence" before each of the explosions. He 'phoned Lowca' and spoke to his dad. He told him not to book the ferry crossing "just yet!"

"Yer mam's determined to come, she's mair worried aboot yer nut cutt'n yer hair!"

Daniel's hair was an issue for Sandra's mum, 'Minnie', also. She had already instructed Daniel not to open his mouth outside the confines of the house. "You will be taken for a soldier."

"With his long hair and his 'mutton chop sideburns'?" laughed Sandra.

"They give them wigs!" Minnie had said.

On the Wednesday Daniel and Sandra had dared to go back to the town centre to get a tie for Daniel and a stanley knife for Daniel to trim some new lino which Minnie had recently installed. On the way back there were two military vehicles and a squad of soldiers on Carlisle Road. They were under fire from who knows where. There was a succession of single gunshots.

Daniel and Sandra turned back towards the shops and found a deep doorway to hide in for a few moments. The single gunshots turned to machine-gun fire. Short half-second bursts. Daniel put his arms round Sandra and pressed her into the corner of the doorway. A girl in a cotton tunic with "McNeills" embroidered on it squeezed into Daniel's back. She was carrying two cardboard cups of 'Marchants' coffee.

She said something in a very strong accent which Daniel could not understand. Sandra firstly said, "No thanks." Then she said, "Yes please," and took one of the cups.

The girl said something else. Sandra replied, "No, it's perfect ... thank you."

The two girls chatted away.

Daniel kept his mouth shut.

Almost an hour passed before there was a long enough silence for Daniel to pop his head out of the doorway. There were no soldiers that he could see.

"We'll give it five more minutes," Daniel said. The shop girl looked at him. Sandra stared at him.

"Let's give it a go, now," said Sandra. "Are you up for it, Mary?" She looked at Daniel. "Me first, then Mary and 'Jimmy', you can be last and take whatever bullets might come our way!"

Daniel did not see himself as a 'Jimmy'.

Daniel phoned his mam and dad as soon as he and Sandra got back to the house. "We got stuck in the city centre because some people were shooting at some soldiers." Sounded so much tamer than most of the television news bulletins.

That hadn't put Tom and Emily off. They set off for the wedding as planned, and here they were on the Friday evening. Lost.

Half-way between Larne and Londonderry, roadworks diverted them into country lanes. What roadsigns there were had been vandalised. Some had been pulled down and lay in a ditch or a hedgerow. But the sun was shining and fields were full of crops.

"Nice drive," said Emily. But they were both getting a bit panicky.

Tom had assumed that if he continued to drive west into the sun, then surely Londonderry would appear before long.

"There's a crossroads cummen up."

"En a roadsign," replied Tom.

"Ballysummat," said Emily.

"Ballybofey," said Tom, "Bloody hell, we're in the Republic." He pulled onto the grass verge and studied the map. "We're miles away."

Tom was thinking about what to say to Emily to stop her going into one of her panics, but it was Emily who said, "It's nut dark yit, we'll git theer, yan way 'er anuther, if we git kidnapped en blown up wid a bomb, we've bin through wuss."

They laughed, both of them.

Daniel tried to help Sandra and her brother Robert with the

"emergency arrangements" but Robert told him, quite firmly, that an English accent would not be of any help.

Daniel made a pot of tea in Minnie's new teapot, but nobody seemed interested. He went into the kitchen and washed the teacups and rinsed out the teapot. He dried them, but not silently enough to stop Sandra glowering at him from the living room.

"I'll go into the yard and do some silent worrying!" he said. Sandra covered the mouthpiece of the phone and mouthed something incomprehensible.

Daniel moved the little deck chair out of the sun and into the shade. He sat up straight in the deck chair.

Daniel's mam and dad were two hours overdue. Daniel had a knot in his stomach. "Butterflies," he said out loud. Was he nervous about getting married the next day? Was he nervous about his missing parents? Was he nervous about being shot or blown up? Was he nervous about not being a good husband? "Allus git butterflies on Friders," he said.

Sandra joined him.

"Flutur!" Daniel said, "Romanian for 'butterflies'."

"Where?" said Sandra. "I'm sorry about all this."

"About all this what?"

Three birds scudded about the little yard making quick shadows on the wall.

"Look! Swallows! Aren't they an omen for weddings and stuff?"

"They might be, but they're not swallows!"

"Yes, they are. Look. They have swallow tails."

"No, they haven't. They have house martin tails, because they are house martins."

"They look like swallows. Are you sure they aren't swallows?"

"What was it you were sorry about?"

"Well, we can't get into the church. Nobody is answering a phone."

"Did yer try phonin' God?"

"Please don't!" Sandra sat on the brick floor and put her arms and her head on Daniel's lap. "Can't get hold of the hotel either."

"If the church is a "no go" area, we cancel the service and get married in a register office when we get back to England." Sandra didn't respond. "If the hotel is already booked and paid for then we go

231

ahead with the reception. We could even have a sort of ceremony at the hotel."

"It needs to be in the church. It's the church that has the licence."

"Look, sweet thing, you know I don't believe in God and all that." Daniel was struggling to get things out properly. He took his time and Sandra knew to wait. "If I did believe in God, I would believe that over the last week or so he has been sending me signals that there is something wrong." He stopped again. He played with Sandra's hair. "The bombs, the shootings, that girl you thought might have been a Catholic, my mam and dad going missing and hours overdue. Even the church is shut."

"Are you saying that we shouldn't get married?"

"I am saying that the only reason that I am still here is that I don't believe all that shit. The only thing I do believe in is us. The 'us' thing is tangible and true. That is why I am still here. The rest is all bollocks. The ceremony. The reception. None of that is real. It is only the 'us' bit that's real. ... And my stupid fucking mam and dad are lost, or blown up, or shot, or having a bloody cup of tea in Limafuckingvady."

"They'll be here soon. It won't be dark for a bit."

"I should have stopped them from coming. If I had been firmer with them, you know me mam, she would tell everybody for years that we wouldn't let them come to the wedding."

"Still, they are coming."

"The car could have broken down," said Daniel, "Or crashed!" Then again,"Or been hijacked by the IRA." Daniel giggled at the thought that the IRA would hi-jack a Triumph Herald.

"You just keep looking on the bright side!" laughed Sandra.

"Shit," said Daniel, "If they have got lost, they are in a car with an English numberplate."

"Well that's cheered us up, entirely," said Sandra, "All we need now is for the hotel and the church to cancel and our wedding day would be complete."

"In the context of what has been going on there would be a kind of cleanliness in that. A purity!" Daniel gently hugged Sandra's shoulders. "This is the furthest me mam and dad have ever been in the car. Dad let slip that up to now they had never driven anywhere that they had not previously been to on a bus."

"That's very sad," said Sandra.

"I would have thought that Dad at least would have driven down all those roads he had walked when he was looking for a job."

They moved the deck chair back into the sun. Sandra sat in it and Daniel sat on an upturned bucket.

"The house martins have a nest under next door's eaves." Daniel pointed.

"They are swallows!"

For all Emily's false optimism, they found the country roads around Londonderry difficult to navigate and it was dark before Tom drove across the "big bridge and straight over the roundabout and up the hill, take the third road on the right."

The door was opened by Sandra before they got out of the car. The couple from the "Bed and Breakfast" at the end of the street, where Tom and Emily were being "put up", came out to join in the hysteria of handshaking, hugging and dropped suitcases.

Minnie had splashed out on a very large tea-set for the wedding and sandwiches had been curling away under teatowels all evening.

The women sat and the men stood and anything that anyone said, however dull, was greeted with smiles and jollity.

Until Daniel said, "The wedding might be off."

It was only Tom and Emily who hadn't known.

Emily was sitting in the armchair by the fireplace. She sat up straight but only to stare at the empty grate. She had imagined that this wedding would be the one thing that her bloody son would get right and that all the pain he had brought to her for twenty-odd years could be put to bed. The three days of labour she had to go through, the numbness and the unknowing of the ceasarian, the ugly little thing in bandages given to her the moment she had woken up, that awful 'sadness' for two years afterwards.

The other people in the room just carried on talking. Emily fixed on the fireplace. Her shitty son deliberately getting lost in the rain just to make her life hell when Tom was out of work. Her bloomen son fighting with every boy in the village just to make her look like a bad mother. Ruining the 'confirmation' by being rude to the Bishop of

Carlisle. Her bloomen son doing his crap Art, instead of doing Maths at Manchester, just to spite her. Just to make people laugh at her.

What would she tell people in Lowca about going all the way to Ireland to have her son call the wedding off and having to come all the way back home in shame?

Tom was standing behind Emily and knew from her stillness that she was getting herself into a state. He caressed her shoulder.

Robert said,"There's a three-hundred-pound bomb in the hotel. We have only just got back."

That created a silence.

"They are sealing the city-centre off at midnight and the church is inside the city wall."

"We have to call the Army people at eleven," said Sandra, "and Robert's waiting for a call from the hotel."

"Mek's ooer la'al ... " Tom stopped himself, "It makes our little adventure ... We came the scenic route." Tom looked at Daniel. He knew that being several hours late must have caused a lot of anxiety, particularly for his son. "Yer cudda been playen cricket termorrer instead ev gitt'n married. Wukki'ten 'er allus asken when yer can play. Billy Moreton rang on Tuesder. Aah tell't 'im yer wur gitt'n married. He wanted ter knoa if yer cud play on Sunder."

"Driving overnight to Workington to play cricket would solve a lot of problems. Should I get my whites as well?" laughed Robert.

The couple from the "Bed and Breakfast" came to help Tom and Emily with their luggage.

"Cummon lass!"

Tom and Emily had never stayed in a hotel and they were both apprehensive. The house was not posh but their room was nicely decorated, the bed had lots of pillows, "proper feathers" as the landlady pointed out, freshly ironed linen and the poshest bit of all, it had its own bathroom, "En Suite" it was proudly proclaimed.

Emily claimed "fuss't go" of the bath and by the time Tom had taken his, Emily was seemingly asleep. The sounds of a city night were an excitement to Tom. He listened for gunfire, but the noises were dull ones from cars and lorries. He thought that he heard the low grinding noise of tanks and he may have been right.

Emily had been awake. She took Tom's presence in bed as a signal to chunter out the litany of pain her son had brought her. Her thoughts when she had been staring at Minnie's fire were poured out more gently on to Tom's armpit.

"En Suite. Eh!"

Robert took Daniel and his suitcase of wedding clothes to stay with cousin Ken across on the other side of the river.

The hotel where the reception was to be held didn't call Robert as promised, so Robert and Sandra called the hotel instead.

"I am calling about the wedding tomorrow, my name is Girvan."

Sandra strained to hear what was being said on the other side of the phone.

"The wedding which is planned and booked for sixty people at two o'clock," said Robert.

"Sandra snatched the phone from Robert. "Let me at her," she said, loudly enough to be heard by the girl on the other side of the call. "Can I speak to the manager please?"

"He has gone home I'm afraid. We have had a very trying day."

"So have I, young woman. You informed us this afternoon that there was a three-hundred-pound bomb in the building. We came to the hotel earlier this evening to find Jessica Clooney's guests hiding in the trees. The manager, can't remember his name, promised to call us by eleven."

"Oh! Sorry! The bomb was a hoax. Mr and Mrs Quinn had their wedding after all. They are still here as you can tell by the noise."

"Well, thank you. My family and friends can sleep soundly tonight." There was sarcasm in her voice, but Sandra was jigging up and down with delight. "I will see you tomorrow," she said, "If there are no more bombs."

"There is a note here for Mr Girvan. Is he still with you?"

"He is, but I can take any messages for him."

"I would prefer to speak to Mr Girvan."

Robert took the phone, Sandra didn't swear.

After a pause,"I will tell her that. Thank you."

"Well ..." cried Sandra.

"Lord Carrington, him from the government, is meeting some Army

235

Generals tomorrow and they have taken over the hotel. The place will be swarming with soldiers and the cars will have to park on the main road. Everybody will have to go through security."

"But we will still have the reception?"

"That's the other thing. The reception has been moved to the bigger "Antrim Room". It makes the security easier for them, but we don't get the French windows and the garden."

Sandra sank into the settee. "Daniel was right, we should have called the whole thing off on Monday."

Robert sat beside her. "When Dad died, I promised Mum that I would be like a father to you." His stutter came back before he finished his sentence,"God knows I haven't been that ... I haven't been a brother to you either." There was another pause, "I know this might not come out as I mean it to, but having to go through all this crap, being scared that we might all get blown up after all ... I mean you and Daniel have had to be really certain about your love to keep ploughing ahead instead of just fucking off back to England and living in sin."

"Where the hell did that come from? Never heard you swear before!" She got up and kissed the top of his head.

"This time tomorrow you will be really, really married."

Sandra cleared up and did the dishes, then went to bed. She was too numb to weep.

Tom woke up just as it was getting light. He wanted to make sure that he didn't embarrass himself, or Emily, or indeed Daniel. He tried to order his day.

First on his list was to find out if the wedding was going to take place. If "the game was on" he would have to shave very carefully. When he was tense, he had a habit of cutting himself when trying to shave too close.

Second was to make sure Emily didn't get into a state. Don't rush her. The odd hug might do well. Make a fuss of her.

Third was Daniel. How to support him? How to say the right thing when the lad must have been a bag of nerves for the last month? He must have been scared when the bombs went off and when he and Sandra had been caught in crossfire. Tom knew that there would have been other things, worse things, that Daniel hadn't told about. "He does get into scrapes," said Tom to himself, but he knew that was just too glib a statement. When Daniel had been caught in that storm coming back from Maryport, it wasn't "getting into a scrape". Tom was always certain that God played a part in that, that God was speaking to him by punishing his son. Why on the very day after the lad's triumph of passing the eleven plus, did he have that Gobbo lad knee him in the face so visciously? And why couldn't his lad have had a normal first date with a girl, with a cuddle and a kiss at the end of the evening, instead of having a nosebleed all over the girl's breasts? And why did God choose that Cup Final to give Daniel three broken ribs and a broken nose? Tom knew that it was God who made him change his mind about going to the Workington Town match and get off the bus to go instead to Daniel's game. He rarely went to Daniel's games. Why did he have to go to that particular one, to witness his son in so much pain? The bombings and the shootings that Daniel and Sandra had witnessed all seemed part of Tom's narrative with God and he was frightened for the day. "What else does God have up his sleeve?" he thought.

Tom rolled as gently and as silently as he could out of the bed and spent some time on his knees praying for his son as hard as he "bloody could".

At seven, Sandra was on the phone to a Major, a Brigadier and then a different Major, sorting out permissions, protocols and procedures to get five cars through the single checkpoint at the city wall which gave access to First Derry Presbyterian Church. The Brigadier would only give permission for three cars.

"I am very sorry, my love, but I just don't have the manpower to make all the security checks." And then, as if to bring an emotional logic to his argument, "A woman brought a bomb in a pram on Tuesday."

"I understand," said Sandra. "Thank you anyway."

"I would set off at least an hour or two earlier than you have planned. There will be long queues!" Then as an afterthought, "You have a wonderful day ... in spite of everything."

Sandra phoned Ken, "Tell that future husband of mine that he is still getting married whether he likes it or not!" She explained the formalities of getting through the checkpoint. "We are only allowed to take three cars so can you and Daniel just walk?"

"He asked me last night if I could fill in as Best Man. I don't mind doing that, but I am not comfortable making a speech."

"You just get him to the church, Ken, and you will be the best 'Best Man' he has ever had." They laughed, "Oh and tell him he has to wear the white shirt and not the pink one with the silly collar."

So, Daniel set off walking to his wedding, a two-mile walk. At Ken's suggestion they put their suit jackets, shirts and ties in Daniel's suitcase, with a towel and some deodorant. "It's a hot enough day." Ken gave Daniel a "City of Derry Rugby Club" tee-shirt to match the one he was wearing himself.

"We'll look cool at least," said Daniel, "Are you up for keeping them on for the wedding ceremony itself?"

"She would kill you ... then she would kill me."

Tom finished his "Irish breakfast". He ate some of Emily's sausages and bacon.

"You ga'an 'ev a bath lass en mek yersel look beautiful. Ah'll ga' en see if owt needs daein'."

He knocked on Minnie's door and was immediately offered a cup of tea. "No thank you. I've had a huge and excellent breakfast, thank you. Perhaps later. I have come to see if there is anything I can do to help?"

Minnie reluctantly asked him to clear out the back yard and move the dining room table and chairs outside as if for a picnic.

Tom was happy. He took pride in arranging things neatly. The furniture made the back-yard look quite roomy. For want of anything left to do he sat on one of the chairs. He heard again the sounds of what he now knew were tanks. Several of them. They made the table vibrate.

Minnie startled him, "Half my relatives and what's left of my husband's family will come back here after the reception and I needed to clear some space. Thank you!" She sat down in the sunshine directly opposite Tom.

"Your Sandra is a bonny lass. I am sure she could do better than my lad."

"She worships Daniel."

"He comes with a lot of baggage."

"They each seem content with their choices."

"Has he behaved himself while he's been with you?"

"He's been lovely. I told him not to speak when he is out, just in case they think he is an English soldier!" They both laughed at that.

"He makes up for it when he is in the house though."

"He's been angry for a long time now. Sandra has calmed him down. How old was she when her father died? Sorry that was a bit personal."

"No, it's not personal at all. She was nine, Robert was fourteen and it was harder for him. Alec was ill for so long, the last few months in hospital. We had a routine when we visited him. Me and Robert, Me and Sandra then me on my own. The visits were the high point of Alec's day and they were happy visits. For Sandra it was time with her dad being funny and loving. For Robert it was watching his dad getting worse every week. Then dying in great pain. In the last few weeks when he was too ill to receive visitors, Robert and Sandra had to stand in the grounds of the hospital so that he could see them one last time. The poor things couldn't see which window Alec was looking out of, so they waved at every window in turn."

"And you?" said Tom, "They will have been watching you all the time, ez well."

"I just chugged on. Like you do. I had Robert and Sandra." Minnie sat up straight, "Robert was good at school, played in the school rugby team, got to do maths at Queens ... very proud of him, but there was always pain."

Tom thought that he should fill the silence with a response or another question; he thought that he had gone too far already. But Minnie renewed her story. "Sandra was always top in every subject at school. When she passed her eleven plus, it was nice, but I couldn't afford the expense on what I earned. All sorts of people came knocking at the door telling me how bright she was and that it would be a tragedy if she didn't go to the Grammar School." She paused again and this time Tom just waited. "Tragedy!" she said. Tom understood. "So, she went; and came top in everything again. She was always very happy. She was a good runner. She was a debating champion. She was the 'All Ireland Temperance Champion'! She has a cup in a cupboard somewhere."

"And here is the 'All Ireland Temperance Champion" hersel!"

"What has she been telling you?" said Sandra from the doorway.

"She has been telling me how wonderful you are, and we both thought that there's still time for you to run away and find somebody better looking than Daniel."

"Our 'first date' was on the Reading University running track. He gave me ten yards start and caught me in sixty! That was good enough for me. If I did 'do a runner' he would always catch me."

"Maybe I should go and put me new suit on," said Tom. He didn't know if people in Londonderry kissed each other on the cheek in such circumstances. He settled for an embarrassed little wave of his hand.

Daniel and Ken caused some amusement at the checkpoint claiming to be on their way to get married wearing rugby club tee-shirts. Daniel slipped his suit jacket on. "Cool," said a soldier. "English?" whispered another. "Good luck, Sir," said an officer.

The cool air inside the church was very welcome. They were ninety minutes early.

Two 'church ladies' showed them to the vestry and offered tea. "You poor lamb," one said,"Getting married with no flowers."

The other 'lady' said, "You can change here. We promise not to peek."

Daniel left Ken to change and wandered round the church guessing at the architectural heritage of the place. "Neoclassical frontage with Scottish Baronial interior." He hadn't expected anything so grand and imposing for something 'Presbyterian'; he had imagined something more 'chapelly'. He hadn't been inside a church since his Confirmation. He wondered if the wedding service would provide some kind of spiritual experience. He wondered if it was supposed to.

Tom and Emily, mindful of "mam's la'al legs" set off early for the walk to the church. The lady from the Bed and Breakfast had given them a small white rose each from her garden. Suitably garlanded they were able to stroll in the sunshine, arm in arm as far as the pedestrian checkpoint. In the small queue they noticed several others wearing the same variety of rose. They each nodded and smiled. The engagements with the soldiers were jolly and polite. Without introductions they all walked together up the imposing steps and into the church. Daniel was in a chair in the vestry. Ken joined him and helped in the flurry of introductions, handshakes and smiles.

"Posh church," said Tom.

Daniel thought that at this time he should be saying something meaningful and uplifting, like a pre-match team-talk. But nothing would come out and he worried that he might screw up his bit of the performance of the service. He suddenly remembered 'the ring', but in his panic of failing to find a little jewel box in any of his jacket pockets, he found the ring loosely stored in the back pocket of his trousers. He gave it to Ken.

"Shouldn't it be in a little box?" Emily asked.

"It's in my pocket now," Ken said. "It's in my hand; my hand is in my pocket. It will stay there until somebody tells me to give it to Daniel, the groom. Why don't we go to our seats and wait to see if Sandra turns up?"

Sandra, her mother, Robert, Melanie the bridesmaid and Auntie Doreen, who was terminally ill and needed to be 'delivered' to the chuch, stood in the living room waiting for the limousine.

Sandra wanted a pee. "Too late now," she said to herself, "I'll just have to thole." In her childhood fantasies she had imagined many times going out through the front door and into the wedding car and the street would be full of cheering neighbours. Her father Alec was always there in these dreams. She followed Robert through the front door. She wanted to say, "Will there be room in the car for my dad?" but she was taken by surprise and silenced by cheering and clapping from twenty or thirty women and children in the street. Doreen, Minnie and Sandra took up the main seat. Melanie sat in one of the ancillary seats.

"Can't change your mind now!" she said. Robert was struggling to lock the front door with the wrong key. He eventually got in the car and when it set off Auntie Doreen said, "All aboard the Skylark."

The traffic checkpoint was a problem. The limousine had to be thoroughly checked and Sandra and her entourage had to get out and be searched. The Major told them that they had to walk the four hundred yards to the church. Minnie shoved Sandra out of the way so that she could let rip at the soldiers about her daughter's "Big Day" and Auntie Doreen and her cancer. "Have you got a comfy chair?" said Doreen, "Leave me here with these nice soldiers and you go on to the church. I'm sure they won't mind looking after me, will you boys?"

A Sergeant whispered something to the young Major and the party was allowed back into the car for the last part of their journey. It wasn't easy getting Doreen up the steps. Robert and Melanie almost carried her. From a small crowd of wellwishers outside the church two men came to help, "You get in there, wee girl, we will get her in and get her sat down comfortably for youze."

The minister was an old family friend of Minnie and Alec and he had come on the train from Belfast and had known nothing about the shutdown of the city. He had problems at the checkpoint and had to open his case to show his robes to the soldiers. He was obviously quite frightened as he greeted Minnie with a "God bless you Minnie! What has become of us?"

"Oh! Sweet child!" He held Sandra's hands together. "God is with us. God is with us. He will see us through."

As Sandra, Robert and Melanie lined themselves up for the procession down the aisle, "Ready?" the minister said, "Hope he's worth it?"

Daniel turned to look at Sandra as the organ sounded. He knew and expected her to look beautiful; he was surprised that his response was that he needed her so much. The traumas of the week, the monotonous terror, the expectation of disaster were all things he could handle. What troubled him was the potential for something spiritual to happen. Something which didn't happen at his Confirmation. For his inadequacies and his isolations to be exposed.

The minister, still full of fright, raced through the service. He unilaterally cut it down to a bit of scripture, two hymns (but not all the verses) and no sermon.

The ring was put on the Bible. The Bible shook to the nervous rhythms of the minister's hands. The ring fell off the Bible. Daniel caught the ring before it hit the floor with a swift swoop of his hand. He kept hold of it until it was time to put it on Sandra's finger.

The minister did not say, "You may now kiss the bride!" so Daniel took it on himself. He may have been a couple of sentences of the service early.

The vestry did not have the same architectural splendour as the rest of the church. It was in every sense, an ante-room.

However, the church had a rich and powerful organ and whoever was playing it was delighting in producing sustained melodic chords.

Daniel said "Bach!"

Sandra said "What?"

Daniel said, "Have we got a proper pen to sign things with?"

Robert, from behind said, "Yes," and offered a small presentation box inside which was a 'Parker' pen. Daniel imagined that it was the same type of pen which his grandmother had kept in her bureau. It wasn't. It was just the same shade of red.

"It was a nice thought," said Daniel out loud.

"It was my dad's," said Robert.

Sandra filled up just a little as she screwed off the top of the pen.

Daniel bent to whisper something into Sandra's ear, but whatever it was, he thought better of it. But it looked like a gesture of love to the little crowd round the big desk.

The minister led everyone swiftly out of the vestry to begin the procession down the aisle. The organist moved seamlessly out of 'Bach' into something Daniel recognised but could not name. Sandra's arm held Daniel back to her own pace.

The church's big doors were slowly opened. They walked in to an explosion of sunlight and warm air and gunfire.

The well-wishers, "confetti addicts", about fifty of them, were scuttling down the steps and into the road below the city wall. The ones who could run, ran. The ones who couldn't run, swung their arms, their hips and their buttocks as fast as they could up the road or down the road. There were several overlapping "God bless youze" shouted back to Sandra and Daniel. There was no screaming. The wedding photographer abandoned his camera on its tripod and scooted round to the other side of the limousine. He crouched as low as he could. He shouted something about getting down the steps and something else about "the line of fire."

Tom and the minister had, on instructions from the photographer, closed the church doors so that he could get a good "shot" of the "couple" on their own at the top of the steps in front of "the church's famous neo-classical façade".

Behind the doors, Tom was anxious. "It's been a bit," he said, "Should I pop oot and have a lewk?"

"Get back in Dad!" shouted Daniel. Tom looked about to see where Daniel was shouting from. Daniel ran up the steps and shoved his dad back through the door. "There's some shooting."

Someone shouted, "Usual procedures please. Back to your pews if you would."

There was no panic.

A different voice bellowed, "William! Some dance music if you would, please."

Daniel danced down the steps to get in the limo with Sandra, the photographer and the driver.

"We're safe here," said the driver. "We're way below the wall. They can only see the upper part of the church."

Six or seven soldiers arrived. Two of them went into the church and closed the doors behind them.

A small military vehicle appeared fifty yards up the road.

A sergeant went to the limo. "Who is in charge here?"

"You are, at the moment," said Daniel.

"Good answer! Geordie?"

"No! Cumberland."

"Forces?"

"With this hair?"

"They give us wigs!"

"I just want to go home with my new wife."

"Well, let's get you out of here."

As he was speaking Minnie and Doreen were being helped down the steps to the car. An extremely armed soldier led the way.

Daniel and Sandra got out of the car to let them in.

Ken put his arms round both Sandra and Daniel. "I should stay back and help clear the church. I know most of the crowd and we'll get them to the hotel, one way or another."

Daniel turned to Sandra. He gave her a small hug. A voice from the church doorway shouted, "Can't you two wait until tonight!" And thirty people, who were trying to escape gunfire, broke into laughter.

"Sandra, Minnie and Doreen in the back," said Daniel. "My mam and Melanie on the bench seats, Dad, sit on the floor, bloody hell, you're covered in brick dust!"

"The shots hit the top of the columns and sprayed grit everywhere," said Robert.

"Happens all the time," said a soldier.

"Robert and me in the front with the driver." Daniel turned to the soldier. "Do you want to ride 'shotgun' with us? There's some beer at the hotel when we get there." Everyone laughed.

"That's very kind, Sir!" he smiled."We have to convoy everybody out of the church and get back to the checkpoints."

"Corinthian!" said Daniel.

"What?" said Robert.

"The columns, they are Corinthian columns."

"I hope there's a beer at the hotel for me when we get there," said the driver.

"Lucky Sandra," said Robert.

The hotel looked a haven of peace when the limousine got through the brief security check.

"I would have thought that the place would be crawling with soldiers."

"It is!" said the receptionist. "You just can't see them. Some on the roof," she added.

"We booked a room for the afternoon ... to change in," said Sandra.

"Room 106, almost next door to The Antrim Room."

"Give us five minutes," Sandra said to Daniel. "Melanie and I need to freshen up." Then she whispered, "I need to pee."

Daniel headed to the main entrance to greet people as they came in.

The guests came into the hotel in large bunches. After parking their cars on the main road and getting through the checkpoint, they slowed down for each other, and others hurried to catch up. Daniel shook hands with a few of them, but nobody offered their name or attempted to make any introductions. Four large men in black suits and polished army boots placed themselves strategically so that the guests were left in no doubt where The Antrim Room was located. Everyone was being watched, very closely.

"A man hasn't looked at me like that since I had a bosom," whispered one.

"It's a good job I have my best underwear on," laughed her friend.

"Photographs," said Robert.

"Just the First Team," said Sandra, "The hotel staff are getting fidgety about timings."

The photographer hovered just outside the main entrance. Daniel and Sandra went to see him. "This place is usually great for background and settings, but the Army have most of them sealed off."

"Where do you suggest?" asked Sandra.

"Just out here!" he said. "No cars about."

The various compilations of families and friends were organised into standing positions. It didn't take long. Everyone was happy, compliant and considerate.

"There's a little copse over in the corner there, some nice romantic shots of just the two of you, away from everyone."

"Sounds lovely." Sandra looked to Daniel for approval.

Daniel said nothing. There was a bank of red hibiscus and pink lavatera in a shaft of sunlight, behind which there was a dark stone wall in full shade.

"What lovely colours," said Sandra.

"I think you will find that the photos will be black and white'," said Daniel.

The photographer smiled and nodded. "'Fraid so! Just relax, stand together as if you love each other. Try not to pose."

Half a dozen shots in the warmth of the sun and the silence of the wood and Sandra said, "I'm happy." She whispered, "I am so glad we saw it through."

"Shit!" said Daniel.

"Sorry! So sorry."

The beautiful red hibiscus was an armed soldier.

"Carry on as if I am not here."

Sandra still could not see him, but she saw his rifle and the top of his helmet. "Don't scream or owt."

"This has to be my best, ever shot," said the photographer. "I'll win a prize with it."

The soldier came up from his prone position and rested on his knees. "Please don't make a fuss," said the soldier.

"Can I at least take a shot with the three of you together?"

"Only if you stop using the word 'shot'. Sir!" the soldier said. "Perhaps the word "photo" would be more sensitive in the circumstances."

Three quick photographs were taken. "Please! As far as your other guests are concerned, this did not happen, and the photographs will remain private." The soldier stared menacingly at the photographer before he went back to being an hibiscus. "Congratulations both," said some leaves.

The Antrim Room was large enough to mingle in and still have room for the banquet. Robert fussed and buzzed round his mother and his extended family. He wasn't sure of all their names. For want of conversation he told each that the vicar had 'escaped' to the train station. People smiled.

The hotel staff ushered the guests to the tables.

"I'll say grace if you don't mind Sandra," said Robert.

When everyone was settled, Robert stood up, put on his teacher's stare and scanned the room. Summoning his "quadratic equations" voice he said, "Dear God, thank you for bringing these wonderful families safely together round this table." He paused, quite deliberately, "Yet another meal which has been the setting of your miracles."

There was a sustained pause, Robert's "Grace" had put the troubles of the day in context. Daniel looked across the 'top table' from Minnie to his right who was already talking to Tom. Melanie was chatting to Ken. "Maybe?" he thought, then "Naah!" To Sandra's left was Emily, then Robert. Emily was in her element telling Robert about 1930s maths and how Daniel had disappointed everyone by "daein' Art" instead of maths "at Manchester".

Daniel ate his meal as best he could. Sandra picked at hers.

"You know that you still have to make a speech."

"Yiss. Aye." said Daniel.

"Do you know what you are going to say?"

"No! Not yet. But I thought that I would say it in "Lowca"so that nobody would understand it and then nobody would be offended."

"Good," said Sandra.

He only needed the first sentence of what he was going to say, then he knew that everything else would follow. "Like singing," Daniel said out loud.

Sandra watched every one of the guests, and if eye contact was made, she smiled. In doing so, she commanded the room. She doubted she would see many of them ever again.

She was "Off."

With Daniel.

She put her hand on Daniel's hand, "Time for you to speak," she squeezed his hand, "Let them have it."

Daniel stood up. He rattled a fork in a wine glass to get everyone's attention.

"Thank you! Sandra and Minnie have been telling me for some time that most of their relatives are teetotal, "drink never passes their lips". Yet how swiftly you all fell silent at the tinkling of a wine glass. I must say that you all seem so much nicer and more civilised than Sandra, Robert and especially Minnie described you. "Daniel paused. "The original 'Best Man', my friend Jugdeep Johal, was very grateful when I called him to tell him that in the circumstances it would not be wise for him to come. When he played Ulster at Ravenhill last season he was constantly asked whether he was a 'Catholic Muslim' or a 'Protestant Muslim'. He was too scared to say that he was a 'Sikh Muslim' in these environs, at this time."

Daniel turned to Ken. "Thank you, Ken, for filling in at the last moment so brilliantly and so courageously."

"Courage is the constant theme of what I have to say. I must pay tribute to Minnie, Robert and Sandra for their enormous courage in dealing with Alec's painful and protracted death when Robert was fourteen and Sandra was just nine. For them to have brilliant careers at school and at Queens University is a tribute to them, as well as Minnie. It would have been so easy on so many occasions to just give up. My family are a courageous lot also, over the years standing up for what is right in a tight and insular community, not only that, but coming all the way from Lowca, via Carlisle, Stranraer, Larne, Ballybofey [I know! I know!] to Londonderry for this wedding. But more than that, it is the courage and dignity of you all, here today, that I must pay tribute to. That you came to the service, in spite of the closure of the city centre and the bombs and the bullets. Sandra and I won't forget the lack of screaming, the lack of panic; how you all calmly helped each other out of, and away from, the church. That every one of you made it here to the hotel for our reception. God, what you all went through just to get a free dinner." Not everyone laughed.

"Today, we all witnessed and were nearly the victims of, one group of Christians shooting and trying to kill another group of Christians coming out of a church. This is an evil beyond my understanding. The spectacular neo-classical façade of that church had its architectural roots in pagan buildings of ancient Greece and Rome, two thousand years ago, and is all the more glorious for that. Christianity was brought to this part of the world thirteen hundred years ago." Daniel paused for effect. "By foreign immigrants."

"Today Sandra and I went into woods over in the corner of the hotel grounds. Several options were open to us. But we opted instead for the photographer taking photos of us away from our families. We stumbled on a soldier disguised as an hibiscus. He was in full military garb, machine gun, various hi-tec bits and bobs patched on to his helmet and bullet-proof vest. He was the same age as Sandra and me; that he was courteous and engaging made the encounter more surreal. Was this a divine joke being played on us? When the photos were done, he reverted to being an hibiscus."

"When I was young, I tried so hard to be a good and devout Christian. I failed rather badly. I have a certain expertise and understanding of European Religious Art. But I don't understand anything of what has happened today and in recent weeks. Love and courage might help. I know that there is plenty of both in this room at this moment."

"Minnie! When Sandra was going off to Reading University a couple of years ago, you said to her,"You go off and get yourself a nice, handsome, young English man who wears a suit and tie for his breakfast." I must have been a great shock and disappointment to you."

"To all of us!" said one of the guests.

When the laughter died down, Sandra looked up to Daniel lovingly and said,"Love you!"

"Whether you are tee-total or not, I ask you to put some wine in your glass, stand up, and help me toast Minnie, Robert and Sandra, as well as Tom and Emily."

When everyone had got to their feet, Daniel said, "To love and courage."

"To love and courage."

Daniel was surprised by what he had said in his speech. He had never been to a wedding before. He had no idea what a groom's speech was supposed to be about. If it was about being upright and strong to honour his bride, Sandra, at the beginning of their marriage then he would find out soon enough if he'd said the right thing. If it was about making a favourable impression on Sandra's extended family, it probably wasn't very good. As for his own family, Emily said for the hundredth time, "Yer tongue will git yer hung," as if it were the family motto. Emily had been afraid of what he was going to say and had tried to focus on a tree outside in the garden, to turn off, to lock herself away from Daniel's horrid jokes. But she sensed a warmth in the room and had started to listen.

It occurred to Tom that he had never heard Daniel 'speak'. He had of course heard him 'talk' in conversation; as a child he was wonderful to engage with as he would excitedly describe things he had seen for the first time. Tom had listened to Daniel's long silences, that time when he was out of work, and wondered what pain he had caused his lad. He had thrilled to talk rugby with Daniel on the bus home from Workington. But Tom had never heard him 'speak', had never heard him give a team-talk in a rugby changing room. He had never heard him give a lecture on Rembrandt, or say anything pre-meditated, thought out, uninterrupted. Daniel's 'Wedding Speech' was a shock to Tom; there was so much in it. If the speech had been written in a magazine by some anonymous journalist Tom would have found it quite interesting, informative and in the the bit about "Christians shooting at Christians", powerful and passionate. But this was his son, 'Speaking'! Making some people laugh, making most people angry. It excited Tom how fluent, eloquent and authoritative Daniel was. Tom thought back to 'the Confirmation' and how beautifully Daniel sang all the hymns, how softly, how pure his voice was. Tom had missed Daniel's rant at the Bishop, but the Reverend Nidd had told him "Daniel was thunderous, poetic even."

Tom filled up a little, either at those old, painful memories or at what Daniel was saying in his speech.

Much later, Tom said in his best enunciated voice, "You still seem angry about things son. Ah'm sorry about the Confirmation thing. It must have seemed like ah stole summat from yer."

Daniel froze a little. 'The Confirmation' had never been mentioned in ten years.

He wanted to say to his dad that over the years he had taken great strength from Tom's religious certainties. Daniel wanted to say also that he would always be grateful that his dad's faith took away a great burden from his thirteen-year-old shoulders and allowed him to grow, to be free and to know who he was. But, of course, it wouldn't come out. "Ah've used up all mi good words for one day," he said as an afterthought. A joke. But Tom was already talking to one of Sandra's uncles about cricket.

CHAPTER 22

Some years later Tom and Emily went to Northamptonshire to stay with Daniel, his wife Sandra and five-year-old daughter Rachel for a couple of weeks. They were half-way through their stay when Tom, catching Daniel alone, said, "I think this might be that lass frae London."

He gave Daniel an A5 white envelope.

"It hezn't bin oppened er owt."

On the top left-hand side of the envelope there was a tiny, hand-written, "Sheila Morrison" and an address in Cheyne Walk.

Daniel opened it and there was just a 6"x 8" photograph. It was indeed Sheila. There was no letter.

Daniel put it back in the envelope.

"Nae worries lad, yer mam hessn't been near it."

"Must be nearly twenty years," Daniel said.

It wasn't until the following day that Daniel could find the space and the time to look at Sheila's photograph. It was a full-length colour print of her standing in what Daniel soon remembered was her mother's purple, shot silk, dressing gown. This time there was no doubt that she was naked underneath. She looked remarkably fit, slim and toned for someone who would now be in her forties. She had long hair flopping over one shoulder, as ever, and it was going grey, very slightly. She was still very, very beautiful. Her nipples pressed against the silk of her gown. Sheila's arms were tucked behind her back.

She was on tiptoe and she was standing by a modern French window.

Daniel checked the envelope and made a note of her address.

She hadn't changed her name then. Did she ever get married?

Daniel couldn't work out why Sheila had sent the photo without at least a covering note, and in spite of Tom's assurances that his mam hadn't been near it, he was sure there was something amiss.

Daniel put the photo back in its envelope. He put it in his studio.

When his mam and dad had gone home Daniel thought about telling Sandra. Sandra knew about the girl that he had bled all over on his first ever 'date', but Daniel thought it best to try and find out if there had indeed been an accompanying letter from Sheila.

"I will write to Sheila," he thought, "Find out if there was a letter with the photo and let her know that I am married with a kid."

That sounded like a good plan.

Except that he forgot, for some time.

Then, while he was waiting in his studio for a life model to arrive, he grabbed a pencil and small sketch pad.

"Dear Sheila,

It was a beautiful shock to receive your photo. It was eventually secreted into my hand by my dad when my parents came to visit. He assured me that the envelope had not been opened, but there was no letter, just your photo!

'Just your photo' indeed!

I was shocked that you still look so stunning, so young. Nobody would comment on our age difference now. I remember the dressing gown in the photo, it was your mother's and you wore it after you showered all my blood off your body that first night that we were together."

This was turning into a love letter and that was not his intention.

"I live in the anonymous Midlands now, only an hour north of London. I did a degree in Fine Art at Sunderland, and then did a teaching thing at Reading. It was at Reading that I met Sandra. Sandra is bright and very beautiful. She laughs with me and at me, she comes to watch me play Rugby, she believes in me and teaches me to believe in myself [an ongoing task], I weep when she is not there.

We were married in Londonderry at the very height of 'the troubles'. We were bombed, shot at, caught in crossfire, all that sort of stuff.

So far, so ordinary.

Then a few years later along comes Rachel, a daughter, and she changed my life, she changed my painting, she changed my sense of self.

Sandra is Head of a local school and I paint, so it is always me who jumps into my car to go and pick Rachel up from school. By the time

Sandra gets home I am lying on the settee with a coffee and a biscuit and Rachel is sitting on my chest with milk and a scone watching Floella Benjamin on the telly.

I am preparing for an exhibition in New York in October and I will miss three games of rugby.

We play most of the big teams in London.

My nose no longer bleeds. It is now more of an extension of my forehead than an adornment of my face. I cannot really breathe through it.

I still go to the Tate, three or four times a year. I always look for you there, especially by the Rodin 'Lovers'. I have a little speech prepared in my mind for if we ever met. I would take you for a posh coffee in the 'Members Café'. We would catch up on twenty years or so. That is the fantasy!

The reality, as we both probably know, is that greeting you with a hug and a peck on your left cheek would turn as quickly as a breath into a full kiss and I would bleed all over you and your [probably maroon!] coat. And before we looked at a painting we would be running down the steps of the Tate and up the road to "try and find a room" I am afraid of that!

I have managed 'the fidelity thing' so far. Sometimes it's easy, sometimes it's tough. Those couple of weeks with you were an important milestone in my life. And you, Sheila, remain one of the most important people in my life. A few Olympian fucks in an accommodating bed, wonderful and life enhancing though they would be, are not worth the loss of what you and I share, nor indeed the profound love of my family. [Did I get those two in the right order?]

I am worried that your photo came without a written note. Maybe your commando breasts pressing against the silk of your mother's dressing gown was message enough. I would very much like to stay in touch.

Please write and tell me everything.

Lots of love
Daniel"

He enclosed his business card and a photo of Sandra, Rachel and himself pissing themselves with happiness in a swimming pool in Las Vegas.

Sheila never wrote back.

CHAPTER 23

Tom had his first stroke soon after he retired from work.

The phone rang, just before dinner. Daniel couldn't work out who was mumbling on the other end of the line. He waited only a few seconds before he hung up.

"Nuisance call," he said to Sandra.

"Probably my 'fancy man'."

Ten minutes later the phone rang again. "Who is this?"

There was the same incoherent mumbling and the background noise of a strong wind. But Daniel recognised his mam's voice.

"Are you all right Mam?"

"Dad's had a stroke an' ah haven't any more change."

And that was it.

Daniel and his family living four hours away was protection for everyone. Though they went up to Cumberland three or four times a year, it was always only ever for a day or two.

Daniel still irritated Emily. He was never the son she had hoped for. She hadn't been the mother she had dreamed of being.

Sandra was Head of a Secondary School now, with a range of all-enveloping responsibilities and Rachel, thirteen, had her own dramas and crises.

"I'll pack some clothes in case I have to stay."

"Are you going right now?"

"I can get there by eleven. That won't be too late."

Daniel meant that he could get to his mam to look after her, to make sure that she ate and didn't get confused. Drive for her. Make sure she went to bed instead of sitting up all night fretting. Rachel had a different interpretation.

"Grandad's going to die then?"

"Put something to eat in a box for me and make me a flask of tea."

He went up to change and pack.

He was only a few minutes, but Sandra had made hot sandwiches with a couple of the lamb steaks they were going to have for dinner. Rachel had a pear, an apple and a packet of chocolate hobnobs wrapped in some foil. She had a letter in her hand, "Please get this to Grandad before he dies."

Rachel had a direct connection to her grandparents which Daniel envied.

Daniel was aware that Emily had once said, "Why couldn't we hev hed her instead ev him?" Actually, she said it quite a lot.

"I'll phone when I get to a 'services'. I'll have to fill up at about Tebay."

"I'll ring people up there, see if they know anything. I bet she'll have called Gwen, or Margaret maybe."

The M6 used to be quite a nice road before it became too crowded, and guiltily Daniel enjoyed the drive. He enjoyed his dinner in the dark of the car. He got to Tebay in three hours. He phoned Sandra and a teary Rachel.

"What's in your letter?" Daniel asked.

"That's private, it's adolescent drivel, it's a 'churchy' thing and I don't want you to read it. You'll only sneer."

She gave the phone to Sandra.

"Your mam rang again. I think she is at the hospital. Margaret is with her and she is more coherent. They will stay at the hospital at least until you get there."

There were a lot of "love you"s in the call.

Daniel got to Whitehaven Hospital and in trying to find the ward that Tom was in, he was, for the first time, filled with the panic that he might be too late. Too late for his dad.

When Daniel got to the bedside Tom did indeed look dead. He had tubes in him, an oxygen mask, and a monitor was bleeping. Emily had nodded off in an armchair. Margaret was of course knitting.

There were silent hugs as Daniel's mother woke up.

"You took a long time," she said.

"Ah couldn't git any sense out 'ev the nurse," said Margaret, "You ga'an smile at her, she'll tell you."

Daniel was directed to Tom's doctor. "The son from far away!" She was Asian, with a Yorkshire accent. She put down her cup of coffee, smiled and shook his hand.

"Your father has had a stroke, quite severe. We have stabilised his situation, but he is not out of the woods yet. As you may have seen, there is a paralysis discernible on his left side."

She got out from behind her desk to take Daniel to his Dad's bed.

Dr Desail looked like Carmen Twentyman, the same posture, the same social command. Eternally eighteen.

She made checks at the bedside, and held Tom's now, 'good hand' with its leather cast. She rearranged a couple of the tubes coming 'from' or 'to' his arm.

"What is this?" She held up Tom's leather cast.

"He broke his wrist and some bones in his hand . . ." Daniel said.

". . . the bones won't knit together." Emily interrupted. She was fully awake now and 'Tom' was her territory.

"What did your father do for a living?"

"He's a check weighman," said Emily. Then she added, "Was." Confused, she filled up.

The doctor smiled but raised her eyebrows as a way of saying, "What the hell does a 'check weighman' do?"

Emily didn't respond, so Daniel said, "He's a sort of factory accountant, logistics, that sort of thing."

"Does that involve any hard, physical labour?"

"It did indeed."

"Stress?"

"Oh yes."

Emily was asleep again by the time Daniel got her home and when they went down the path she couldn't find her house keys. The contents of her handbag spilled out onto the ground and she got herself into a state.

"It's all right Mam, I'll try the back door."

"Back door is shut," she said sharply.

"So is the front door."

The back door was of course, open.

Daniel weaved his way through the kitchen, the dining room, the living room, each time searching for a light switch that he should have just felt for by instinct.

He got to the back of the front door in the hallway and opened it.

"Ken yer nut put a light on fer ez."

Daniel picked up the remnants of her handbag, which by now she was wearing on her arm like the Queen does.

"I'll make you some supper."

He made cocoa. They split a toasted teacake with marmalade.

"Couldn't yer put jam on it?"

"Couldn't find the jam."

"It's on't top shelf in the pantry."

"That may well be, Mam, but it isn't on yer teacake."

"It's allus on't top shelf."

"You must be exhausted Mam. You won't be much use to Dad if you fall ill."

"Ah'm oahreet."

"You have a lie in. In the morning, I'll go to the hospital first thing and see how things are, then come back for you."

She was starting to nod off again.

"Come on I'll help yer upstairs."

"Ah'm oahreet, ah said."

She had been angry with Daniel for forty years.

Daniel woke before dawn. The living room was merely untidy. The dining room was spotless and neat. The kitchen was a mess.

He did what cleaning he could in the kitchen, more as a penance than any desire to be kind and helpful. Through the kitchen window the dawn came very slowly. St Bees Head and a quiet sea, the other side of the valley going from Bransty to Moresby to Pica emerged in flat greys.

"I don't know how to do this caring thing," he thought.

He set a tray of breakfast out for his mam.

The kitchen didn't look too bad.

When he got to the hospital, he had to do some persuading to get to his Dad's bed.

"Breakfast 'n pills," said a nurse.

"I've had breakfast."

"No, I meant that the patients will be taking their breakfasts and their medications."

She smiled and looked at her paperwork. She glanced down the corridor. "Tom, isn't it?" she said. "Yes, go on then. You might just catch the doctor with him."

"Doctor Desail, is it okay for me to come in?"

Carmen Twentyman smiled at Daniel too, and held out her hand.

"Have you been here all night?" he asked.

"Your dad has been awake. He is a lovely man, isn't he?"

"Er! Yes! What's the prognosis?" he nervously added, "Will he live?"

"Oh yes! I think that he'll fight his way through this. He'll be here for a bit though. We will keep him asleep for a day or two."

Daniel could see that Dr Desail wasn't Carmen Twentyman, but he didn't have to know that.

Daniel went back home for his mam. She was up, bathed and dressed and sitting in the dining room, drying her hair in the sunlight.

"Ah've hed a cuppa tea." She had ignored the breakfast tray that Daniel had laid out for her.

"Would you like me to take you out for a proper breakfast?"

"Yer doahn't hev te."

"I know I don't. But dry your hair properly and put your best coat on."

Daniel took her to the Wheatsheaf Hotel where Aunt Eva had once taken him for tea.

Guilt was the family currency and Emily was the treasurer.

Emily and Daniel did shifts sitting by Tom's bed.

They sat together for two hours with only the interventions of the nurses for dialogue and amusement. Emily had read that stroke victims can still hear and take in the surrounding conversations even when they look at their most comatose.

"What are you going to say, after forty-five years of marriage, which will upset him?"

"Even so."

"Besides, you and me sitting here saying nowt, will upset him more."

"Don't start."

A small deposit in the current account.

After a while Daniel stood up. "Would you like a magazine, or a paper? I'll go to the shop."

"How can a'ah read at a time like this?"

"Would you like a tea or a coffee?"

He took the silence as a signal for tea, milk, no sugar.

He brought her 'The People's Friend', 'Woman's Own', and as a special treat, a copy of 'Cosmopolitan', just so that she could reject it out of hand as "Bloomen rubbish."

"Just like a normal day. Cuppa tea and yer magazines."

"Shhh, Dad might hear." Daniel moved the bedside table round and put her tea and biscuits with her magazines.

"Write a shopping list and I will do a shop before I go home tonight."

The tears started after she had finished her tea.

They both knew that Daniel staying another night would drive her mad.

They both knew that there was nothing that either of them could do about Tom. "He's in the hands of better people than us, and we should accept that."

"You shudda bin' a doctor," Emily said.

"Where did that come from?"

"Lazy," she stuttered. "Ower many daft ideas."

"Let's get you home."

They both knew that Daniel wanted to go back home to Sandra and Rachel, that he would want to take Rachel to 'Orchestra', first thing on Saturday morning.

They both knew that he was in the middle of a heavy-duty painting.

They both knew that the team he coached, Rugby Lions, were playing Saracens at home on Saturday.

They both knew that, "Hevvin' te leave his dad's bedside just fer a rugby match," would be the story that would enter family folklore.

And who is to know that it wasn't the truth?

"You stay here, Mam, and I'll go and do a shop. Give me a key and I'll put it away before I come back here."

It was a lovely day and the supermarket was bathed in sunlight. Daniel bought the usual fruit, vegetables, salads and breads. He bought toilet rolls, cleaning stuff, polish. He remembered all the stuff they did not have in the house that time when his dad was out of work. He bought ten 'dinners for one' and a load of microwavable stuff. But mostly he bought everything he could think of which Emily would give him a hard time for 'forgetting to get'.

He took it all home and did a blitz on the kitchen to make room for everything he had bought. He did all the dishes, the cooker and stripped out the fridge and 'brilloed' all the pans.

While he was at it, he went to the downstairs loo and looked above the cistern to see if his 'hidey hole' was intact. It was, and he found a stack of old letters from his London friend, Sheila, and a very old copy of 'Penthouse'. He read every letter. He didn't really need to. He had learned them all by heart thirty years before. He put them in the bin and hid them under the older rubbish.

In the dining room sideboard he found a cardboard box full of the match programmes from his rugby playing days. His dad always asked him for them. Tom knew that Daniel used to make post-match notes in them, match scores, scrum scores, notes on hookers or tight head props. They looked a bit like his dad's notes in the match programmes at Workington Town. There must have been a couple of hundred of them.

Tom must have read, and studied, every one of the programmes.

Daniel put all the programmes back in what he thought was the order in which he found them.

The box itself was made of thick, heavy duty, pressed cardboard. A label on the underside indicated that it was a container for some kind of valve which had been manufactured in the USA. It must have been a Sellafield thing. Like his marbled edged ledgers were 'a Micklam thing'.

The ordering of the programmes, and his cataloguing, was perhaps Tom's way of numbering off Daniel's strides. As Daniel had once done for him.

Daniel thought about taking them home.

"But Dad's going to live," he told himself. Perhaps out loud.

"He'll want to browse them. He'll want to show them off again to his friends in the Brains Trust or at the cricket."

Daniel had a small weep.

Two hours later he was back at the hospital and Emily was in a better mood. She had seen Daniel coming down the corridor and quickly shoved the 'Cosmopolitan', which she had been reading, under Tom's bedsheets.

They sat there and happily talked about what Daniel had bought, and where he had put it.

Daniel was relieved that he was leaving.

Soon, there was a parade of Auntie Elsie, Margaret and John, and a woman called Beverley, from Church, bearing 'get well soon' cards from a dozen 'Church Women'.

Amid all the jollity and innuendo Daniel gave his mam a hug and a kiss.

Daniel wanted to do the same for his dad, but settled for, "Yer 'ave all these women chasen efter yer Dad, yer divvent need me." Then, "Aah'l be back on Munder."

He might have heard.

And that was the pattern for the next few weeks. Tom left the hospital. Got a wheelchair. He oversaw the installation of a ramp from the front door up the path to the road. He did the physio and the speech therapy.

Daniel went up regularly over that summer, sometimes with Sandra and Rachel, mostly on his own. They were happy visits, in their way.

Daniel had always tried to do drawings of Tom whenever he visited. It went right back to Daniel's schooldays. Sandra was never allowed in to Daniel's studio and was certainly never allowed anywhere near 'a sitting'. So, when Daniel took over the living room in Lowca to draw his dad this made her uncomfortable. However, it allowed for watching rubbish on television. Rachel thought that her dad was being selfish and that he was opting out of 'family stuff'.

"I'm not allowed to watch rubbish on television," she would say. Then, "Isn't it great?"

Daniel never drew his mam. She always refused. "Doan't like bein' stared at."

But when Tom and Daniel were alone, Tom not yet having fully regained his speech, Daniel sat drawing and Tom sat 'sitting', facing him.

This was new to Daniel. He had always drawn his dad 'dae'en summat', reading a paper, watching television. So, 'eye contact' had a new immediacy for both of them. Daniel struggled at first. In his normal portrait commissions, he preferred to have his sitters looking straight at him, at least for the initial stages. It gave him 'command'.

Men were often intimidated, surrendering to the situation by talking, telling stories, asking questions, "confessing". Women reacted to Daniel's gaze in many different ways. Some "posed". Some shrunk. Some melted.

But when Daniel was drawing his dad 'face on' he realised that most of their life had been 'side by side'. Walking together to rugby matches. Sitting on the front seats of the top deck of the Gosforth bus to let Tom smoke a quiet woodbine. Standing staring at the 'tippen oot' of the Bessemer converters by Harrington Bay. Sitting in the front pew of St Bridget's Church waiting to see if God would come to visit one, or both, of them.

In these late days when Daniel was looking at Tom and Tom was looking at Daniel, the 'looking' was enough. Tom, in his 'silent days' when he had just come home from the hospital, had rehearsed several versions of a speech that he would one day make to his son. He would apologise for the 'Micklam Time' when he couldn't put food on the table and Daniel went hungry and had difficulties in talking. He would apologise for not understanding how painful for Daniel it was when they got confirmed together. He would tell him that he now understood that his young son's courage in the front row of all those retreating scrums was the same thing which gave Daniel the unique power and elegance in his paintings.

When Tom's speech improved slightly, "Neether 'ev 'ez 'ev owt ter say!" was Tom's jocular way of saying that he quite liked the silence. That he quite liked being 'relaxed' with his son.

"Three 'ooers wid nae arguments. Eh! Is that a record fer us?"

Every drawing was the same pose; the head, sometimes the shoulders were drawn in to show the withering of the muscles on the left side; sometimes a couple of lines sufficed to support the position of the head. Daniel used the same sketchbook but used whatever pens and pencils were at hand in the Lowca house.

But each drawing explored the dimensions and spaces of 'this new face' Tom had, with its collapsed left cheek and eye, its drooping lop-sided mouth.

It was still 'his dad'. The same one he had been drawing for thirty years.

In one of the sittings, out of nowhere, Tom slowly, slurringly, said

"Aah'm glad yer ..." he stopped to regather his words, "Glad yer didn't gaa ter that public school."

"Where did that come from?"

"It wudda killed yer mam."

"It was Mam who wanted me to go," said Daniel, "Desperately, if I remember."

"Yer were the oaney thing that kept her ga'an."

Daniel carried on drawing.

Then he said, "It sometimes didn't quite feel like that."

"Nowt's ivver what it seems."

In another drawing session Tom, in more enunciated speech, came out with another rehearsed phrase. "You must repay all her love when I am ... ." he stuttered, then had almost to shout the final word, "DEED."

A little later, "Yer knoa wot aah mean."

CHAPTER 24

For thirty years or so, every time Daniel and his family went 'up to Cumberland' during the cricket season Tom would tell him to 'bring yer kit' and play for Workington. Daniel hadn't played for Workington since he was twenty or so.

"David Cordle is allus asken 'es te' tell yer te' cummen play when yer up."

"Dad, I've lost it. I just play now for the fun, and for the exercise."

"Yer were good when yer were young," he said, then, as an afterthought, "Yer've nivver done owt just fer't fun 'ev it."

It was Sandra who persuaded Daniel to play. She had talked to Emily on the phone to confirm the arrangements, "Tom sez ter tell Daniel ter bring 'is cricket kit."

"You tell 'himself' that." Sandra handed the phone to Daniel. He took it, thinking that it was still his mam on the phone, but it was Tom.

"David Cordle wants yer te play on Saterder if yer cummen up."

"Okay," Daniel said, "But tell him I am only playing for the seconds."

"Oah'reet." He sounded really pleased. "Mind on, mek sure thet yer kit's proper clean."

"Yes, I'll make sure that Sandra makes sure that my kit is clean."

"Hev yer got proper pads?"

"I bought new pads three years ago. They are perfectly white. I don't bat often enough or long enough to get them dirty!"

"See yer on Saterder." There was triumph in his voice.

"We're coming up on Friday. Late Friday. About ten."

"Whativver."

Sandra made a special effort with Daniel's cricket shirts. She ironed them as if they were dress shirts. She did her best with the grass stains in the 'whites', then ironed them too.

"You should really get a new set of whites."

"I'm packing in this season."

"You've been 'packing in' for the last twenty years."

"I don't usually get nervous before a game of cricket these days, do I?" On the way up the M6 Daniel had to stop twice for 'comfort breaks'.

"Haven't seen you like this since your rugby days."

"Don't worry Dad. You'll get a hundred and take four wickets. That's my prediction." Rachel reached forward from the back seats and kissed the back of her dad's head then returned to her book.

"I can't believe after all the front rows that you played against that you have let yourself get into this state. What's a game of cricket compared with all that? If you had ever been any good at cricket there might be a point in getting the pre-match shits."

"Thank you for your support and encouragement. For some reason it's important to him. I hope I don't let him down."

"You have been letting him down since you were ten years old."

Sandra had way of allowing Daniel to know his place.

"Y'ev ter play in't fuss't team terday."

"Dad." Daniel took a deep breath, "I told you that I would only play in the 'seconds'."

Tom looked hurt.

"It pissed down in the night," Daniel said. He looked out of the dining room window for signs of a cloud. It was a beautiful, hot, day. St Bees Head looked only a hundred yards away, "Tides out."

"'Seconds' 'er et Ulverston terday. Yer mam en me wuddent be up fer cummen ter Ulverston."

"Mam's never been to a cricket match in her life."

"She's seen yer play rugby."

"No, she hasn't."

"Hessent she?"

"Who are we playing against?"

"Whitehevven."

"Whitehaven?" Daniel said, "Of all the bloody teams to play."

"Aye."

"At least I'm too old for any of them to know me."

"Ther's a few ev them still aboot," he said, "Yer nut rigister'd and yer mightn't be able ter bowl."

"He hasn't been able to bowl for twenty years," laughed Sandra with a small hug.

Daniel had planned to set off from the house at one o'clock, but everybody was dressed and ready at twelve thirty.

Somewhere in the twenty-minute journey to the cricket ground in Workington it was decided, silently, that Emily, Sandra and Rachel should be dropped off at the shops.

Tom and Daniel got to the ground and Tom was packaged safely into his wheelchair. He was disappointed that the ground was too soft for him to take his wheelchair to look at the wicket.

They were much too early. "Tek 'es fer a push roond."

They were half-way round the boundary when someone waved and shouted to them from the pavilion. It was the captain, David Cordle. He ran over to say hello. "You still look fit."

"Raging against the dying of the light, David," Daniel said.

"I was talking to Tom," he laughed.

"How are you Dan?" They shook hands. "You are still playing I hear?"

"In a manner of speaking."

"Warwickshire League though."

"Bottom end of."

"You two ga'an 'ev a lewk et track," said Tom, "A'ah'll sunbathe ovver 'ere."

The rain had got under the covers during the night and created linear patches of wetness across the pitch.

"I'm glad I will be batting at number eleven," Daniel said pointedly.

"I will have to ask 'Mr Hogan' where I can bat you."

"Is Alan still Whitehaven's captain?"

"Still a good player."

"We were in the same maths class at school."

"We have to win the toss today. I hope you have brought some luck with you."

Daniel got his cricket kit from the car. There were not many players who were around when he last played at Workington. He made a real effort to commit some names to memory.

One of the younger, louder ones said, "I know who you are. You played rugby with my grandfather."

Everyone laughed.

When the lad said who his grandfather was, Daniel was able to say, "I danced with your mother!" He hadn't really. "You will give her my love, won't you."

"Is that oah yer did?" said one of them.

That made everyone laugh and gave Daniel a little 'acceptance'.

Workington had lost the toss and were, of course, put in to bat.

Daniel walked round the boundary to join his dad.

Tom was with several of his old cricket friends. Daniel had played with three of them, but he could not remember their names. There were three men who he recognised from the "Brains Trust" at Workington Town. Introductions were not made. It was assumed that Daniel would remember their names from twenty odd years previously, as they had remembered his. They all wanted to talk more about rugby than today's cricket game and some chairs were harvested to sit round Tom.

Two wickets went down before everyone settled.

"Where are yer batten Daniel, lad?" asked somebody.

"Eleven."

"Ah wouldn't git settled. Hev yer seen't track?" He turned to Tom, "It's like a Zebra crossen Tom, asser."

As he said that, another wicket fell.

"Tell't yer."

Sandra, Rachel and Emily arrived and Tom's pals each proffered their seats with old fashioned manners.

"I had better go and pad up."

"Good luck Dad. Go and hit a century."

Workington were forty something for nine after only twenty-one overs when Daniel went in to bat. David Cordle was still batting.

"We need to bat out the overs, so no heroics Dan."

He was a different man with a bat in his hand; authoritative, cold, and that was comforting.

There was a quick bowler and a medium pacer operating, and Daniel was able to get his pads in the way a few times and give David the strike with his leg byes.

Daniel had gone a few overs without making a run; actually, without hitting the ball with his bat.

There was a lot of meaningless abuse. It got more personal and spiteful the longer they stayed. David went up to Daniel, "Don't let the slagging put you off your stride."

"I get sledged by my own family. This is soft stuff."

The two opening bowlers were brought back on to bowl short at Daniel. That cut out the leg byes. He took quite a few balls in the ribs and the shoulder. There was a huge variation in the bounce of the ball off the hard, dry bits and the damp patches. Daniel didn't wear a helmet.

Daniel gave Alan, their captain, a smile. Daniel remembered that when they were at school together they shared a girlfriend. Alison. Well, Daniel had once walked her home to Low Moresby in the dark after a school athletics trip. The walk took longer than everyone thought.

Nothing had happened, but words had been exchanged at the time.

"I wonder if he remembers now?" Daniel thought.

Daniel started getting somewhere near the ball with his bat, but he was bowled out in the final over.

Daniel had batted for twenty-seven overs and he had only got a dozen or so runs.

As David and Daniel were being clapped off, Alan Hogan shook Daniel's hand, "New bat?" he said. "Still getting used to it?"

"Fifteen seasons old Alan, good as new!" They laughed.

Rachel had pushed Tom to the pavilion.

"Paint's dry now lad."

"Nearly well-done Dad. I worked out that it would have taken you until Tuesday afternoon to get that 'hundred'." She hugged her dad then hugged her grandad.

Workington did indeed lose the game, but only by a couple of wickets. Alan Hogan had 'advised' David Cordle that as Daniel was not registered with the league, he would not be happy if he was to bowl.

"That was so nice of him," said Sandra.

In return, Daniel decided not to ask Alan to, "Give Alison my love."

Tom was happy with the day.

In those incoherent months, those waiting months, Emily found something heroic in herself, a depth of unconditional love and patience in coping with Tom's difficulties and humiliations. His difficulties were in the small details, and the painful intimacies of his new circumstances. Emily even found the strength to push Tom, in his wheelchair, up the ramp, and even more difficult, hold him back going down. Tom crashed into the front door several times. Each time must have been extremely painful. Emily would panic. She would blame Daniel for not being there. For living so far away. For living with Sandra and Rachel. Daniel understood that, for the time being at least, his role as 'whipping boy' or 'scapegoat' was a positive thing for him to accept. Emily couldn't have given so much, so unselfishly, to Tom if she didn't have someone to shout about, and at. When she called Daniel to tell him of the latest accident or catastrophe there was a bit of her which was saying, "I have learned to love again. Your dad needs me again. I have a caring purpose again."

Daniel took some time to realise that he was part of a loving family again, even for such a short time.

Emily explained to Daniel that Tom only ever got "weepy" in private. Daniel was pleased to be brought into that small intimacy.

Tom's speech recovered erratically. When Daniel, Sandra and Rachel visited he was keen to talk about everything and anything. Sandra struggled to understand him. It wasn't so much the slurring of his speech, but the Lowca accent. She could just about handle a conversation with Tom face to face, but on the phone, she had no idea what he was saying. She was once bold enough to say to him, "Tom, please slow down, I'm struggling to understand your accent." Tom was sharp enough to reply "Pardon? What was that you said lass?"

Rachel adapted more easily and sometimes adopted and imitated Tom's intonations. She did this first as a way of trying to be amusing but then, over the weeks, she found that it became a natural way, a closer way, of talking to her grandad. It made it easier for her to listen to him.

The first big trip that Tom and Emily undertook after that first stroke was to go to Rugby by train for Rachel's 'Confirmation'. From the taking of a taxi to Whitehaven, no small thing for them, to the train to Carlisle. Changing platforms to catch the "London train" with luggage and a wheelchair must have been heroic on Emily's part. The long stretch to Rugby in the crowded compartment was an ordeal for them both.

At Rugby Station, Daniel guiltily and a little humbly, picked them up.

Rachel was devout and sincere in her Christianity. This made Daniel uncomfortable. All the baggage of his own Confirmation, side by side with his dad, came to the surface. If Daniel had been able to find an excuse for not going to the ceremony, he would have been happy to miss it. He never missed Rachel's violin performances, or the Youth Orchestra concerts.

"If Rachel had been a boy, and a boy who played soccer, would I have gone to watch him play?"

"Of course you would," everyone chorused.

Daniel held back saying that his parents didn't come to see him play rugby, but Tom beat him to it by addressing Rachel. "Aah once paid real money to watch yer dad hevv'n the shit kicked oot 'ev 'im."

"We have all done that . . . and enjoyed it too," laughed Sandra.

But Daniel surmised that if Rachel and Tom were to share some spiritual bond in the Confirmation ceremony, which Daniel had not been able to share with his dad thirty years previously, then he was glad.

He wasn't jealous, but he was amused that for a short while, his mam and dad had "got her, instead of him."

Over the months after Rachel's Confirmation Tom had a few setbacks and he realised that he was never going to recover in a meaningful way. "Aah pump aluminium 'en weight lift balloons 'en stuff," he said. "But I oaney gaa fer't nurses!" he winked.

Each time Daniel visited, Tom looked worse. He lost weight. His shoulders, his 'sack of coal' shoulders, just shrunk away from him.

Then Sandra took a phone call from Emily saying that Daniel should go up. She was surprisingly calm and commanding, "Best that the three of yer come up."

Friday evening traffic was very slow, and Sandra wanted to stop and find a hotel in Kendal, but Daniel was determined to press on to Lowca "just in case!". When they arrived it was after eleven. The lights were on and when Daniel tried the front door, he found it open. Emily was asleep in her armchair by a dying fire. Tom was awake. "Wheesht! Doan't wake 'er up."

A tray had been laid out in the dining room with tea and scones, jam and biscuits. Emily woke up, stood up and said her 'hellos'. Between them Daniel, Sandra and Rachel took their coats off, poked the fire into life, then set about their supper.

Emily got Tom up and out of his chair and over to the doorway to the stairs. "Matron sez aah hev ter gaa ter bed!"

Amidst the welter of 'goodnights' and 'goodneets', Emily said, "See you in the morning."

And that was it.

Daniel was pleased that his mam was coping, indeed seemed to be enjoying the leadership and the responsibility of "Tom's situation!"

Of her husband of fifty years dying.

"Can I do the dishes Dad?" said Rachel.

In the morning Daniel woke early. The bedroom curtains had not been drawn properly and a thin shaft of sunlight cut across the bedclothes. He slipped on his clothes 'from yesterday' and went to the downstairs loo for a pee. The kitchen was spotlessly clean. Rachel had 'done the dishes', put everything away and wiped everything down. He went to the fridge to get an orange juice. The fridge was full, neat and clean. He thought that he might make everyone a proper breakfast. He thought that he should wait until his mam was up and check that he wasn't invading her territory.

He went out into the back garden and was shocked to find Rachel standing on the small patch of lawn. She was fully dressed, had her mum's coat on. She was gazing out to St Bees Head.

"Is this what you used to look at every morning?" She wasn't crying, but she had been.

Daniel wrapped his arms round her from behind. "Why are you up so early? Couldn't you sleep?"

"No. I slept like a log."

"Would you like a walk to the shop?"

"It's a 'Christian' thing dad, and you wouldn't understand."

"We could get some eggs and make 'egg 'n crumb'."

"It's a 'witness' thing."

They bought eggs, The Guardian, The Independent, bacon, milk and sliced bread.

When they got back to the house Rachel asked if she could set the table.

"Very silently! But bring a pair of scissors out to the garden."

There was a line of four ten-inch terracotta pots.

"There's herbs in these pots."

"What kind?"

"There's thyme, marjoram, I think those are chives, this might be basil."

"Are any of them poisonous?"

"We won't know 'til we try!"

They cut a small handful of each and took them back into the kitchen.

Emily was filling the kettle.

"Would you like me and Rachel to cook a breakfast?"

Emily was going to say that she had everything under control, that she would get Tom downstairs, then she would make breakfast. But what Rachel meant as a 'good morning' hug was taken by Emily as something more meaningful and she let out a long, low wail. Almost silent. She had wanted the hug from her son. But this embrace from her grand-daughter was unconditional, genuine, without baggage. It had just flicked a switch in her.

"Ken aye 'ev a love 'es well!"

It was Tom on his zimmer-frame, almost upright in the doorway. Behind him was Sandra, who proudly announced, "I helped him down the stairs."

"Shit dad, you took your life in your hands there, didn't you?"

In the laughter Emily was able to turn her head away and pretend that she hadn't cried.

The first pot of tea was made. Emily, Tom and Sandra were persuaded to sit at the dining table and between them shuffle all the plates, cups and cutlery into neat and orderly places.

Daniel and Rachel chopped the herbs, crumbed the bread and whisked the eggs and served the 'egg 'n crumb' with an accompaniment of bacon, Cumberland sausage and fried tomatoes.

"Delish!" said Rachel.

"Delish!" repeated the others.

Daniel took everyone for a good drive, through Lorton to Buttermere, stopped for great ice cream. "Just git me a la'al 'rum'n'raisen', doan't want ter git fat, eh Rachel?"

"I'll get you a double scoop of 'rum and raisin' with a scoop of 'mint' on top." She smiled. "Anything you don't eat, I'll have instead. I'll get fat on your behalf."

They went up and over Honister Pass and stopped at the slate mine.

Daniel told Rachel that he had worked there one summer when he was a student. He explained the difference between gunpowder and dynamite.

"That's a very useful thing for me to know Dad."

"Whatever! But working down this mine was a more profound sculptural experience than anything I ever got from Art College."

"Bet ther' wuz nae coal down the'er," said Tom.

"No shale or fireclay either."

Daniel and Rachel left the others at the splitting sheds and they raced each other up the winding path to the old mine entrance. Rachel was no good at any of the school sports, but she was a mountain goat up a hill. Daniel had to be strong to beat her to the top so that she didn't do anything daft like fall over the cliff. They rested by what used to be called the 'carbide shed'. Rachel gasped happily, she knew that she had pushed her dad, engaged with him.

"We wore safety helmets," said Daniel when he had got his breath back. "We had a little pot on the front of our helmets into which was pressed some 'carbide'. White, crumbly, like salt."

Rachel was going to ask a question, but she was trying not to look and sound knackered after her 'hill climb', so she let the question go.

"Then the gaffer put the required amount of water into the pot, gave it a 'la'al rattle', then screwed the top on and lit the wick."

"Didn't you have any electricity down the mine?"

"No."

"When there were five or six of us in the 'hall', the lamps surprisingly provided enough light to see quite well."

"Why didn't the union man kick up a fuss?"

"No unions," he said, "This is the Lake District, it's all Toryshire here. Besides, the mine manager was captain of Egremont Rugby Club. Nice man. Tory though!"

"Let's race down to Nana and Grandad."

"No, we'll walk down carefully."

Daniel took them to the Castle Inn and Tom and Daniel each had 'a posh pint' of Jennings. 'The Ladies' had, what were to them all, exotic fruit drinks, each with ice and a sprig of mint.

"Why don't we have an early dinner here?" said Sandra.

Tom and Emily weren't keen. "We're not best dressed." Then Emily said, "Tom might get too tired."

"Daniel will pay. We were going to take you out for dinner tonight anyway."

Tom and Emily looked at each other. "Eating out" was still alien to them, 'not sure about their dress', 'not too sure about their table manners'. It was a 'Lowca thing'.

But there was something else wrong. Did Tom need the bathroom? Did he need to take some pills?

"Are you alright?" said Daniel.

Emily took a second or two, got hold of Tom's 'stroke' hand, "Yes Daniel, we are alright, we are going to have our dinner here and you are going to pay. I might even have a glass of wine."

"Bloody hell lass. Steady on," said Tom.

Tom and Emily went quiet, still holding hands.

Daniel, Sandra, Rachel were each sensitive enough to respect their silence. At least until the waitress arrived with the menus. Rachel was still excited about her 'little climb' and enjoyed this rare moment of family harmony. She jumped over a stool and sat down a little roughly beside her grandad and held his 'bad hand' with its leather cast.

The following day, Sandra took Rachel and Emily to church. Tom, holding on to his zimmer-frame tried to wave them off at the front door, but he could not support himself on one hand and nodded to the car instead.

"Divvent like 'Matins' ennywez!" he grumbled.

"Sit down and I'll get you a cup of tea and the paper," said Daniel.

"Er yer ganna dae a drawin' ev 'ez?"

"Can do," said Daniel, surprised.

Tom sat with the paper on his lap, not really reading it. Daniel picked a flat "woodworker's pencil" from the mantelpiece and began drawing. The flatness of the pencil lead guided his hand into straight lines and shallow curves and he soon found a rhythm for the drawing of the droops and the collapsed flesh of his dad's face.

"This is me!" said Tom after a while. It was a minute or two later that he completed his sentence with an angry "Fucked."

Daniel was well into the drawing before he realised that Tom was 'posing'. Tom was staring at Daniel with the gaze of a man saying, "Here, draw me like this, this is how I want to be drawn."

And Daniel responded. His pencil did not move any quicker than it normally did, but it moved insistently. Daniel had an eraser in his left hand, not to rub out any mistakes and exaggerations but to modulate the rapidly darkening tones of the graphite and to create highlights in the flesh and greyness in the hair.

"Ambipedaled," said Tom.

"What?"

"Bein' 'ebble ter kick wid both feet."

Daniel smiled.

Daniel just drew. There were no thoughts that this might be his last chance to draw his dying father, or that this drawing would be a preparatory drawing for an oil portrait. It was just another chance to sit and "BE" with his dad again in an ordinary, mutually agreeable, activity. Like in his youth.

"Wur yer enny good?" said Tom.

"What?"

They were interrupted by the clamour of Emily, Sandra and Rachel coming through the back door, then the kitchen door, then the dining room door.

Tom's question hung in the air. "Any good at what?" Daniel thought. "Art? Painting? Being a dad? A man?"

In the excited account of the church service, the useless vicar, "The crap organist" according to Rachel, the people outside the church who said "Remember 'es ter Daniel," Tom managed to catch Daniel's eye in a gap between Emily and Sandra to answer the unasked question.

"Ah meant the hewkin'. Wur yer enny good at the hewkin' bit 'ev yer rugby?"

"We met one of your old girl-friends, Dad," announced Rachel teasingly.

"No, it wuzzn't," interrupted Emily, "She was just a lass who was confirmed at the same time as your dad."

"What was her name?" asked Daniel, but nobody seemed to hear the question.

After a surprisingly good lunch, prepared in rare, quiet, harmony by Emily, Sandra and Rachel, Daniel busied himself digging the garden, cutting a whole load of roses back, hard back, and strimming the small lawn under the dining room window. Tom acted in a supervisory capacity from inside. He had the window half open. It was a lovely, but cold, day. St Bees Head was clear and sharp, there were two cargo boats anchored off Whitehaven Harbour, and Daniel was happily digging and sweating to avoid facing up to his dad's imminent death. "Here I am," he said to himself, "'atoning' again."

The gardening, and the incongruity of Tom, sitting in his wheelchair by the window directing operations, gave plenty of opportunity for laughter.

Rachel brought out coffee and a sliced cake. She served her grandad through the window.

"What's in the boats?" she asked.

"Phosphates fer Marchon."

"What's a phosphate for?" she laughed.

"It's guano," said Tom, then in a conspiring whisper, "It's bird poo. Thousand-year-old bird shit."

"Are there many thousand-year-old birds in these parts?" Rachel was pleased with her joke and shouted it to her dad as he came for his coffee.

What wind there was, died and the sun bounced back off the house wall and they each stopped to take in the warmth.

"Yer nivver answered mi question."

"It's a hard question to answer honestly." Daniel drank his coffee.

"The best hookers, the international hookers, are usually sandwiched between international props."

Rachel put her right arm round her dad's waist, "I'm your prop," she said and squeezed, spilling a little coffee on to a geranium.

"They usually have huge packs behind them, but mostly they practise, practise, practise. They all get their feet in the right position on their own ball. They practise getting the timing of their forward shunt on the 'put in'. They practice the hooker flapping his hand for the scrum half to put the ball in. They practise to the inch the exact spot in the grass where the ball is to be struck, then they all straighten their legs and shove like ..." Daniel mouthed a "Fuck" to Tom.

"Heck," said Rachel. "I think Dad means they shoved like 'heck'. Not the word he just whispered to you."

277

"Indeed, they all shove like 'heck' at the same time and shunt you back yards."

"Er yer mekken excuses?" asked Tom.

"No, quite the opposite, Dad." Daniel put his coffee cup through the window and placed it on the ledge. "There's no way we could out-shunt these teams. They get everything perfect. And that is their weakness ..." Daniel took hold of Rachel's right hand and pressed the flesh between her thumb and forefinger onto the flesh of his own left arm just below his elbow. He flapped his left hand, "Did you feel that?" he asked Rachel.

"Yes!" she replied trying to be a little cool and casual. But then she said, "I bet that happens when I do the fingering on my violin." She was now quite interested. She placed her hand on her own arm and felt for its twitching.

"All I have to do to win the ball is react quicker to the hooker's signal than their scrum half does. And that's easy because they have practised, practised, practised; to get their rhythm and their timing just perfect. Sometimes I close my eyes so that I can focus totally on the feel of the hooker's signal. Sometimes I try to take my mind out of the equation and let my body just react."

"D'yer ivver tek many?"

"One or two, usually. It's the best feeling in the world. So beautiful when you feel the ball on the inside of your foot and you know that for a microsecond that you have won it before he knows that he has lost it."

"I sometimes went to the big games to see Dad play," Rachel told her grandad.

"If I took one against the head there was always a kick or a punch to follow from their second row."

Tom is listening intently. It is the sort of trivia that he revels in, would want to understand, would want to annotate and make notes on.

"The music of the scrums." Rachel tried to be sarcastic, but it came out quite reverential.

"I go underarm onto my loose-head to make it easier to twist my arse round and point it to their scrum half as he puts the ball in. That way I can get more reach to strike. Also, I can strike downwards much quicker."

He demonstrated lifting his right leg directly upwards to his head, then in another movement stamping it downwards like a cat's claw. Rachel copied her dad's strange movements laughing out loud.

"No! Wait!" she said still giggling, "Guess who this is." And with that she repeated the leg movements but this time she pressed her nose sideways with her fingers across her face to resemble her dad's broken nose.

She roared with laughter and then went to her grandad and the two of them embraced in hysterical, uncontrollable giggles. Daniel joined in, but his joy was triggered by the sight of his daughter and his dad hugging and laughing.

Emily and Sandra came out to see what all the fuss was about.

"Dad," said Rachel, still laughing, "You are a seriously weird man. You have spent half your life going all the way round the country, to wave your leg up in the air and wave it down again, you wave your bottom at the scrum half just so that you can kick a ball backwards with your eyes shut. And then you would get a black eye!"

Tom and Rachel re-joined their hysterical embrace.

"And you think that it is a spiritual event, like church, or me playing "Lark Ascending".

Emily and Sandra looked on, laughing, but not really understanding what was so uproariously funny.

"Then during the week ..." said Tom, "he paints women in the nude!"

"I know," said Rachel. "You have to feel for those poor women when Dad comes into the studio, takes off his clothes and picks up his brushes."

Emily tried to scowl and say something about the Sabbath but even she was taken up into the hysteria of the moment.

The laughter did eventually abate, until Rachel pressed her nose sideways again and it all broke out once more.

A waft of cold air came off the sea and killed the moment.

"Mair tea?" said Emily and they all retreated indoors.

Daniel took a bath in the local soft water. There was 'palmolive' soap laid out, but Daniel found some small scraps of 'carbolic' in a dish under the sink. He luxuriated in the bath while Sandra packed, ready for a daylight departure for home. Daniel had got used to the regular four-hour journey home, but for Sandra and Rachel it was an ordeal once they were beyond Stoke on Trent.

Emily had made sandwiches with rough cut bread, with cheese, ham, chicken and corned beef. There was a pork pie and some hard-boiled eggs, a flaskful of coffee made with boiled milk. She always went over the top with such things, but this time it seemed like a genuine gesture of love and affection.

"Are yer nut ganna play yer fiddle fer ez lass?"

"I didn't bring my music stand."

"A'ah'll 'od yer music fer yer."

Rachel had her Grade 8 exam in two weeks. She had to play the largo from a Mozart Violin Concerto.

'Number 3 in G'!

There are, as the film said, 'a lot of notes' in Mozart and there were sixteen pages to negotiate.

Tom gripped the music sheets in the fingers and thumb of his 'good, bad hand', the one with the leather cast on, the right one. While Rachel was tuning up, he struggled with gripping the papers, so he took off his leather cast.

"Nae point in it noo anywez."

Daniel looked at his mother, but she just smiled a little wanly.

"Riddy lass?"

"Aye asser marra." She nodded, pleased with her little bit of the vernacular.

The first few bars on the first page establish the cadence of the piece and Rachel had that almost imperceptible dance that fiddlers have in their upper body as she approached the bottom right of the page of music. She was trying to tie in the turning of the page, 'in time'. However, Tom, with a flick of his thumb, had turned the first page over so that Rachel didn't need to break stride. Only the slight raising of an eyebrow registered that this was 'a good thing'.

Getting to the bottom right of page three, there was the same anticipation of 'the turning of the page problem' and she gave a nod of her head in her grandad's direction, but Tom had the page turned anyway, with impeccable timing.

By the turning of page five the trust had been established and Tom was joyously playing a tiny part in the playing of the music, the playing of Mozart, the playing of music together with his grandaughter. Daniel fell into the music: glorious, glorious stuff which until now he had only heard from his daughter's bedroom. However, it wasn't until more than half-way through that he realised for the first time that his dad could read music. He could read Mozartian violin music with all its unique notations and signals.

To Daniel's 'shame', that word again, he had not known that. Tom did not play an instrument. At the band, with Grandad Cragg, he had never even thought of blowing a trumpet. At Church he sang a quiet, unmelodic hum, the words of the hymns undiscernible except to himself and the God he was singing to.

The Reverend Nidd had once said to Daniel. "I think your dad has spent some time in his life looking for bushels under which to hide his lights."

Daniel wondered now if his dad's profound understanding of rugby, of cricket, and his ability to read music were accomplishments honed so that one day he might, in his dying days, turn the pages of Mozart with his grandaughter. Was it a measure of his life that he could talk meaningfully with his son about hooking and scrummaging, watch his son score thirteen runs in thirty overs and understand that it was sometimes good to be ordinary? That it was not always good, or indeed bad, to be excellent. That things were often just the way they were. His strange boy pushing his bike up Harrington Hill in the hungry howl of a storm was just the way he was, irrespective of what Tom had perceived as his failings as a father. His strange boy grew to be a strange and independent man, and he was none the worse for that.

Rachel played beautifully, fabulously. Maybe it was the spirit of the occasion, but she had never played better. She had never played with such command, such authority. Maybe in those moments she understood what music was for, as she played for her grandad, with her grandad, to give 'everlasting comfort' to him as he faced death.

Nobody clapped.

All five of them knew that they had witnessed, shared, something special.

As Sandra, Rachel and Daniel put their coats on and headed, with their bags, and Daniel's folder of drawings, for the car, Tom got up, and with Emily made it to the front door. Everyone knew the effort and courage those few short steps had taken.

It was not a time for hugs and kisses.

Daniel, Sandra and Rachel turned and took in the sight of Emily, and Tom, in the doorway.

Tom strained to stand up straight, and Emily did also.

Nobody said goodbye.

The journey east to Penrith and the M6 was made in a good sunset, made glorious by the top half of each of the mountains bouncing domes of fiery red back to the west.

The sandwich feast was eaten on the downward journey from Shap.

"Nice coffee," said Sandra.

"Nice restaurant," said Rachel. She reached forward from the back seat and kissed both her mum and her dad. She tidied the dishes and the cutlery away in the space behind the driver's seat and made a small bed for herself using her violin case and a jacket as a pillow.

"Played well today." She was asleep as it got dark.

CHAPTER 25

Sandra usually made Daniel breakfast in bed, but the next day Daniel was up at six, set the kitchen table for breakfast and was in his studio before Sandra and Rachel were awake. They knew not to disturb him, they showered and dressed downstairs, ate quietly and left for work, and school, in silence.

Daniel didn't notice them go. He had a canvas primed and ready on his easel. He had traced one of the drawings of Tom into the damp paint. He set about laying a full palette on to an A2 sheet of thick white glass. The careful process of squeezing the paint out of the tube into small turds on to the pure white of the glass gave Daniel the opportunity to engage with and relearn each individual colour.

All the time he was working on Monday, Daniel thought that he was doing well. He was in a hurry, but he laid down his paint in a careful, methodical manner. He was only working from a line drawing, but he was pleased with the flesh tones. His dad's life-long suntan had faded since his strokes, his skin looked dry now, almost transparent.

By the end of the daylight when Rachel came home from school, Daniel felt that he had built the structure of a good portrait. He happily made a curry dinner while Rachel practised her Mozart in her room. Before he changed out of his painting clothes, he went into the studio to tidy up his mess and clean his brushes. It was dark now and the yellow light of the room's bulbs changed the colours of the painting. He was shocked at how weak it now looked. He knew that it would look better in the daylight of the next morning. He knew that he would be a grumpy arsehole over dinner.

In the morning the painting didn't look better to Daniel. The memory of seeing it in the yellow artificial light the previous evening haunted the way he looked at it. He was angry with himself and attacked the picture, challenging every mark and brushstroke he had made. The anger brought energy and he tried to use that. He sustained that anger throughout the day and by the time Rachel came home he had an exciting painting. The colouring was vibrant and accurately caught the chalky complexion and the dark shadows of the eyes. The drawing under the paint held the picture together and it did indeed look like Tom.

But it wasn't right.

Daniel phoned Lowca after dinner and talked to his mam about trivial things. She put Tom on the phone and they talked about Rugby League, then about Rugby Union. Tom was animated about the lack of basic handling skills in Rugby Union, even in international games. "Couldn't pass wind," was his assessment of one England fly-half.

Daniel gave the phone to Rachel. She had obviously misheard her grandad and launched into a long story about the school Art class before realizing that Tom's question was about Mozart.

"Oh! Sorry Grandad ... MozART."

Daniel left the two of them laughing and took Sandra up to the studio to show her the painting.

"It's your dad to a tee," she said.

"Not the one I know," said Daniel.

"Oh!" she held his hand, "You're always low at the end of a painting. It's the spit of your dad." She let go of his hand and went up close to the picture.

"It's a different person close up, but it's still your dad."

"I have it in my head that I have only a short time to do the thing before he dies. To show it him. Parting gesture ... sort of!" With a certain finality that Sandra knew she shouldn't challenge, he said, "I can't show him that."

Wednesday was "sunny with cloudy spells" or "cloudy with sunny spells" and the light was constantly changing. Daniel had taken a four foot by two foot board which had the early stages of a painting of a ditch on it. He didn't really know what he was doing except scraping his palette clean of superfluous paint, but he was plastering the board with the paint in vaguely "Tom-like" shapes. He soon put the board onto his main easel and began painting his dad without reference to his drawings. He did not paint with the same wild energy which had taken him over the previous day. He did not refer to his drawings because he had a constant vision of Tom in his mind, built up of nearly fifty years of looking, listening, sharing things. A broad image of Tom first mingled with, then dominated, the image of the ditch underneath the new paint. But the old paint was incorporated into the picture where it was tonally appropriate. A small flat headed screwdriver was used to incise lines into the new paint and a viable graphic image of Tom emerged. Viable enough for Daniel to engage with fully. He grabbed a handful of mixed brushes and reached for his "sitting down chair", the old wooden one with big, solid, arm rests. He lowered the painting on its easel and just started working.

He,"let go".

His eyes and his hands, his brushes and his big palette of colours were programmed by the confluence of the image which was developing in the paint and "that eternal image" which Daniel had of his father. Daniel's controlling intellect was kept at bay as he trusted in his natural gifts.

In the fire of a rugby scrum he only had to suspend his cognitive mindset for the two or three seconds it took to position himself, arse pointing to the ball in the scrum-half's hands, and strike the ball against the put in. Sitting at his painting, the brushes came and went from his hand, the paints on his palette presented themselves to the hairs of his brush. Daniel witnessed his father emerging slowly, sometimes hesitantly, in the transcendent paint on the board.

A toilet break, a pork pie break, and several hours later Daniel had something which he knew was on its way to working. He set up the fan heater for the evening hours to dry the paint for the next day's work.

He didn't tell either Sandra or Rachel what he had done that day and he locked his studio door.

In the evening he called Lowca at what had become "the usual time". Emily had some story about an application for a powered wheelchair. Some male nurse had dismissed the idea because neither of Tom's hands was capable of operating the levers safely. There was an offhand remark about "how long would it be needed for" and this had upset her. When she had finished her story, she gave the phone to Tom, who said something in such a weak voice that Daniel was shocked.

"D'yer still nut ga'a ter chutch?"

"Funerals and stuff. But Sandra and Rachel go every week."

"That's nut an answer." He replied rather aggressively. "What're yer ganna say ter Sent Peter when yer time comes?"

"If you get there before me, which is not certain, I have been trusting that you would put in a good word for me."

"That's just flippant."

"I gave 'the chutch' my best shot, Dad."

There was a silence. Daniel could hear the sound of the television through the crackling of the phone. He was worried that his dad had dropped the phone for some reason.

"A'ah knoah lad."

Another silence and the phone was put down at the Lowca end.

The next morning, Thursday, Sandra brought Daniel coffee and a biscuit in bed. She was dressed and ready for work. She had to leave early for a senior staff meeting at the school. She listed all the issues of the day before they heard Rachel's violin across the landing.

"You go off to work. I'll sort her breakfast and have a word with her."

Daniel waited in the kitchen for Rachel to come for breakfast, but she was still playing her violin, not very well. He banged on her bedroom door.

"Breakfast is served, modom, sausage, bacon, mushrooms, toast, tomatoes, six poached eggs and a black pudding."

The music stopped. Rachel charged past her dad and down the stairs. She had been crying.

By the time Daniel caught up with her in the kitchen she was gulping down some orange juice.

"Why don't you slow down, eat your cereal and I'll drive you to school?" He moved to put his arm round her, but she shrugged him off, grabbed her bag and charged out of the door, leaving it open.

Daniel ate her cereal.

The studio was stiflingly warm. He had left the fan-heater on all night, but Wednesday's paint was touch dry. He tidied up his palette and squeezed gobs of fast-drying clear medium into spaces between key colours. He had six new, thin, flat brushes. He pressed his thumb and forefinger round their fibres and began to paint.

There was no order to the making of his marks.

He was just painting.

He did not put right the exaggerations and mistakes of the previous day.

He had new painting to do; and he would make new, better, mistakes.

He had shadows to bring to those deep spaces between the nose and the eyes. He had to give new shape to the lid of the left eye. But these were simultaneous acts with the need to repaint the septum and other unnameable parts of the face and its flesh. Soon the six different colours on his six different brushes had to be cleaned, wiped and reloaded, each new colour to be addressed to its rightful place in the painting. The thousand calculations per minute involving size, shape, tone, colour, degree of transparency, gesture were Daniel's litany and the music of the movement of his brushes would soon overtake the mathematics of his looking. This was painting. And Daniel trusted in his hands and his eyes and his vision. And in this particular time, he carried the vision of his father. Not his father's 'character'. Not his father's 'soul'. Just his father, Tom. Just a person reconstructed in paint. Daniel recognised when his brain was operating in top gear, and he knew, after twenty years of painting full-time, that his hands and his eyes understood things which his brain could not grasp, could not believe in, did not have access to. Sometime in the process of the painting of his dad, in the transition from the fierce intellectual control of the drawing and the manipulation of the paint, to the surrendering to the authority of his natural gifts, Daniel recognised that he had finished the painting of his father. Something in the arrangement of paint was telling him that he had to stop.

It was only a painting.

It would not change the world or make people's lives better.

It was just a painting.

It took some time for Daniel to be able to 'see' what he had done.

It would be hard for him to separate himself from the making of it. It would be hard for him to accept responsibility for the painting, to take ownership of it, to take pride in it.

He would be very nervous about showing Tom the painting, not because it was an inaccurate portrait or that it did or did not define a very fine man. He was afraid that Tom would recognise that 'strangeness' again which so alarmed him when Daniel was a boy. He was even more afraid that the painting had stepped into the realms of 'spirituality' and that Tom would say, with a hint of triumphalism in his voice. "So, yer did find God efter oah? Eh?"

Daniel still had lots of technical work to do on the painting, but he was already planning to go on his own to Lowca for a quick visit after the rugby game on the Saturday. Rachel had orchestra practice on Saturday morning and her Grade 8 violin test was coming up. Sandra's headship was all-consuming, of her time and of her spirit. Taking the picture to his dad was a personal thing and full of risks. He didn't want Sandra and Rachel involved in the emotional minefield that was his mam, his dad and his own self. He knew that the painting would drag up forty odd years of intimate family discordance, not because it was a bad painting, but because it was so fiercely good. It would remind Tom and Emily of so much pain. But getting the painting to his dad was still the most urgent thing in Daniel's life.

The phone call at eight o' clock on Saturday morning was still a surprise.

"He died at two this mornin'."

Daniel had rehearsed this scene many times since Tom's first stroke. He was aware that there were so many things that he could say that his mam could take the wrong way or misinterpret.

"Aa'h didn't want ter wake yer up," Emily said.

"Are you on your own?"

"Margaret's 'ere."

"Have you called the doctor?"

"It's ower late fer a doctor." And this small stupidity set Emily off on a long, low wail.

The phone died.

Sandra had already gone to Rachel to tell her.

"We have to get packed," Daniel shouted upstairs.

The cancelling phone calls were made, bags put in the boot with Rachel's violin and stand, Rachel was hugged, coffee and sandwiches made, the house was locked up in only ten minutes or so.

"Can I take some work with me?" said Sandra.

"Shit! I should call me mam back."

Emily had settled down. "We'll be there about two, we can do everything between us when we get there." There were even a few "I love you"s.

Rachel was in the passenger seat of the car. "Mum can work in the back seat and I can look after Dad and read the map."

It was ten to two when they arrived and Daniel struggled to park near the house. He could see figures through the window, but the front door was closed. He rapped at the door gently with his knuckles and after some time a fat woman in a tartan coat opened it. He did not know who she was and evidently the woman did not know Daniel.

"Helloah," she said.

The noise from the living room sounded like a party and for the first time Daniel felt the immense weight of his father's death. He had kept his emotions at bay for the whole of the journey, even delighting in Rachel's map reading and the earnestness with which she performed her task. Sandra and Rachel were behind him now, outside, waiting to get past this stupid woman in her silly coat, to see his mother and address his father's corpse.

Auntie Elsie saved the day. "Let me git past, May." She pulled the woman out of the way, "Come in Daniel lad," she said. "Yer mam's in't front room." She kissed him on the cheek and whispered in his ear. "They've collected yer dad already. The Doctor and the Co-op were here this morning and sorted things out."

Silent hugs were exchanged with Sandra and Rachel and the four of them pushed past the stupid woman and into the living room. There were six middle-aged women, each in coats, all of them seemed to be talking. Emily sat in her armchair and waited for Daniel, Rachel and then Sandra to go to hug her.

"Cuppa tea love," Elsie called to Sandra and ushered Daniel and Rachel into the dining room and the kitchen where Tom's sisters Eleanor and Margaret were on 'tea duty'.

"Yer dad's groupies frae't chutch," said Margaret.

"Live on biscuits and tea, this lot. Can yer ga te't Co-op Daniel lad and buy a load?" said Elsie. "And milk! Mebbe some tea bags en'oah!"

"I'll boil kettles," said Rachel.

"You gaa' wid Daniel," whispered Margaret to Sandra. "Daniel's dad 'es just died. He won't 'ev tekken it in yit."

The Co-op in the village had packets of loose leaf lapsang souchon tea which Daniel once drank with his Aunt Eva. They bought four packets to take home. They had plenty of exotic teas at home. Buying some in a shop in Lowca seemed to have a significance which Daniel couldn't quite define.

Daniel and Sandra bought two big tins of mixed biscuits, as well as the standard quartet of custard creams, gingersnaps, chocolate digestives and 'rich tea'. "Parents' evening biscuits," said Sandra.

The shop still sold bottles of 'Camp' coffee, which was labelled "coffee essence". It wasn't really coffee, but it was all that was available in Britain during the War. It was all that was available for many years after the War as well. It was all that Tom and Emily could afford when Tom was out of work. They bought two bottles of it, "One for Mam", and one to take home.

Emily of course was offended by the bottle of 'Camp' and thought that it was a deliberate gesture on Daniel's part. "D'ye hev this stuff et yewer hoose'?"

"We got some proper coffee as well."

The 'Camp' coffee would have been good enough for the vicar. The Reverend Nidd had long gone and this one was just another in a long line of former public schoolboys. They came to Moresby Church for two years before moving on to 'a less challenging parish'.

"Come on a bike and leave in a car."

The place was spotless when the vicar came, a good fire was stacked up, and the tea and the biscuits were served in the best service.

He kept calling Emily, 'Amelia'. Daniel kept repeating "Mam's name is Emily."

"I have some suggestions for the hymns," he said.

Daniel was incensed when he said, "How about 'There were ninety and nine that safely lay'? Then there is 'Morning has broken', that's always popular. Cat Stevens used to sing it ..." He was halfway to listing 'All things bright and fucking beautiful' when Daniel interrupted him, "That's fine Vicar. Thank you."

Emily had her own list in her hands. She and Tom had been planning this funeral for the three years since Tom's first stroke. They had initially set out the hymns in desperation together at Tom's hospital bedside. Then, over that limbo period, when he was recovering and declining at the same time, they put together the hymns and readings which suited them, meant something to them. Tom had written everything for the service in a small hard-backed notebook. There were also, on separate pages, in chapters, instructions for Emily about insurance policies, the phone numbers for the Doctor, the undertaker, the cricket clubs, there was a list of the "Brains Trust" at the rugby, there were still members of the Lowca Colliery Prize Silver Band alive. He had drawn a family tree of all the brothers and sisters, the grandchildren and great grandchildren and the three great-great grandsons of his parents John and Mary. He did a parallel family tree of Emily's relatives going back to William and Sarah Carr.

And all this was colour coded like his cricket score books. Copper plate handwriting in reds, yellows, greens and some in 'pink ink'.

On a separate page, in black ink, were listed the names of...

Les Thornton

Len Clayden

John Dee

"That lot 'ev hed letters tellen 'em nut ter come."

So, when the vicar was off on his own little trip, Emily was able to open Tom's book and, with assurance, tell him what the service would be. What hymns would be sung, what prayers would be offered.

None of this meant anything to the vicar.

Exasperated with his difficulties in listening to his mam, Daniel spoke for the first time.

"Both my parents are ..." he stuttered, "Both my parents have each served on the Parochial Church Council of St Bridget's Church for many years. My dad served on it for over thirty years."

The vicar didn't make eye-contact.

"My dad was the archetypal committed Christian. Until his stroke, he never missed Evensong in over thirty years. He did 'bible study' every Tuesday evening. He mended half the pews in your church for goodness sake."

"That's good, that's very, very good," the vicar said, writing something down, but still not looking up. "Tell me. Did Thomas have a middle name?"

"No," said Emily.

How could Daniel tell this stupid man that the significant moments in his dad's life could be listed as ...

Teaching Daniel to read, with his silly nursery rhyme.

Holding his hand at Micklam and watching the steelworks light up their world.

Being honest and strong in resigning from Micklam.

Beating the shit out of Les Thornton, so beautifully, and bringing him down with a David Duckham tackle. Then, glory of glories, carrying a hundredweight sack of coal all the way from Ghyll Grove to Parton.

Later, when working at Sellafield, in a job which did not accommodate his skills or his fastidiousness, he spent twenty-five years defined as an 'unskilled labourer', bending without being broken.

Learning to read music, not as a public affectation but as a private accomplishment.

These things defined Tom as a good man to Daniel. They defined a set of values for Daniel to live by. They informed his painting, his rugby, his loving.

As a eulogy, standing in front of a funeral congregation in a church, Daniel's list would perhaps be open to misinterpretation.

However, when the vicar stood up at Tom's packed funeral and said that, "Thomas worked down the pits ..."

"He was a check weighman," Emily muttered loudly.

"... and his 'hobbies' were rugby and cricket, and he was a regular churchgoer."

That was just about it.

The cricketers in the congregation, the 'women' from the church, Tom's rugby mates, all of Lowca, none of them knew who he was talking about.

It had been written in a late note, in rather shaky handwriting, in Tom's book that when the coffin was taken back down the aisle at the end of the service, Rachel, upstairs in the balcony at the rear of St Bridget's with Sandra, would play the Mozart that she and Tom had shared only a few days before. She had played several bars when the organist started playing something, drowning her out, but one of

Tom's friends from church had the presence of mind to go and physically take the organist's hands off the keyboard to allow Rachel to play on. Rachel had not broken stride. She did not need Sandra to turn the pages for her. She 'knew' the music in every sense. Tom had played a part in that.

As the congregation came out of the church to follow the bier to the grave the weather had turned nasty. Only the family, and with Tom's tribe, that was still about forty, joined the interment party. Daniel had his mam by the arm and moved round to protect her from the rain and the wind. At the turning of the path, he saw a red service bus stop at the church gates. But the pits had all closed, Micklam had gone, the coking ovens too. All the miners, all the workers had gone. And the red bus had stopped, not to pay respect to Daniel's dad, but merely to negotiate the funeral traffic.

Across the other side of the beck, Lowca's great sphynx-like slag heap had been bulldozed to a large, rounded slope and covered with soil and grass, to hide the shame of history. Where the tar plant had been, there was the field and the new clubhouse of Lowca's Amateur Rugby League Club.

One large horse grazed the whole of the 'slag heap field'.

The bier turned right again and there was some shelter from the wall dividing the churchyard from the remains of the old Roman fort.

Emily turned to see the main congregation scattering to their cars out of the squall. "A lot of people," she said.

"Upstairs was full as well," Daniel replied. Emily took comfort in that. The number of people at your funeral was important in these parts. A good turn-out at your funeral was an important testimonial to present to St Peter when the time came.

They turned left, and the gaping grave was a shock to Daniel as well as to his mam.

Rachel tried to hold an umbrella over Emily, but it disintegrated in the fierceness of the wind. Daniel traced the line of the road from where the prefabs once were, down past the Ship Inn and where the Brethren Chapel had been, then it disappeared behind the hill they were standing on.

A single carriage train crossed the bridge over the beck, very slowly. There was a very low tide.

A great blast of rain and wind came up from the shore seemingly bringing half the sea with it. Daniel imagined that it came through and over Les Thornton's Parton house at number 129, to pick up the strength to charge up the cliff before hitting everyone as they tried to form a circle round the grave. Daniel put his arm round his mother to hold her close for fear that she might be blown into the grave before Tom had got there. Rachel and Sandra took this as a signal that they should all hug together in a nice tight foursome.

The 'useless' vicar's surplice was billowing all over the place and nearly took him airborne. His well-rehearsed graveside intonation was lost in the squeal of the wind.

Daniel picked up a gob of mud and gave some to Emily to throw on the coffin.

"'All aboard fer Lowca.'"

"Yiss lad."

Lightning Source UK Ltd.
Milton Keynes UK
UKHW011108290622
405126UK00001B/81

9 781789 632491